About the Author

Jennie Ensor is a Londoner descended from a long line of Irish folk, which may be why she sometimes sneaks off from writing novels to indulge her other love, writing poems, preferably with a bar of Lindt chocolate. Her poetry tends to inhabit the darker, bleak and surreal side of life. It is published in a range of journals and magazines.

Jennie's first degree was in physics and astrophysics, on which she blames her ancestor William Parsons, the third Earl of Rosse (who observed the first spiral nebulae with the gargantuan telescope he built in Birr, Ireland).

While on an extended trip to Australia – a six-month working holiday somehow turned into 12 years – Jennie was inspired by investigative journalist John Pilger. She completed an MA in journalism and became a freelance journalist, focusing on the environment and social justice issues. Her articles covered topics from forced marriages to accidents in coal mines to the fate of Aboriginal Australians living on land contaminated by British nuclear tests.

For much of her life, Jennie has been a wandering soul. But now she is settled with her husband and their cuddle-loving, sofa-hogging Airedale terrier in a lively part of north London that's perfect for wandering from café to café with a Kindle, and chasing disobedient dogs.

BLIND SIDE

BLIND SIDE

JENNIE ENSOR

Unbound

London

This edition first published in 2016

Unbound

6th Floor Mutual House, 70 Conduit Street, London W1S 2GF

www.unbound.com

ISBN (Paperback):978-1-911586-00-5

ISBN (eBook): 978-1-78352-976-6

A CIP record for this book is available from the British Library

Design by Mecob

Cover images:

© iStockphoto.com / Anna Omelchenko (face)

© Shutterstock.com / Stephen Finn (skyline)

© Shutterstock.com / YurkaImmortal (skyline)

© Shutterstock.com / joingate (skyline)

© Shutterstock.com / igor.stevanovic (skyline)

Textures.com (smoke)

This book was produced using Pressbooks.com, and PDF rendering was
done by PrinceXML.

For Stuart

Dear Reader,

The book you are holding came about in a rather different way to most others. It was funded directly by readers through a new website: Unbound.

Unbound is the creation of three writers. We started the company because we believed there had to be a better deal for both writers and readers. On the Unbound website, authors share the ideas for the books they want to write directly with readers. If enough of you support the book by pledging for it in advance, we produce a beautifully bound special subscribers' edition and distribute a regular edition and e-book wherever books are sold, in shops and online.

This new way of publishing is actually a very old idea (Samuel Johnson funded his dictionary this way). We're just using the internet to build each writer a network of patrons. Here, at the back of this book, you'll find the names of all the people who made it happen.

Publishing in this way means readers are no longer just passive consumers of the books they buy, and authors are free to write the books they really want. They get a much fairer return too – half the profits their books generate, rather than a tiny percentage of the cover price.

If you're not yet a subscriber, we hope that you'll want to join our publishing revolution and have your name listed in one of our books in the future. To get you started, here is a £5 discount on your first pledge. Just visit unbound.com, make your pledge and type HELLOYOU in the promo code box when you check out.

Thank you for your support,

Dan, Justin and John
Founders, Unbound

Super Patrons

H Awan
Wendy Beauchamp-Ward
Helena Boland
Jessica Bromberg
Maria Burberry
Chris Burroughes
John Carter
Lauren Carter
Stuart Carter
Runilla Chilton
Annabel Christian
Dale Christian
Mark Christian
Tom Christian
Sean Clarke
Sarah Courtauld
Lumiel Cunin-Tischler
Rosamund Davies
Peter Dunn
Sam Elwin
Dianna Fatseas
Elizabeth Flanagan
Stephen Freeland
Justine Gilbert
Miranda Hampton
Tina Hill
Rosalind Horne
Kerensa Jennings
Kristen Johnson
Bharat & Ann Khaneka
Zac Kombou
Evelyne Le Gall
Anja Lohse
Seonaid Mackenzie-Murray
Duncan MacLean
Margaret
Gavin Mitchell

Tim Parkinson
Karim Rehmani-White
Emily Roberts
Phyllis Richardson
Nathalie Romani
Amanda Smith
Cindra Spencer
C T
Nick Tischler
Elizabeth Tucker
Julie Anne West
Roxy Wilding

My kisses across your breast, like water from a jug!
They'll have an end, and soon, our days of summer heat.
Nor shall we every night rise up in trailing dust
The hurdy-gurdy's bellow, stamp and drag our feet.
I've heard about old age. What ominous forebodings!
That no wave will lift again to the stars,
That waters will speak no more; no god in the woods;
No heart within the pools; no life in meadowlands.
O rouse your soul! This frenzied day is yours to have!
It is the world's midday. Why don't you use your eyes?

From 'Sparrow Hills' in *My Sister Life* by Boris Pasternak, translated by Eugene M.
Kayden

Prologue

I'm maybe three or four metres away when he sees me. The gun swings across to point at my face. The barrel opening glints in the sun, a perfect circle. I close my eyes and wait for him to kill me.

A blast rattles my eardrums. I open my eyes. He cocks the hammer once more and straightens his arm.

But already I'm running towards him. Moments later, my foot finds his groin. He makes a grunt tinged with a yelp, like a dog whose paw has been trodden on. His body hinges at the waist and the satchel falls from his shoulder.

The gun is still in his hand. He raises his arm.

I lunge at the gun, knowing I have one last chance. My hand grips his, firmly clasped over the handle. The gun wavers between us, pointing at the sky, at him, at me...

Then everything is silent.

1

Julian has been quiet since he arrived. His rigid posture, stick-thin back and clump of pale hair suddenly make me think of a scarecrow.

'What's the matter, Jules?'

His eyes fix on mine with an uncanny intensity. Instead of his studious-looking black plastic-rimmed specs – 'Joe 90s', I call them – he's wearing his new contacts. They transform the uncertain haze of his irises to a precise blast of metallic blue. The effect is disconcerting.

'Oh, just things,' he replies, finishing his glass of wine. He prods a piece of the tandoori chicken from the local Indian as if a slug has crawled onto his plate. 'I've been feeling a bit off lately.'

Come Away With Me, Julian's favourite album, is playing low in the background. Norah Jones' sweetly sad rendition of 'Don't Know Why' seeps through my flat, adding to the melancholy mood.

'What things? Bridges?'

Aside from his shiny black Jaguar XK8 and watching Formula One races, Julian's thing is bridges. He specialises in bridge design at his civil-engineering firm.

He scowls. 'I don't want to go into it now.'

'If it's to do with the earrings… I'm sorry if I upset you.'

'Don't worry, it's nothing. They look nice, by the way.'

'Thanks.' I pull my hair back and turn my head to show off my ears, each adorned with a disc of lapis lazuli set in a spiral of silver. 'I do like them. I didn't mean to be ungrateful. I was a bit taken aback, that's all. We never give each other anything for Valentine's Day. We're not like that… ' I wait for him to look up from the table. 'Are we?'

'Apparently not.'

Since he gave me the earrings two days ago – he thought I'd appreciate them because I didn't get any Valentine cards – they've sat in their box inside my dressing-table drawer, where I keep things that I'm not sure what to do with: foreign coins, spare buttons and a collection of brooches, scarves and other items my mother has given me over the years. I put them on for the first time fifteen minutes before Julian arrived. Julian has never before given me jewellery; on our birthdays we buy each other silly cards and maybe a cake or a bottle of wine.

'What do you mean?' A woolly unease gathers inside me.

'It's OK, Jaf. If that's what you want, I understand.' He turns his attention back to the table.

Jaf, originally Jaffa, was Julian's nickname for me at university, when I had a thing for Jaffa Cakes. I got to know him in my final year; we both hung around the same local pubs where certain bands played. At first I saw him as a bit of a geek, obsessed by puzzles and anything with an engine. But it didn't take long to find the humour beneath his reserve. I got Julian in a way that some people didn't. Like me, he had issues with his mother. She died unexpectedly, soon after we finished uni. It struck me as odd that he decided he 'couldn't be bothered' to go to her funeral.

Julian sighs, his shoulders slumping. 'Hey, why don't you open another bottle?'

I find the bottle of Haut Medoc that my father gave me. The contents smell like a dusty library but taste pretty good. We chat about the dangers of stilettos; Julian's sister caught her heel in a drain cover while running for a bus.

'No one knows what random fluke is going to strike next,' Julian gazes around the room as if expecting a meteorite to crash through the ceiling. 'A car accident, an incurable disease… '

'You're in a cheery mood.'

Julian pushes himself up from the table. 'It's Saturday night 'n' all. What about a film? I brought a DVD over.'

I take the wine and glasses into the living room and tend to the DVD player. As I sit down on the sofa beside Julian he gestures to the magazine on my coffee table. It has a full-page, near-naked male model on its back cover.

'That hunk's been there for a while. Your bit of hot totty, is he?'

'Well, you know how it is for us single girls,' I smile. 'I fantasise about him ringing my doorbell late at night, wearing just Calvin Kleins under his coat. I give him a shot of whisky and he unbuttons the coat, really slowly.'

A small crease appears above Julian's nose, and rather than laugh as he'd normally do, he says in a low voice, not looking at me, 'I don't know why you bother with all these guys. If you don't want a relationship, why go out with them in the first place?'

'What guys? There's been about three in the last six months.' I scowl at him. 'I *do* want a relationship. Just not with anyone.'

'Not with me, you mean.' He says it under his breath.

Something has changed between us, a micro shift. I take a slug of wine.

'You've been acting really weird lately,' I say. 'Do you want to tell me something?'

He rubs the bridge of his nose, not meeting my eyes. I feel a surge of irritation.

'Jaf.' A blotch of red creeps up his neck. 'You know I've always... fancied you.'

Julian has never hidden from me that he finds me attractive. Sometimes he compliments my legs or how I'm dressed. A few months ago in the Hampstead Everyman as we sat in the dark waiting for the film to start, he told me my face had the perfect bone structure. I giggled, nearly choking on my popcorn. Julian is shortsighted and on the scrawny side, whereas the only man I've ever been in love with and most of the guys I've dated have been strapping fellows. He has a high forehead, straight nose and wavy hair, lighter than mine. Handsome enough in a studious, slightly effeminate way. Like me, he went to a private school. An aristocratic overtone sometimes enters his voice, as if he's asking the butler to bring him the newspaper.

'Well, yes, sure,' I reply. 'But I didn't think... ' I'm up-ended for a moment. 'We're pretty close, aren't we? But we've always kept it on one side of the line. That's what I really like about us. It's not like we're in each other's pockets, we're not fuck buddies or anything. Are you saying you want to... Well, what *are* you saying?'

'Sorry, Georgie, I didn't mean to confuse you. It's just... ' He sighs, running his hand through his hair. 'I don't know. Can we talk about it another time?'

Now we're finally getting to the nub of the matter, I don't want to let it go. I wonder what's going on; we can usually talk about anything, pretty much. His dread of losing his hair and his hope to one day become a father. My loathing of being photographed and my secret wish to get a tattoo of a seahorse at the top of my left thigh. His ambition to be his firm's/the UK's/the world's number-one bridge designer. My uncertainties over what I should be doing with my life. The real purpose of bras. The components of dust. And the top ten ways to die – skiing off a mountain (accidentally or on purpose) is the only item we agree on.

The film is in French. I try to follow the plot but I've drunk rather too much. It's all beautifully shot scenes of couples quarrelling and making up and climbing in and out of each other's beds.

When it's over, Julian yawns and stretches. 'Another bottle? I feel like getting wasted.'

'It's late. I've had a hectic week.'

'Come on, it's Saturday night. You're getting boring. Once you're thirty you can drink a mug of hot milk and go to bed at ten every night.'

I slap his arm playfully and get the wine.

'We could play that game we used to play,' Julian says.

We're slumped on the sofa now, side by side, feet on the coffee table.

'Which game? I don't think I could manage anything except dominoes.'

The third bottle is almost gone and so is my brain. The rest of my body is struggling; what it most wants is sleep.

'We swap confessions – bad things we did years ago, secrets we haven't told anyone, that kind of thing.'

'OK… You go first.'

'There was this girl at my school. Hannah. She was the cool type, popular. I was mad about her, but to her I was invisible. After a while, I came to my senses. I decided to pay her back.' His eyes gleam. 'I took a mouse from the biology lab and put it in her sports bag.'

'You didn't!'

'I hung around outside the girls' changing room. There was a huge scream. I heard that the mouse ran right up her leg –'

'That's terrible. The poor girl.'

'Your turn.'

'I can't think… OK, I was thirteen. I was pissed off with my mother for not letting me go to the shops on my own. I took two tenners from her purse, went down to HMV and bought some CDs. She didn't say anything about the missing money. She left us three days later. I felt really bad for not owning up. I used to have this idea that my stealing from her was what made her leave.'

Julian doesn't speak for a long time.

'I never told you about the time my mother left me, did I?'

I come back from my reverie with a start. 'I don't think so.'

'My mother, my sister and I were in the car coming back from my grandmother's. It was the summer holidays. I was nine. My sister and I were flicking elastic bands at each other – my mother blamed me, as usual. When she stopped to fill the car, I got out for the toilet. I came back to find them gone. She'd driven off without me.' Julian's voice sounds small and hollow, as if he's become that little boy again.

'On purpose?'

'She said neither of them realised I wasn't in the car. But I was stuck in that place for fucking ages. I think she did it to teach me a lesson.'

'That must have been awful.'

'Shitty things happen. But life goes on.' He reaches over and touches my cheek. 'You're beautiful, did I ever tell you?'

I stare at him. My mind has slipped out for a while, leaving no one in charge.

'I want you so much, Jaf. You've no idea.'

His voice is strange, reckless. He leans over to kiss me. Instinctively, I pull away.

'What's the matter? Have I got bad breath?'

'I don't want to have sex with you, Julian.'

'Are you sure?' He puts his hand on my thigh and gazes at me with bluer-than-blue eyes.

'I don't think this is a good idea… ' I catch sight of the bulge in his jeans.

'How do you know, if you never give it a chance? We could be amazing together.'

'It would spoil our friendship,' I insist. 'It would change everything.'

'Come on, Georgie, don't be so uptight.'

My intuition tells me not to do it. But suddenly I feel weary, worn down. What the hell, why not give it a try? Perhaps it'll be wonderful and I'll change my mind about wanting to just stay friends. If it's not wonderful, the sex thing will be out of the way and we can go back to how things used to be.

'I've got another confession to make,' Julian says as we lie on my bed afterwards. I'm naked; he still has his shirt on, half unbuttoned.

I look at him, only half listening, still coming to terms with what we've done. My vagina feels tender. I put on my pyjama top that's hanging on the bed post, pulling it firmly over my breasts.

'I love you, Georgie.'

I recoil. It's as if he's lobbed a brick at me. 'You love me? Since when?'

'Long enough. It wasn't a lightning-bolt kind of thing. More a moss-growing kind of thing.'

'Why didn't you say anything?' I push myself up onto the pillows and try to get my bearings.

'I knew you'd take it badly.' He laughs, a tepid gurgle in the back of his throat. 'Hey, it's one of those things. I know you don't love me back – that's not the sort of girl you are.'

I don't know what to say. This is all wrong.

'I'm sorry, Jules. You're a wonderful friend... But that's all.'

Julian gets out of bed and picks up a sock from the floor. I can't see his face.

After an age, he speaks. 'I'm sorry too, Georgie. This is all my fault. I've had way too much to drink.'

'Me too.' I try to stand but wobble and sit back on the bed. 'I'm sozzled.'

'I shouldn't have pushed it. You didn't really want to.'

'It's OK, don't beat yourself up about it. I said yes, didn't I?'

It isn't OK, though. Why did I do it? Where have all my principles gone?

I try to think of something to say to clear the air. But there's an awkwardness between us now that won't go away. Julian starts to dress; I take a long shower.

'I'd better be off,' he announces on my return. 'I promised Rob I'd go trout fishing somewhere in the back of beyond... I'll text you later in the week. Let's get together next weekend, shall we?'

His tone borders on casual, as if nothing has happened.

Next morning I don't wake till midday. For a few moments I savour the sensation of being not fully awake with no need to go anywhere or do anything. Then dismay pours through me.

Julian. I went to bed with him. How could I have done something so stupid?

The night before rushes back. His sloppy dog kisses. His eager, slightly clumsy foreplay, interrupted by me fumbling with the bedside lamp for a packet of condoms. My increasing discomfort while I wait for him to finish. The grip of his hands on my arms, his harsh breath in my face. Closing my eyes and wondering if I should say something. The weirdness of it all.

I feel a surge of anger with myself for being such a dolt. After all my intentions to get things straight between us, I've gone and had sex with him. Then I feel angry with Julian. He encouraged me to drink to excess. Did he plan this all along?

It's coming back now. There's something else, even worse. Julian is in love with me.

I swear aloud. Why hasn't he told me before? Why did I never realise?

After the 'bee guy', as I mentally refer to him, I built a barrier to ward off love in its various manifestations. Not on purpose, it just happened. I've dated guys on and off, quite a few over the years, wondering if one day I will meet one who will be different to the others, who might make me want something beyond some interesting conversations and good sex. But I haven't considered the reverse – that someone might fall in love with me.

More than once lately, I've sensed something going on beneath the surface in Julian. He'll look at me without speaking and not admit what he's thinking about. I never imagined he was in love with me, though. He kept that well hidden. He told me not long ago how glad he was that we were friends, that a good friendship is better than a relationship because it can last for ever. I agreed, joking that we would probably still be friends in our eighties, sharing Christmases at our care home. Still, I always hoped – expected – for him to find a proper relationship sooner or later, perhaps with a leggy girl who loved obscure French films and could cook a perfect *melanzane*.

But now I know for sure. There isn't going to be someone else. It's me he wants.

2

I leave the office late and follow my usual route towards King's Cross. The sky glares down, a dirty yellow. Along Regent's Canal, converted warehouses hem in narrow streets.

Usually I enjoy the walk. But tonight my document-clogged bag feels as if it's been packed with stones. My mind is weighed down too. Julian begins to burrow into my thoughts.

Some way on, I realise I've missed my turning. I take the next street, recalling from the *A–Z* that it joins up with my usual route. After a while, low-rise blocks of flats sprinkled with sandwich shops and cheap cafés replace gated office buildings. There's little traffic. A heavily perfumed teenage girl in four-inch heels click-clacks towards me; concrete walls return the sound like a volley of bullets. A man tethered to a heavily muscled Rottweiler passes by on the opposite side. I pause, wondering if I'm still headed towards the station. But there are no turnings off. I'll have to retrace my steps, or keep on.

Ahead, in time with my footsteps, a distant percussive thump grows louder. I approach its source – a traditional-looking pub, name hidden by a scrawl of ivy. But a cosy glow shows behind the steamed-up windows and between guitar riffs I catch snatches of animated voices. I glance at the message chalked up on the pavement blackboard: TONIGHT 8PM THE KITTYHAWKS.

I'm not sure exactly why I go in. To take my mind off Julian, or the long, demanding day – and a sudden sense that it's time to do something different.

Inside, cigarette smoke mingles uneasily with chip-frying smells. One large room, more crowded than I had imagined. I make my way past a group of youngish guys in suits towards a gap at the bar, peel off my new camel coat, half price in the Harvey Nichols' sale and order a bottle of Becks. As I wait, a couple of leather-jacketed men hunched over their pints look at me enquiringly. Their lined faces and yellowing fingers don't entice me. I grab my beer and make a beeline for the only free table. A stained beer mat graces it, along with a small heap of ash.

The band is squashed into a corner at the far end of the room. From time to time I glimpse a nattily dressed chap on keyboard and the guitarist's head as he leaps into the air. My foot begins to tap.

At the next table, a lone old man dips into a bag of Liquorice All-sorts. I watch him herd the round, dotty ones into a clump beside his empty glass.

I'm halfway through my lager when my mobile bleeps. A message from Julian.

What are you up to Saturday night? Can we talk?

I hesitate. We often see each other on Saturday nights, now we're both unattached. A few drinks at the pub, a takeaway, then a DVD. A trip to the Roundhouse, maybe. But perhaps it's given out the wrong message, encouraged him to see me as something other than a friend. I text back.

Busy Saturday. 12ish Sunday?

My thoughts are interrupted by the drummer pounding on his high hats as if getting even for a deep grudge. Someone announces the band will be taking a break, the old man dips his hand into the bag for another Allsort and I slump back into my chair, thinking I ought to find a way home.

It weaves in and out of my awareness, a tendril of sound seeking sympathetic ears. I look up. Someone is playing the keyboard, not the guy from the band. The music is totally different too; it has a delicate, wistful quality. A handful of notes repeat with subtle variations, softly and slowly at first, then swirling and surging, forming intricate textures of sound. Snatches of melodies come and go like smoke.

A lump comes to my throat. The music is strange yet beautiful.

I crane my neck to see the player better. Finally I glimpse him. Creased brow, parted lips, stubbly jaw. Dark hair needing a cut, flopping into his eyes whenever he moves his head.

A little later he looks up, as if remembering he's not alone, abruptly gets to his feet and disappears into the crowd. A small delay is followed by ragged applause and a fiendish whistle, and I'm jolted back into that unremarkable pub with its ash-specked tables and smell of stale cooking oil. Nudging aside my disappointment I reach for my coat, recalling without pleasure the Sainsbury's Thai Red Curry awaiting me at home.

On my way out, I spot the guy who's been playing. He's standing alone by a pillar, holding a pint glass.

I go to him. He smells lemony with a faint tang of something else, something earthier. His mouth has the sort of lips that makes one think of kissing.

'I just wanted to say – I loved what you were playing.'

He doesn't seem to hear, though the band hasn't yet restarted and I'm standing close to him.

I lean in and speak louder. 'Hello –'

In a split second his forearm swings up towards my face. Instinctively I swerve out of the way, a moment before the edge of his hand would have connected with my jaw.

I stand staring at him, then at his dripping glass and the puddle of beer at his feet. Words I can't understand spill from his lips.

'I'm sorry,' I say, not sure whether I'm more annoyed with this man for his total overreaction or with myself for being foolish enough to intrude on him.

'No, I am sorry, I am idiot.' His accent is strong, Eastern European. He's staring at me, still holding on to his glass as I retrieve tissues from my bag. 'I don't know what I do... I am sorry.'

He sounds so contrite, I smile. 'At least my self-defence classes came in handy.' I take off my coat and dab hurriedly at its soggy sleeve. 'I thought you were going to clobber me.'

'You move fast for girl.' He wipes a beery hand on his thigh.

'I assume that's a compliment? Here, have a tissue.'

'Thank you. I will pay to clean your coat.'

'It's nothing, don't worry. Anyway, it was my fault... mostly.'

He smiles. 'OK, I will buy you drink... Please, I would like.' He digs into his jeans pocket and brings out a ten-pound note. The end of his sleeve is frayed.

I hesitate. 'All right, just one.'

Part of me wants to go home. This guy has an edge to him. He isn't the sort of guy I generally spend time with: professional types who never leave the house unless their shirt is ironed and a Black-Berry is tucked into their jacket pocket. But something about him stops me leaving.

He brings our drinks over and puts them on the ledge. He's in his mid-twenties, I guess, a few years younger than me and six foot or near enough, though the thickness of his upper body makes him seem shorter. As he stands there, legs apart, feet planted firmly on the floor, it strikes me that not many men would be able to take him on and win.

'I am Nikolai.' He says it as if he's the chieftain of some tribe, and reaches for my hand.

'Georgie.' Taken aback at the formality, I return his grip. 'You're Russian?'

'Yes, Russian.' The 'r' is rolled excessively.

'I didn't recognise that music. Who wrote it?'

'Me, I write.'

'That's amazing… Where did you learn to play like that?'

He shrugs. 'My mother was pianist. She teaches me everything about music.'

'You must practise for hours.'

'Not now, I have no piano since I come to London.' He sighs, looking at the floor. 'But tonight, I am in mood to play.'

'Have you been in London long?'

'Five weeks… I like London but I am… homesick.' Again, he makes that exaggerated gesture, half shrug and half orator making a point, head tilting as he lifts a shoulder, accompanied by a broad sweep of his upturned palm. 'I lived in Perm, it is day on train from Moscow.'

'I've never heard of it.'

'It is big city with big river – beautiful river. Boris Pasternak once lives there. He takes Perm into his book –'

'*Dr Zhivago.*'

'That's right. But he is poet first.'

'It sounds like a great place,' I say, adding before I can stop myself, 'I'd love to see it one day.'

'It is my home.' A peculiar look crosses his face. '*Was* my home.'

He reaches for his glass, exposing a thick, purplish welt on top of his wrist. I try not to stare.

'I am sorry I fight you earlier,' he says, following my eyes. 'It is not usually my way to meet girls.' He smiles, an amused, teasing smile that makes me smile back.

'I'm glad to hear it, Nikolai. Where did you learn English?'

'It is so bad?'

'Not at all; it's very good.'

'My sister helped me. Irina. She is tourist guide in St Petersburg.'

Behind us, a clatter as the band returns. Someone pushes past me, nearly spilling my drink.

'Do you write music for a living?'

He cups his hand against his ear – the sound level has gone up several notches. I repeat my question against the thrash of percussion.

'No, I would like. But for now I must do other things. I have job in restaurant, for two weeks now. I peel potatoes, chop potatoes. I am getting good at this. Soon they will let me loose on the carrots.' He steadies his eyes on mine, making my heart beat triple time. They are close to black; the thick frill of lashes could have come out of a box. 'And you? What is your work? You are clever woman, I think.'

'Oh, yes, very clever.' I smile. 'I work in marketing.'

'Marketing,' he repeats with a frown.

'I work for a company that sells food supplements,' I explain. 'Tablets for women who need extra vitamins, extra iron or whatever.' His frown deepens. 'I work on promotion, advertising and so on.'

'I am impressed.'

I think he might be teasing me; a smile waits behind his lips. He's standing just a few inches away, his eyes roaming my face.

'What made you leave Russia?'

His jaw tenses. 'It was time for me to leave, that is why.'

It's as if someone else is speaking. A muscle at the corner of his eye begins to twitch. Then an eruption of raucous laughter from two teenage girls sitting nearby. One thumps the table and swears loudly.

'I learn many words in your pubs,' Nikolai says in a changed voice, level and friendly. 'Girls in London, they swear like men.'

It takes me a second or so to respond. 'How many swear words do you know?'

'Good God, Jesus Christ, Christ Almighty, damn you, fuck you, fucking hell… ' He rattles them off like an announcer going through a list of railway stations. 'I think this is all.'

'Bollocks.'

He gives me a quizzical look.

'It's not as bad as "fuck". You can say, "Oh bollocks!" if you miss your train. And if you don't agree with someone you can say, "What a load of old bollocks!"'

'Thank you, this is very useful,' he says, perfectly seriously. 'I will practise at home… What a load of old bollocks!'

'You devil!' I laugh; he sounds just like me.

He smiles. 'I am mimic, I am sorry. At school my teachers all tell me I am devil.'

'Oh, I forgot. If you really like something you can say it's "the dog's bollocks". Be careful with that one, though.'

'This beer,' he replies without hesitation, reaching for his glass, 'it is the dog's bollocks.'

That cracks me up.

'That is right?'

'Absolutely.'

As he drinks, my eyes are drawn again to the scar on his wrist.

'It is ugly, no?'

'How did you get it?'

' From… ' – he gestures impatiently, gazing around as if hoping to pluck a word from the air – '… grenade.'

'You were in the army?'

'I fight for Russian army. They send me to Chechnya.'

I'm about to ask more; I don't know anyone in the military and know next to nothing about Chechnya. But he doesn't let me.

'So, Georgie, what about you? Where you live, it is near?'

I tell him I live near Hampstead Heath, a few miles to the north and handy for the office, where I spend much of my waking hours.

'And when you are not working? What do you like to do?'

'Oh, the usual things.'

'The usual things?'

'After a hard day I love wallowing in the bath with the lights down and a CD playing – the blues, Beethoven… I go climbing and hiking a lot. Well, I used to, not so much now. It takes me most of Saturday to recover from a week at the office.'

A crease appears on his brow. He's studying me again.

'You have busy life, I see. You have time for boyfriend?'

'Not any more. I'm not looking for one, either.' I try to keep my voice light, though his directness is unsettling.

His eyebrows raise a fraction. 'Why is that? You do not want love?' Again, that frank stare.

'I didn't say that, did I?' I don't quite succeed in keeping the annoyance out of my voice. My eyes are smarting from the smoke and I'm hungry enough to eat a 12-inch pizza. I don't need to be interrogated by a guy I've only just met. 'I'm sorry, I don't mean to be rude. But I must be getting home; I've had a long day.'

'I will come back here next Thursday, Georgie.' He smiles warmly. 'Maybe you will too?'

'Maybe.' I can't help but smile back. 'And thanks for the beer.'

'It is my pleasure. I am sorry again for your coat.'

He helps me on with it and I leave, wishing I hadn't been quite so sharp with him. But as I hurry towards King's Cross, after checking I'm going the right way, I have no intention of seeing the Russian again.

3

Saturday dribbles by. I wake late then go back to sleep. After breakfast in bed I run a bath, then think of phoning Ella. Usually we chat on Saturday mornings and arrange to meet for a coffee in the afternoon, or go to see a film. But I'm not in the mood for talking to anyone, not even on the phone. A kind of haze is enveloping my mind. It keeps going back to the pub, and the Russian guy.

I get on with chores around the flat then flop onto the sofa with an old Murakami paperback I've never got round to finishing. After a while I put it down, realising I've read the same page twice. I spend a while decluttering my desk then sort out the fridge and start on the cupboard drawers.

Buried under elastic bands, Sellotape, utility bills and old postcards, I come across the photograph of my mother, unframed, one corner slightly worn. It's the only picture I've kept of her, taken in the garden of a villa overlooking Lake Garda where my parents and I stayed one summer when I was small. I found it months ago in my father's photo album. Wavy, straw-toned hair tumbles down from under my mother's scarf, its shade exactly matching her vermillion lips, caught mid-laugh. A simple cotton dress shows off her narrow waist. She looks 100 per cent happy, the opposite of the distracted, weary expression I remember. I think that's why I keep it. I often wonder how things might be different if she'd stayed happy.

Standing there, photograph in hand, studying my mother, the usual stirrings of anger and regret fade. For the first time what strikes me are the similarities in our looks, not the differences. I know I don't have the can't-tear-your-eyes-away kind of beauty my mother had. But I recognise an echo of her beauty in my own face; I have her cute nose, pointy jaw and greenish-grey eyes.

I take the photograph into the living room and put it on the mantelpiece. Through the window, a buttery blob of sun is smeared across the sky. Shadows creep up walls and trees, removing each patch of brightness in turn.

I'll go for a walk before it gets dark; that might help lift my spirits. Something is nagging at me, trying to find a way in.

A sprinkling of people are still about on Hampstead Heath, throwing sticks for dogs or standing around, hands in pockets, gazing at the ponds. Geese flap across a pale, cut-out moon.

As I follow the path towards the woods, the question the Russian guy asked a few days ago keeps repeating like an infuriating advertising jingle.

You do not want love?

Although the only child of divorced parents, I'm hardly alone in life. My father and I get on reasonably well. I have friends I can rely on and confide in. Aside from Julian and a sprinkling of more recent friends, there's the gang. They keep me cheerful, most of the time. But who can I cuddle up to on cold nights and warm my feet on? Who can I hold hands with, whisper silly things to?

And yet... I tried love once and it came to nothing. Worse than nothing.

The stillness of the church that afternoon comes back. The hours I sat gazing at the statue of Christ, the bee guy's cruel words leeching into my mind. If this was love, I decided, I want nothing more to do with it. It's too painful, too futile. Everyone I love will leave me in the end.

I stop at a cluster of oaks. One tree is slightly separated from the rest. I touch its trunk, thick and grooved like armour. An ache presses at my throat. I can't risk falling in love again.

4

'Hiya.'

I step into his flat. Julian has his Joe 90s back on. His hair is damp from the shower, sticking up at the front. He smells pleasantly fragrant.

'Coffee? Glass of wine?'

He busies himself in the kitchen, which occupies a corner of the expansive living area. I go over to the ceiling-high glass doors that lead out to the deck. I wonder how many times we've sat out there among the potted palms, chatting over beer, oblivious to passing time. And if all that will now have to change.

Clinking sounds bring me back to the present. Julian is taking an age to pour two glasses of wine.

'Do you want some help in there?'

'I'll just be a moment. Sit down, chill.'

I walk over to the framed photographs and drawings on the wall of his favourite bridges: the Millau Viaduct, the Clifton Suspension Bridge... Below them, bridges that have come to an untimely end: the first Quebec Bridge, Silver Bridge, Tacoma Narrows...

Julian emerges from the kitchen and hands me a glass of cold white wine. He meets my eyes with an awkward smile.

'Sorry about Saturday night. It was a bit of a disaster, wasn't it? I shouldn't have come over in the first place. I definitely shouldn't have got you to open that third bottle.'

I sit on one of his stylish but uncomfortable leather armchairs on either side of the coffee table.

'I hope I didn't hurt you or anything,' he continues, settling into the other chair. 'When, you know –'

'Never mind. What's done is done.' I take a large gulp of wine. This is excruciating. 'What you said, about... being in love with me. I'm glad you told me. But I really wish you'd said something before.'

'I'm sorry, Jaf. I thought you wouldn't be able to handle it. I thought you'd say we'd better not be friends any more.'

A lump comes to my throat. Julian has always been around in my vision of the future. If not with me in person, he'd be at the other end of a phone line in New York or Hong Kong, telling me about the latest findings in quantum physics, or his conversation in the local supermarket with some girl who looked totally like Audrey Tautou. Could I really just say, 'Bye then, see you around some-time'?

He's shaking his head. 'Couldn't you just forget that I love you? Pretend I never said it?'

'It's not that simple. We can't just go on as before.'

'I don't see why not.'

'I would only end up hurting you, don't you see?'

My hand latches on to my glass. Cool, honey-tasting liquid slides over my tongue. The flat hums with silence. Julian stares into the distance, fingers tapping on the arm of his chair.

'So now everything has to change?'

'I don't know, Julian. I just know that I don't feel the same way as you do. I don't –'

'You don't want to walk off into the sunset with me, holding hands. I understand.'

He pushes himself up, takes a few steps towards the glass doors and looks out, his lean figure dark against the sky. His arms hang by his sides, seeming slightly too long for his body. Then he turns to me and speaks, so quietly I can hardly hear.

'I knew it would frighten you.'

'What?'

'You won't let yourself fall in love with anyone, will you? You're too scared you'll end up losing them, like that guy who dumped you.'

A flash of anger goes through me. 'That was below the belt.'

'I'm sorry, that was mean.' He comes over, perches on the arm of my chair and grasps my hand. 'Georgie, listen.' He looks at me expectantly. 'Can't we go on being friends? I promise not to propo-sition you again. Or do anything I shouldn't.' He grins. 'Scout's honour.'

Eventually, I shrug. I'm not sure about anything any more.

'I suppose we could stay friends for now, and see how it works out...'

'Come on, you idiot.' He rolls his eyes. 'You're my best friend, near as damn it. There's no one else like you.'

I don't know what to say.

'How about a walk?' Julian gets to his feet.

We merge with the crowds in Camden Market, picking at items

displayed in stalls, then order coffee in a café. We watch people walking over the narrow arched bridge that crosses the canal. Some stop to photograph each other posing. A lip-studded teenage girl in torn jeans takes a small package from an older guy in a long coat and dark glasses.

I'm grateful for the distraction provided by this activity. Our conversation is stilted; short bursts breaking long silences. The rules between us have changed. I feel as if I'm driving a car for the first time, trying not to stall the engine or rev it too much in case it goes out of control.

'Fancy catching a band later?' His voice is hopeful.

I spoon the froth off the top of my cappuccino. 'I'm tired, I don't want a late night.' It's true enough.

Neither of us speaks for a while. Julian folds over the unused portion of his sugar packet.

'Where were you when I called?'

'What?'

'I called Thursday night, after I got your text. You didn't answer.'

'Oh, I was in the pub, that's all. The music was pretty loud.'

'The pub?'

'I popped into one after work.'

'That's not like you. I thought you said you had loads of stuff to get done for your campaign.'

'I just felt like it, that's all. I took the wrong turn and saw this lively-looking place... '

'So, did you meet anyone interesting?'

'Oh, loads. I had to fight them off.'

'Something happened, didn't it? You met someone.'

'Only some Russian guy who tried to karate-chop me.' I wouldn't have told him if he hadn't asked. But I don't like to lie if there's not a good reason.

Julian sits up straight. 'Go on, tell me the rest.'

I briefly describe the incident.

'Russians – they're all over London, these days.' He says this as if they're cockroaches. He looks at me intently. 'You're going to see him again?'

'I doubt it,' I reply. 'He was an interesting guy – but I'm not sure. There was something a bit... edgy about him.'

Julian's face is blank, as if everything behind it has shut down.

The only movement in his body is his chest as it rises and falls. His lips are slightly parted and I can hear his breathing.

'He sounds a total arsehole.'

I pull my hand away, shocked. Julian never uses that kind of language.

'If I were you,' he adds, 'I wouldn't have anything more to do with him.'

5

The last of my colleagues departs, leaving me alone at the table. Around me, bathed in garish orange from low-hanging lamps, the other diners carry on talking and eating. I drain my bottle of Kirin and stare out of the window into sludgy darkness, now empty of shop and office workers.

The excitement of the evening's impromptu celebration has been replaced by relief. Thank God the campaign is over. The relaunch of ImmunoBoost ('Wonder Woman pills' to the mostly male managers) has been my biggest project to date at Whole-Health, and the most exhausting. Getting my head around key messages, online metrics and the like within a constant stream of deadlines left me so frazzled I decided to personally test a bottle of ImmunoBoost capsules. (They made me feel pleasantly woozy and produced some lurid dreams.)

Two couples nearby laugh loudly. Suddenly I don't want to be alone. What do I have to occupy my time now? My non-existent love life? That foolish escapade with Julian? Work has at least kept unwelcome thoughts at bay. I feel disorientated, as flat as a week-old pancake.

Outside, a couple walk by, his arm around her back. I wonder how it would be to do that again, to hold someone's hand. Before I know it, I'm thinking about the Russian. His full lips, parting in a lazy, skewed-to-the-side smile. Words tumbling from his lips with that endearingly not-quite-right pronunciation, the stress on the wrong syllable or the wrong word. All day long he's been there, in my head, daring me.

It's Thursday night, exactly a week since I met Nikolai. I've already decided, at least five or six times, there would be no point in seeing him again. We're too different. He isn't settled in London; he might leave at any time. What could it ever come to, except a few passionate nights? I would be better off going home to soak in the bath... In any case, it's too late to go to the pub.

I check my watch – 9.55 p.m.. It isn't too late. Not yet.

I get up from the table. Pulling on my coat as I walk, I hurry outside and break into a run, narrowly missing a cyclist as I cross the road.

By the time I reach the pub, I'm sweating and panting, my face flushed. I slow and walk in casually. The air is still hazy with smoke but the place is much quieter than it was last time. People are getting up from tables, putting on coats and scarves. The band is packing up.

Shit, shit, shit!

In a moment, I've scanned every face in that drab room. The students and tourists, the blokes nursing their pints, the red-lipped blonde in a fuck-me dress tapping on her phone. I inch along the bar, double-checking faces. Has Nikolai left already? Or has he decided not to turn up after all?

Then I see him. He emerges from the door at the far end of the room, head lowered, strides long and unhurried, the hems of his jeans dragging, canvas bag slung over his shoulder. For a moment I think he's seen me, but he turns away and goes to sit at a table bearing a pint glass, half finished. Heart pounding, I escape into the ladies' toilets.

The mirror confirms it: I'm a mess. Face pink and shiny, shirt stuck to my back, hair everywhere. I splash cold water over my face, wipe it off with toilet roll, then apply a smear of lipstick and a shot of Miss Dior down my cleavage.

When I return, Nikolai's head is lowered, his shoulders hunched over. I go to the bar and order a Scotch and soda. It's no big deal, I tell myself. I'll just walk up to him and say hello.

But when I look over to the table again, Nikolai has gone. Panicking, I scour the room.

'Georgie! I think you will not come.' He's standing beside me. In my confusion, I nearly spill my drink.

'Oh, fuck,' I say under my breath.

'You forget my name?'

His accent seems stronger than before. A faint hint of lemons again; shower gel, perhaps.

'Nikolai.' I smile helplessly, feeling like an idiot. 'Hello again.'

'Call me Nikky, if you like. It is what everyone calls me.'

He brushes a frond of hair from his eyes, which stray to my lips and travel downwards. I grope for a stool, feeling my face warm.

'Let me.' He pulls the stool over for me and props himself against another. 'Why do you come so late?'

'I was with people from work,' I mumble. 'A sort of celebration. I'm so glad you're here.'

'And I am glad that you are here.' He gives a big smile, showing dimples and shiny teeth. 'I come at seven, full of hope to see a special girl again. I look everywhere but there is no sign. I eat chips, listen to very bad music, watching for her. Then it is nine o'clock and I start to lose my hope. I go to sulk and get drunk… Then, a miracle.'

I laugh, yet my heart skips with delight.

'You have a silver tongue, Nikolai. You must have had lots of practise charming the ladies.'

'You take me wrong way, Georgie. I have eyes for one lady only.'

'Don't be silly.' I take refuge in my drink, downing half of it. 'I'm sorry I came so late… How are you, anyway?'

'I have not been so happy. It is difficult for me lately.' He sighs, the brightness leaving his face.

'Are you at the restaurant still?'

He shakes his head. 'No, I finish there. I spend these last days looking for work.'

'No luck?'

'Everywhere they ask for my references, my union card, history of my life from when I am child. I am not sure what is wrong. My English is too bad, or it is how I look? I do not have nice clothes, I am not pretty like dandelion.' He frowns. 'Not dandelion.'

I can't help laughing, conjuring an image of a huge straggly dandelion sitting opposite me.

'Dandy, you mean?'

'Dandy, that is right!' He laughs too. 'I hear in old British film.'

'What sort of work are you looking for?'

'Construction worker, labourer… The pay is better than restaurants. I have done before, in Russia.'

'Won't it damage your hands? For playing the piano, I mean.' I study the large hand resting on the bar between us, with its bold veins and long, strong fingers.

'Maybe. But I must work to survive.'

Before I can reply, the background music stops mid-song and the overhead lights come on. Staff begin to go around collecting glasses and ashtrays from tables. Nikolai glances at the door.

'My father owns a construction business,' I say quickly, afraid he might get up to leave. 'He uses an agency to get temp workers. It's in the City somewhere, you could try it. I don't think they care about people having the right documents.' My father told me that the agency uses mainly foreign workers and doesn't bother with all the red tape imposed by larger agencies.

'Wait, I write down.' He lifts his bag from the floor, rifles inside and produces a stub of pencil and a scrap of paper.

I give him the scant details I can remember. 'I think that's the right name. You can check the number in the phone book.'

'Thank you very much, I will try tomorrow.' He looks at me with a frown. 'What is name of your father's business?'

'Cameron Construction.'

'It is big company?'

'It's got over a hundred employees. They specialise in substructures – excavation, basements…'

A draught hits us as someone opens the door. Nikolai glances quickly around the room, then reaches for an ancient-looking leather jacket.

'You are going to take the Tube, Georgie? I go to King's Cross.'

We walk quickly, keeping a small gap between us. Last year's withered leaves swirl at our feet. The cold air makes my nose and ears tingle.

'It is good night for walk,' Nikolai says.

'It is, yes. Where do you live, Nikky?'

'Finsbury Park. You know?'

'Not well.' I went there once, to buy a *tagine*. It's always seemed a rundown, slightly depressing area, though only three miles east of my flat, which is in a well-heeled part, a short walk from Belsize Park and Chalk Farm Tube stations, Hampstead 'Village' and Hampstead Heath – my favourite bit of London. I vaguely recall reading in the paper that a man was stabbed to death by Finsbury Park Station.

'It is not so bad. I take what I can afford.'

We lapse into silence. Another bus rattles past, empty of passengers. I cast around for something else to say.

'Did you volunteer for the army?'

He looks at me as if I've suggested he eat a piece of rotten fruit.

'No, I was conscript – they force me to be soldier. It is the way things are in my country. If you are boy, when you finish school you go into the army. Except if your family has money or they know people who can help you – or you go to university. I was not good student. I do not pass exams and my father cannot pay enough to bribe the medical officer.'

'Were you there long?'

'I start in 1998. Everyone must serve two years. The first war is over, we think we will go home without fighting. But then another war starts and we are sent to fight in Chechnya.'

'That must have been a shock.'

'I was ready to fight. I hated the Chechens – we all hated them.'

'Why did you hate them? It's probably a stupid question, but isn't Chechnya part of Russia?'

'Russians have always hated the Chechens and the Chechens hate us back. For hundreds of years, we do terrible things to each other… ' His voice becomes animated. 'Many Russians think Chechens will shoot you in the back or cut off your head. When I come into army, I too think that Chechens are not like us. Our commander tells us of madmen in Chechnya who will do anything for Islam.'

'I can understand why you'd hate them,' I say.

'I do not hate them, not now. They are people, aren't they? They are not so different to us. Except they wear different clothes, say different prayers… But enough of this. I have enough of war and army. I would rather talk about you.' He slows and touches my arm. 'Georgie – it is your real name?'

'My parents called me Georgina – I've always hated it. It sounds like someone who goes to dinner parties and belongs to the Young Conservatives. Georgie isn't like that.'

'What is Georgie like?'

I think for a moment. 'I'm quite independent, I like to do my own thing. I'm quite into my career, at least I was… ' My mind goes blank. What else could I admit to?

'You are good person?'

I hesitate. 'I try to do the right thing, yes. I'd help someone who was in trouble, if I could, I suppose.' I smile. 'But I'm no angel. There's definitely room for improvement.'

'Tell me.'

'I'm bad tempered, I haven't got much patience. My plants are always dying because I forget to water them… I'm not so good with people either, to tell the truth.' I sense I might be saying too much but words are spilling out of my mouth. 'Maybe it's because I'm too used to being on my own… Sometimes I feel there's something missing from me. Like I'm a recipe that's gone wrong, someone's left out an important ingredient.'

'Me too, my recipe has gone wrong. Whoever eats me will spit me out.'

I'm laughing; we're both laughing. This conversation is crazy. I feel lightheaded, as if I've just swallowed a bottle of Wonder Woman pills.

We walk on, towards a fuzzy moon. For the second time, I notice Nikolai turn to look behind. Surely he isn't scared of being mugged? He nudges my arm, pointing to a narrow street lined with parked cars.

'We go this way, it is quicker.'

I follow him without thinking. Ahead, a black taxi stops, discharges a man holding a briefcase, then drives off before I think to hail it. Further along, some street lights are out. As we walk into the gloom, I wonder why I've let Nikolai bring me this way. Why have I trusted this guy, who I scarcely know?

We approach an enclosed garden or small park. Behind metal railings, blackness yawns.

'Wait, Georgie.'

I stop. He moves closer and puts down his bag. We're standing in a pool of darkness; I can't see his face clearly. But I can see the slope of his chest, thick and powerful. Above us, something flits among the branches of an overhanging tree. A breeze scrapes the branches together, fluttering the dead leaves at our feet. I pull my coat tighter.

'You are afraid of me?'

I shake my head, though I think I am, a little. But long ago I decided never to become the sort of woman who scurries around afraid of her own shadow, staying indoors for fear of what some guy might to do her.

He pulls a strand of hair away from my face.

'You are beautiful woman. A woman I would like to know.' His voice becomes sad. 'But I am not like you, Georgie.'

'What do you mean?'

'I have no job, no money, no home... I have nothing except my music.'

'It doesn't matter. Not to me.'

He doesn't answer. I see the slight bend in his nose and the tiny lights reflected in his pupils... The smell of him encloses me. His lips touch mine; I kiss them back. Soft and warm, they make me catch my breath. I put my arms around him. He pulls me against his body and kisses me, deeply. Desire wells inside me. I want him, there and then. In that moment, I want never to part from him.

Finally, Nikolai pulls away. He picks up his bag, puts his hands in his pockets and gazes into the trees.

'We'd better go,' I say, suddenly unsure of myself.

We walk on in silence. The street turns into the main road and everything is well lit again. When we reach the station, Nikolai stops just ahead of the escalators and turns to me.

I'll never see him again, I think, and ready myself to say good-bye.

But he rummages in his bag, finally removing the same stub of pencil and scrap of paper as before.

'Can I have your number, Georgie?'

I look at him in surprise.

'Please, give to me.'

6

After work the following Wednesday I go over to my father's. I'm looking forward to a chat, just the two of us. My stepmother Alicia has her weekly hospice meeting today.

My father greets me at the front door, reading glasses perched on his nose and a stained tea towel slung over his shoulder. The old house, once the family home, is a five-minute walk from Hampstead Heath.

Inside, everything is the same as always. The whiff of furniture polish, the grandfather clock dominating the hall and an antique Italian chair too precious to sit on. Sometimes I half expect my mother to waft down the staircase and ask me to take off my muddy trainers.

In the steel and marble kitchen, my father pours me a large glass of red wine.

'Good day at work, sweetie?'

'Not really.'

My father peers at me over his glasses. 'How did your presentation go last week?'

'It went fine. Jake told me I'd done a great job with the campaign.'

'You don't sound very pleased.'

'Don't I?'

The campaign results showed everyone at work what I'm capable of; more importantly, I've proved to myself how capable I am. Yet now it's all over, I'm not sure why I let myself get so caught up in it all. Jake is pleased with me and hinting about another promotion... Is that worth all those extra hours I put in, I wonder.

A wave of gloom washes over me. I have to admit it: I don't enjoy my job any more.

'Georgie, I don't often say it, I know. But I'm proud of what you've achieved.'

I recall how my father encouraged me to study marketing when I was veering towards the biosciences, imagining myself as a researcher discovering something valuable to humanity. A new vaccine, or how to prevent a crippling inherited disease. As ever unsure of myself and my abilities, I listened when he told me that

31

bioscience research was highly competitive, a field few could succeed in.

My father stares into the middle distance, forehead crumpled.

'So, Dad, how are things with the business? Still having trouble with the union?' The business has been around for as long as I remember. I learned long ago that its fortunes and my father's moods are linked by an invisible cord.

He groans and tops up his glass. 'Now they're demanding that members only do jobs that are one hundred per cent safe. I was accused of trying to drive out the union.'

I say something sympathetic. Though his views often seem harsh, I always try to see my father's side. Judging from this and similar reports, workplace relations are particularly strained of late.

'But that's the least of my worries. Health and Safety were over at the Watford site the other day – we weren't expecting them.' He rubs his eye, a habit he has when under stress. 'They found breaches of the rules: equipment not checked according to schedule, men operating diggers without certificates.'

'Is it serious?'

'It doesn't look good. They're going to prepare a report, we'll see what they say... Anyway, enough of that.' He dismisses the inspectors with a flick of the hand.

We take our glasses into the spotless living room. The carpet shows signs of recent vacuuming and the furniture is dust-free, as usual. I think back to the dusty radiators in my mother's time.

'Blair's going to have a fight on his hands. The Conservatives mean business.' My father gestures at the muted TV, once again filled with politicians' faces.

I carry on flipping through the *Daily Telegraph*. The sooner the general election is over the better, as far as I'm concerned.

'How's Julian? Have you seen him lately?'

'He told me something the other day... I could hardly believe it.'

'What's that?'

I hesitate. My father and I usually avoided personal subjects; there are too many words that have been left unsaid between us.

'He's in love with me.'

'And you don't love him.' My father studies me from underneath raised eyebrows. 'It's a pity. Julian's a decent bloke. You could do a lot worse.'

'He's not the one for me, Dad.'

My father purses his lips, picking at the edge of a fingernail.

'Georgie, there comes a time when… Well, you know what I'm trying to say. You won't be young for ever.'

In September I would be 30, a fact that had begun to stir feelings of unease. But I can't put it off for a while, like a dentist's appointment. As I cast around for a change of subject, a key rattles in a lock. A small thud as the front door closes, then Alicia's dainty figure appears in the doorway, an extravagantly large, furry black hat perched on her head like a curled-up cat.

'Hello, love! I didn't know you were coming over.'

Her hat comes off. I get to my feet and submit to a kiss on each cheek followed by a full-blown hug. For once I'm pleased she's interrupted us.

'I'll see you both soon,' I say, edging towards the door.

7

As he doesn't seem in a hurry to leave, I hand Julian a beer. He came over to my place soon after I got in from work, supposedly to pick up some CDs he lent me, which for some reason I don't quite understand he now needs. I suspect this visit isn't just about his CDs.

We're in my living room, both standing. It's dark outside. The police drama I was planning to watch on TV has started. I've muted the sound and glance at the screen from time to time. I haven't eaten dinner yet and I'm hungry, only I don't want to feel obliged to ask him to join me. I'm tired and I don't want company. Julian's company, in particular.

'Do you remember the night we listened to this?' He picks up the CD on top of the small pile: 'Sweet Dreams (Are Made Of This)'. He's wearing his contacts again. He's quite good looking really, minus the glasses.

I shake my head.

'It was my 23rd birthday. We went to a pub on the King's Road and drank about ten Singapore Slings in a row.' He pushes his hair back from his brow. 'It was happy hour, baking hot.'

'Oh, yes, I remember. Some horrible druggie guy tried to chat me up and you ended up buying a load of dope to get rid of him.'

'Then we went to a graveyard and smoked it. Well, a few joints. You were worried that it was disrespectful to do that near the dead. We lay there for hours, talking and laughing. We were totally out of it.'

'It was a beautiful night, wasn't it? It was like being in India.' The air was warm and sweet, I remember. We were beside a hibiscus and a huge moon lit up the graves.

'We went back to mine and I put on that Eurythmics CD.' His eyes are watering. 'I remember thinking that this might be the best night of my life.' His voice drops. 'That's when I knew how much you meant to me. I knew you probably wouldn't ever feel the same way about me. Not for a long time, anyway.'

We stand there looking at each other, wordless. For the first time I wonder what might have happened if things had been different. If we'd met later. If the bee guy hadn't fucked with my head… But I shouldn't be thinking like this. It isn't going to do any good.

'Is it really too late for us, Georgie?'

I put my hand on his arm and blink back my tears. 'I'm sorry, Julian. I don't know what to say.'

'OK, OK. I know when it's time to go.' He puts down his empty beer bottle and picks up his jacket. 'Have you seen the Russian chap again?'

It sounds like a casual enquiry, no more. Again I feel the foreignness of Nikolai, the scent of him. My heart beats faster.

'I saw him the other day,' I reply, trying to sound equally offhand. 'At the pub.'

'Oh, really?' Julian's eyebrows rise. 'What happened?'

'Nothing happened. We talked for a bit.' My voice sounds almost defiant. I swig the rest of my beer.

'So, when are you seeing him again?'

'Saturday. We're going for a walk.'

A ripple moves over his face. Displeasure, or something worse. 'That's nice.'

A chill goes though me, almost too quickly to notice.

'Where are you going to walk?'

I shrug. 'Hampstead, probably.'

'Let me know how it goes, OK?' Julian puts his hand on mine. 'Jaf? You can still talk to me, you know.'

I say nothing. I know something isn't right. He's keeping something from me.

He turns towards the door. 'See you soon, then.'

8

She's standing there, across the lane. Close enough for me to call out hello. Blue jeans, padded jacket, short boots, the furry insides folded over at the tops. Not much make-up. Hair loose, tickling her shoulders. Scarf draped chicly about her neck. With her long legs and silky hair she could pass for a model.

Every so often she looks at her watch. She's getting agitated, chewing her lower lip, staring at people passing by. Men, that is. Her hair keeps getting blown across her face and each time she pulls it off with an impatient flick of the fingers. The wind has a nip in it today. She hugs herself and rubs her arms. She pushes her hands down into her jacket pockets, rocking from one foot to the other.

It's busy in this quaint little lane. People ducking in and out of boutiques and bakeries, yakking in French, supping their Saturday morning cappuccinos. Old ladies creaking along in cashmere coats and sensible shoes, trendy mums pushing designer kids. Oh, yes, and little old me loitering in a doorway, watching.

A burly man in a khaki jacket strides into view from the direction of the Tube station. His hair is hidden by a beanie. She checks him out too. A sharp turn of the head and the expectant look on her face is wiped in an instant. He disappears into the gallery.

Russell Brand, or his lookalike, emerges from a florist. Diamond earring, pirate beard. She looks again at her watch, ignoring him. Her mouth twists in frustration. She jams her hands in her pockets and strolls along the lane, away from me.

I drain my coffee, ditch the plastic cup. She stops and looks into the florist's window. I go closer, almost close enough to reach out and touch her.

Her long earrings nestle into the curve of her cheekbones. She's wearing gloss on her lips. A trace of light perfume reaches me. Something new, inviting. I feign an interest in the garish display of tulips, unnatural yellows and reds. Funny how dark glasses and a hat can make such a difference. She doesn't recognise me, doesn't even see me.

9

Twenty minutes past twelve and still he hasn't come. I turn away from the second-hand bookshop and move along the cobbled lane, inspecting shop windows. The breeze nips at my nose and cheeks. I catch sight of myself in a window, my slim figure swathed in layers of wool, jeans tucked into ankle boots, beaded earrings swaying.

He's not coming, there's no point waiting.

I check my mobile. No message. I decide to wait ten minutes more then go home.

My stomach feels empty with disappointment. All morning I've looked forward to seeing Nikolai again. I've spent the longest time ever getting ready. Shaping my eyebrows, cleansing, toning. All that girlie stuff I never usually bother with.

I turn and walk slowly back towards the bookshop. Standing outside is a man of Nikolai's height and build. My heart quickens. Hands in pockets, head lowered. Nikolai looks up and waves.

'Georgie!'

He's wearing a sheepskin jacket and the same scuffed trainers. In daylight, his face is less pale. His hair and eyes aren't black, but have a peaty hue.

'Sorry I am so late.' He grasps my hand in his. My heart does a little skip and hop. 'I go wrong way at Camden Town.'

'It's OK. I haven't been waiting long.'

He smiles back, shifting the canvas bag that hangs from his shoulder.

'I am pleased you wait.'

We set off up the lane, passing a row of postcard cottages.

'So, you've found another job? That's great news.'

'I go to the agency you give me. The man asks me lots of questions. Have I worked on building site before? I say yes, in army I build barracks. He asks where I come from, I think he will tell me to go away, then he tells me they need labourers on a building site near Old Street. It will be offices, apartments, very big project. He says can I start tomorrow? Of course, I say yes.'

'So, how's it going?'

He stops walking and pats his right thigh. 'My leg does not like. But this work is simple enough. There is just hole in the ground now, for foundations. I carry things up and down ladders, I break the concrete, I put rubbish in skips.' He sighs.

'Is it temporary?'

'For six months, maybe more. If my body does not give up first.'

'You're OK to walk now?'

'Sure. I am not –' He frowns.

'Disabled?'

'That is it, yes.' He fishes a battered Russian–English dictionary out of his bag. 'I use all the time. I sit with my dictionary and TV to learn more English. I do not let one word escape me.'

I smile. 'What do you watch on TV?'

'*EastEnders* is my favourite. And Sunday afternoons I watch old movies. I try to speak English like my sister. I try to sound like English gentleman.'

'Not too English, I hope. I like your accent.'

'And I like yours. It is beautiful in my ear, like mountain stream.'

I give him a stern look, wondering if he's pulling my leg.

We make for Parliament Hill, avoiding the dogs and kites. At the top we look down on the London skyline, towers glinting like cut glass. A bitter wind pierces my jacket. I pull down my sleeves as far as they will go and fold my arms across my chest.

'You are cold.' Nikolai takes my hand between his and rubs it, as though we've known each other for ages. He does the same with my other hand.

'Thank you.'

'You are excellent guide,' he says, voice serious. 'Where you will take me next?'

We carry on, stopping at a pond to watch moorhens rippling through opaque water. The sky is starting to cloud over. We trudge up a hill and skirt another. The bare trees do little to shelter us from the wind. Our path crosses another, wider one. I stop and search for a landmark.

'We are lost?'

'We must have made a wrong turn, that's all. Let's go back.' It is 2.30 p.m.; we've covered a far larger chunk of the heath than I'd intended. 'Are you hungry yet?'

'Hungry? I am biting off my fingers.'

I look at him sharply, then realise he's teasing.

'Sorry, it is clown in me. I thought I lose him but he is back.'

More tramping over muddy paths. Nikolai stomps through a puddle, splashing his jeans. My ears are frozen and the insides of my boots are damp.

'Sorry for putting you through all this,' I say. 'It's not far now.'

'I have done worse things than this, don't worry.'

The sky darkens further. A raindrop wets my cheek.

'Bollocks! I didn't bring an umbrella.'

Nikolai doesn't reply. He's peering into a tangle of shrubs beside the path.

'What is it?'

'I think I see someone.'

I hear a rustle and see a quick movement of something dark, low in the undergrowth.

'It's a bird, that's all.'

Nikolai looks around some more then sets off at a faster pace. A few minutes later the path veers and we join the avenue of trees leading to the road.

The fire is giving off enough heat to put the sensation back into my fingers and toes. I sip my large glass of Merlot, grateful to be somewhere dry and warm. The pub is crowded. Couples with strollers huddle over the weekend newspapers.

Nikolai insists on paying for our drinks. 'No,' he says, waving dismissively at my tenner. 'I pay.'

'But that's not fair.' I earn more than he does, I imagine.

'Please, I invite you. I do not expect for you to pay.'

We order lunch. Nikolai takes the seat closest to the wall. When our meals come he eats quickly, looking up from his food every so often and glancing nervously about the room.

'What's the matter? Is there someone after you?'

Nikolai doesn't answer. He swallows several forkfuls of mashed potato in rapid succession. I watch a small boy feed his family's leftovers to the Labrador under a nearby table.

'I do not want to stay here,' he says as soon as I finish my meal. 'We will go somewhere else.'

I fight an urge to laugh. 'OK, if we must.'

'There are things you don't know. I must be careful.'

'What things?'

Nikolai pushes away his plate, drops some notes on the table and reaches for his jacket. 'We go now.'

On the way out, I scan the room. There's nothing out of the ordinary.

I almost have to break into a jog to keep up with Nikolai. He strides up the hill towards Hampstead High Street, checking behind two or three times without slowing. I check too. No one except a couple walking hand in hand and a boy on a bicycle.

At the top, the pavement is churning with Saturday afternoon shoppers. Nikolai points at a café and leads me inside.

Most of the tables are taken; Nikolai heads straight to one at the back, pulls out a chair for me and sits down.

'Nikolai, are you all right?'

His face is pale. His lashes flutter against the dark patches under his eyes. I wonder what I would do if he fainted. He puts his elbows on the table and shields his face with his hands, digging his fingertips into his brow. He hasn't removed his jacket.

'I am sorry, Georgie.' He places both hands on the table. I notice their prominent veins, the long, capable fingers.

'What's happening?'

He shrugs.

'You think someone's following you? Why would they want to do that?'

'It is nothing.' He lowers his head, biting his lip. 'I am too worried today. I am frightened of my own shadow.'

'I don't understand.'

'It is difficult to explain. I come from a country where bad things happen. It is different from here. Here, you can go to the police if you need; they will protect you. In Russia, it is not like that. People make their own rules –'

'But you're not in Russia any more.'

'Of course. I do not expect you to understand.'

I'm irritated now as well as disconcerted.

'I apologise,' he says to the table, his voice low, 'for leaving so quickly. You will order something to drink?'

'I'll have a coffee.'

We sit in silence. Nikolai removes his jacket and a waitress takes our order. I wonder again about this man I know so little about. Is the threat he fears real, or does it exist only in his imagination? That's just as alarming, somehow.

Two cups appear in front of us. Nikolai clears his throat.

'You think I am crazy man, no?' He rolls the 'r' in 'crazy' extravagantly. 'You expect for man in white coat to take me to home for madmen.' He clasps his wrists together. 'Handcuff me so I cannot escape.'

I feel a tug at the corner of my mouth. He drains his espresso cup.

'And you do not know worst. At night, I change to evil wolf. I leap on helpless virgins while they sleep. They scream, I sink my teeth into their necks and suck their blood. At home they call me "Mad Nikolai", you know. All the people in my town, they are afraid of me.'

A smile overruns my face.

'I know,' he carries on, eyes wide, 'I am not what you are used to. I am little bit crazy, I know. But I will be good to you, I promise. Please, have mercy on me.'

'I don't know if I should.'

'I am kind to cats.' His face stays deadpan. 'That is sort of man I am.'

I can't help laughing.

He starts telling me about a stray cat he looked after in a room he rented in a house in Perm, though pets were strictly forbidden by the landlady.

'One evening it is snowing, I open the back door to put out my boots and cat comes in. I put it out but cat comes again. Every time I open door it comes. So I make place for cat to sleep. He has broken ear and bite in his leg – he is a fighter. And always hungry… Anything I give him, he will eat. Peas, rice, *borscht*.'

I lose track of what Nikolai is saying. Instead I watch the complex dance of his expressions and listen to the rise and fall of his voice, the continual bursts of heavily accented words. A rush, a hesitation then another rush. His thick, curving lips that always seem about to break into a lazy smile. His eyes, dark and vital, that could scour my face in a fraction of a second and miss nothing. His pianist's hands moving to accompany his words.

'I'd love to visit Russia,' I say when he's finished his story. Since meeting Nikolai, I've spent hours reading *War and Peace* and have restarted *The Gulag Archipelago*. I've even bought a Russian phrase book and tried to learn a few words, though I'm hopeless at languages. 'It's so different from anywhere else. It seems to have a kind of Jekyll-and-Hyde personality. There's the crazed, evil side – nuclear weapons, Gulags, Stalin. Then there's the romantic, poetic, magical side.'

'It is like person, yes.' Nikolai dips his head and falls silent. When a plate clatters loudly nearby he sits up with a jerk, startled.

'Where were you?'

'I was thinking about my life. Of things that happen before.'

'You looked sad.'

He shrugs, his hands sweeping the air. 'Often I am sad. Sometimes it is like I am in small, dark room and I can't get out. The only thing I can do to escape is to play music – Chopin, he helps. Sometimes Tchaikovsky, Brahms, Shostakovich. Or I play the blues very loud until man next door bangs on wall.'

'I love the blues too. Ray Charles and Nina Simone are my favourites.'

'Ah, Ray Charles. I like him too.'

'So, you have a keyboard now?'

A guy he met at the launderette helped him buy a second-hand Yamaha for thirty pounds on eBay, he explains. 'The sound is not as good as my mother's piano. But it will remember all the notes I play.'

The waitress leaves the bill on the table. Before Nikolai can put his hand in his pocket, I open my purse.

'My turn. We're in England now.'

'So,' he says, zipping up his jacket. 'We are friends again?'

Daylight is fading as we walk slowly along the pavement, avoiding the people rushing in and out of shops. Nikolai stops and I realise we are outside Hampstead Tube Station. I think of the evening I had in mind before leaving home: pasta, a DVD then an early night before Sunday's ten-mile hike with the gang. It seems dull now.

'Maybe I come back to your place, Georgie? I could cook something.' He smiles and leans closer. 'I am good cook.'

I imagine how it would feel with this man beside me. His warmth, the touch of his hands.

'I don't know,' I say. 'I have things to get ready for tomorrow.'

'Another time, then.' He squeezes my hand. 'Goodbye, Georgie. I enjoy today very much.'

I walk home, caught up in my thoughts. Why did I refuse his offer? Do I need to be so scared of getting involved with him? Undoubtedly, there are good reasons not to. I have no idea how long he'll be around. Apart from that he's troubled, to say the least. His idea that someone was following him… Is he delusional?

10

I meet up with Ella, Cath and Tim the following Tuesday at our usual tapas bar in Tufnell Park.

'The guy's a screwball! He spent fifteen minutes telling me about this bloody parrot he imported from Ghana. Then he had the gall to tell me he doesn't like small talk and he'd like to have sex with me; thinks we'd be fantastic together. Jesus in heaven, I ask you!'

Ella is telling us about her recent date. Her Irish accent grows stronger as her voice grows louder. She tosses a curtain of brown hair over her shoulder and sits straight-backed, cheeks flushed.

'At least he was honest,' I say cautiously.

'He obviously needs a few tips on chatting up women,' Tim adds.

Cath giggles.

Ella slams her bottle of Corona onto the table. 'That's the last time,' she hisses, 'I'm going on a date with any more dickheads from the fucking Internet!'

There are four of us left in 'the gang'. We did the same marketing course at university and are all still more or less unattached. We manage to meet up most months, and I usually see Ella in between, though I haven't seen or spoken to her lately, except to tell her over the phone that there's been an 'incident' with Julian.

Ella works for Islington Council and puffs around London on a mud-splattered bicycle. Despite our frequent spats, she's my closest girlfriend. Cath has a wicked laugh, a happy disposition and an undemanding HR job; Tim, when he isn't watching re-reruns of *Blackadder*, offers his services as a 'marketing consultant'.

'How's Julian?'

I hesitate over Cath's question. We're hovering on the brink of a new topic of conversation, having squeezed Ella's date dry.

'Do you want the long version or the short version?'

'Just hurry up and tell us, Georgie,' Ella says.

'He came over to my place. We ended up in bed.' I explain what happened, ending on his declaration of love.

Tim breaks the silence. 'And you're not in love with him?'

'Don't you think I would have said something by now?'

'Georgie.' Ella's thick brown hair sways as she shakes her head.

'What are you going to do? Are you going to stay friends with him?'

'I don't know. I can't drop him just like that, after eight years – nearly nine.'

'You could fall in love with him,' Ella quipped. 'Then there wouldn't be a problem.'

I pull a face at her. She's teasing, I know, but I'm not in the mood. Ella and I have different attitudes to sex and relationships; she never takes her clothes off for anyone until she practically has an engagement ring on.

Ella swigs on her Corona. 'At least you could look out for someone you *can* love.'

'I *have* met someone, actually.'

All three stare at me. Ella speaks first.

'So? Who is he?'

'His name's Nikolai. He's Russian, he hasn't been in London long.'

'Where did you meet him?'

'In a pub. I went up to him to say hello. He was so startled he tried to knock me down – some kind of martial arts move. I got out of the way just in time.'

'My god!' Cath's eyes light up.

'I hope he apologised,' Ella says. 'Is he into martial arts, then?'

'I don't know. He was in the army.'

Tim grabs a handful of olives. 'What's he doing in London?'

'He works on a building site.'

'So, what is he? An engineer?'

'A labourer. He writes music in his spare time.'

Another silence. Ella's eyes meet Tim's. Tim is about to toss me another question but Ella gets there first.

'Has he taken you out on a date?'

'Sort of. We went for a walk on Hampstead Heath last weekend.'

'What's he like?' Cath smiles. 'Tall, dark and handsome?'

'He is, actually – and quite mysterious. He's not like anyone I've ever met.'

Ella looks doubtful. 'When are you seeing him again?'

'Saturday. We're meeting at Charing Cross.'

Cath gives me a thumbs up.

'I hope it goes well, Georgie,' Tim says. 'What does Julian think about Nikolai?'

'He's jealous; he thinks I shouldn't see him. But I don't care if Julian doesn't like it.'

I watch Julian's lean figure as he waits at the small theatre bar, trying to attract attention by jabbing a rolled-up note in the air. He looks very Jude Law-ish this evening. His gelled hair is combed back neatly. His dark blue jacket fits him perfectly, not bagging at the shoulders as his suits sometimes do.

Minutes later, not long before the play is due to start, Julian returns to our table with two glasses of wine. He's wearing the red silk tie from Liberty – the one I bought him years ago for his birthday. I feel uneasy. Is he trying to impress me?

'You're looking very smart.'

The brightness leaves his face. 'I went to lunch with a client.'

It's Friday evening, the day before I'm due to see Nikolai again. The play was Julian's idea. He insisted I go with him to make use of a ticket originally intended for a work friend, who cancelled due to a bad cold. It's more bleak than funny. It's in one of those cramped old West End theatres with seats that numb your bottom after fifteen minutes. Instead of following the plot, I think gloomily about my friendship with Julian.

After the play we go to a nearby restaurant, but my appetite has abandoned me.

'Is it as bad as that?'

'I can't eat any more.' I toy with a ribbon of pasta floating in lukewarm sauce.

'Have the rest of my pizza, if you like.'

'No, thanks, I'm not hungry.'

Julian looks at me suspiciously. His contacts seem metallic blue in this light – so blue they could zap me into a puff of smoke.

'How's it going with Nikolai? You haven't mentioned him in a while.'

I shrug. 'OK, I suppose.'

'When are you seeing him next?'

'Tomorrow. We're going to some galleries.'

A dark look crosses his face. 'Is there something you're not telling me?'

I jolt upright. 'What?'

'You know. Are you sleeping with him?'

I pluck a piece from my bread roll and squeeze it into a ball.

'I haven't slept with him, no.'

'But you'd like to?'

'Maybe.' Anger seeps through me, warming my cheeks, making my voice loud. 'I can sleep with whoever I want, I don't need your permission.'

A man at the next table glances at us. Julian wipes his hands on his serviette. I try to catch the waiter's eye.

'This isn't going to work, Julian,' I say calmly, 'if every time I show interest in a guy, you're going to take it as a betrayal.'

We wait for the bill in silence.

Julian looks at me, unblinking. I can't read his expression. I wipe crumbs off the tablecloth and fiddle with my handbag. I just want to go home and forget all about him.

11

Nikolai downs his double espresso in several gulps. Shadows encircle his eyes.

It's late morning, a week since our Hampstead visit. We're sitting in a café not far from Charing Cross Station. When we last talked on the phone, Nikolai was cheerful, telling me he was looking forward to seeing me again. But the man I face now is different. It's as if he's left part of himself behind somewhere.

'Is something wrong?'

He doesn't respond. His head stays tilted to the side, his eyes unfocussed.

'Hello? Anyone there?' I wave at him.

His head snaps towards me. 'Excuse me?'

'Are you OK? You look like you've gone to another planet.'

He nods, his eyes slipping away. 'I am sorry. I will be OK after another coffee.'

I smile. 'You must drink a lot of coffee.'

'Last night I have bad dreams. I wake and cannot go back to sleep.'

'What did you dream about?'

He shrugs. 'There is woman – she is always in my dreams. She will not let me go.'

I'm wondering whether to ask about the woman when he speaks again.

'I prefer not to talk of these things. They are not… nice.'

He reaches over to a table beside us, picks up a copy of the *Guardian* left there and slowly turns the pages. I've turned my attention to my mobile, replying to a text from Ella, when he mutters under his breath.

'What is it?'

'They have killed Maskhadov. Four days ago. Russian troops have blown up the house he stays in.'

'Maskhadov?'

'Aslan Maskhadov. He was the Chechen leader in the first war. No one expects that they can defeat our army, it is incredible to everyone. For this, the Chechens make him their president – until Putin replaces him.'

'Why did they bother to kill him if he'd been replaced?'

'Because Putin calls him terrorist. He must be killed because of the war on terror.'

I stare at Nikolai, taken aback at the anger in his voice.

'Maskhadov is not terrorist,' he goes on. 'He is not radical like Basayev. He always said it was wrong to take the hostages in Beslan, it is wrong to use innocent people for your cause. Last month he asked for peace talks with Russia and our government tells him to go to hell.' He tosses the newspaper away. 'And now, Russia has made thousands more enemies. To the Chechens, Maskhadov was their hero. They will not forgive Russia for this.'

He glances around the café then takes his wallet from his leather jacket, scowling.

'We go, is that OK? I would like to walk now.'

'Fine by me.'

We head towards the river. Though the morning is nearly over, a colourless sun leaks light through thin cloud. An uncertain warmth replaces the earlier chill.

I ask how his job is going.

'It is difficult,' he replies. 'Last week we are told we are behind schedule, we must work one hour extra every day. Some guys say we must resist the bosses, it is not safe. But most do not care, they just want to take the money.'

I am uncomfortable. Whenever my father complains to me about workers downing tools at the least provocation, I take his side. I've never had any reason not to.

'Why not look for another job? One that's not so tiring?'

'It is good money.'

We pass a car reversing into a tight parking space. There's a thud as it hits the car behind. Nikolai yelps and jerks away from me.

I stare at him. His face is paler than ever.

'I am sorry,' he says. 'I frighten you.'

'Are you OK?' I put my hand on his forearm.

'It is nothing, don't worry.' He stares at the ground. 'Lately I am wound up too tight, that is all. At any noise I jump like cat.'

We walk along the South Bank, passing huge concrete concert halls poised above the turgid river. Nikolai says little.

I try to find something to engage him.

'Have you been to Moscow? What's it like?'

'It is flashy bauble for tourists,' he replies scornfully. 'Not like Perm. There people stop to talk when they pass in the street. The streets are wide and straight, and everywhere is water... ' His voice becomes wistful. 'I grow up in big, old-fashioned house. The trams go past and from top floor you can see the river.'

'It's beautiful, you said.'

'Yes, the River Kama. It is nothing like this grey little thing.' He gestures dismissively at the Thames beside us.

'You love Russia, don't you? Why come to London? Not just to get work, I take it?'

His face goes blank, as a shutter slips over a window. He speaks in a flat voice.

'It is not for work I come. Something happened... I do not wish to talk about it.' He rummages inside his bag, starts to remove a dented packet of cigarettes – a brand I don't recognise – hesitates and puts it back.

'I didn't mean to pry. I'm sorry.'

He looks at me for a long time. 'I do not wish to lie to you, Georgie.'

His mobile rings. It's the first time I've heard it ring. He always has it with him in his bag but never seems to pay much attention to it.

'Hello, Vakha... I am so glad we speak at last. I hear many good things about you.'

He gestures for me to excuse him and takes a few steps away. I wait by the wall, one eye on Nikolai and one on the river beyond.

He walks in short lines back and forth, staring at the ground, absorbed in conversation. I can't hear much but I can tell he's getting agitated. I pick up snatches of Russian, then for a while it's mostly Russian with a few English phrases interspersed.

'Your father? Yes, yes, I talk to him.'

Nikolai hits the wall with the heel of his hand and talks louder, forcefully. It sounds like he's trying to persuade the person about something.

'I am on your side, Vakha.'

More Russian. Animated. I find myself straining to catch the snatches of English.

'See you next week... Don't worry, I will be careful. Thank you for this, Vakha.'

He turns to me, smiling, and puts his phone away.

'Sorry I am so long. You will show me the gallery now?'

I pick up my bag and we resume walking. After a minute or so he hasn't said anything about the phone call.

'Who was that you were talking to?'

He glances at me and doesn't reply for a few seconds.

'It is just a guy I know. He agrees to what I ask, it is good.'

'Oh, right. What did you ask?' I know I'm prying again but I'm curious.

'It is not important. Come, let us enjoy the day.'

His mood has changed. At the Tate Modern he laughs at one bizarre exhibit and examines others at length with a bemused expression. On the way back, we stop at a crowded café overlooking the river. Nikolai talks fondly of family trips to the mountains every summer when he was small, before the end of the Soviet Union. I sit across from him, watching his eyes glint in the watery light as streams of words spill from his lips. I want to take his hand and kiss him.

'Me and my sister are outside our *dacha* one evening,' Nikolai says after we've eaten. 'We are having meal; the others are in kitchen. A bear comes out from forest and goes to Anna. Not so big, but the smell! She looks to him and screams like it is the last seconds of her life. The bear just picks up her plate and puts out his tongue for pancake. Then he walks away with cream dripping off mouth. I am laughing so much, I cry… She tells my father that I leave her. I tell him I know this bear will not hurt us. But I must stay in all next day for punishment.'

'He was very strict, your father?'

'He wanted most for us to be obedient, to be respected in the community.' He crushes his serviette into a ball and drops it on the table. 'My mother is different. She is kind to everyone, always. She says the most important thing is to be kind to each other.' He meets my eyes. 'Enough, I talk too much.'

'No,' I say. 'I could listen to you all day long.'

We take the footpath over Hungerford Bridge back across the Thames, away from the giant hamster wheel of the London Eye and the Houses of Parliament in the distance. Halfway across we stop and lean over the railing, arms touching, watching a laden tugboat cleave through the dirty grey water towards the low arches of Waterloo Bridge. I point out St Paul's and the Gherkin's glassy curves. Without warning, Nikolai cries out and pulls away from me. For a second I think he's been shot. Then I register a deep bellow from below and look down. Metres below, water sloshes against a steel girder. A passenger boat emerges from underneath the bridge.

'What's the matter with you? It's only a boat.'

Nikolai is breathing heavily. His face, damp with sweat, contorts in what looks like serious mental effort. I watch anxiously as he removes the packet of cigarettes from his bag. There are three left. He lights one with a plastic lighter, hand trembling.

'I didn't know you smoked,' I say.

'I hate fucking cigarettes.' He kicks the railing viciously. 'For years, I try to give up. But they help when I am like this.' He draws on the cigarette with quick, nervous movements then tosses it down and stamps on it. 'I am OK now.'

Questions I dare not ask form in my head. What has made him like this? Was it the war he fought in, or something else? And amid my concern and curiosity, I feel a twinge of fear. He's like a box of fireworks that's been stored for too long, one that might explode in your face at any moment.On the other side of the river, Nikolai takes my hand and leads me into Embankment Gardens. Tiny yellow flowers peek out of the earth, trembling with each breath of wind.

'I am sorry, Georgie,' he says. 'I am not good company today.'

'You're right,' I huff. 'Maybe you should have stayed at home.'

He looks at me for a while then bends down to the flowerbed. 'Keep still.' I let him place a crocus in my hair. 'You are so beautiful today. And your hair... When the sun shines it has so many colours, I cannot count.'He steps off the path and stretches himself out on the neat grass. I lie down beside him.

After a while he sits up and removes a pencil and some folded sheets of music manuscript paper from his bag. His hand sweeps across the stave. When he reaches the end of the sheet he puts it behind the others and continues on a fresh one.

'I have idea,' he says, at last putting down his pencil. 'It is for opening of the piece I work on.'

The paper is covered in a torrent of crotchets and quavers.

'Is it like the music you played in the pub?'

'It is many stews in one pot. Gypsy, folk, classical... I will wait to see what comes – if I can finish.'

'Don't you think you will?'

'I don't know.' He sighs, carefully placing the sheets back inside his bag. 'One day, I will finish something. A-ny-way... ' He puts his hand on mine. 'I am excellent cook, Georgie. If you let me, I will come to your place and cook you dinner.'

I'm only slightly taken aback. 'Well if you put if like that, how can I say no?'

12

At last, here she is.

She's back. With him.

He is at her side, clinging on to her arm like a creeper up a rose. He has a limp in one leg. He looks worn out, some bum off the street who has nowhere to go for the night. But he's got somewhere to go.

They go up the steps and inside. For a moment I see into the hall. It's lit, there's a pile of envelopes by the door.

The front door closes. I move out from my hideout and cross the road.

After a while a light comes on in the living room. The curtains are still open. I shift my position. The sofa looks empty but I can't see the chairs. Is he in there, with her?

The bush is in the way. There's not enough gaps to see properly. I move to the other side of it, into the front garden and stand against the bins. If anyone comes I'll duck down behind them.

The curtains are shut now. She shut them. Her hair is loose. She's wearing nail polish. She never wears nail polish.

The light's still on. They're in there still. What are they doing? He's probably all over her by now, slipping it to her on the sofa. Or on the carpet maybe or against the fucking mantelpiece.

There's no noise from inside. There's a party a few houses down and one across the road. The flats round here are full of people dancing, people kissing, people undressing. People screwing. They're all at it round here.

It's cold and dark. The thermos was empty ages ago. I get out the bottle of Bell's and take a swig. I don't need to be here. This is crazy. This is worthy of some stupid comedy.

But I'll stay a bit longer. I need to see him leave. I just need to know he's left.

13

I stand in my kitchen watching Nikolai chop a clove of garlic with enviable speed.

'How come you know how to cook? Isn't cooking a woman thing in Russia?'

'I enjoy, that is why.' Nikolai puts the knife down and seizes a frying pan. 'Many men let their girlfriends cook, yes. But I like to cook myself, even if I have girlfriend.'

'If I was your girlfriend, I'd willingly hand over the cooking.'

He glances at me. 'You have boyfriend before?'

'A long time ago.'

'Tell me about him.'

'I met him the year I finished university. He was researching the navigation mechanisms of bees, he could talk about them for hours. Two weeks after we met, he asked me if I'd go with him to Berlin; he had to present a paper. It was very exciting at first.'

'You loved him?'

'He took over my life in a way. I'd never been in love before – I didn't think it could end.'

Nikolai tosses onion and garlic into the pan, followed by chilli, soy sauce and the rest of the vegetables.

'What happens?'

I watch him shake the pan over the flame, sputtering oil over the cooker.

'He said he had to leave me because he was going to marry this woman, an ex-girlfriend. He'd only mentioned her once. He proposed to her and she said no, then she got in touch again. I didn't cope very well.'

Nikolai moves the pan away from the flame and turns to face me, his expression curious.

'It was worse than when my mother left.' I think back to the pain and near desperation of those times, and can hardly recognise the person I was. 'I don't know how I let myself get into that situation. I was so stupid –'

'It is he who is stupid, not you. Not all men are like him, Georgie. You were unlucky. Next time, it is another story.'

Next time – or this time? I smile, hoping to disguise the sudden flutter of my heart.

We eat by candlelight. I watch shadows play over Nikolai's face. His hand rests on the table, near mine. I place my hand over his for a few moments. My fingers, long for a girl, are dwarfed by his.

'So this guy,' Nikolai begins, 'he breaks your heart... You give up with love?'

I scrape a fleck of wax from a candlestick, not sure how to explain.

'I suppose. For a while. I set off to have adventures, to make myself forget about him.'

'And after this, there is someone?'

'No one serious. I've got male friends – Tim, you haven't met him yet. And there's Julian –'

'Julian?'

'He was a good friend... ' I run out of words.

'Not now?'

'It's not like it used to be.'

I wish I hadn't mentioned Julian. It would be too awkward to explain. Nikolai picks up his glass, a puzzled look on his face.

'It's your turn now,' I say. 'Tell me about your mother. She played the piano for a living?'

His mother had been a professional pianist. In the evenings the family would gather round the piano and listen to her play Tchaikovsky and Borodin. But she was hit by a car and had to give up performing to teach piano instead. She taught Nikolai and encouraged him to practise every day.

'When I am fourteen, I have enough. I am bored with this music. I play other things, and no more lessons. I play only when I want to play. My father tells me I am lazy, I do not enough study, I will make bad end to my life. My mother is happy that I still play, she does not care what it is.' He settles back in his chair, his expression becoming wistful.

'She must miss you a lot.'

'Of course, she is Russian mother. She writes every week – always proper letters.'

'What about your father?'

A hard edge enters his voice. 'He does not write.'

I wait for him to go on.

'I am not the son he hoped for. Always I disappoint him. He wanted me to be doctor – but I have no wish for this.' Nikolai looks away from me, deep creases on his brow. 'We fall out when I come back from army. I have pain from my injuries, I do not sleep. Sometimes I get up in night to smoke marijuana to calm me. One day my father tells me to leave his house. I am bad influence for my sister. So I rent room in the city… The place with cat, remember?' He drains his glass and moves his chair away from the table.

We sit in the living room. I sip my coffee, watching the gas fire flicker as Nikolai tells me about the cat's unexpected return months later. I'm pleasantly tired after the meal and the day's walking – and alongside that, I feel a twang of nervous anticipation. The Russian guy is here, in my flat, beside me.

'It is your mother?'

Nikolai's gaze rests on the photograph I've moved to the mantelpiece.

'Yes, it was taken a long time ago. Before my parents split up.'

'What happened to them?'

'My mother was seeing another man. She went to Spain to be with him.'

He looks back to the photograph. I think back to that surreal evening after school, weeks after I turned thirteen. My mother pulling me away from my peanut butter sandwich and hugging me almost tight enough to break my chest. She had to go away for a while. There was a man she loved; not my father. She was going to stay with him in Barcelona. Whatever happened, she would always love me and she'd always be my mother.

'It was a relief not to have them constantly fighting,' I explain. 'But I missed her so much. I couldn't understand why she'd gone, how she could love this guy more than me. After a while it was easier if I pushed her away.'

'You think she was wrong to leave?'

'I used to. But I can see it wasn't easy for her. She was seriously depressed. Her marriage was falling apart, then she met this man who promised her a new life. I don't blame her for doing what she did.'

My last words come out with a certainty I don't feel. At least I believe them with my head, not my heart.

'What did you do after you left school, Nikky? You never studied medicine?'

'It is good profession but it was not for me.' He sighs heavily. 'I took long time to learn to read. I would muddle up letters, make into nonsense. I was good only at music and sport – instead of studying, I play football and make up tunes on piano. When I fail my exams, I tell my father I am not going to university. He tells me they will send me to Chechnya and I will be killed. "The war is mad," he says to us, "no one can win. No one wants another war except the generals and politicians."

'I tell my father that I am not afraid to serve my country... It was not true. I hear stories of soldiers and how they run from army because they are bullied – and mad Chechens who cut off our heads.'

As he speaks he rubs his thigh in the absent, tender manner that one might stroke a cat.

'How did you hurt your leg?'

'Yes, the same.' He touches his stomach. 'It gets me here too.'

'What happened?'

He looks doubtfully at me, then shrugs.

'We were in the forest, outside Grozny. We lie in snow for hours, my fingers are frozen on my rifle. I wonder if I will be the hero... I want to kill as many Chechens as I can.' Nikolai gives a wan smile into the fireplace. 'But they find us first – we have no chance. There is explosion, very close. I think my end is come. Someone tells me to get up but I am frozen. After this, I cannot remember. When I wake, I am in the hospital. A doctor has taken out the metal in my body. He tells me I am lucky, I will mend soon.'

Nikolai's face contorts. When he speaks again, the intensity of his voice makes me start.

'My injuries, they are nothing. The guy beside me – I try not to think about what I saw that day.'

He has paid a high price, I think, for the honour of serving his country.

'I have seen too much,' he carries on. 'I have seen men treat other men like animals – women, children too. Russians, Chechens, there is no difference. At night I see things, it is like video playing inside my head. I try to turn it off but it comes back.'

Despite the heat of the room, I shiver. He looks at me with an expression I can't work out, then buries his head in his hands. I rest my hand on his shoulder.

'I am afraid, Georgie. Sometimes I want to leave this world. I want to go where no one will scream in my head at night.'

His voice falls away and sorrow seems to engulf him. My throat tightens. I can't bear to see him like this. I grip his hand.

'You're not alone. I can help you.' The words come out as if of their own accord. I have no inkling how I could help.

He raises his head and touches my cheek. Moments later, his lips are pressing into mine. My tongue reaches for his.

I shouldn't be doing this. I definitely should not be doing this.

He takes me into the bedroom. He unbuttons my shirt and unclasps my bra. I pull off my ankle boots, undo my belt, step out of my jeans and underpants and stand naked in front of him. His glance lowers to my breasts. Then I forget everything except my desire to kiss this man in front of me, to love him with my hands and my lips, with every part of my body.

After Nikolai leaves, I go to my computer and type 'Chechnya' into the web browser, not knowing exactly what I'm looking for. A long list comes up.

I flip from site to site. There are pictures of war and devastation. Armed men waving from tanks, landscapes of endless ruined buildings, sorrow-laden women in headscarves picking through rubble. I read about the history of the region and opinions as to how the two most recent conflicts started. I find an article on the Human Rights Watch website. Despite the conflict in Chechnya taking a huge toll on the civilian population, it says, the international community has done little. Indiscriminate bombing and shelling have resulted in thousands of civilian deaths. Crimes have been committed by both sides. Chechen rebels brutally attacked civilians; Russian forces tortured suspected rebel fighters and buried them in mass graves. Then I come across an article about how thousands of Russia's armed forces who served in Chechnya are now suffering from post-traumatic stress disorder. Its symptoms include depression, nightmares and explosive anger.

It clicks. Now I know for sure. Nikolai is one of those traumatised soldiers, surely. He is doing his best to overcome his injuries, both physical and mental. Yet, as far as I can see, he has a long way to go.

On the spur of the moment, I decide to Google Nikolai. What is the name he told me? Konstantin? No, Konstantinov, that's it. Nikolai Alexandrovich Konstantinov.

There's no one with the same name, except someone who filed a patent back in 1965. That can't be him.

For days after that first night with Nikolai, I have a feeling that something has been done that can't be undone. I wonder if I've made a mistake, giving in to my desire. We had sex without using a condom, something I'm usually careful about. The omission is a symbol, somehow. What else might I have overlooked?

But another part of me doesn't care. Whenever my mind wanders, fragments of that night come back. The unexpected heaviness of his body on mine. The tenderness of his touch. The devout concentration on his face as he fucked me. And afterwards, his slow smile, filling his eyes with a quiet joy. How can I put all that behind me?

14

The phone rings as I'm eating the remains of yesterday's pizza. Another party political broadcast gushes from the TV.

'Hello, stranger.'

It's Julian. I brace myself for whatever might come next.

'What is it?'

'I won't keep you long. I just wondered if you'd like to have a bite to eat sometime. I've been missing you.'

'I don't know, Julian. I've got a lot on at the moment.'

'Next week, then. Thursday?'

'I don't think I can make next week, I'm sorry –'

'You're seeing that Russian, aren't you? Nikolai.' He says the name with disgust.

'I see him occasionally, yes.'

A long silence.

'Why don't you just come straight out and say it? You don't want to see me any more because you're shagging him.'

I take a deep breath. 'Julian… '

I can't do this any more, I'm about to say. But I can't end our friendship in a phone call. That would be a coward's choice. However hard it may be, I have to do it face to face. So I arrange to meet him at the Island Queen in an hour.

The pub is a short walk from Angel Tube Station. I get there early and nab a table. I watch people collecting at the grand, curving bar. My untouched bottle of Becks sits beside my phone in front of me.

Julian is late. When I look up he's standing to the side of my table, looking at me, coat still on.

'Hiya, Jaf. Sorry to be late.' He stoops as if about to give me a kiss, then stops and unbuttons his coat. 'I had trouble on the Tube; someone got stuck in the doors… Have you been here long?'

'Not long.' I don't smile.

'Can I get you another drink?' His cheery tone jars.

'I'm OK, thanks.'

He folds his coat over the chair beside mine. Five minutes later, he comes back with a pint of beer and a bowl of cashew nuts.

'Thanks for making the time.' He picks up his beer and puts it down again. 'I'm glad to get a chance to see you. I wanted to tell you something. It's not easy on the phone.'

'I've got a few things to say too.'

'So, who's going first?' He smiles. 'Toss for it, shall we?'

'You go first.'

'It's not anything earth-shattering. Just that... I want so much for us to have fun again, like we used to.'

'I don't think we can.' I search for the right words. 'You've been a good friend, Julian. A wonderful friend. But your feelings for me –'

'It's love, Georgie. Something you seem to have forgotten about.'

The bitterness in his voice makes me wince.

'This isn't going to work, Julian. You know it isn't.'

'Surely you're not going to let Nik-whatever-his-name-is come between us?'

'I really hoped we'd be able to stay friends, once you got used to the situation. But –'

'Come on, Georgie.' His mouth puckers. He wraps his hands around his glass. 'You're getting this all out of proportion.'

'I don't want to hurt you, honestly I don't. But I don't see any other way.'

He is silent. I stare at the specks of foam above his top lip. People around us carry on talking and drinking, paying us no attention.

'I don't want to be without you,' he says at last.

'I'm sorry, Julian, you have to let me go. There's no point in dragging this out any longer. That would only make it harder for us both.'

He smiles, an odd little smile that makes the back of my head tingle, as if I've seen a particularly ugly spider. His eyes flick around the room. He seems to be fighting to stay in control. I cross my fingers under the table, my heart beating hard. Finally his eyes return to my face.

'Fuck you, Georgie. You have a heart of fucking ice.' His eyes glitter with tears. He grabs his coat and lurches from his chair, nearly knocking over our drinks. 'Fuck off to that Russian prick then, if that's what you want.'

I watch him stride away, head down, pushing people aside as he goes.

Then he is gone. I shut my eyes, replaying his words in my

head, wondering how things have come to this. After all, he once changed the direction of my life.

It was after the bee guy. James Woods, his actual name was. I was 21, just out of university, stepping hesitantly into my first job. He was 28, a lecturer in the Zoology department of a top university. He'd lived in three countries, spoke four languages and had more friends than anyone I'd ever known. We met during the interval of a performance of some modern opera at the Royal Opera House that I'd only gone to because my friend who worked there had a spare ticket. He and his friend approached us and started chatting. He bought us each a glass of champagne and a programme (we were both short of cash and dithering over a lemonade or a Coke) and an ice cream in the next interval. I said I didn't get the opera at all – it was my first time, the prices were ridiculous and I wouldn't be going to any more. He said he would have to take me to another opera in that case; he could guarantee that I'd love the next one. (He was right.)

He was the first guy to get through my defences, deploying all his charm, wit and experience to make me believe I could trust him. A month after we met he persuaded me to come with him to his friend's gloomy chateau in the Loire Valley, where over three days we drank endless bottles of musty wine from an enormous cellar and had sex in every room, on rugs, tabletops and under tables, then finally in the moonlight on a terrace overlooking the river.

After this we saw each other four or five nights a week and every weekend. Ella, Julian and a few other friends tried to warn me that I ought to stay grounded, but I didn't listen. The bee guy took over my life. He bought me perfume and took me on trips to Europe. He said he loved me and I believed him. I loved him back in that naïve way that only the never-heartbroken can.

Our relationship ended after five months and five days. Over the final weeks he became cooler, less available, but I hoped this would be temporary. When he finally told me about that previous girlfriend who'd unexpectedly turned up and whom he realised he still loved, part of me wasn't surprised.

Emotionally, I imploded. This confirmed what I'd known all along, didn't it?

For a short time I did consider ending it all, I admit. But thinking about how to do the deed – a leap from a high place? A dip in a fast-flowing river? A slash of the wrists? – was too scary. I wasn't ready for such a drastic step. Instead, I went on a sort of pilgrimage to the Dark Side. On evenings and weekends I drank way too much and had sex with whoever happened to be around. I went on long, arduous walks alone, ignoring risks of serious injury or worse – the more dangerous, the better. With barely adequate equipment I sought out precipitous trails and narrow, windswept mountain ridges. While I was walking in the Scottish Highlands a thick mist came down, obliterating the path. I was too cold to stop and kept on in the direction I thought was right until the mist cleared, and I found myself five feet from a cliff edge. While not actually intending to die, I seemed to be beyond caring whether I stayed alive.

My friends tried to instil some sense into me. Ella suggested I see a therapist about my unresolved childhood issues; Cath asked if I wanted to go to a nudist camp with her. Tim said I should take up boxing or join the navy. Julian, who had a girlfriend at the time, made me promise to phone him whenever I needed to talk to someone or felt like doing something stupid, even if it was in the middle of the night. He didn't want anything to happen to me.

I decided to take three months' unpaid leave and go backpacking around Europe and Asia. The week before I left, my mother came over uninvited with handmade gifts and asked me to stay with her in Spain; I said something horrible and she left. My father said I needed to sort myself out, then got really angry and said I was acting like a 'fucking loser' and to 'fuck off, then', see if he cared.

Alone in unfamiliar places, I felt free to indulge in whatever foolish whim took my fancy without the possibility of anyone I knew finding out. I stayed in cheap, squalid hostels and encountered questionable people who suggested questionable things. My friends left me text messages and called sometimes to see if I was OK. It's an adventure, I told them. So what if I'm a woman alone? Yes, I know I'm going a bit crazy. So what?

The dramatic finale of my trip came in northern Thailand. While zooming from village to village on an ancient scooter, I took a bend rather too fast and ended up sprawled on the rocky hillside, scratched, bruised and shaken, my knee in agony and the scooter unrideable. Then I realised I was on a deserted road, miles from anywhere.

Ten or fifteen minutes later, an ordinary-looking middle-aged man in a Toyota saloon pulled up. He was the first to drive by. I was relieved not to be stranded given there was no signal on my phone. He offered me a lift to the next town where he thought there was a hospital. On the way he offered to 'fix me up' if I had sex with him. He had drugs, money, whatever I wanted... I declined politely, repeatedly. We arrived at the town and I started to breathe easier. But as I was opening the door, the guy lunged at me across the car. I managed to pull away and hobbled into the nearest shop, some kind of pet sanctuary, where I begged the shop assistant to let me use the phone. I was in a desperate state, picturing the guy coming through the door any second to abduct me.

Julian took control. He told me, calmly and firmly, to call a cab to the hospital. As soon as I'd got my injuries checked and felt well enough to travel, I was to get a bus to the airport and take the first flight home, he said. He'd check the travel situation and call me back with the details, and transfer any cash I needed to my account.

Sometime during that long flight to Gatwick, it dawned on me that he was right. I'd had enough adventures. I needed to get back to my life, while I still had one.

Julian and his then girlfriend met me at the airport, drove me home and made sure I had food in the fridge.

'Is it really that bad?' he'd say sometimes after that, when I sat staring into my drink, as though the world had just entered nuclear winter. 'Everyone goes through bad times when relationships don't work out. What do you want on your headstone? "Here lies Georgie, a girl who gave up on life because of some stupid bastard?"'

This time I didn't say no when Ella and Cath insisted I join them to do wacky things. We cycled from London to Brighton and spent a week in a draughty old building in Shropshire, forced to get up at 5.30 every morning to meditate in silence for the rest of the day. I pushed myself harder to enjoy work and got promoted. No more serious relationships, I promised myself. I would enjoy life, have fun with my friends and be successful in my career – that would be enough.

My father and I made up, more or less; he encouraged me to buy a flat and helped me out with practical advice. My mother and I didn't. She still phoned occasionally but seemed to accept that I didn't want her in my life. Some of my outdoorsy friends drifted away, perhaps realising that I was a 'trainee basket case' as Ella sometimes joked.

Julian and I got closer, though. He seemed to understand how difficult it was to 'get back to normal'. He didn't press me to go out on dates as other friends did. And I couldn't forget how much he helped me after the Thailand incident.

15

I stuff the piece of paper with Nikolai's address into my handbag and check my appearance in the hall mirror. My freshly washed hair gleams. Even my eyes, usually a murky pond green, look clear enough to swim in.

When Nikolai asked me over to his place for the first time last week, I declined. I sensed his impatience with me but didn't know how to explain my reluctance. He attracts me, physically and mentally. His creativity fascinates me; his past intrigues me. He's reached out and touched a part of me I'd forgotten about. Yet none of that seems quite enough to risk my happiness. OK, I'm not wildly happy... But I'm not miserable or desperate, either. Do I really need a traumatised ex-soldier in my life?

The second time he asks me over though, with a big smile, fluttering his long lashes, a little current of pleasure goes through me. I decide it would be rude to say no. Anyway, it will be interesting to see where he lives. Saturday night I have a get-together with some climbing-club friends, I tell him, but I'll be free on Saturday afternoon.

Nikolai warned me that parking would be difficult, so I park as soon as I find a space and walk the rest of the way. As I get closer to his place, the streets became more crowded, more diverse. Women wear all sorts, ranging from black hijab and brightly coloured saris to tight jeans. Groups of bearded men congregate in cafés. Two small boys pass me, deep in conversation. 'I can write my name in Arabic,' one says. I pass an Islamic bookshop, a betting shop, a hardware shop and an 'Any Style £4' barber, before hurrying on to a row of three-storey terraces with small, inhospitable front gardens. Forlorn, concrete-covered rectangles are piled with building materials, shadeless lamps and slashed armchairs. None has any greenery except one – a creeper-covered hedge and a collection of potted plants, all dead.

I note the Chinese medicine and acupuncture shop and the '£1 Bargain Shop' that Nikolai has mentioned, then spot a building matching the description on my scrawled note: three stories, four buzzers beside the front door and a boarded-up top-floor window surrounded by stained bricks. The paint on the lower window frames is peeling badly.

My spirits sink. How could anyone live in a place like this?

I cross the paved strip of front garden. Four refuse bins huddle in a corner, their lids plonked over bulging plastic bags. Buzzer number three is labelled with a heavily crossed-out name. After three presses, a crackly voice and a loud answering buzz, I step into the hall, to be greeted by a smell of disinfectant and a stack of *Yellow Pages* slumped against a wall. I climb the stairs to the first floor. The first door on the right is unmarked.

Before I can knock, it opens. Nikolai is facing me, barefoot, a thick jumper over his jeans. He leans towards me; I kiss his bristly cheek. He smells like the fresh-baked raisin and rosemary bread I get from my local delicatessen.

'Come, I show you my place.'

I step onto worn beige carpet. There's a faint whiff of mould, almost masked by cooking smells and a hint of cigarette smoke. Once-white paint covers the walls. The room seems large, possibly because there isn't much furniture. On a battered card table lie several open CD cases, a folded Russian newspaper and a Russian–English dictionary. Near by are two collapsible wooden chairs. A shirt is draped over the back of one. Along the wall facing the window stand a sofa draped in a blanket, and an electric bar heater. Apart from the sofa, the upright Yamaha keyboard is the largest piece of furniture.

'Where do you sleep?'

He gestures towards the sofa and shrugs. 'I am sorry, it is not so nice.'

'It's fine,' I say quickly.

We go into the kitchen, separated from the living area by a waist-high counter. I stand on the narrow strip of linoleum floor, wondering how on earth he manages to cook anything. The few available surfaces are mostly hidden under stacks of jars and tins. A large saucepan bubbles on the stove.

'That smells good.' I put my plastic bag on the counter and ask for the bathroom. He points to a door. On the other side, a toilet, basin and shower just about manage to fit. The tiles are grimy and cracked, and the shower curtain has come off its rail. I wash my hands in a gush of cold water, catching sight of a rust-specked face in the mirror.

When I come out, Nikolai is sitting at the keyboard. He frowns as his pencil hovers over a handwritten sheet of music. I sit down at the card table.

After a while he looks up, surprised, as if he's forgotten I'm there.

'Will you play me something?'

'What would you like?'

'Something Russian.'

He plays a sad, gentle waltz that I don't know. Fascinated, I watch his hands working the keyboard.

'That was beautiful.'

'It is by Alexander Borodin. My mother used to play it. Now I play something else by another Russian.'

It is as strange and arresting as the music he played in the pub. A delicate melody, repeating and shifting, becoming darker and ominous, fracturing into a series of jangling chords, rising to a crescendo. Then a ghost of the melody resumes, serene, like a glimpse of heaven.

'This is what you've been working on?'

'This is part one of my sonata. You like?'

'It's –'

'Weird?'

I shake my head. 'No, it's amazing. Where did that come from?' I don't believe in God most of the time, though sometimes really beautiful music or those incredible photographs of distant galaxies seem like evidence of something like it. 'You're lucky to have such talent. There's nothing I'm much good at, except wondering what to do with my life.'

He slaps the top of the keyboard. 'We eat now, dinner is ready. I can eat three horses.'

I follow Nikolai into the kitchen. He opens a cupboard and removes jars of pickled cucumber, mustard and relish. The window rattles in its frame as a lorry rumbles past.

'How much rent do you pay?'

'Ninety pounds a week. It is cheap, that is why I take.'

It isn't much compared with my mortgage of nearly six hundred pounds a month. But you'd have to pay me to live in a place like this, I can't help thinking.

We eat at the table, slightly uneven and just big enough to hold two dinner plates. The stew contains cabbage, potatoes, carrots and tender pieces of lamb. It tastes marvellous.

He gets up suddenly and returns with a jumper, way too big.

I drape it over my shoulders. I've been warming my hands on my bowl. The room is cool, though I don't like to say.

'So, Georgie, how are your Wonder Woman pills?'

I tell him the latest work news – continued good sales of ImmunoBoost for the second post-campaign month, up 30 per cent on the same month the previous year. But I'm not in the mood to talk about work. I wish I could escape somewhere where no one cares about brands or market share. I ask about his week.

'Yesterday the guys at work take me to pub and buy me beer. I drink two pints to show respect for British customs.' On his face, a wisp of amusement.

'Are they friendly at work?'

He hesitates. 'Most of them. There are Poles, Ukrainians, Romanians... Some English and Irish guys say that they come here to steal their jobs. I have friend, Malik. For him, it is worse. They shout "Hey, Paki!" and make jokes at him.'

'Is your leg coping?'

'I will survive.'

'You can't cut back your hours?'

'It is not possible. We are told we must work harder or we will not finish on time. One guy, he is off sick for three days. The fore-man phones him, says do not come back.'

'That's tough.' My father might be hard-boiled, but he wouldn't treat his workers like that. I nibble a fig pastry, watching Nikolai add a huge dollop of aubergine dip to his Turkish bread.

'This job is hard,' he says between bouts of chewing. 'But it is better than jobs I have before.'

Nikolai tells me he worked in a timber yard in Perm after his military service. The job aggravated his injuries, so he left after a few months. Then he had a string of temporary jobs, including sev-eral months as a security guard.

'Every week is different. I work in bars, casinos, nightclubs... At night, some of the customers drink vodka until they will try to fight everyone. One day, I cannot stop myself fighting back.'

I study the hand that grasps the remains of his sandwich – a capable hand, far bigger than mine, knuckles hard as walnuts – and imagine it clenched in anger.

'What happened?'

'A guy comes to the door; he has nice suit and gold Rolex. He is drunk, shouting at me to let him in. I say he must stay outside. He swears at me, tells me I am no good, I am scum from army.' Nikolai wipes his mouth and meets my eyes. 'I hit him. After this, his face is not so pretty.'

He looks out of the window. I try to collect my thoughts. How badly had that man been hurt? I picture a bloodied, broken face.

'I say enough. You do not want to know this.'

I start to protest but he's already pushed back his chair.

While Nikolai is in the bathroom, I scan the room. There are a couple of shelves crammed with notebooks, papers and various objects. I pick up a small box and examine the finely carved wood. The lid bears the outline of a male and a female figure, entwined.

'It was present. From girl.'

Startled, I turn to Nikolai, now standing behind me.

'Olga. She was my girlfriend. She made boxes like this to sell at the market.'

He sounds sad. I return the box to the shelf.

'Sit with me,' he says. 'It is more comfortable here.'

I join Nikolai on the sofa. He rubs my shoulder through the wool of my borrowed jumper.

'You are like ice. Come closer.'

I move so that my arm is touching his.

'Tell me how it is when you are child,' he says.

'I was on my own a lot. I always wanted a brother. When I was small I pretended I had one. He'd watch out for me, share my secrets. My mother was ill quite often. She used to go to bed for half the day sometimes, or go and stay with friends. And then she left –'

'Your father looks after you when she leaves?

'He did his best. He still had to run his business, so I didn't see much of him during the week. My aunt came over quite often, though.' I stop, seeing the concern on Nikolai's face. 'But I had Sam,' I say in a lighter voice. 'He was our Golden Retriever. My dad bought him when I was seven. The two of us used to walk him on Saturday mornings. He was always stealing food and sniffing strangers' bottoms. When he died, I cried for days… What were you like when you were small?'

'I like to make my sisters laugh. Sometimes I play tricks on them. My father was very serious man, reading newspaper every day, telling us what is right thing to do, what we should know about this world.'

'What was his job?'

'At first he makes weapons.'

His father qualified as a chemist, working for the Soviet military. During the Cold War, Perm had been a centre of production, closed off from the rest of Russia. Then the Soviet Union collapsed and his father lost his job.

'He tries to get another job but he cannot. He opens shop to sell medicines. He says to sell medicines is better than killing people. But he is not good at business. He was member of Communist Party – he does not believe in capitalism; he would prefer to live in the old Russia.'

'It must have been very hard for your parents.'

'Of course, for everyone. I was child, I do not understand what happens. I must pull out potatoes and turnips after school. Once I go to see my friends instead and my father is very angry with me. Every year, my mother says she cannot stay in our house for another year. The roof lets in rain, the windows cannot close.' He laughs. 'It was tough for my family, yes. But I was happy.'

The afternoon is fading. Weak sunlight slants through the window, striking dust motes.

Neither of us speaks. My hand falls onto Nikolai's thigh.

'My family always had plenty of money,' I say. 'I don't think it made us any happier, though. My father was always thinking about work. He thought his duty was to provide for his family. He encouraged me to study hard. All his hopes were focussed on me.'

'And your mother? She is pleased for you?'

'I'm sure she is.' He gives me a questioning look. 'She would have preferred me to become an artist or a scientist. She thinks I'm too influenced by my father.'

'Are you?'

I hesitate. 'I used to be.'

Nikolai yawns, raising both arms above his head. A band of flesh gapes above his belt, revealing the scar above his belly button. I've only glimpsed it before. It's several inches long, curving in opposite directions at each end like a snake.

'Touch, if you like.'

I place a finger on the bluish ridge.

'He is like old man who grumbles in bad weather, he reminds me that always I have his company.'

'I like him. He's part of you.'

He pulls down his jumper. 'Not everyone thinks like you, Georgie.'

'Is Olga waiting for you in Russia?'

'No, she has gone.' His eyes glisten in the fading light. 'She did not like to see my scars. The ones in here.' He taps his head.

We fall into silence. I nestle closer to Nikolai, enjoying his warmth. The only sounds are the occasional click of the electric heater and a steady drip, drip from the kitchen tap.

I wake with a start, not knowing where I am. The room is unevenly lit by a street light and the glow of the heater. Beside me, Nikolai is asleep, breathing noisily. I get up quietly and go to the kitchen for a glass of water.

On the way back, I find myself heading towards the shelves. I glance at the mess of papers on the lower one, along from the wooden box. I might learn something about Nikolai, I suddenly think. I could take a quick peek while he's asleep.

I pick up a cut-out newspaper article. It's dated 1 March 2005, 25 days ago:

Seven Russian soldiers have been killed in separatist Chechnya in clashes in the past 24 hours. Four men died and four were injured in a battle near the southern Chechen town of Nozhai-Yurt. Two separatists were killed...

I put the article back. Then I notice a sheet of paper with a note in pencil on it in Nikolai's handwriting:

Vakha Dagayev – Caucasus Action
Meeting 5 p.m. Thursday – Chemistry Building Imperial College
Agenda – local action – agree date & location – prepare – roles

I stare at the words for a while as if they might tell me what they mean. They provide more questions than answers.

Vakha Dagayev – is this the same Vakha I overheard Nikolai speaking to on his mobile phone? Caucasus Action – could that be part of the Chechen separatist movement? Has Nikolai been to a meeting of this group? Is the meeting still to come? What does 'local action' mean? A protest, or something more sinister? Is this group preparing for a violent incident of some kind? Why would Nikolai be interested in something like this?

Nikolai says something in his sleep and moves his head from side to side. I put the paper back quickly. Four or five times he repeats the same short phrase in Russian. With a moan, he jerks upright. He turns to me, his face and chest coated with sweat.

'I have the same dream as before... ' His voice sounds as if he is half asleep. 'I must go into a house, I don't know why. I see a woman lying on floor. Her face is white, her mouth is open. She does not breathe. I look down and see that my shirt is red. I know at once, it is her blood.'

A shiver goes down my spine.

'Don't be scared,' Nikolai says, switching on the lamp. 'It is only dream.'

I wonder who the woman in his dream is and why he dreamed such a thing. But there's no time to ask. It's gone six. I say I'd better be going or I'll miss my dinner. I should have left twenty minutes ago.

'If you miss your dinner, does it matter? There is good place I know to eat, very close.' He smiles. 'If you wish.'

'I'm sorry, Nikky. I'd better go. My friends are expecting me.'

It's true. But more than that, I feel unsettled by this man and the violence that seems to permeate him. What I've seen on his shelf is disturbing too.

I hand back his jumper and collect my things.

'Wait, it is dark. I will walk with you to your car.'

'No, don't worry, I'll be OK.'

Nikolai opens the front door. I stand in the doorway ready to kiss him on the cheek. But his hand goes to my back and urges my body closer, until the gently sweet, herby smell of him surrounds me. My lips press his back, without question. Then, while I still can, I gallop downstairs.

16

My father takes off his reading glasses, puts down the menu and raises his glass. As always on a weekday he's impeccably dressed, this time in a grey pinstripe and a turquoise tie.

'Here's to my favourite category manager.'

Our wine glasses meet across the table. It's lunchtime; waiters in head-to-toe black churn between tables of banking and media types. It was my father's idea: lunch at Langan's, just like old times. He took me there the week I started my first job and again after my recent promotion.

'What's new at work, then?'

'Oh, nothing much,' I reply. 'I can't stand the politics, the jockeying for position. And Jake's more demanding than ever.'

'Don't worry, things will sort themselves out.'

'What happened with the health-and-safety inspection?'

My father groans. 'The report wasn't good. They're coming back again soon to do more checks. It means a ton of extra work for us, which we could well do without. But never mind... Who are you going to vote for in the election?'

'Who knows – Labour and Conservative are as bad as each other.' Although more right-wing than some of my friends, I'm not nearly as conservative as my father.

'Blair will win easily, if the polls are anything to go by. But the Tories still have a chance on immigration.'

'The Conservatives are clutching at straws, Dad,' I protest. 'They're trying to convince us the country is being overrun by immigrants and asylum seekers.'

'I sympathise with genuine asylum seekers,' he replies. 'We can't just tell them to go home. But immigrants are another matter... Do you have any idea how many people are in this country illegally?'

I shake my head.

'And no one else does either – that's the problem.' He skewers a piece of steak.

'But your business benefits from foreign workers, doesn't it?'

'We've got our share of them, I can't deny. Who would do all the jobs the Brits won't do if it weren't for the Poles and the Eastern Europeans?'

'I know someone recently arrived from Russia,' I volunteer before I can think better of it. 'He's working on a big building site near Old Street Station.'

My father gives me a probing glance. 'So what's this chap do?'

'He's a labourer. I gave him the name of that agency you use – they found him something straight away.'

I can almost hear my father's disgruntled response, unspoken. My daughter consorting with labourers – what next?

He leans back in his chair, smoothing non-existent wrinkles out of the tablecloth. 'You're friendly with him, are you?'

I shrug. 'We meet up from time to time. I'm going to see him again this weekend.'

Since Nikolai's overnight stay last week, we've met up a couple of times recently in a King's Cross café after work.

'Has he always been a labourer?'

'He was in the army before. He fought in Chechnya.'

'That doesn't sound like fun.'

'He was injured in a grenade attack. Quite badly.'

My father looks thoughtful again.

'Dad?' I'm not sure if it's a good idea to involve my father, but an idea has popped into my head. 'I wonder if you could do me a favour?'

'Sure, what is it?'

'You have a friend who's quite high up in the Met, don't you?'

'Jimmy, yes. He's not been well lately.'

'Do you think he would be willing to run a check on someone to see if they've been in any trouble with the police?'

He raises his eyebrows.

'I'll ask him for you,' he says doubtfully, 'but I can't promise he'll do it. The police are stricter about who sees what, these days. What's the name you want checked?'

I take out a piece of paper and write down 'Vakha Dagayev'. My father folds it in two and tucks it into his wallet.

'What's this all about?'

'I can't really say.'

'Come on, Georgie. If I'm going to do this, I'll need to know something. Who is this guy?'

'It's someone Nikolai knows. I saw something the other day that seemed rather odd. It's probably nothing. I just want to make sure that there's nothing to worry about.'

'OK, I'll do my best. What's the latest with Julian? Are you two still friends?'

'No, I can't be friends with him any more.'

'I don't see why you can't stay in touch with him.'

'It's not that simple, Dad. Julian is really jealous of Nikolai. I didn't want to have to choose between them, but he's forced me to.'

My father swirls wine around his mouth. He's observing me as he sometimes does – as if I'm a painting that fascinates him but he can't quite get. It pleases him that I've chosen to go into business like him and that I've done well in my career. But he can't understand why I have no boyfriend.

'Are you sure you're doing the right thing, sweetie? Julian thinks the world of you, you know.'

I roll my eyes.

'You're my only chance, Georgie,' he says in a lighter tone.

'For what?'

'Grandchildren.'

I give an exaggerated sigh. My father leans towards me.

'I admit I'm not the most adept bloke on the planet when it comes to relationships. I've got some experience, that's all.'

'With your two marriages, you mean?'

He doesn't reply for some time.

'Love is a strange thing,' he says, gazing at his hands. 'It makes you behave in ways you don't expect.'

17

I'm in a changing cubicle in a Hampstead boutique dragging on a third pair of jeans when my mobile rings. I lurch towards my bag, expecting it to be Ella; she promised to call me after work. But it's Julian.

'Hello, stranger,' he says brightly.

I slump onto the bench, jeans gathering at my knees.

'What do you want?'

'I'm sorry about that stuff I said in the pub, Georgie. I got upset, I didn't mean it.'

I don't know what to say. The ambient music blasts into my ears; I have to speak loudly to be heard.

'That's all right. Is there anything else?'

'Actually,' he replies, 'there is. I've managed to get tickets to a Joss Stone concert, fantastic seats. How about coming with me?'

'Julian, you know what I said –'

A double rap on the door is followed by a strident female voice. 'Going to be long, luv?'

'I can't talk now,' I hiss into the phone.

'Just one sec. I thought you might be tempted to put aside your principles for once.'

'No, I –'

'I'm not asking you to marry me, for Christ's sake. I'm just asking you to a concert. Come on, Georgie, what do you say?'

He sounds so upbeat, so together, that for a millisecond I nearly relent. What harm could it do to go to a concert with him? Aren't I the one being unreasonable? We've had plenty of differences before and got over them… But this jealousy is different. There's something off with the way he's seeing things now. Something is eating up the Julian I've always known.

'I'm sorry, Julian. I'm not going to change my mind.'

I'm about to end the call when he speaks again in a different tone, one I don't recognise.

'You're making a mistake, a big mistake. You really shouldn't do this.'

Three more raps on the door.

'Hurry up in there, will you? Some of us are here to shop.'

'I have to go, I'm sorry.' I switch off my phone and sit there, my palms cold and clammy, all thoughts of shopping gone.

Next evening I'm finishing putting on my make-up, half listening to the radio, when the doorbell rings. I decide not to answer. It's bound to be either a charity collector or a Jehovah's Witness.

A second ring, longer. I wonder if it might be Tess from the flat above mine – a woman in her late sixties who seems to camp outside her front door, ever ready to discuss the latest affliction of her cat. But she never rings my bell after 6 p.m..

The bell goes again, a long push and two short pushes in quick succession. Some kids having a laugh? Swearing, I fling down my mascara and hurry down the hall. Through my inches-open front door, I see Julian. He stands on the porch, thumbs hooked into his jeans pockets, whistling. Trying to, anyway. He never quite got the hang of it.

'Thought you'd never answer.'

I stare at him. He smiles, a best-of-mates smile. His light fragrance wafts over. It doesn't mix well with the churning in my stomach.

'Aren't you going to invite me in?'

'Why have you come here?'

He looks me up and down.

'You're looking very nice. Going somewhere?'

'I am, actually. I have to leave in ten minutes.'

'Can I come in? I won't keep you long.'

'I'd rather you didn't. As I said, I have to leave in ten minutes.' I feel irritated and anxious in equal measures.

'That isn't very hospitable.'

'I'm not feeling very hospitable.'

He doesn't reply.

'Julian, I've told you how things are. What is it? Why are you here?'

He pats his jacket pocket. 'I've got the tickets with me. Just in case you want to change your mind.'

My patience reaches breaking point. 'No, I'm not going to change my mind. Don't you understand?'

An ugly scowl. 'No, I don't understand. One minute I'm your best buddy, the next I'm chucked out in the cold like a fucking leper!'

'You know why we can't be friends. You want too much from me. You'd be jealous of every guy I looked at.'

'Like I'm jealous of this guy you're humping now?' He laughs contemptuously. 'I'm not stupid, you know.' His gaze travels over me. 'You're all made-up, you've got your best jewellery on. You don't dress up like that to see your friends.'

I keep quiet, hoping Tess might come out – or anyone at all.

'The Russian, is it?' He leans in towards me, smiling coldly. 'Nikolai.'

I don't answer.

'What's he like in the sack, then? A good fuck, is he?'

'How dare you?' For the first time, I feel a dart of fear. 'Please will you sodding well go away and leave me alone.'

His face hardly changes. There's only a flicker of his eyelashes before he turns and walks down the steps, past the parked cars and onto the pavement. I wait on the doorstep, my heart pounding. I don't go back inside until I hear the Jaguar's low growl build to a powerful roar, then slowly fade into silence.

By the time I've driven to Finsbury Park, parked and found the restaurant where Nikolai and I arranged to meet, the incident has shrunk to manageable proportions. I decide to say nothing to Nikolai about Julian coming over. I've only known him for a couple of months; why burden him with Julian's jealousy? He doesn't know what has happened with me and Julian; I would have to explain everything. He might think that the situation was all my own doing.

As it probably is, I think miserably. I've done everything wrong. First I encouraged Julian by having sex with him. Then, instead of ending it cleanly, I dragged things out in the vain hope of salvaging our friendship. The less I tell Nikolai about Julian, the better.

Nikolai is waiting for me at a corner table. He's smarter than usual. He has on a black jacket and a white shirt, open at the collar, over his jeans.

He picks up my hand and kisses it. '*Tu es très jolie, ma chère.*'

'I didn't know you spoke French.'

'I speak only what is essential.'

'For chatting up girls?'

He smiles. 'If you like.'

He orders a glass of Malbec for me and hands me the menu

inside its plastic sleeve. We both decide on battered haddock, chips and mushy peas.

'It's not pretty, this place.' He gestures around the room. 'But it has good food.'

He's right about the food. Two huge fillets arrive, the tastiest fish I've eaten in ages, and the chips are crisp and hot.

'What is the matter?' Nikolai puts down his knife and fork. 'I see on your face, something is not right.'

'I've had a bad day, that's all.'

'Why is that?'

'Oh, this and that. Things not going as they should.'

Over our desserts – chocolate fondant with ice cream – Nikolai tells me about an incident at work involving his Pakistani friend. Malik's work boots have gone missing from the drying room for the second time in two weeks; he was upset at having to buy yet another pair and suspected that someone took them.

'He is getting shit from some of the guys. They think he is going to put bomb under them. They call him "dirty Paki".'

Nikolai pushes away his empty plate; I carry on picking at my dessert. Normally, I wolf down anything containing chocolate.

'What is wrong, Georgie? Something worries you, no?'

I nearly mention Julian's visit. But I don't want to spoil the evening.

His eyes stay on mine as if they might find the answer if they look long enough. Then he leans back and his face relaxes. We talk about cats, religion and global warming, the Russian films Nikolai has recommended, which I've taken out from my local video shop, and Boris Pasternak's poems – Nikolai has lent me a disintegrating paperback containing both the Russian and a translated version. I've stayed up half the night reading them.

Without warning, Nikolai leans towards me.

'You are beautiful, tonight. That dress, it is perfect. I never see you like this.' He puts his hand on mine. 'I would like to be close to you, Georgie. If you will let me.'

I am taken aback. It is the seriousness of his voice, perhaps, as much as the sudden change of topic.

'You do not like to hear.' He withdraws his hand. 'I am sorry.'

'No, don't be silly. It's just that – well, I'm English. We're more reserved than you Russians.'

'It is *you* who are reserved, not the English.'

His tone is sharp. It shocks me, like the sudden scratch of a cat that has been sitting contentedly on your lap.

The tone of the evening has changed. We finish our coffees; Nikolai doesn't speak except to ask for the bill. When it comes, we split it as usual, then I drive him back to his flat. Despite my attempts to get the evening back on track, he hardly speaks during the journey.

I stop the car outside his building. Before he can open the door, I put my hand on his arm.

'Please don't be upset, Nikky. I like you – very much.'

'What are you afraid of?'

'I've never met anyone like you – I can't quite work you out.'

'Life is not for ever, Georgie. We must live while we can.'

With that he steps out of the car, slamming the door behind him. A surge of dismay goes through me. Before I can think better of it, I'm out of the car and on the pavement, shouting at his retreating back.

'Nikky!'

He walks on.

'Please, Nikky. Come back!'

Finally, he turns. I breathe again. Thank you, I whisper, watching him walk slowly towards me until there's no distance between us. I touch his hand; it wraps around my fingers.

He takes my hand in his and we set off towards his block. A surge of adrenalin goes through me. I want to stay and at the same time I want to run away.

Inside, Nikolai switches on the lamp, starts a CD of Chopin's Preludes and hands me a vodka and tonic. I drink it while he unfolds the sofa-bed and arranges sheets and blankets. The alcohol burns my throat, makes my brain fizz.

We undress and lie down beneath the covers.

Suddenly I remember condoms – or the lack of them – and curse myself for forgetting a second time. It would be the sensible thing to do, but... Do I trust him or don't I?

He kisses me, and I decide.

I pull him close, breathing in the tang of his sweat mixed with the remains of his lemony scent. His lips find my nipples and play with them, nudging and gently pulling. An ache grows between my legs until I'm sure I will go crazy with desire. My hands become bold, exploring his chest, his torso, everywhere. I don't care what this might lead to. I want him, all of him.

Time vanishes. I hear his cries mixed with my own and lay my head on his heaving chest.

'You make me feel like I am new in this world,' he says. 'There is nothing better than this.'

My eyes fill with tears. I kiss him, over and over. I'm falling and I have no idea of how long it will take to reach the ground.

18

Nikolai pushes away his empty mug, folds his *Evening Standard* and places it on the plastic-clothed table with a sigh. I put my mug of milky tea down beside my teaspoon and squeezed-out PG Tips bag.

The café is our regular after-work rendezvous, chosen both for its location (close to King's Cross Station) and its cheapness (a mug of tea costs ninety-five pence). A red-cheeked, out-of-breath woman trots up and down the narrow aisle, offloading plates of sausages and chips. I usually stick to a toasted ham and cheese sandwich.

'Saturday night,' Nikolai says. 'You are going to this party?' His tone is casual.

'My father's party, you mean? Yes, of course.'

'So I will not see you this weekend.'

'I thought we were going to meet on Sunday.'

'On Sunday I must visit Ruslan.'

'Weren't you going to meet him the weekend after?'

'Ruslan texts me this afternoon, he changes the date. Now I will see him this Sunday.'

Nikolai has mentioned that he's planning to visit his friend Ruslan in Leicester, the brother of a woman he used to know. I sense he doesn't want to tell me anything else; there is no point asking.

My gaze moves to the mirror fixed above the pale green wall tiles. The young, businesslike woman reflected there has crisply cut hair to her shoulders, a fashionable short-skirted wool suit and Bally shoes. Opposite her is a guy with untidy hair, a stubbly jaw, frayed jeans and mud-caked boots.

'Well,' I say. 'I hope your meeting goes well.'

'And I hope you will enjoy your party.' As if he doesn't care one jot. 'There will be many guests?'

'I should think so. Alicia's invited a ton of people. Friends of my father, relatives –'

'I have not met any of your family – or your friends. You are hiding me away?'

I open my mouth to defend myself, and shut it. I haven't introduced Nikolai to anyone, it's true, nor have I told anyone how I feel about him, not even Ella. To the gang, he's just 'the Russian guy' I see from time to time.

We are lovers; he occupies my thoughts more and more. I imagine him in his tiny kitchen cooking stews, or at his keyboard feverishly scribbling down crotchets and quavers, or leafing through his Russian–English dictionary as he watches TV. I imagine him in my bed, in his bed, doing to me what I crave. Yet, in a way, I'm still keeping him at a distance.

Because he is a struggling labourer, living in a less–than–desirable part of town?

No, it isn't that. OK, we're on different levels of the social pecking order. I live in an affluent suburb and am firmly lodged within the privileged middle classes, whereas Nikolai has a precarious existence, living in a shabby block of flats without secure employment. But I don't care what job he has or how much money he has or where he lives. The real reason why I haven't yet introduced him to my family and friends is... What? I dare not let him disturb my cosy little world?

'I don't want to hide you away,' I say.

'For that, I am pleased.' He doesn't sound it.

'Do you want to come to my father's party?'

He shrugs, a lazy movement travelling from his shoulders to his spread palms.

'This is your invitation?'

'Will you come with me to the party, Nikolai?'

I wait for him to tell me to shove the party.

'Of course, I would be delighted,' he says in a spookily upper-class accent.

19

Nikolai raises the knocker for the second time.

'They do not hear us.'

'No, someone's coming.'

A breeze catches my skirt, swirling the flimsy fabric. I steal another glance at my escort, not 100 per cent believing it's Nikolai and not an identical twin he's forgotten to mention. His hair is combed so you can actually see the parting and his fingernails are clean. He looks striking in his black jacket and red silk shirt over black jeans and polished black shoes.

My stepmother opens the door, welcoming smile ready. Her shimmering powder-blue dress matches her eyes and her hair is gathered into a complicated knot. My father waves, emerging from the living room. He wears a sleek grey suit – Armani, I guess.

'Glad you could make it, darling.' He bends for me to kiss his cheek. 'And your friend – Nikolai, did you say?'

'Nikolai Alexandrovich,' Nikolai replies in a flash, clasping the proffered hand. 'Good evening, Mr Cameron. I am very pleased to meet you. And Mrs Cameron, I am very pleased to meet you.'

'Alexandrovich...' My father looks puzzled.

'Nikolai Alexandrovich Konstantinov is my full name, but you can call me Nikolai.'

Alicia ushers us inside. The living room is thick with people; the carpet is no longer visible and a heady mixture of smoke and perfume replaces the antique-shop smell. The guests are mostly older than us, in their forties, fifties and up, many quite formally dressed. Looking around at the luxurious dresses, I feel out of place in my simple outfit.

'I haven't heard very much about you, Nikolai,' Alicia says in her guest-charming voice, hailing one of the girls delivering champagne and canapés on silver trays. 'Except that you're Russian and you work in construction like Vincent.'

'I am also composer. One day I hope to make my living from music.'

My father raises his eyebrows. 'A hard way to earn a living.'

Nikolai looks at him steadily. 'Yes, it is true.'

'What brought you to England? You didn't just come to escape the cold winters?'

'No, Russian winters I do not mind,' Nikolai counters. 'There are many opportunities here – also I can practise my English.'

I wonder if this was something he invented for the benefit of people who asked awkward questions.

'London has such a lot going on,' Alicia cuts in, her frown at my father switching to a radiant smile as she turns to Nikolai.

'Georgie, can I –' my father begins.

But Alicia interrupts. 'Come with me, both of you. I'll introduce you to some people.'

I take Nikolai's hand as we weave among the guests, stopping here and there to meet people I've never met or have long ago forgotten.

'Hello, Georgie! Thought it was you.'

I turn to a baby-faced guy with spiky hair. 'Hi, Sean, long time no see. This is my friend, Nikolai.'

'Pleased to meet you.' Nikolai offers his hand.

'Sean is my father's godson,' I explain. 'His father and mine took the same City & Guilds course, years ago.'

Sean turns to Nikolai. 'Where are you from?'

'Russia, a city called Perm. Don't worry, no one has heard of it.'

Sean enthuses to Nikolai about university and his career plans, and I relax. Nikolai might not always construct his sentences perfectly but he's quite able to grasp what is said to him and make himself understood. In fact, his social skills are superior to mine, I have to admit. He's enviably quick-thinking and knows exactly what to say to put someone at their ease.

As Nikolai scoops up several caviar-laden blinis from a passing tray, I see Alicia's discreet glance in our direction. On the other side of the room, my father is deep in conversation.

'Did anyone see that programme on TV the other night?' An elderly man in a dinner suit takes a puff on his cigar and continues in his resonant bass. 'About immigrants from Eastern Europe.'

'Fright'ning it was, quite fright'ning,' says a leathery-faced man with a loud tie. 'How they're straining the system and ruining the country.'

The elderly man puffs more acrid smoke. 'One has to ask whether a country as small as Britain can cope with such an influx. What's going to happen to the countryside?'

'It's gonna be buggered, that's what.'

'And what about all the failed asylum seekers? And all the ones who slip over here in the backs of lorries?'

'They should be deported, the lot of 'em!'

'They are fools,' Nikolai says, loudly enough for others to hear. His face is flushed.

I turn to urge him to keep his voice down, and find myself looking straight at Julian. His sullen expression vanishes as our eyes meet. His hand rises to greet me. He's standing by himself by the wall, not far away but hidden by the crowd of guests. How long has he been there – and what the hell is he doing here?

I touch Nikolai's arm to warn him.

'Hello, Georgie, how nice to see you again. And you must be Nikolai.'

Julian extends his hand, his face radiating goodwill.

'I'm Julian. Georgie and I have been friends for a long time.' He glances at me.

'I am pleased to meet you.' Julian's handshake is politely returned.

I stare at the shiny gold buttons on Julian's blazer, my anger rising. How does he have the gall to introduce himself as my friend?

'I hear you've recently come from Russia,' Julian goes on. 'What's it like there now? I've read that the corruption's not much better than it used to be in Soviet times. There's a lot of very rich people around, I've heard.' He takes a spring roll from a passing tray and dips it in soy sauce.

'It is true,' Nikolai replies, taking two spring rolls. 'The rich get richer; they can exploit the rest. But people without jobs – the old, the sick – they have hard life. Russia is not good place to be poor.'

A sneer passes over Julian's face. 'You're better off over here then, aren't you?'

Nikolai's brow creases. 'I do not come here because I have no money.'

'Why *are* you here?'

Julian waits for Nikolai to speak. Cigar man, watching the exchange with interest, also turns to Nikolai.

'It is not your business,' Nikolai replies.

'Julian,' I say. 'Will you please leave?'

'Pardon?'

'You heard. I don't want you here. You've no right to be here.'

'Your father invited me.'

Speechless and conscious of my warming cheeks, I stare into his fake blue eyes.

'Nikolai, it was good talking to you.' Julian pats Nikolai's arm. 'Maybe we can continue our conversation another time.'

'I don't think so,' I splutter, not bothering to keep my voice down. Heads turn in our direction. 'And I'd appreciate it if you would keep well away from me from now on.'

'Sorry, Georgie. I didn't realise my presence would be such an affront to you.' With that, he saunters across the room and out of the door.

'He shouldn't have come here,' I mutter to Nikolai. 'Excuse me, I have to talk to my father.'

My father is talking to his cousin, who runs a chain of boutiques in Hong Kong. I plant myself beside her flowing gown and wait for my father to finish.

'What is it, sweetie?'

'What was Julian doing here?'

'I invited him.'

'You know we're not friends any more. I told you.'

'He phoned a few days ago, Georgie,' he says in a tone that one might use to a small child. 'He explained that you two hadn't been getting on so well and asked if I could suggest anything that might help. I said he'd have to sort it out with you. He said he can't, that you've refused to speak to him – so I told him he'd be welcome to look in on my party. We're hardly strangers, after all. I felt for him, I thought it might be a chance for you two to settle your differences.' He sighs, glancing at his cousin. 'I'm sorry, Georgie, if I did the wrong thing. I tried to warn you he was here but I never had a chance –'

'Thank you so much, Dad, you've been a great help.' My voice comes out high and tight. I feel the cousin's pitying gaze. 'The guy won't leave me alone. The last thing I expected was to bump into him here.'

I don't wait for my father's reply.

We take the Tube back. As the carriage lurches towards Finsbury Park, we sit side by side in silence.

'I'm sorry for rushing out like that,' I say. 'We should have stayed a bit longer.' I've ruined the evening, I think.

Nikolai keeps his eyes on a poster advertising a hair-loss treatment. 'You did not want to say goodbye to your father?' His eyes flick onto mine and away.

'He knows why I left.'

'Because your friend comes, who you do not expect?'

'Julian isn't my friend, Nikolai. I've already told him I don't want to see him any more. I made it perfectly clear. Then my father goes and invites him to his sodding party.'

'Julian. He is in love with you?'

I keep my eyes on the empty seat opposite me, aware of Nikolai's steady scrutiny of my face.

'He said he was. A while back. I didn't realise how he felt about me, not till it was too late.'

'He was your lover?'

'No, a friend. A close friend.' I feel my hands twisting in my lap. That's not the entire truth, is it? 'I made a mistake – things happened that shouldn't have.'

'Like the things that happened with me?'

I turn to him. 'No, it was totally different with you. It is totally different.'

Nikolai looks away.

'What if you see him again? What will you do?'

'I won't see him again.'

'You are sure?'

I hesitate. I hope that now he's seen me and Nikolai together, Julian will finally realise that he has no chance with me. It's creepy the way he was secretly watching us, though.

'I think he's got the message this time. If he comes near me again, I'll go to the police.'

'You would like me to speak to him?'

'There's no need for that,' I say quickly. That will make things even worse, I'm sure. 'Look, it's not even ten o'clock. Do you want to go somewhere for a drink?'

From Finsbury Park Station we walk a short distance to a plain, harshly lit Victorian pub full of men draped in football scarves. We're overdressed – that's obvious from several glances towards us. Nikolai goes to the bar while I make my way to an empty table. Around me, fragments of conversations collide.

'What about the result, then?'

'The bleedin' ref should be shot –'

'Did you 'ear about the new Pope? They reckon 'e's a Nazi.'

'Cardinal Rat Slinger, you mean?'

'God's Rottweiler, they're calling 'im.'

Nikolai returns with his pint and my half. We're discussing the spate of wealthy Russians buying up mansions in Kensington when an alcohol-bloated voice barges into our conversation.

'Another bleedin' Ruski, is it?'

This comes from a youth standing a few feet away. His eyes are fixed on Nikolai. He has close-cropped hair and a long scar on one cheek. A leer spreads across his thin lips. He mutters something to his companion and saunters up to our table, jolting Nikolai's arm. Beer spews across the table. Russian words explode from Nikolai's lips. The youth looks on impassively. Nikolai, face distorted with rage, springs to his feet.

'See what you have done? You spill my beer all over this table – all over me!' He holds up the drenched sleeve of his jacket.

'No need to get so upset, mate. It was an accident.'

'It's all right, Nikky,' I urge. I've never seen a pub brawl and I don't want to see one now. He ignores me.

The youth turns and speaks loudly to his companion, who's appeared at his side.

'You can't get away from 'em these days, can yer?'

Nikolai takes a step towards them. 'What is it you say?'

'They can't even fuckin' speak proper English,' the youth adds, looking straight at Nikolai.

'He's only trying to provoke you,' I say, standing and tugging at his arm. 'Please, let's go.'

Nikolai's hands flutter at his side; he gives no sign of having heard. Several men at the bar turn to us. Everyone around us has stopped talking. Before I can say or do anything, Nikolai grabs the youth by his jacket collar and shakes him. His head flops up and down.

'Shut your mouth, idiot. You shut your mouth!'

The youth bares his teeth and snarls. 'Let me go, you cunt! Fuckin' let me go!'

The other youth steps back, mouth hanging open. Neither of them looks any match for Nikolai. People nearby put down their pints and shift their chairs to get out of the way. Helpless, I watch the two men face each other with hate in their eyes.

Nikolai wrenches his adversary away from the table. With one hand he holds the youth in position and with the other he delivers a blow to his face. His head jerks back with a horrible crack. Someone yells at me to get out of the way but I can't move. Nikolai pulls his fist back again. I can't see where it lands. The youth moans, totters backward and collides with the empty chair beside me. I stand there in shock as shouts ring out around us.

'Fuckin' madman!'

'Call the police!'

"E's gone crazy. Get him out of 'ere!'

Nikolai gestures towards the door. 'Georgie, we go now!'

In a flash I snatch my bag and follow him. I have no thought of disobeying, my legs are propelled by some force that has nothing to do with me. I run as fast as I can, afraid that any second I will trip over. Not far off, a police siren wails. We take right and left turns seemingly at random through poorly lit streets, until my windpipe hurts, my shoes are throttling my feet and I can't take a breath without feeling a sharp pain in my side.

'Stop, please.' I bend over, gasping for air.

Nikolai scans the street, left and right.

Leaning against a low wall, I inspect a blistered heel. The siren has stopped. A baby starts crying from an upper window.

'We must go.' Nikolai moves towards me, wiping a ribbon of spittle from his mouth. A street lamp turns his face a sickly yellow. His eyes have disappeared into shadowy sockets.

'Who are you running away from? The police have gone; no one's going to find us. What the hell got into you back there?'

'Please, let's go now. We will talk later.'

He takes my hand and walks at a normal pace. When we reach the entrance to his building, Nikolai puts his hand on my arm.

'Come up, stay with me tonight. Please.'

20

We stand in his cramped kitchen under the stark light of a grimy fluorescent strip, gulping down tumblers of tap water. Nikolai pours two glasses of Stolichnaya and hands one to me. He downs his in one and immediately pours another. I take a mouthful. The blaze of heat in my belly does nothing to subdue the turmoil inside me.

'What happened to you back there, Nikolai? Why did you have to hurt that guy like that?'

'You do not hear him? He talks like I am the shit he walks in.'

He removes his stained jacket and wipes his face and neck with a tea towel. A large damp patch has spread across the back of his shirt.

'But he was just an idiot who'd had too much to drink. You didn't have to clobber him like that. God knows what you've done to him.'

He looks past me, through the curtainless window. 'He insults me. He should not say those things.' Nikolai leans against the sink, staring me out.

'Like that guy who insulted you when you were a security guard?'

'You want to know what happened to him, Georgie? I break his nose, his arm. After this, my boss tells me I am fired and my father says it is the end for me, unless I change. I agree to help in his pharmacy. I promise him never again will I let out my anger... ' He looks away from me and speaks quietly. 'But I fail him. This anger, it never goes away. It comes out without me agreeing and I don't know how to stop it. I am no longer man, I am crazy dog.'

Shocked by his words, I down the rest of my vodka and pour myself another one.

'You're here illegally, aren't you? That's why you're so afraid of being caught.'

'Why do you ask this?'

'I'm not going to report you, don't be stupid. I'd just like to know, that's all.'

He laughs without humour. 'Yes, you are right. I am one of the illegal scum everyone hates.'

I stare at him.

'OK – I will tell.' He pulls himself straight, eyes defiant. 'In Moscow I buy visa for UK, it is valid for six weeks only. I must leave Russia quickly – it is only visa I can get. At Heathrow I give false address. I say that I visit friend, I have money, I will be here for three weeks. I do not say that I need to work so I can find place to live. When I show my passport at employment agency, they tell me my visa is not good for working. They tell me to go to place where they will help me with what I need for construction job. I see man in betting shop, I pay him three hundred pounds and he gives me construction worker card with my photograph and number. I go back to employment agency, they are happy. Everyone is happy.' He speaks scornfully. 'In Russia, if you have enough dollars, money will buy anything you want. I come to London and it is not so different.'

'Is your passport fake too?'

'No, it is not fake.' His voice is taut with suppressed anger.

'Is it in your own name?'

'Yes, it is in my own name. You want me to show you? I do not lie to you.'

I've wondered for some time whether Nikolai might be working illegally. It's a shock to hear him admit it, though.

'What if someone finds out you've no right to be working here? You could be deported. Why risk that?'

He looks at me as if I'm stupid. 'I came here because I had to leave Russia. And I have to work or I cannot live.'

'Why come to London?'

'I can get visa for UK quickly, no waiting. Also there are many Russians in London.'

'But why did you have to leave Russia in the first place?'

'I have to go somewhere far away,' he says in a quiet voice. 'Where no one can find me.'

'What?'

'I had to leave. I had no choice.'

'But why?'

'I cannot tell you.'

'You don't trust me?'

'Georgie, please.' He grips my hand so hard it hurts. 'I trust you. Only it is better you do not know everything.'

'What are you afraid of?'

He releases my hand. 'I am afraid you will hate me, and then you will run away from me.'

I nod, not saying what's on my mind.

Later, I call a cab to take me home. All of the way back I ask myself: *What could make me hate him?*

21

I'm pleased when Tim phones and invites me to join him, Cath and Ella for a picnic on the weekend. 'Your Russian friend is welcome to come too,' he adds. 'You know we're all dying to meet him.'

'I will look forward to it,' Nikolai says when I call to tell him.

I ask how last Sunday's trip to Leicester went.

'It was good, thank you. Ruslan cooked big meal for me. The two of us talk for long time. His son Vakha is chemistry student at Imperial College. He is in final year, he lives in Bethnal Green.'

Something clicks in my brain. Vakha – this must be the Vakha Dagayev I saw in the note, the guy who Nikolai was talking to on the phone. So, Vakha is the son of Nikolai's friend Ruslan.

'Vakha is a friend of yours too?'

Nikolai looks at me sharply. 'He is friend, yes.' A long pause. 'His father Ruslan is the brother of a Chechen woman who was once my friend. Ruslan came to UK five years ago with his wife and son – the only son he has left. He claims asylum here.'

'Why?'

'Their lives were in danger, that is why.'

I don't ask more. I've not yet heard anything from my father about the police check on Vakha. I wish I hadn't done that now. It was an overreaction, a breach of trust.

Nikolai says he'll see me Saturday, he will count the days.

22

04 May 2005 22.08
   To: Georgie Cameron
   From: Julian Lewis
   Dearest Georgie,
   Sorry to be bothering you yet again. But they say to strike while the iron's hot, don't they?

   I'm not in the best of spirits these days, I have to admit. It's hard to grasp how things can change so quickly. One day you're on cloud 99, the girl of your dreams is at last within reach. The next you're on your knees, gutted, a clown who's just seen the red blob on the end of his nose.

   I thought I had a chance to win your love, if I was patient. And I was, until he came along.

   Every day now I wake up and try to accept what you've told me, that it's over between us. I'm like a clock with its insides taken out, my hands are still going round from force of habit but there's nothing left inside. When I think of you with that Russian, I want to die. Not literally, of course, I wouldn't go quite that far. But you know what I mean.

   Our brief chat the other evening with your boyfriend was most illuminating. I still can't quite believe that after those hours we spent together in your bed you could run off with a ruffian like him.

   That night is now, without question, the No. 1 night of my life. I'm sorry I got a bit carried away towards the end, my sweet girl, but oh my lord, I was unprepared for such delights. You were a panther, eyes ablaze, cunt on fire. I won't ever forget your flailing claws and your wild cries as you abandoned yourself to me.

   How can I go on knowing I will never experience this again? I dream of your heavenly lips all over me, just once more. I long for you, I can't help it. Now I've tasted 5-star Michelin-guide gastro paradise, how can I go back to Kentucky Fried Chicken?

   Did you really think the best way to get rid of me would be to shag someone else? Were you so scared by the idea of me loving you that you had to do that? I know you're as fucked up as I am, my love, so I am doing my best to forgive you. Just don't think I'm going to slink away nursing my wounds. I'm not going to give up so easily. I'll be patient this time. I'll wait for you, I promise.

With all my love,
Julian

I find the email on my computer before going to bed. I reread the message several times, guilty, alarmed and appalled in turn, until what little sympathy I had left for Julian is gone.

I have a horrible sense of being caught out, as if someone has secretly photographed me dancing around naked in a moment of joy and pinned it up on the office noticeboard. While I can't reconcile those descriptions of me with what actually happened, I imagine there may be a kernel of truth in what he says. I was admittedly drunk and totally out of it by the time we had sex. Much of it, mercifully, I've forgotten. Yes, I enjoyed what we did together, once I got over the weirdness of it and before he got 'carried away' and went at me like a pile driver. Yes, maybe I did yell and go a little crazy. Why should I feel bad about that? I'm a single woman – don't I have as much right to enjoy sex as any man?

But I do feel bad. I imagine what Nikolai would think if he saw these words and I know I can't let him see this email or tell him of its contents.

Try as I might, I can't comprehend how my relationship with Julian has transformed into this unnatural fixation, this stubborn refusal to face facts. 'I'll wait for you.' What does he mean by that? This can't be love, surely. It's closer to obsession. A shiver goes through me. Has Julian transformed into a deranged stalker? No, of course he hasn't. I've watched too many thrillers. This is Julian, my old friend from university and a highly qualified professional, not some psycho.

Even though it's late, I phone Ella.

'I've just had an email from Julian,' I tell her. I paraphrase it and read out the final line, about him waiting for me.

She says it is worrying; perhaps I should go to the police.

'I could never show this to the police,' I tell her.

'They probably won't be able to do anything useful, anyway,' she says, then tells me again the story of how she was harassed by an ex who kept on turning up uninvited at her office, shouting and clutching a bottle of Johnnie Walker. 'When I went to the police,' she growls, 'they treated me like I was some neurotic bitch who'd forgotten to take her medication.' The police told her not to respond to the guy in any way whatsoever and he eventually disappeared, and she advises me to do the same with Julian, but to keep his email somewhere – 'just in case you need it later'. This is all my own fault for being daft enough to have had sex with him, she adds.

Before going to bed, I delete Julian's email. I don't want to look at it again and I don't want it on my computer for someone to accidentally find. Sooner or later Julian will get fed up with hassling me, I tell myself. I've just got to last out longer than he does.

23

He comes out of the construction site and walks down the street towards the café. It's raining and he's walking faster than usual. No umbrella, his hands in his jacket pockets. He's taken off his work boots this time. He's got his fancy black shoes on. A bit incongruous with his worn-out jeans, like a bovver boy in a cravat.

He turns a corner and disappears. I speed up to keep him in sight. The rain drums on my big umbrella. A bit further along he starts to whistle. Jaunty. He's going to break into a Fred Astaire routine at any moment.

He goes inside the café and sits down by the window. She's not there yet. She won't be there till five fifteen or five thirty. He takes off his jacket, yawns and picks up the Standard. *Sits there turning the pages, elbows on the table. He rubs his eyes, yawns again and rubs his nose.*

I wait outside, looking at my watch then down the street like I'm waiting for someone. It's not raining so hard now but I keep holding up the brolly. No one can see my face under this contraption. It's just the thing for spying.

Spying, yes. The word has a ring to it. MI5, men in trilbies. I guess that is what I'm doing.

A waitress comes up and puts a tall glass in front of him. Pepsi most likely, his usual beverage next to the old London Pride. He gulps it all down then gets up from the table. Off to pee, I should think.

She arrives at 5.09, earlier than usual. The rain's almost stopped. She's carrying her work bag over her shoulder. No umbrella. She's a bit weather-beaten. Her hair is back in a ponytail, loose bits straggling down, damp from the rain. Low-heeled, mid-calf boots. Her raincoat trails the tops of her boots. There's a smudge of make-up below one eye. She hurries past me into the café, out of breath. She goes over to him, takes off her coat, dumps it then retreats into the back.

I move to the bus stop a few yards down from the café. I lean against the wall, hidden by the crowd. Brolly down, baseball cap on. I've found the perfect American tourist outfit, no one would ever think it's a Brit in this get-up: Levis, sneakers, red and white college boy slouch jacket. A new pair of Ray-Bans, '50's style. Hair parted on the far left, gelled down. Ron Howard would be proud of me. I've even found an old leather satchel in

Oxfam to carry my library books. I feel a right prat. But she won't twig it's me in a million years.

I wait a good while then head back towards the café.

She's sitting with him now. They're facing each other, not talking. Her hand is on his arm. He's looking serious, so is she. Her smudge has gone. She's put on fresh lippy.

I stop. I'm right outside the window. They could see me if they looked up but I know they won't. The moment I've been waiting for is coming up.

She moves her face close to his. A smile breaks out all over it like she can't help herself, showing her small, even teeth. She flicks back her hair. It's falling free to her shoulders now, soft and shining. She's beautiful. He moves his mouth to hers.

My heart squeezes into an iron fist. For a brief moment I want to pull his horrible mug off her and stamp on it until it's not his any more. I walk away as fast as I can and keep going, way past the bus stop. Why don't I just go home, leave them to it? Take a shot of something strong and wipe them away.

I pull myself together. Something is drawing me back. A terrible itch I have to scratch. It's like when you've been attacked by mozzies. You know the next day you really mustn't scratch the bites or they'll itch like hell all day long. But once you start to scratch you can't stop yourself, no matter that the skin ends up red and sore and the itching torments you worse than ever.

I know I shouldn't have started to scratch it. This itch is taking over my life. I can't work properly any more, I can't sleep. But if I leave it alone, it will drive me fucking crazy.

I walk back again, brolly up to hide my face, lingering on the pavement a little way from the café window. It's not raining any more but no one seems to notice that some twat still has his brolly up. They are both eating now. She, a hunk of overflowing sandwich, he a plate of egg and chips. She's pecking at hers like she's wary of what she might find inside. He's tucking in like he's not eaten all day. I get the feeling she's not quite sure of him. She stares at him sometimes when he's not looking at her, like she's trying to work him out.

They'll go their separate ways soon. He's peering out of the window. It's a wet Wednesday evening. It doesn't look like they're about to pop back to hers for spot of dessert. But I may as well stay to the bitter end, just to make sure.

Some kind of pervy fascination has come over me. I dare myself to stay a bit longer, go a bit closer. It's like being at the zoo. He's a croc, a real saltwater beastie – the kind that could snap you in two if he wanted. There are no enclosures in this zoo, just a flimsy glass wall and this make-believe outfit. But he doesn't scare me. I'm the watcher and they're the watched. I have the tranquilliser darts and a rifle slung over my shoulder, just in case.

I follow them back to the Tube. They get the escalator down and stop at the arch going into the Northern Line northbound platform. He pulls on her arm and gives her a quick kiss on the cheek. A chaste little brush. Then he carries on to the Piccadilly Line.

It's crowded inside the compartment, making it easy to keep out of sight. Sometimes she gazes in my direction but I quickly tuck my head behind the conveniently fat woman in front of me and pull down the peak of my cap like a born PI.

I follow her all the way to her flat, keeping a respectful distance. As fast as lightning she gets her key out and nips in, as if she's expecting someone to grab her and drag her into the bushes. It's a shrub with yellow flowers, tall and bulky enough to block the view into the living room, unless you stand really close, that is, and peek through the gaps. There's always too many people around to be loitering on the pavement, though, unless it's well past pub closing. But I can usually see the two of them coming and going well enough from over the road, behind old codger's palm tree. It's on the spiky side and there's not much room here squashed up against the wall, but hey. He's deaf and his curtains are always closed. I don't think anyone else can see me.

Once she's safely inside, I head to the main road and grab a cab back to mine.

I slump into the back seat, ignoring the driver's prattle. Just as well she's not far away, haha. Maybe next time I'll take a wander down the little alley round the corner. It would be nice to have a view of her place from the back.

I close my eyes. I can see her face inside the train. Her skin, dull white under the glare. The shiny lips pressing together for a moment then relax-ing, opening. The cute little nose and the wrinkle above that forms from time to time as she reads her paperback.

24

Tim pauses at the top of the long incline to check the plastic-encased Ordnance Survey map hanging from his neck. He has assumed leadership of our expedition, and looks the part in his Australian bush hat and multi-pocketed khaki trousers. Cath is panting beside him, looking terribly '70s in her flared jeans and garish headband. Ella, Nikolai and I follow a few paces behind. All of us wear sturdy hiking boots except Nikolai, whose trainers look like they might expire at any moment.

The weather isn't ideal for a picnic. Each time the sky clears, fat clouds nibble at the sun. But we're far enough from London for the air to smell of manure rather than exhaust fumes. The hedgerows and trees are startling in shades of yellowy green, as if we've walked into a children's picture book.

'So,' Tim says, as he sets off again. 'It looks like we'll have to get through another four years of Tony Blair.'

'Anything as long as the Tories don't get back in,' Ella shoots back.

Tim laughs, glancing over his shoulder. 'Do you follow politics, Nikolai?'

'I follow what I can.'

The response comes so long after the question, I think Nikolai hasn't heard. Since mid-morning when we all piled into Tim's station wagon he's spoken little, answering any questions politely but briefly and keeping out of general conversation.

'Blair,' Nikolai continues, clearing his throat. 'He is not respected like before, I think. After he took your country to war against Iraq.'

Tim's reply is interrupted by Ella pointing to a nearby field and yelling that she's found the spot for our picnic.

We spread out our collection of plastic containers on Tim's rug as far as possible from the intermittent dried-up cow-pats. Below us, hills roll into a violet haze. A pair of horses clip-clop down the lane.

I watch Nikolai bite the meat off a chicken leg. He's sat on the edge of the rug, away from me. It strikes me again how distant he's been all day, apart from taking my hand briefly in the back of the car. He puts down the remains of the chicken leg and gazes into the hills, lost in some unknowable place.

'It's fabulous here,' Cath says.

Nikolai turns to her. 'I have not seen the English countryside. Except on the train to Leicester.'

'The train to Leicester!' Cath's exuberant laugh gurgles out. 'It's not the best way to see the countryside.'

Tim gives me a pointed look. 'You've been neglecting your friend, Georgie. Life doesn't stop north of London, you know.'

Cath smiles at Nikolai. 'You're a musician?'

'I play the piano, yes.'

'And you also write music?'

'I try my best. It takes long time, I don't know if I will get to the end.'

Tim cuts in. 'You work on a building site, I hear.'

'That is right. I move things from here to there – timber, cable, bricks. I clear mess when they are finished. I dig holes, I open gate for deliveries. You name it, I do it.' He laughs. So do the rest of us, except Tim.

'Not a job you'd recommend, then.'

'Sometimes I like, sometimes I do not. The work is hard for body. Last week I am digging holes for cables. The jackhammer is thirty kilos; it is difficult to hold for long time. When weather is bad… ' He says something in Russian under his breath. 'Sometimes we make mistakes.'

'Really?'

'Last week, there was accident… ' He stops. 'But this work is not so bad. I have done worse.'

'Are you planning to stay in London for long?'

'I would like to stay to end of this year, maybe longer.'

'You'll go back to Russia?'

'Of course, one day. Russia is my home.'

For a while, no one speaks. Nikolai picks a stem of clover. Tim drains his plastic cup.

'So,' he says, turning to Nikolai as if they've just been discussing the subject, 'do you think Blair was wrong to send troops to Iraq?'

'I think he was wrong, yes. The invasion was revenge for 9/11. He doesn't care about innocent people killed –'

'But thousands of innocent people were hurt in 9/11.'

Tim's voice has an edge. I glare at him.

'So it is OK to kill thousands more?' Nikolai speaks no louder than before, but now there's anger in his voice.

'Come on, guys,' Cath urges. 'We don't have to fight about this, do we?'

Tim carries on.

'What about your president? Putin invaded Chechnya, didn't he? To fight the terrorists there. Was he wrong to do that?'

'Some people in Russia agree with him.' Nikolai's voice is low, controlled. His body is stiff as he plucks at the clover. 'And some do not. They do not call Chechens terrorists for defending their land against Russia. They say Putin was trying to win votes in the election. He wanted to keep Russia's power over Chechnya – and to get their oil.'

'What's your opinion?'

'I see this crazy war close up. I see it is not only so-called terrorists who are killed. The old and sick, the mothers and grandmothers, the babies and children – they are targets too.'

'You didn't believe in what you were fighting for?'

'None of us knew what we were fighting for.' His tone is contemptuous.

'What are you saying? There were – are – no terrorists at all in Chechnya?'

I gobble a potato crisp. Like the others, I'm awaiting Nikolai's reply.

'Some Chechens are terrorists, it is true. Those who take schoolchildren hostage in Beslan last year, of course they are terrorists. But it is small number.' He releases crushed clover onto the rug. 'Many Chechens hate Russians for what they have done to them. You know that Stalin moved half a million Chechens out of Russia in the Second World War? He tells them they are spies for Nazis, they betray Soviet Union. He sends them to Kazakhstan, to this useless place they have never seen. Many of them die on the way, or when they arrive. You think that they will love Russians after this? And many Russians hate Chechens back, because they are Muslim, because for years we are enemies. But most Chechens want to live in peace; they want food and water and electricity and chance to make their living. They are angry at the Russians for invading their land and bombing their houses. So some take guns and fight back. They fight how they can. They do not have tanks and rockets like Russians so they fight in other ways.'

Nikolai wipes his brow with the back of his hand.

'It sounds as if you're justifying terrorism.'

'I do not justify terrorism.' Nikolai's tone is chilly. 'I do not justify anyone who kills ordinary people who have done nothing wrong. I wish for peace, not war. But I know that when one person hurts another, that person will fight back.'

For a few long moments, silence. I crunch another potato crisp.

'What was it like – to fight in a war?' Tim is bolder now. 'To have to shoot people because they're on the other side?'

Nikolai hunches over his knees, eyes on the grass. He replies without looking up.

'By the time we go into Chechnya, most of us are ready to fight. It is better than watching bodies of others come back. It is better than someone kicking and punching you because they know you can do nothing. It is tough in Russian army, you know.' He gives Tim a hard look. 'Two guys in my unit, they run away, they go to prison... I learned how to survive. But it was terrible to be in place like this. When we are sent to fight, I am glad.' A deep furrow has formed on Nikolai's brow. 'I am sorry, I do not wish to be rude. But I do not wish to say any more.'

We watch him get to his feet and stride across the field. I turn to Tim.

'Why did you have to upset him like that?'

'I didn't mean to,' Tim protests, refolding the map. 'I was interested in what he went through.'

'He's fought in a war,' I say, flinging down my crisp packet. Its contents scatter across the rug.

'And it's obviously had an effect on him. I'd tread carefully, if I were you. He's been through some pretty heavy stuff. You told us yourself you've got concerns about this guy.'

'I'm worried too, Georgie,' Ella cuts in before I can reply. 'First you fall out with Julian, then you get involved with a flaky soldier.'

'Ex-soldier.' Stirrings of unease dampen my temper. I want to defend Nikolai but I'm aware that my friends are only expressing what I too have been thinking. 'I know it's not the most sensible thing to do.' I struggle for words. 'But it's like I've no choice.'

'What if he's just stringing you along so he can get what he can from you? Maybe he just wants your money.'

'No, Ella. That's not how it is.'

'Are you sure?'

I roll my eyes. 'I'm not a complete airhead. I'm not about to marry him – or hand him my credit card.'

'Well, I like Nikolai,' Cath says firmly. 'I think he's a decent guy. He might not be the perfect boyfriend but I think he'll be good for you.'

Ella raises her head, a teasing smile on her face. 'It's about time someone found Georgie's heart.'

I toss a piece of cheese at her.

'I'll drive you home,' I say to Nikolai as we wave at Tim's departing car.

'Thank you, but I will take Tube. It is no problem.'

'OK, but come in for a cup of tea before you go.' I'm glad not to have to go out again; I long for a hot bath and a few hours alone before another week at the office.

Nikolai's gaze sweeps around the kitchen, taking in the heap of saucepans and dishes waiting to be put away, the pile of unwashed clothes by the washing machine, Cath's year-old postcard from Easter Island propped against the biscuit tin and a six-pack of toilet rolls on the hall step.

'Sorry it's in such a state.' I remove the vase of flowers, which have deposited a sticky mess on the table, and make two mugs of tea.

He lowers himself into a chair, face muscles tensing. I get him a couple of Nurofen for the pain, then sit across from him as he drinks his tea. He looks more handsome than ever. His face is golden in the last rays of sun.

'I have concern about something,' he says, massaging his right thigh with the heel of his hand. 'What I tell you before, about how I come to London, about my visa... I tell you so it is honest between us –'

'I'm glad you told me.'

He carries on as if I haven't spoken. 'What you will say when people ask about me?'

'I'm not going to tell anyone you're here illegally. If anyone asks about your visa or permission to work, I'll just say you haven't told me – I don't know what your situation is.'

He stops massaging his leg. 'It bothers you that I am illegal?'

'I don't judge you for it, if that's what you mean. The only thing is –'

'What?'

'Well, you could be found out. You could be deported. There's thousands of people working in the UK illegally though, I'm sure no one bothers to go round checking on them all. Did you hear about the Chinese cockle pickers who drowned last year? No one tried to stop them working or to throw them out of the country.'

Nikolai says nothing. A grimace passes over his face as he stands up.

'Before you go, Nikky. What was the accident at work last week?'

'Malik, he is hurt. He is standing by stack of bricks and they fall. Someone drives into them with the dumper.'

'How is he? Will he be all right?'

'I go to see him at home. He is not so bad, just his leg is hurt. He has luck of devil, he says. If he stands a little closer he will be dead... The doctor says he can go back to work in three weeks. But it is hard for him. His wife is cleaner; she has two jobs already. They have two children. If he cannot work, his family is in trouble.'

'He's not on sick leave?'

'He is temp worker like me – he is paid by agency every week. He will get no more money now. The management say it is his fault that he was hurt so he gets no compensation.'

'I don't understand. How can it be his fault? Isn't it the fault of the guy who drove this thing that went into the bricks?'

Sighing, he shakes his head. 'Ricky is driving the dumper, he has full load. He says he reverses too far and hits bricks by mistake. He does not expect anyone to be standing behind – it is not his fault, it is Malik's for being in wrong place.'

'What was Malik doing there?'

'He goes outside to make a call. He stands by bricks, he does not see Ricky.'

'Do you think he did it on purpose?'

'It is possible.' He scowls. 'Ricky is loudmouth troublemaker, everyone knows this. Malik tells me he cannot believe what happens. He says the dumper is long way off, Ricky sees him go behind pile of bricks and hits them on purpose. But there is no evidence. No one else sees anything – some guys are laying pipes in the trench, they look only when they hear Malik shouting.'

'Did you see Malik after the bricks fell on him?'

'I run out with the others and help to pull the bricks off. He is lucky they do not hit his head.'

I shudder, picturing the scene.

'Why didn't you tell me about all this?'

'It is not nice for you to hear. I do not want to worry you. A-ny-way, I must go now, Georgie. I need to rest or I cannot get up tomorrow.' He puts his arms around me and pulls me close. 'Thank you for today. I enjoy very much. I am sorry I am not good company. It is normal for me. I have bad dreams again; they stay in my head.'

I kiss him goodbye. 'Look after yourself, Nikky. Be careful at work, won't you?'

25

The cup slips in my fingers and shatters against the sink. Cursing, I place another one under the coffee machine. Nikolai leans against the table sipping his coffee, watching me with a bemused expression.

'You are not good at making coffee.' He opens his arms. 'Come here, Miz.'

Ever since Nikolai overheard me on the phone to my bank saying pointedly that I prefer 'Ms Cameron' to 'Miss Cameron', he's called me 'Miz' with an exaggerated buzz.

I go to him.

It's late. After leaving the office I met Nikolai at the Sir Richard Steele, my local pub, where we stayed until closing time. And now he's in my flat, supposedly for a cup of coffee before getting the Tube back to Finsbury Park.

My body tells me otherwise. I want that creeping intoxication again. His closeness, his smell, his warmth. The slow glide of his hands and lips on my skin. I want that impossible desire to take me over, to take away everything except him.

Lying on my high wrought-iron bed, naked under the quilt, we watch shadows play over the walls. Cool air ripples through the open window, tickling my bare arms.

'I like this room,' Nikolai says. 'Your spirit is here.'

I laugh, following his gaze to the mantelpiece crammed with the collection of curious, useless objects I've salvaged over the years: feathers, stones, seashells, a warped yet beautiful piece of wood I found on Hampstead Heath after a storm.

'There's too much stuff,' I say.

'It is good to have stuff. I move many times and each time I take less. This time I take only myself and what will fit in my bag – and what is in my head.'

I let my hand fall on the hairy slope of his chest. It feels good to be with him like this – and strange, as if I've never lain beside a man before.

Nikolai rolls onto his side, props up his head on an elbow and gazes into my eyes.

'You are beautiful woman. Sometimes I feel you – it is like you move away from me.'

'Maybe I'm scared of what might happen.'

'What might happen?'

'I might let you get to me.'

'That is bad?'

'No… But then I'll no longer be me, but me with a bit of you mixed in.'

'And I will be me with a bit of you mixed in.'

He kisses me, languidly. His thick lips caress mine, opening to let my tongue slide into his mouth. He puts his hand on my breast. Though his touch is light, I feel my breath suck in. I close my eyes, my desire for him becoming a need. He pushes back the quilt and moves his head between my legs; I hear my cries unfurl like huge flowers into the room. One orgasm bursts upon the next, each more intense than the last. Finally, he pulls me onto my knees and stands behind me. I cling to the bed post, half out of my mind as he makes love to me, slowly at first then with a furious energy that shakes the bed and bumps my head repeatedly against the wall. But such is my bliss, I scarcely notice.

Nikolai falls on the bed, panting. Black fronds stick to his brow.

'You've taken me to heaven,' I whisper. 'From now on, I will worship you.'

Hours later, I'm woken by a sound that is barely human. It resembles an animal in pain; a series of whimpers slowly rising in pitch until they become a sort of wail. Something about the pitiful sound forces me to listen. In it is fear – and something worse.

I open my eyes. Nikolai is writhing on the bed beside me, eyes shut, mouth open, legs thrashing the mattress. '*Nyet,*' he repeats over and over. At last he rolls onto his side and his body stills, and all I can hear is the sound of his breathing.

Later I'm woken again by a stab of pain in my lower back.

'Jesus Christ!' I switch the lamp on. 'You frightened the life out of me.'

'What is matter?' Nikolai blinks in the light.

'You kicked me,' I replied, furiously rubbing my back.

He raises himself and wipes his damp face with the sheet. 'Where did I kick you?'

'Right here. That's a powerful right foot you've got.'

'I am sorry.' He touches the place where I point. 'It was not you I kick, it was someone in my dream.'

'Who were you kicking in your dream?'

He doesn't reply.

The next time I wake, the other side of the bed is empty. My alarm clock shows 4.42 a.m.. Nikolai's jeans and cotton sweater are gone from the chair. Picturing him trudging towards Finsbury Park, I put on my dressing gown and go into the kitchen. The light isn't switched on and a glass of water sits on the table. Through the glass panel of the door leading to the garden, I glimpse the back of his head. I open the door, coughing so as not to startle him. He continues to stare into the distance. He's sitting on the step, elbows resting on his thighs, hands cradling his jaw.

'Are you OK?'

He doesn't reply. I pull my dressing gown tighter around me. His feet are bare. I fetch a blanket and drape it over his shoulders.

'Thank you,' he says as I'm about to go back inside. 'Stay, will you?'

I sit down. He adjusts the blanket so that it covers my legs too. Night is almost over. A few stubborn stars linger in the sky.

'Can't you sleep?'

'It is my dream. It won't go away.'

I hesitated. 'Do you want to tell me about it?'

He looks down and doesn't answer for ages. Then he speaks, quietly, halting every so often.

'There is a man and a woman, close to him. Her face is not clear. The man is going to do something terrible to her if I do not stop him... I must stop him, I must do everything I can to stop him. With all my strength I try to fight him. But my legs cannot move; my hands cannot hurt fly. I am useless.'

'Do you know who these people are?'

'In the war, I met a woman. She was on the other side, a Chechen. But she was my friend. She died because of me.'

'How did this woman become your friend?'

He gets up, leaving the blanket with me, and sits on the patio wall. As he talks, the brownish-black sludge of the garden behind him slowly transforms into the purplish mouths of poppies.

'I tell you how we are friends. It was early spring when I met her, the war was nearly over. My unit is in village near Argun River, near the mountains. We camp in school there. We have taken this area but some Chechens are hiding out in the hills; sometimes they attack us at night. One morning, I am with my mate Leon. We are hungry because our rations have not come – they are always late. Sometimes women in the village give us food, or we find scraps of meat left outside for us.'

He sits hugging his knees, gazing into the ground.

'This time we go different way, along street on edge of village, up steep hill. There is house at top with yellow flowers at the windows. We smell fresh bread – to us, it is smell of heaven. A window is open and behind is loaf of bread. Leon reaches in to take. Then woman comes into the kitchen, she sees us. Leon runs away with bread – I am too ashamed to run. She says I do not need to steal from her, she is pleased to give me more bread, also fresh cheese. If I come in she will get for me. There is small boy drawing pictures at the table. I smile at him but he moves away like I will eat him. She says her name is Zara. She hates to see thin faces on young men, she says, even if they are Russian soldiers. She says I look like her brother's son who was taken by the army. It is a friend's son she looks after now; his mother was killed by rocket.'

He digs his fingertips into his brow.

'I do not speak much. I see she is proud woman, not afraid of us. She is alone – her husband was killed in first war. Not so old. When she was young she was pretty, I think. But now her hand is like old woman's and her teeth are yellow... I thank her for this bread. She tells me to come back in one week, she will have more.

'Next time I go without Leon.' Nikolai bites his lower lip. 'I ask her why she does not hate Russian soldiers for killing her husband and taking her brother's son. "I will not get my husband back by hating them," she says. I say goodbye and go back to camp. I ask myself how it is she does not hate us. I wonder if this woman is wise and I am fool.'

'What happened to Zara?'

'You really want that I tell you?' he says slowly.

'I'd like to know,' I say.

He pushes himself off the ground. 'First, I get cigarette.'

I get up and shake the stiffness from my legs. The garden is no longer flat and ghostly but solid with colour. Nikolai returns and takes up his position on the wall. After a few drags of his cigarette, he looks at me.

'Zara did not have a good death, you could say.' A blast of

smoke, an imitation of a laugh. 'I go back to her house three times. She gives me bread and cheese and little honey cakes. I tell her about my life in Russia. Leon asks me why I go to this woman so often, why always I go alone, if I have sex with her. I say, "Of course not. I talk to her – that is all."

'The next time I see her, it is different. We have order to check village for the resistance. The day before, they kill four soldiers on road to Grozny and escape into the hills. Our commander gives order for *zachistka*. We must search each house in the village for Chechens hiding in their cellars. I go in truck with Leon, Pavel and Lieutenant Krizsky. It is early, the sun shines, the birds sing. Not a day for doing bad things. But I have bad feeling in my bones, I am sick of fighting. I know that in April my two years in the army will finish. I do not want to make trouble in this village; no one has done us wrong.'

Nikolai stubs his cigarette out on the wall. His gaze is steady in my direction, yet he doesn't see me.

'We drive from house to house asking if they are hiding men who fight us. We search everywhere. The lieutenant is shouting about Chechen pigs, we must clean up their filthy houses. He breaks up photographs, kicks their stuff onto floor. He tells us to take jewellery, watches, war medals, whatever we like… We find no one hiding in cellars. All the men who can fight are gone. Only boy, about fifteen. He has no hair on his face. He is in yard milking cow, he does not stop when he sees us. I think at first he is slow in the head.

'The lieutenant asks him, "Where are your friends who fight us?" The boy says he has no friends here. The lieutenant takes his rifle and shoots cow in the belly. He tells us to put the boy in truck and take him for questioning. Then he says to me, "Where is your friend, the Chechen bitch?" He is angry, red in face, but I say nothing. He looks at other two, I pray they will not speak. Then Leon tells him. He says Zara's house is at top of hill; it has yellow flowers in the windows.

'We kick on door until she opens. "We are searching for our enemies. We know they are here," Lieutenant Krizsky says. Zara says there is no one for them to take. He says he knows she has Chechens hidden in cellar. "Leave me in peace," she says, "I hide nothing." Then she sees me. She thinks I have betrayed her. I want to tell her that I do not, but it is impossible.

'We search her cellar. There is no one. We go to kitchen. The boy's drawing is on table but he is not there. Zara has eyes shut, her hands together like she is praying. The lieutenant shouts, throws plates to floor. He asks her if I am the only Russian soldier she fucks. "It is lie," I say. "She is good woman." He tells me to shut my mouth. "Everyone in unit knows that you go with this woman," he says. "Leon tells us." Then he puts his hand on Zara and asks if she will fuck him too. She looks at the lieutenant, does not speak. Then she spits in his face. It is good shot, straight in the eye. His mouth opens like fish. He takes his gun and hits her across the mouth. It is so quick, no one expects. She cries out and he laughs. He tells Leon and Pavel to take her to the cellar – they can do what they want to her.

'I try to stop them but the lieutenant points his gun at me. He says I must let them take her or he will make me regret the day I am born. I want to take the gun and kill this fucking lieutenant. I cannot believe he can do this to innocent woman. But I can do nothing. He has gun, not me. And I am soldier, I cannot go against officer. If I do, they will lock me up, maybe shoot me… So, I am in kitchen with the lieutenant; he eats the honey cakes she leaves in the oven. All the time I can hear what they are doing to her… I am never so angry, so ashamed in my life. The boy runs out from behind big sack and the lieutenant tells him to go and play.

'I do not see her again. I go back to her house one week later, first chance I get. It is locked. Someone in village tells me she drowns in the river. It is then that I see how it really is. I know that not all Chechens are barbarians. I know that we Russians also do terrible things. In my heart, I am ashamed to be Russian.'

I notice the stubble on Nikolai's jaw and shadows around his eyes. A bird begins to pipe tunelessly; the sky glows with dawn.

'I say enough,' he says.

Until now, war has been something that happens to other people in other places, something you watch on the news then forget about. I can't speak; I feel utterly useless. Nikolai has confided in me, let me be his witness. But I'm not up to the task.

26

I wake at midday to the phone ringing. It stops as I reach to pick up. I leave Nikolai sleeping, take a long shower and make some strong coffee.

'I should not tell you that story,' he says as I come into the bedroom with the coffee. 'It upsets you. You were shouting in your sleep. I was worried for you.'

For the rest of the night, frightened women and children had flitted through my dreams. I sit down on the bed beside him.

'Do you regret telling me?'

'I tell no one before.' Nikolai bites on his lip. 'You are the only one.'

I ask if the army ever did anything to help him deal with what he went through in Chechnya.

'They give me name of doctor. He tells me he sees many soldiers who leave Chechnya with the same problems as me. It is reaction from war – it is normal.'

'Was he any help?'

He pulls a face. 'He says I must rest often and try to relax. He gives me sleeping pills. I take only one, it makes me feel like I am in the grave already.'

'I was wondering… Do you know what happened to the lieutenant?'

'Nothing happened, probably. I do not hear he is in trouble.'

'But it was a crime, what he did.'

A flash of anger. 'You think for every crime there is trial, with judge who thinks only of what is right? The Russian system does not care what happens to women like Zara. Ordinary Russians do not care.'

Before I can reply, the phone interrupts. It's my father. He's called several times before, he says, sounding irritated. He needs to talk with me – could he come over?

'There's no need to go,' I insist to Nikolai. But within twenty minutes he's showered and left.

My father arrives fifteen minutes after Nikolai leaves. He looks troubled.

'Coffee, Dad?' I usher him into the kitchen.

'Thanks, I will. Late night?'

I pull my unbrushed hair off my face. 'A bit.'

'Hope I didn't interrupt anything,' he says without humour.

'Sit down, if you want.' I make coffee and sit at the table. 'Is something the matter?'

He's leaning against the table, eyes roaming the kitchen. They come to rest on the music manuscript book beside the toaster – Nikolai must have forgotten to take it. My father picks it up casually and examines it. I know without looking that 'Nikolai Alexandrovich Konstantinov' is written across the cover in black capitals, together with his address and mobile number.

'So, you're still seeing this Russian of yours.'

He drops the book then sits at the table opposite me, his back rigid. His eyes, unblinking, bore through my composure.

Of course. My father has come to talk about Nikolai. No doubt Julian has given him the benefit of his views.

'He was here just now, actually.'

'I'm surprised, Georgie.'

'At what?'

'Do you know what his plans are?'

'His plans?'

'How long is he planning to stay in the country?'

'He wants to go back to Russia later this year, or next year. He's not going to stay here for ever.'

'And in the meantime, he'll keep on working?'

I let out an exaggerated sigh. 'I think so. Why are you so interested?'

My father returns his cup to the saucer with a clatter. His face is stony.

'What do you know about him?'

'What do I know about him? He's twenty-five years old and he's from a city near the Ural mountains. He fought for his country in the second Chechen War. He works as a casual labourer and in his spare time he writes music. He hasn't got much money and he isn't from a rich family. What else do you want to know? What colour underpants he wears?'

'Georgie, stop!' He thumps the table. 'I know how much you like this guy. But you aren't that naïve, are you? Surely you have concerns about him?'

I draw in my breath and release it slowly.

'Yes, I do, as a matter of fact. I'm concerned that he gets

depressed and he doesn't get enough sleep. I'm concerned that he has to live in a dump of a flat and he's risking his health day after day working on a sodding building site.'

My father leans forward so his nose was only inches from mine.

'This guy appears out of nowhere and before you can say "Bob's your uncle" he's got you lapping up his hard-luck stories.' His voice hardens. 'Have you ever considered that he could be using you? He's found a nice girl with her own flat, a well-paid job and a loaded father. He must be licking his lips. Next he'll be asking you to marry him so he can stay in the country permanently.'

I look at him, too stunned to speak.

'That's bollocks,' I say at last. 'I can't believe what you've just said.'

'You know he's probably working illegally, don't you?'

I don't reply.

'The recruitment agency that hired him – I know the sort of people they use. Most of them don't have the right to work here. They buck the system, hoping no one catches them out.'

I recall my father saying that his HR manager turned a blind eye to certain less-than-rigorous employment agency practices. I imagine my father has hired temp workers who conveniently enough have been helped just like Nikolai.

'What are you going to do, report him to Immigration? I don't think so. You wouldn't want to risk immigration officers poking around in your business, would you?'

My father's face reddens.

'This guy's bad news, Georgie. For God's sake, let him go now before he causes you real problems. '

He puts his cup in the sink, walks down the hall and lets himself out.

To hell with him. The idea of Nikolai being with me for my money is laughable. If my father knew how difficult Nikky makes it for me to pay for the smallest thing. As for him wanting to marry me in order to stay in the country… It's ridiculous. How on earth did I let my father influence me for so long? I put him on a pedestal, believing everything he said to be right. In reality, he's a business-man with no compassion or imagination, incapable of seeing any-thing beyond his own relentless pursuit of wealth. How dare he tell me to stop seeing Nikolai just because he doesn't fit with his ugly view of the world?

I resolve that from now on, I'll banish all traces of doubt as to whether it is a good idea to keep on seeing the Russian. For once, I will do what my heart is telling me.

27

11 June 2005 04.33
  To: Georgie Cameron
  From: Julian Lewis

Georgie,
This wasn't what I was hoping for. Did you think I would just
go away like a good little boy while you're dropping your knickers
for him?

I don't want to give you a hard time, sweet girl. But please,
spare a thought for one who suffers, who right this minute is nursing his battered heart. I can't go anywhere without seeing you and
him together, his eyes leering at you, his broken English in my ears.
I can't bear the thought of his grubby paws on your skin.

Please, tell him to go away. He's not in your league, Georgie.
His fancy manners don't fool me. He's an urchin, a chancer. Can't
you see underneath that sneaky Russian charm of his? He's a guy
who can't make it who's latched onto a girl who has.

I wonder what he would say if he knew how much you
enjoyed our night together? You haven't told him, have you? No,
I didn't think so. He might be surprised to learn what a shameless
vixen you became under the influence of a little excess vino and the
enticements of yours truly. You didn't expect weedy old Julian to
be so well endowed, did you? Your hunger showed in your eyes
and in your hot little breaths. You couldn't pretend it away. Those
noises you made, dear one, they weren't the noises of a lady.

Just give him up, that's all I ask. Please, Georgie. Do this one
thing for me and I'll never ask anything of you again.

I love you with all my heart.
Julian

At first I almost burst out laughing. Shameless vixen? Hot little
breaths? Oh, dear me. Julian really has lost the plot.

This absurd, half hectoring, half begging message... Does he
have no pride left? Does he really think I'm going to let his jealous
ranting influence me? Does he imagine he has a cat's chance in hell
of coercing me to give up Nikolai?

A nauseous feeling settles in the pit of my stomach. I want to punch Julian. I compose a reply laced with four-letter words, then delete it.

I phone Ella and read her a heavily censored version of the email. She has the same reaction.

'What a complete tosser!' she shouts down the phone. 'He needs a good slap.'

'I don't know if that'll help much.'

'I only ever met him a few times,' she says, 'but I got to quite like him and his morbid sense of humour. But now he's turned into a complete dick-brain.'

'Do you think he'll keep on hounding me?'

'He'll give up in a while. He probably just needs to vent his feelings. You should ignore anything else he sends you. Can your father do anything to help, do you think?'

'I told you, we had a fight about Nikolai. We're not speaking.' After what he's said about Nikolai, I certainly don't intend to ask for his help.

'It's probably not a good idea to tell Nikolai – not if there's stuff about you and Julian having sex. You know how men are. Russian men especially. He'll either dump you or try to beat the crap out of Julian.'

She's right, I think when I put the phone down. God only knows what Nikolai might do if I told him. He would stand up for me, perhaps, and I might feel safer with his protection. But if he did 'beat the crap' out of Julian, he could end up killing him. He'd go to prison for years and his life would be ruined. I couldn't let that happen. Besides, Nikolai would want to know everything, wouldn't he? Why I went to bed with Julian and what I've done to make him so obsessed with me.

I've asked myself the same questions, over and over.

28

As summer gets under way, Nikolai and I set about discovering London on the cheap. We make the most of the long June days, spending much of our free time visiting markets, museums and parks, watching films at student-filled cinemas, listening to free concerts at the South Bank and riding buses around London. It's fun to be with him doing things that I would never normally do.

Nikolai seems to be enjoying our outings too. He's sleeping better, he isn't so jumpy and he's generally cheerful. Whenever he goes quiet, he'll invariably take out his sheet music and a pencil from his bag and jot down fragments of music. His composition is going well, he tells me; he works on it every day in whatever moments he can find.

'I must be good for you,' I say early one sunny Sunday morning. We're sitting squashed together in the front seat at the top of a double-decker bus looking down at Piccadilly. Nikolai is humming a recurring motif he's been working on, which is becoming familiar to me.

'It is true, Georgie,' he replies, putting down his peanut butter sandwich. 'You are the best medicine I can ask for.'

My caution is slipping away; Nikolai has become part of my life. I enjoy my time alone less and look forward to time with him more. We've even planned to go away to Devon together in the last week in June. The idea gives me a tingle of anticipation whenever I think about it.

I squeeze two rolled-up beach towels into the boot of my MG, on top of a tent, portable stove, rucksacks, bags of provisions and the rest of our camping paraphernalia.

Nikolai opens the driver's door and climbs in. He turns the ignition key. The engine, freshly oiled and watered, growls contentedly.

'You'll take it easy, won't you?'

'Of course.' He pats the dashboard. 'Don't worry, I will not hurt your car. I know it is your pride and joy, no?'

'Exactly. Don't you forget it.'

I added Nikolai to my insurance after he produced his Russian driving licence and he has driven the MG several times with admirable care, I remind myself. We'll be going a long way now, so it seems sensible to let him share the driving.

It's a fine morning. The sun had risen shortly before into a clear sky; already there's a hint of warmth. I put on my sunglasses and lower the window. At last, a week of freedom ahead, just the two of us.

The trip was Nikolai's idea. He rejected my suggestion of a week in Spain or France, saying he couldn't afford a flight and hotel room. Even budget B&Bs and hostels he dismissed as too expensive.

'We will take tent, OK?' he announced one morning over breakfast, when I'd given up on us ever agreeing on where to go. 'To Devon, if you like.'

'Camping?' He might have suggested a trip to Pluto.

'Why not?'

Why not? I've spent a total of one night in a tent in my life, in the middle of my 12-year-old best friend's garden. The night was interrupted first by rain, then Lily getting up to check on a leak in the roof and, lastly, a hedgehog.

But camping with Nikolai would be different, I told myself. He's spent weeks camping in muddy fields and snowy forests while in the army and is proficient at putting up tents, cooking with portable gas stoves and all those outdoorsy things I haven't a clue about. So I booked five days at a campsite by the sea in Devon, and we agreed to split the cost.

We've turned onto the North Circular and are going at a steady 50mph as I instructed. After a few miles of near-empty roads, traffic builds. Nikolai glances at me.

'I am looking forward to this time with you, Georgie. Of course, I am sorry we are not going to Paris or Monte Carlo –'

'Come on, you know I don't care about that.'

'And that we will have to sleep outside –'

I thump his leg. 'Shut up, will you? I don't have to stay at the Ritz and drink champagne every night to have a good time, for goodness' sake.'

I study the dark shadows around his eyes. He needs a holiday more than I do.

We approach a roundabout too quickly, in the wrong lane.

'You shouldn't be in the left-hand lane if you're turning right.'

'OK, boss.'

We turn off the North Circular and drive towards the M3. I bring out a bag of roasted peanuts.

'I have finished a poem yesterday,' Nikolai says between crunches.

'I didn't know you wrote poems.'

'In Russia, I write some. This is my first in English.'

'Can I see?' I retrieve a thin folded sheet of lined A4 paper from his bag.

> *You come to me one day,*
> *a butterfly I cannot hold*
> *bringing me closer*
> *as you fly away.*
> *The colours in your wings*
> *lighten my darkness*
> *take away my sadness*
> *make my heart sing.*

Tears come to my eyes.

'It is for you, Miz.' His smile flashes white against his tan. 'You don't like?'

'No, I like it. Very much. No one has written a poem for me before.'

The car stereo is on, J.J. Cale is singing: 'But I'll make love to you any old time.' I watch Nikolai's hands manipulating the steering wheel in deft, easy strokes and think of how the two of us make love. Sometimes we fuck urgently, as if it were the planet's final hour. Other times, it is slow and gentle, as though we really are making love. He'll take my hand, look into my eyes and kiss me. But he's never said he loves me and I don't believe he does. Not the sort of love where your heart races upon a glimpse of your loved one and you lose sight of everything else in life, anyway. That isn't the case for me, and I don't think it is for Nikolai, either. Perhaps, though, there's another kind of love. A love that creeps up on you without you knowing it. A love you don't have to talk about, that's just there.

We stop for petrol at a motorway service station. It will take most of the afternoon to reach the campsite, I've estimated. We agree that Nikolai will carry on driving for another hour then I'll take over.

'What is it?'

He doesn't answer.

We're belted up in the car ready to go, engine started. But

Nikolai is staring into the rear-view mirror as if an alien spaceship has landed behind us. I look over my shoulder. Nothing out of the ordinary, just a car filling up – and further away, a dark blue BMW. There's a man in the driver's seat. I can't see much except for his straw hat and sunglasses.

My chest presses against the seat belt as the car shoots forward. 'What are you doing?'

Nikolai spins the steering wheel, paying me no attention, swerving the car through the exit and into the inner lane of the motorway just behind a passing car. I grab the edge of my seat with one hand and the door handle with the other and jam both feet against the floor. The MG straddles the middle and outer lanes, the engine's thrum rising in pitch as the speedometer moves up to 70, 80, 90…

'Fuck, what's the matter with you? We'll have an accident – watch out!'

We pass a lorry in the middle lane, missing it by inches. Nikolai lets out expletives as we accelerate in the outside lane, rapidly closing on the car ahead. He honks until it moves out of the way. 100mph… Finally, after checking the rear-view mirror several times in quick succession, he slows to 80, no faster than other cars in our lane.

'It is OK now,' Nikolai mutters. His face is pale.

I let go of the door handle and wait for my heart to stop trying to rupture my chest.

'We get rid of him.' For the first time, his eyes flick to me. 'Sorry, I do not mean to scare you.'

'You nearly gave me a heart attack. What the fuck is going on?'

'The BMW. I see it outside my place last week, early in the morning when I am on my way to work. The same guy inside in sunglasses. He has same hat. He is sitting in car across the street, doing nothing. I think it is strange that he wears sunglasses and hat when there is no sun. I am going over to the car and he drives off.'

'And he was definitely the same man as the one just now?'

He hesitates. 'I think he is the same. But I may be wrong. I did not see him for very long.'

'Did you get the registration number?'

'He is gone before I can see it.' He sounds sheepish. 'This time, I do not think to look.'

'He could just have been a guy waiting for his girlfriend or whoever, couldn't he? Maybe he got fed up with waiting. And maybe he just likes wearing sunglasses when he drives. That's not unusual.'

Nikolai is silent. I try to make sense of it all.

'If it is the same man,' I say, 'he must have followed you to my place last night. Or maybe he was already at my place this morning, saw us leave and decided to follow us all the way out here. Why would anyone want to do that?'

'I don't know, Georgie.'

A creepy thought comes into my mind. Julian.

No, surely not. It's too weird to even think about.

'The guy wasn't close enough for you to see him properly. It's probably just someone who looks similar, driving a similar car.'

'Maybe you are right.'

I say no more.

'I take different road now,' Nikolai announces a little later. He takes the next exit. We find ourselves on an industrial estate surrounded by warehouses. Nikolai's eyes still keep flicking to the rearview mirror. From time to time I find myself peering into the wing mirror, and I'm relieved when the dark blue BMW behind us transforms into a black Ford Mondeo.

It's the same weird thing again. Someone is following him – but it's in his head, surely. My stomach starts to churn.

'Hey, pull over will you? I need to get some air.'

I step out onto the narrow pavement beside a high fence and wait until I'm sure I'm not going to be sick.

When I get back, Nikolai is leaning against the bonnet, frowning. He doesn't look up.

'Please,' I say, getting in behind the wheel, 'will you explain what the hell is going on? What happened to make you leave Russia? Were you running away from someone?'

He sits down beside me, silent.

'For Christ's sake, Nikolai. This is beyond a joke.'

He taps on the dashboard, not meeting my eyes. 'OK, I will tell you when we get to camping site.'

'And please – don't ever drive my car like that again.'

While Nikolai sleeps I drive, raking over my father's accusations. I still think he is wrong about Nikolai. That stuff about him trying to sponge off me and plotting to marry me is plainly ridiculous. Yet so many things puzzle me about the Russian. His evasiveness about his contact with Vakha and Ruslan. His refusal to explain what made him leave his home in Russia. I know he's hiding something from me.

In recent weeks he's revealed more to me about his earlier life. The harsh, numbing routine of the Russian army before his posting to Chechnya. How in his last few months he came close to deserting. What it was like leaving the army – being surrounded by people who have never gone to Chechnya and couldn't understand what he went through. His struggle not to give way to drink, drugs and depression. How music kept him going: listening to CDs, playing the piano, his early attempts at writing music. But of his final days in Russia and the incident that triggered his departure, he has said nothing.

By late afternoon we're driving on higgledy-piggledy roads past cow-strewn fields, roof down, the sun out and music blaring, laughing at Nikolai's attempts to pronounce the names on signposts. I've stopped thinking about the incident on the motorway and look forward to arriving at the campsite.

'I didn't think it would be like this,' I say, taking in row after row of caravans. Behind them, a trek from the invisible beach, a city of tents.

We trudge back to the reception and an adjacent shop, raising our voices to overcome the noise of children screaming in the pool.

'I do not like this place,' Nikolai says.

'It's dreadful,' I agree. 'But we've paid for two nights. We won't get our money back.'

He looks sullenly at me.

'I'm too tired to look for anywhere else now,' I say. 'We can stay the night here and look for somewhere else in the morning.'

'No,' he says, walking away. 'I do not wish to stay here.'

By now, on top of being tired, hot and thirsty, I'm pissed off. We've ended up at a dud campsite and now we're squabbling like a married couple.

I follow him to a grassy bank. On the other side of the road is a strip of sandy beach, or what would have been sand if it weren't for the crush of bodies.

'I have idea. We will camp on beach. These people will be gone soon.'

'You must be joking,' I mutter, wishing I'd insisted on a hotel.

On the beach is a large sign indicating no dogs, no fires and no camping.

'OK,' he says, 'we find another beach.'

'We'd be better off looking for another campsite.'

Unfortunately, I didn't bring the directory. Back in the car, we pore over our map. There are no campsites marked. The tourist office would be shut by the time we got there. In any case, the nearest sites would probably either be full or just as crowded.

'There.' Nikolai stabs his finger at a yellow strip on the map, several miles away. 'It will be better, I think.'

Pushing aside my concern over the likely lack of amenities, the possibility of getting lost or not finding anywhere suitable to pitch our tent, I start the engine. I don't want to argue any more.

After ten minutes the road begins to climb steeply and switch back on itself. We round a bend and a sheet of blue appears far below. Every so often we glimpse the shoreline, a series of smooth white crescents separated by jagged black rocks.

Suddenly, Nikolai yells for me to stop, pointing through the windscreen at a gate. A path behind leads towards the cliffs. I park behind a lone station wagon. We study a sign showing the route to the beach, two miles away.

'How do we get there with all our stuff?'

He looks at me as if I've asked how to breathe. 'We walk.'

We agree to take what we need for one night.

The path cuts down through brambles, gorse and scrubby slopes dotted with twisted trees, narrowing as it goes. The heat of day has gone. The wind scatters our voices and whips hair across our faces. My lips taste of salt. Way out in the distance, white scribbles of breakers move in slow motion towards a dark finger of land.

An elderly couple trailed by a West Highland Terrier dip their heads in greeting as they pass us. I stop to gulp water, letting Nikolai go on ahead. The cliff forms an overhang here, protecting me from the buffeting wind. A peculiar reddish light bleeds from the rocks and twisted shrubs. The only sound is the hum of bees.

I take a few steps towards the edge of the cliff. I can now see a sweep of white sand below, empty of people. My legs are scratched and my rucksack is heavy; I long to lie down and drink a cold beer. But I feel exhilarated. This place is as beautiful as it is remote. And we'll have it to ourselves, most likely.

The thought produces a surge of excitement, making my heart gallop. There's no one either behind us or below us, as far as I can make out.

Nikolai stands in the dappled shade of a group of pine trees. I go to him, tug off my load and collapse onto a mixture of pine needles and strips of bark. This is all we could have asked for. The sea, gently lapping. Sand, shade and a light breeze.

'Georgie, wake up. It is not time to sleep.'

His tone is coaxing. I look up. A strange, three-zoned creature stands naked on the sand: white in the middle with dark brown arms and legs.

'Come with me.'

'I want to sleep. And it'll be cold.'

He runs to the water's edge. I watch his calves disappear, then his thighs. I pull off my T-shirt and shorts and lie down once more.

I wake again to find myself being lifted into a breeze, flinging salty air. Soon I'm high off the ground clinging to a slippery torso, swaying sideways each time Nikolai's feet sink into the sand. I look down. His legs are disappearing beneath the foam.

'No, Nikky. Don't!'

The coldness of the water shocks me, as though I've been engulfed by a giant stinging nettle.

'You devil!'

I thrash my legs as hard as I can, sending a fountain of water over him, then start to laugh. Nikolai swims away towards the horizon. I swim slowly, parallel with the shore, gazing down at smooth stones and shoals of tiny fish.

I'm floating on my back when I feel a tug at my bra, which begins to slide down my arms. I watch as it flies away, landing on the sand just beyond the foam. Another tug, at my underpants. I cry out, trying to fend him off. But he removes the flimsy garment and sends it flying.

'Now you are like me.'

His hair is strewn like seaweed across his brow. His eyes rest on mine, tender and serious. I wrap my arms around his shoulders and my legs around his waist. His lips press against mine. I kiss them back.

'I love you,' I say.

I'm not certain if he's heard me or if my voice has been carried away in the breeze. I didn't mean to say those words. Until this moment, I didn't know them to be true. 'Race you back!' he cries out suddenly, pulling away from me and launching himself into the water. I can't catch him.

Nikolai waits for me in the foamy shallows. He takes my hand and we run across the beach. He leads me towards the pines, then down onto a rough bed. Drops glisten on his lips and eyelashes. I pull hair off my face, place my hands on his shoulders and lower my mouth to his.

I won't ever forget these moments. Our wet bodies clinging together. His erection, hard and hot against my belly. My tongue in his mouth, stirring his salty tongue. Astride him, riding him. The shudder deep inside me, the surprise and delight on his face. His eyes, wet with sea, opening wide and losing focus. How afterwards I sprawl over him, drunk on him, knowing something inside me has been set free.

While Nikolai puts up the tent, I slice dark red tomatoes with my Swiss Army knife and place them on paper plates beside bread rolls, hard-boiled eggs and legs of roast chicken. We eat the meal with our hands, seated on low rocks, watching the sun lower into glowing threads of violet and gold. Neither of us has mentioned his promise.

After the meal, we gather pine needles and pieces of driftwood. The pile begins to burn as soon as Nikolai lights it, cracking, popping and spitting, sending out a fierce scent of pine.

'Are you going to tell me now?' I put down my beer. Suddenly I can't wait any longer. 'What you are so frightened of? What made you leave Russia?'

He doesn't reply straight away. With his bare heel, he's digging a groove in the sand.

'When I tell you,' he began, 'you can judge me as you wish. But first you must know – I judge myself more than you ever can. I know that what I have done is wrong. I can never make it leave me, it will always be there. When I wake, in my dreams.'

My heart thuds.

'First, I tell you about Ivan. He was friend of my father for long time. Two, three years ago Ivan hears my father is having trouble with his business and he offers to help. Someone from my father's *krysha* tells him he must pay more so they will look after his shop. They want five hundred dollars every month – it is too much, my father tells them he cannot afford.'

'Protection money?'

'*Krysha,* it is "roof" in English. You pay money to *krysha* to stop anyone hurting your business. It is the way in Russia. If you are lucky, you know someone in the government, or you have money to pay for security. Anyway, Ivan knows the boss in another gang, his name is Anton. This gang is bigger, it covers many more businesses. My father agrees to pay Anton instead – Ivan will arrange; he is pleased he must pay only what he pays before. I am not pleased, I do not trust Ivan.

'After this I hear that Ivan is not happy with my father's business. He puts his money in and he helps with *krysha*, now he thinks he is boss. He wants it to sell other things, things that will make more money than medicines and ointments. When I am helping in the shop I hear them talk of selling chemical that is used in weapons – it is very expensive on black market. Ivan says he has supplier and he will find people to buy. My father says it is bad idea. I think it is because of what he does before, when he makes weapons for the Soviet Union.'

Nikolai shifts his position on the rock. He has deepened the groove into a channel. His eyes gleam yellow in the firelight.

'One day last year, Ivan comes into shop. I am serving customers but I see he has sour face, maybe he is drunk. He goes to the office at the back where my father is working. I hear them shouting. My father says, "Ivan, why don't you get out of my business?" Ivan says, "It is not *your* business, it is *our* business." Then I hear nothing. I am scared. When the customers leave I go see what happens. Ivan stands very close in front of my father, holding him by chin, forcing head back.'

He closes his eyes, leans over his knees and rocks to and fro.

'You hurt Ivan, didn't you?' My mouth is dry. I don't want to hear any more.

'I hit Ivan in the head. Five, six, seven times. I am angry, so angry I cannot stop myself. I hear my father calling my name, shouting for me to stop. But something happens to me, I cannot explain. It is like another man takes my place – he has strength of one hundred men. I think of the lieutenant, how I wish it is him I hit, not Ivan. Then Ivan falls to ground, he does not move. My father is on his knees. I listen for Ivan's heart but there is nothing.

'My father tells me I must go before police come. He says Ivan is respectable man, a businessman. They will call me murderer and send me to jail for many years. He says Anton will put his gang on me for what I do to Ivan. I must go far away where no one can find me, and I must not come back.'

He rubs his arms briskly up and down then resumes his slow rocking.

'I say I cannot leave, he will not be safe. But he pushes me, tells me to go, he will take care of everything.' Nikolai lowers his voice. 'I am ashamed now. I was too scared to think of what will happen to my father. I think only of dark cell where they will lock me, where I cannot see the sky. I run away. In the shop on my way out there are two women. They look at me like they know what I have done – like they think I will kill them too. I take train to Moscow. The next day I buy visa and flight to London. I think London will be a good place. It is far away, big city, big enough to swallow me.'

The fire has dimmed. Nikolai's face is a dull red.

'I don't understand.' I can hardly hear my voice.

'What do you not understand? That I kill someone for no reason? That I am a murderer?'

'You were trying to protect your father.' Smoke rises from the dying fire, making me cough.

'Ivan had no weapon... I lose my reason. I want to hurt him until he is nothing. That is what I can never explain.' Nikolai's face is contorted with emotion. 'I am sorry, Georgie. I did not want to tell you this terrible thing.'

I can't take in his words. He's a murderer? No, it isn't possible.

'You say nothing?'

I can't.

Nikolai stands and stares into the faintly glowing pile. A few sparks shoot into the darkness. Then he begins to walk. His barefoot figure shrinks as it moves along the beach.

'Nikolai! Where are you going?'

The breeze carries away my voice. I run after him, shouting. I can just make out foam spilling onto the shore. I run faster. My foot catches something hard, my leg buckles. I sprawl onto the sand. I try to get up but pain stabs my ankle.

'Nikky!'

I scan the beach. But darkness has swallowed him.

I'm not sure how long I lie there, visualising against my will what Nikolai has told me. The blows, the cries, the blood, the horror of it all. Now I know why he ran away and why he was afraid to tell me the reason. He killed a man in a frenzy of violence, using only his hands. My stomach clutches into a tight knot, my breath comes harsh and uneven.

What if he were to lose control with me? What might happen late at night on a deserted beach?

But he wouldn't hurt me, I know that. I remember the gentleness in Nikolai's eyes as we kissed in the sea and the way he sometimes brushes his finger softly against my cheek, as though trying to memorise my face. There's an explanation for what he's done. He had to stand by, unable to help, when Zara was raped. Then, when Ivan intimidated his father, perhaps his pent-up anger towards the lieutenant was released – too much to put back inside.

My thoughts race on, tripping over themselves.

He has killed someone – for whatever reason. What is to stop him killing again? How can I stay with him knowing what he's done, knowing that such a thing might happen again?

I stare up into the sky. It isn't sludgy like London sky – it's a perfect, unbelievable black. When did I last see so many stars? When I was small, six or seven, my mother took me into the garden and pointed out the constellations… I've not thought of it for years. I remember the faint lavender scent of her skin and feel the firm coolness of her hand pressing into mine. My mother is back again, her voice reassuring me that everything will be all right.

I'm dreaming, or delirious. Time passes. Water slurps and sucks. The sharp pain in my ankle becomes an insistent throb. My head floats, far away…

I wake as a gust of wind catches my hair, piercing my thin cotton blouse. If I stay here, I will freeze. I sit up and look around. No sign of Nikolai. Virtually nothing of our fire remains. I make out only the outline of the rock that he sat on and, further away, our tent, just visible among the pines. Is he sitting on a rock somewhere, afraid to come back? Has something happened to him? I picture him wading into deep water.

'Please, Nikolai,' I say aloud. 'Come back.'

I hobble over to the tent, crawl inside and fall asleep to the rustle of branches and the sea's soft murmur.

29

I jerk my head up. Shuffling, snuffling sounds outside, getting louder. Someone – or something – is coming into the tent. A head shoves through the opening. Thick black clumps of hair hide the face.

A smell of seaweed. Then I recognise Nikolai, crawling towards me in the half light. His face is smudged with dirt, sand and what look like tear stains. He picks up the water bottle on the groundsheet and begins to drink. I push off my sleeping bag, sit up and wait for him to stop gulping.

'I thought you weren't coming back,' I say, relief spilling into my voice. 'Why did you go like that?'

'I was afraid that you will not understand. That you will hate me and I will not see you again.'

He's right, I don't understand. I don't hate him, but I hate what he's done.

'It is true,' he says in a low voice.

'No, I –' I try to reach out and take his hand. My ankle gives a spasm of pain that makes me cry out.

'You are hurt? Let me look.'

'I tripped on something. It's not so bad now. I took some Nurofen.'

Nikolai kneels beside me and inspects the injury, gently touching the area around the joint. Then he goes to his rucksack and rummages inside.

'Wait,' he says, crawling out of the tent. 'I come back soon.'

I hear thudding feet, getting fainter. Minutes later Nikolai comes back into the tent, breathing hard, his calves splattered with wet sand. I gasp as something cold and dripping touches my foot. He's bandaging my ankle with his sock, firmly and without hesitation. When he's finished he passes me the water bottle, pulls my sleeping bag over me and removes his sweater and shorts.

He sits beside me, eyes locked onto mine. 'Tell me,' he says. 'What you are thinking.'

'I don't hate you, Nikky. I just want to understand what... what made you do such a thing. But you have to help me.'

His brow furrows. 'For so long I try to make sense what I do. I am angry at Ivan because he treats my father like shit, he thinks he can ask for anything because Anton will protect him.'

'That's all?'

'I know it is Ivan I hurt, I know I am in Russia. Then it is like I go far away, into another place... I cannot explain.'

And I'm too tired to think.

'Nikky, this guy you think is following you – could he be in the gang that was protecting your father's business?'

'I do not know if anyone is really coming after me.' He strokes his stubbled jaw thoughtfully. 'I think it is my fear; it makes me imagine what is not there.'

'But it could have been Anton or someone from his gang? He could have got someone to track you down?'

He gestures dismissively. 'It is not Anton, for sure. Anton is much heavier, bigger in the shoulders. It is possible he asks someone to find me, but I think it is too much trouble. England is long way from Russia. How will anyone find me? It is not so easy. I am not in phone directory. I do not have sign on my head –'

'What about the Russian police? They could contact the British police, couldn't they? They could find you.'

He sighs, shaking his head. 'I am here for six months now. No one has tried to arrest me.'

'Do the Russian police know you killed Ivan?'

He pauses before replying.

'I get letter from my mother after I come to London. She says the day after I leave, the police come. One of the women in shop tells them she sees blood on my shirt, the other says I run out like crazy man. My father tells the police I do it because I try to help him. He says I was soldier in Chechnya and when I come back I am not like before. He tells them I do not deserve to go to prison. They laugh. They say that I will be old man when I come out. So, he offers them money. Two thousand American dollars.'

'And they took it?'

'They take, yes.'

'So now they'll just forget about you? They won't try to arrest you if you go back?'

His voice is weary. 'If I am lucky, they will forget. In Russia, people are shot every day and the police do nothing. Outside Moscow, they have no money to catch criminals. Anyway, they are busy with other things – to make people afraid of them so they can take their money.'

He rubs his eyes. He looks exhausted. I want to put my arms around him and hold him. Only I have one more thing to ask.

'Could you… Could you ever do that again? Could you ever get angry enough to kill someone?'

'I make promise to myself when I leave Russia. I will never again hurt anyone, no matter how angry I am.'

I think of the youth he hit in the pub. 'But you didn't keep your promise, did you?'

'No, you are right. I have failed already.'

'And what about me? Could you ever hurt me?'

'I promise, Georgie, I will never hurt you. It is the truth, you must believe.'

His face is just a few inches from mine; he can hide nothing. I see the drops of sea and grains of salt on his skin, the restless flicker of an eyelid. I smell his unwashed body, his fear.

'Do you regret what you did?'

'Every day I regret. What I do to Ivan – and what happens to my father.'

'What happened to him?'

'My mother writes me what happens. Two weeks after I leave Russia, Anton sends his men onto my father, then they set fire to his shop. He gets out alive. But my mother says he is old man now. He gives up his business, all his plans.'

He closes his eyes for a while then continues.

'It is my fault. When I leave, I do not expect him to take my punishment. My father tells me to run, so I run. I am frightened, I do not think of what will happen to him. And now my mother writes that he wants to forget me. He tells me to go away so I will be safe; he will take Anton's revenge instead of me. But he cannot forgive me for what I do. He says to my mother that this war has made me into everything he hates. He does not want to see me. He does not write. My letters, he never opens. The money I send for him, he will not take. My mother tells him it is from my sister.'

Nikolai looks straight at me.

'I understand if you want to say goodbye to me, Georgie. Now you know what I do I think it is better for you to let me go.'

I blink back tears and reach for his hand, taking in the strong fingers, the proud veins strung between his broad, deep knuckles.

'I don't want to let you go, Nikky. I believe in you.'

He wipes his eyes with the back of his hand.

'You are... how to say? Before I meet you I am lost, I am always in the dark. You make my world bright again.'

We spend the rest of the day on the beach. Nikolai insists I rest. He tends to my ankle, brings me meals and whatever else I need and fetches supplies from the car.

My horror at what he's revealed has not gone away. But I try my best to understand rather than judge. Something – perhaps many things – drove him to that crime. The violence he witnessed and committed himself during that war: how could any man leave it behind, unaffected?

I told Nikolai I trusted him; he reassured me that he would not let me down. But now, I wonder how he can be so sure.

Nikolai says little. We're drinking beer by the tent. I've been thinking and suddenly it spills out of me:

'Tell me about Vakha, will you? Why are you having all these secret meetings with him that you can't talk about? And what is Caucusus Action all about?'

Nikolai's mouth falls open. 'This name, Caucusus Action, how do you know? I do not tell you.'

'I saw it on a piece of paper in your flat. When I came over for the first time. I shouldn't have looked but I was curious –'

'It is not your business, Georgie.'

'I need to know what's going on, Nikolai.'

He stares me out. 'I am sorry. There are things I still cannot tell you.'

'Really?'

'Please, trust me. There is reason why I meet Vakha. It is not bad reason.'

'So why not tell me what it is?'

'It is not safe for me to tell you. It is something... sensitive. I will tell you when it is the right time.'

I don't know why, if it's because I'm being naïve, or plain stupid – or because I'm in love with Nikolai. But something makes me trust him.

The following morning my ankle has recovered enough for me to manage the cliff path. We drive inland and find a quiet campsite by a river, driving distance from the coast, and we stay for the rest of the week. We swim, take boat trips and explore fishing villages. No more men in BMWs trouble us. I brush aside thoughts of sinister men hiding in bushes or the police taking Nikolai away. He seems easier in himself, as if a burden has been removed. But now the burden is with me, and it's heavy.

Sometimes, when he holds me close or caresses me, I can't believe that what he's told me is true; the awfulness of it overwhelms me. He has killed a man, then run away, not thinking of the consequences. He has committed the ultimate crime. How can I carry on as if nothing has happened, knowing what he's done? Yet how can I condemn him when he's already condemned himself? He has confessed to me, trusted me with his secret – I can't throw it back at him. And I believe in the power of Nikolai's promise.

We're lying together, side by side in the darkness of the tent. Scraps of birdsong make their way to our ears.

'I make a fool of myself,' Nikolai murmurs. 'I make a fool of my life.'

The edge in his voice strikes me. He sounds on the verge of defeat.

'But you can do things differently in future, if you want to enough. Don't you believe that?'

'I don't know. Maybe to try is not enough.'

Perhaps, I think, my faith and his will combined will not be enough, and I'm a fool to think otherwise.

'So many times I wish I could go back and put it right with my father. To start over and be clean, like the new snow. But I know it can never happen.'

'What you did to Ivan,' I reply. 'You'll always have to live with it. But what someone does once doesn't make them a bad person for ever. What matters is how you choose to live from now on. I know you're a good person, in your heart.'

'I will try to keep your faith in me.' He finds my hand and holds it tight.

30

Thursday morning. Another tedious day ahead, I think, as I cling to the handrail of the Northern Line train. A meeting about corporate branding, another meeting about something else and a stack of emails. Three days back at the office and still I'm in that no man's land between holiday and the routine of work. Everything is an effort: getting out of bed, the journey to the office, not to mention work itself. I can't imagine how it once seemed so important.

The train waits between stations. King's Cross, next stop. I check my watch. We're on time, a few minutes after 8.30. The lights dim and come on again a few moments later. Nothing seems out of the ordinary. People cough, mutter, adjust clothing, fan themselves, sip water and stare past each other. I read someone's newspaper, a few inches from my nose.

With a jolt and a long metallic screech, the train begins to slow. A guy bends over to retrieve something, causing a woman lodged behind him to emit a cluck of irritation. I pull my bag closer and stare at the doors, urging them to open. Sweat pools in the small of my back. At last, the darkness of the tunnel gives way to the brightly lit platform. Propelled by the thrust of bodies behind me, I emerge from the compartment into the hustle for the escalators.

Outside, the air is warm and humid. I hurry to leave behind the commotion of King's Cross, slowing as soon as I reach the back streets. It takes 12 minutes to arrive at the office at my usual pace. Perhaps if I walk slowly enough I won't get there at all.

Through the high gates into the old brick building. I take the lift and walk to the end of the aisle. My neighbour smiles, I smile back. I turn on my computer and click into my emails.

It's nearly an hour before I realise something is wrong. The usual purr of activity has stopped. I look up to see seven or eight people gathered around a desk, craning their necks to look at a computer screen. I go over. They're watching a news report.

'... explosions at Liverpool Street, King's Cross... '

'Fuckin' hell,' someone says.

There have been several underground explosions, the reporter says; a power surge could be responsible.

More people gather behind me. Glancing around, I see other groups forming around other desks. The news cuts to a reporter in

Russell Square. Police have cordoned off part of the square because a bus has just blown up; there are fears that terrorists could be responsible. I leave the stunned faces around me and return to my desk, silently thanking the universe for my uneventful exit from King's Cross.

A hush falls over the office. Then a phone on a nearby desk rings, followed by another and another, until everyone seem to be talking on their phones or mobiles. I pick up my mobile and try to reach Nikolai until someone shouts that the mobile networks are down. He's safe, I reassure myself; he would have passed through King's Cross Station well before me on his way to work.

I'm searching on the Internet in case there's a phone number for the site office, when my father calls to check that I'm OK. He was out of central London, having driven to his office in Hertfordshire as usual. None of my friends have been caught in the bomb attacks, as far as I know. I wonder about Julian. But his office is on the fringes of London and he normally drives in.

Mid-morning, Nikolai calls from his site office. A surge of emotion goes through me as I hear his voice. He tried calling my mobile for ages and couldn't get through but found my office number in his wallet. As I thought, he got off the Tube well before me. Less than ten minutes later, my mother phones from Spain. She is at home, listening to the radio.

'Thank God,' she says as soon as I pick up. 'I thought –'

'I'm all right, Mum.' I explain that I was on the underground earlier, well before any of the explosions.

A short silence.

'I love you, darling,' she says.

I want to tell her that I love her too. But I can't say it. The words sound wrong somehow, like a line in a sentimental Hollywood film. Or perhaps they're simply too difficult to say. I just tell her not to worry, I'll call soon.

As the morning passes, more news comes in. Everyone seems to be either watching the latest news on their computers or standing around talking about it, ignoring their work. The Tube network has been suspended and no buses are running in central London. People are confirmed to have died in the explosions. The police say that this could be a 'co-ordinated terror attack'.

I stay at my desk, watching the latest headlines on my computer, trying to process what's happened. Jake has emailed that our meetings are cancelled and there are rumours that the office will close early. I don't expect my phone to ring and a voice to announce that there's a Mr Lewis waiting for me at reception. For a second or so it doesn't register. I don't know anyone called Mr Lewis.

Then it hits me. Julian is waiting for me. I've heard nothing from him since his second email a month ago, and have dared to hope that he's finally accepted the end of our friendship. I nearly ask the receptionist to tell him to go away but I don't think he will – he'll just hang around till I leave the building.

As soon as I emerge from the lift, he bounds over from the waiting area and wraps his arms around me.

'Jaffa,' he murmurs, squeezing me tight. 'I thought you might be hurt.'

'I'm perfectly OK.'

I try to pull away. We're standing in full view of the reception desk and anyone who might be passing. He's pressing into my body with his; I feel him getting hard. Repulsion washes over me.

'Hey, let me go.'

He steps away, surprise and hurt plainly marked on his face.

'You're OK, then,' I say. 'I didn't think you'd be in central London.'

'I had to see if you were all right. I was on my way to Harley Street to see my shrink.' He makes an amused titter. 'Just kidding, it was only my dentist.'

I edge towards the door, thinking of how to extricate myself from him.

'Let's go outside, we can talk out there.'

He follows me around the side of the building, towards the bench next to the canal. I don't sit down. Julian stands facing me, too close.

'It's so good to see you again, Georgie. It's been tough without you around.'

'How dare you say that after those disgusting messages you sent me?'

'I was only telling you how I feel. Is that so disgusting to you? Or maybe it's how you behaved that's so disgusting.'

'I told you, Julian, I don't want to see you any more. This is –'

'Come on, Jaf. Let's not fight. We could go and get a coffee somewhere, if you like... ' He reaches out and caresses my hair. A chill goes through me.

'Get your hands off me! I said I don't want to see you any

more. Why can't you get that into your fucking head?' I run into the building and up the stairs, not waiting for the lift.

Thank goodness, after this there's no sign of Julian. But my hands are shaking for about an hour and I can't stop seeing his cold, creepy little smile.

Not long after midday, the managing director tells us all to go home.

It's a relief to be away from the office. I head north along pavements clogged with people, passing lines of barely moving vehicles, all thoughts of Julian gone. Every taxi is taken, the Tube isn't running and there are scarcely any buses. In any case, walking seems the safest option.

Outside barred Tube station entrances, newspaper headlines yell 'Capital Under Attack!' as if London has been invaded by Martians. I see my own sense of shock and disbelief in other people's faces. The reality is soon evident, though. In a crowd at a taxi stand I glimpse a man in a suit, bandages wrapped around his head. Outside a florist, a woman swears into her phone. Her eyes are reddened and teary. She hasn't noticed that the bag at her feet has fallen over, spilling kiwi fruit across the pavement. Later on I see a man sitting on a bench near some traffic lights, elbows on his knees, face hidden by his hands. His white shirt is specked with black, as are his trousers. A filthy backpack lies beside him. His back and shoulders are shaking.

At home, I watch Tony Blair on TV denouncing the bomb attacks and telling everyone to carry on as normal. There's talk of suicide bombers and possible Al Qaeda involvement, and warnings of further attacks. I put aside thoughts of changing my clothes and lie on the sofa, compelled to see the next unbelievable scene unfold, as if I'm watching a horror film. How are such things possible in a country where we queue for everything and complain about the weather? Wars are fought in far-off places like Iraq, not here in London.

My father phones as I'm about to go to bed.

'Nigel and Liz haven't heard from Sean,' he says. 'He was on his way to a meeting in central London when the bombs went off. They think he might have taken the Circle Line. They can't get him on his mobile.'

Sean is down there, I think immediately. He's a hundred feet underground, trapped inside a wrecked train.

'He might have got distracted and forgotten to call,' I say. 'One of his friends could have been hurt.'

'He would have called straight away if he was all right.'

'Have they called the hospitals?'

'Yes, none of them have got him. But people are coming in all the time. He might be in a bed somewhere waiting to be put on a list.'

I say I'll be right over.

The three of us sit in the kitchen, waiting for the phone to ring. Alicia makes cups of tea and moves things from one place to another. My father stares at his crossword, getting up every half hour to turn on radio news bulletins. Many people who travelled into central London that morning are still missing, they say. Rescuers are trying to reach dozens of people still trapped inside the bombed Tube trains but no one knows how long it will take.

Eleven p.m. passes, then midnight. At 12.30 my father phones Sean's father for the third time. He puts the phone down immediately.

'There's no point in us waiting up all night,' Alicia says. 'Nigel will call as soon as he has news.'

'Georgie,' my father says as I stand by the front door. He looks at me as if he's about to tell me something important. 'Take care of yourself, won't you?' is all he says.

Early next morning I'm woken by the phone. Sean has been admitted to the Royal London Hospital with minor injuries, my father tells me. He was stuck inside the bombed Circle Line train until firemen managed to cut open his compartment.

After work I turn off my mobile and flop in front of the TV. The news is dominated by the previous day's bomb blasts. Police are now certain that suicide bombers are behind the attacks; more people have been rescued from underground but some are still trapped inside tunnels.

I doze off, waking abruptly in the darkness to a rapping on my front door. Outside is Nikolai. He takes hold of both my hands.

'I wanted to see you,' he says, 'after all that happens.'

'I was going to phone but I fell asleep.'

He pulls me towards him. A trace of cigarette smoke. I close my eyes, glad that he is here.

Inside, we stand looking at the TV, which shows a distraught

Muslim man. His daughter has been killed in one of the bombs, the man says.

I say I don't understand how people can kill in the name of religion, that maybe it would be better if there were no religions.

'Then there will be other reasons for us to kill each other.'

Suddenly I remember what he did and turn away, in case it shows on my face.

'I know someone who was hurt yesterday,' I say. 'Remember Sean?'

I tell Nikolai what happened and the latest news – Sean has been released from hospital. He is astonishingly cheerful, according to my father, telling everyone how lucky he is to be alive.

That night I lie tightly wrapped in Nikolai's arms, listening to his steady breathing. It takes me a long time to fall asleep. Our lives have changed, I think. London, a city that always seemed quite safe as long as you were careful, has turned into a war zone.

31

It's not going how I hoped. I've tried to forget you and move on to fresher pastures but all the time you're in my head, in my dreams. I can't get rid of you. Your gauzy green cool cat stare, that curious paw toying with me. I'm your mouse, still half alive.

You shut down your emotions and you tried to shut down mine too. We're better off as friends, Jules. I don't want things to get complicated.

But I saw it in your bed, that night. Your need for me. It was the best fucking night of my life.

Then it's All change, please.

I made a mistake. I'm sorry, Jules. I had too much to drink, you're just not the one for me. Let's just be friends, shall we? Oh, no, we can't be friends any more, sorry about that. I'm off with Count Nikolai von Superman. I'm really really sorry, Jules but I can't see you any more. You understand, don't you? And please don't come to my office any more. Don't come near me, not even if World War III has started because can't you understand, I don't give a monkey's about you and I never ever ever want to see your face again.

Cunt.

You think you can still play with me, don't you? You think you can just shove me aside like a piece of smelly garbage and nothing bad will happen. Well, my sweet, think again.

32

The following Monday things are getting back to normal at work. Everyone is still trying to come to terms with last week's events. Some of my colleagues refuse to go on public transport and they cycle or walk instead. I spend my Tube journey pondering the chances of my carriage being bombed, or the one beside it. There could be further attacks. At the same time, it seems a little cowardly and not very public-spirited to dwell on such things.

When I get home I vent my grim mood on a medley of weeds and ivy threatening to overtake the garden. Half an hour in, the landline rings.

'Hello?'

No response.

'Hello? Anyone there?'

I'm about to hang up when a loud screech in my ear nearly makes me drop the handset. A gut-clenching yowling like the sound of mating cats carries on for several seconds, until I let the phone clatter to the kitchen floor. Heart thumping, I retrieve it, check the caller's number. It's withheld.

It's from someone who wants to upset me. Someone who doesn't have the guts to identify themselves.

Julian. It has to be him.

I've hardly thought of him since he arrived at my work last week; the bombings have crowded out everything else.

Suddenly, I'm angry. I'm not going to hide this any more.

I phone the police and ask to speak to a female officer. I say I've had a disturbing anonymous phone call and I'm concerned it might be from a man I used to be friends with who came to my flat and then my office after I said I didn't want to see him. Without going into any detail, I explain about the two emails asking me to give up my boyfriend and how jealous he's been, making sure to give her Julian's full name.

She asks if this man has threatened me. He said he'd wait for me, I reply. I try to recall anything he's said or written which might be considered threatening but nothing is, not really.

The woman sounds sympathetic but says there is little she can do right now. She tells me to contact the police again if I receive any specific threats involving actual physical harm. Also I must log all contact I have with him, as well as any further anonymous calls. She confirms that it is better not to respond at all, as this might encourage him.

I get on with preparing a salad, feeling a little better. At least there's something now on record about Julian's behaviour. I renew my resolve not to respond to him in any way. I'm not going to give him the pleasure of knowing he's got to me.

After dinner Nikolai phones and tells me about his day. He sounds cheerful. He went for a pint after work with a few of his workmates to celebrate someone's birthday.

'I had a really odd phone call earlier,' I say when he's finished.

'From who?'

'They didn't speak. I just heard this horrible noise. I have this feeling it might be Julian,' I say. 'He came over to my office last week, the day of the Tube bombs. He said he wanted to know I was OK. Something isn't right about him. He doesn't listen when I say I don't want to see him any more.'

'Why do you not tell me?'

'I got distracted with everything that happened... Anyway, I've reported him to the police.'

'The police? You really need to do this?'

'I told them he's been harassing me and won't leave me alone.' I hesitate. 'Also there's been a couple of emails. Julian is jealous of you. He wants me to give you up.'

'You do not tell me.' His tone is accusing, as if this is all my fault.

'I didn't want to bother you with it all. I thought he'd stop pestering me if I just ignored him.'

'Will you show the emails to me? I would like to see.'

'No, I can't. I deleted them. They're mostly just him mouthing off about you.'

'Mouthing off?'

'He said some nasty things – not just about you, about me too.'

'You want me to go to his place and talk to him? I will tell him to leave you alone.'

No, that's the last thing I want, and I wish I hadn't told Nikolai anything. I imagine Julian showing Nikolai the messages he sent me, then gleefully filling in every detail of that night we spent in my bed, and how exactly I gave him the most wonderful sexual experience of his life. It would be the perfect way for Julian to get one up on Nikolai. He would revel in it. And God only knows what Nikolai might do to Julian in return. I can't let that happen.

'I honestly don't think that would help, Nikky. He would just deny the call was from him. And I suppose he only came over to the office that day to see if I was all right. I doubt I'll hear any more from him.'

'You will be OK, Georgie?'

I imagine Nikolai's concerned face. I want to be safe in his arms, knowing that no one can hurt me.

'Yes, I'll be OK. Goodnight, sweet dreams.'

We can't see much from where we are standing, only a mass of people up to the other side of Trafalgar Square. A succession of church and trade union leaders, politicians and celebrities address us from a distant platform. Their figures are practically invisible but their words boom out clearly through the PA system.

'We must not let them break down our communities! We must not give in to fear and hate, or we will give victory to those responsible for this atrocity!'

'Good on yer, mate!' someone shouts. In front of us, an ear-splitting whistle from three teenage girls. Ella begins to clap; I join in. Sucked in from its ragged edges, we've become part of the crowd.

It was my idea to go to the rally, held in memory of those killed in the bombs seven days ago. Despite the uniformed police officers everywhere, there's an almost joyful defiance – a collective decision to tell the departed bombers that we won't be cowed by their deeds. Standing there in the evening heat, the vibe begins to get to me, normally the most unsentimental of people. I brush off Ella's observation that this would be a perfect opportunity for another suicide bomber to strike and feel proud to be a Londoner resisting a common enemy.

We leave before the end and order food at a nearby pub. Someone has left the *Evening Standard* on a table, opened at a headline about recent arson attacks on mosques.

'Christ, that's better.' Ella puts down her depleted glass of Guinness and wipes foam off her mouth.

I tell her about Julian's visit, the weird phone call and what the police officer said when I reported his unwanted contact.

'I didn't think the police would do anything – I've been

through it, Georgie… Do you really think the call came from Julian?'

'Who else would it be?'

'I suppose it could be him. It seems unlikely though. What's Nikolai up to this evening?'

'He's meeting this guy, a student at Imperial College.'

'You're not happy about it?'

'He won't tell me what they're meeting about. I'm worried in case – well, that Nikolai might be involved in something he shouldn't be.'

'Like what?'

'Something illegal. I can't say any more.'

There isn't much to say, in any case. I have nothing concrete to go on except an overheard conversation, a short newspaper article and a scrawled note about a meeting that could have meant anything.

Ella gives me a dubious look. 'How's it going with you two?'

'OK – more than OK. He's been working longer hours lately and I haven't seen so much of him. I miss him.'

'You've really fallen for this Russian guy, haven't you?'

She finds the answer in my face.

'There's something about him…' Ella pauses. 'Don't take this the wrong way, Georgie. I'm just saying how it seems to me.'

'Go on.'

'He's damaged – in his head. It's that look in his eyes, like something's broken.'

She's being over-dramatic as usual, I think. All the same, I'm tempted to confide in her about Nikolai's revelation. But what would she say if I were to admit that the man I love is a runaway killer? She would tell me to leave him, just as my father has done. What's more, Ella might be tempted to tell someone else, who might tell the police. I feel bad enough for asking my father's police contact to check on Vakha; I can't take the risk that someone in the police might start rummaging into Nikolai's past.

'Hey, listen to this.'

Ella leans over the *Evening Standard* and starts to read from an article about the suicide bombers. Not only were they British and brought up in Yorkshire, they were apparently harmless – hard-working, cricket-loving lads from moderate Muslim families.

'God, this is creepy. One of them worked in a primary school. They reckon the kids thought the world of him.' Ella peers at the page disbelievingly. 'All that time they blended in so well, no one suspected what they were really like.'

'You'd think someone would have realised.'

'Perhaps they did, but they didn't want to believe it.'

Our haddock and chips arrives and the conversation turns to the latest goings-on at Islington Council.

On the way home, an Arab-looking guy gets into the Tube at Camden Town, sits down opposite me, places a backpack between his legs and begin to flick through a *Metro*. I have an urge to move down the train but stay where I am.

It's only while I'm getting ready for bed that I recall what Ella said about Nikolai: *Like something's broken.* It makes me shiver, thinking about it now. I switch on the radio to dispel the silence. Surely, Ella is overreacting? Her fears are unfounded, stirred up by this outbreak of mass hysteria and fear of the unknown – aren't they? But deep inside me, I know she's right.

33

How many ways can an 'accident' happen?

I was thinking about that yesterday evening as I walked round his workplace with my new friend. Let's call him R. I won't mention his name in case he gets into trouble with Mr Plod. We wouldn't want that.

We had a good old prowl around in our hard hats. It was dark and the whole place was empty except for us, which was a bit spooky. R took me up to the fifth floor – they've got one floor more to go, he reckons. The rails are still going up and the temp ones look pretty flimsy. I suggested he could just go up behind someone and give him a shove and it would be, Oh dear, down he goes. He didn't like the sound of it, though – too much like murder. I asked if he couldn't do a sudden reverse with a dumper truck as can happen from time to time, so I've learned from a construction health-and-safety video. R wasn't keen on that idea either. He mentioned that he'd already been accused of all sorts for an incident involving a dumper truck, a Pakistani and a pile of bricks. He said everyone would point the finger at him if anything like that were to happen again.

We were nosing around the lower floors for inspiration when R had a eureka moment. He ran over, his eyes flashing like Belisha beacons and a big grin on his face.

'What I'll do,' he cried out with sociopathic enthusiasm, 'is get them on their own and wait until they're busy with something or other, then I'll take away the manhole cover! I could knock out a few lights too. With any luck, sooner or later they'll not look where they're going and come crashing through the hole.'

Simplicity itself. This plan has the added benefit that a misplaced manhole cover does not appear malevolent – it's just the momentary forgetfulness of an overstretched construction worker.

After the site tour we stop in a nearby pub to cement the deal.

I buy R a pint and shepherd him into a quiet corner while he moans about all the Arabs, gypos and Pakis cluttering up the bloody building site and how London isn't the same any more. They even have the audacity to pop into his Enfield local these days. If he had his way, they'd all be chucked off the fifth floor tomorrow.

His eyes light up when I hand him the envelope. He looks around *furtively like he's not sure if it's bad form to count it in front of me, then does so anyway.*

Seven hundred smackers. I reckon five hundred would have done it, but, hey. When I tell him who the victim is, he's positively ecstatic. He's more than happy to let your Ruski stumble into a hole leading to a very unwelcoming concrete floor ten feet below.

I hope you won't be too upset, my sweet girl. I'm not a cruel person, really. I just can't bear to see him with you any longer.

I tried. I tried to go home and forget you. I even spent the night with a girl in Soho who did some unspeakable things to me. But everything in my life reminds me of you. Everything in my life is Not You.

Sorry if this sounds drastic. I guess I've never been good at half measures. I remember you told me once I was obsessive about everything – cars, bridges, Formula One. I guess you hit the nail on the head there.

I warned you, didn't I? That nothing good would come of this. You had your fun with your beloved and now it's over. He's going to get what he deserves for taking you away from me.

Ah, here he is, late again. Dishevelled hair, bags under eyes, feet dragging – all the better to fall down holes with. He must have had a hard night by the look of him. It's all right for some.

We'll see how many lives Niknik has soon. I can't wait. It's making me hungry, all this waiting for something to happen. I've eaten my miso soup, the packet of crackers and a massive apple. Should have popped in for a Big Mac on the way. How much longer is this going to take? The suspense is killing me, haha. There's something splendid about waiting, though. It's that delayed gratification thing, like holding off from an amazing orgasm. You know when the moment comes you'll relish it all the more.Another batch of workers head up the road, minus Niknik. With any luck he'll be on his own in there by now – except for R, of course. Maybe he's already a heap of broken bones.

Lord knows what R's playing at. Playing hard to get, scarpering off without reporting back. All he has to do is text me a 1 or a 0 – you'd think he could manage that for seven hundred quid.

Uh oh, something's up. Chaps are running in and out of the place like angry bees, shouting into walkie-talkies. And is that a siren I hear?

An ambulance has pulled up outside the entrance. That's a good sign.

Someone's coming out now.

It's him.

Oh lordy. He's walking. He doesn't have a scratch on him.

34

The next day, Friday, I strenuously apply myself to my outstanding tasks at work, forgetting I promised to call Nikolai about our plans for that evening.

It's just after 4 p.m. when he calls.

'Sorry I didn't get back to you,' I say. 'I've been caught up with things here.'

'I had accident, Georgie.'

It takes me a second or so to register what he's said.

'An accident? Are you hurt?'

'My arm, my ribs. It is not so bad, nothing is broken. They get doctor to see me, he bandages my arm and says I must go home and rest. They call cab for me.'

He was moving pieces of timber, he explains, when he fell through a hole in the floor. Fortunately a pile of plywood sheets on the floor below broke his fall.

I tell him I'll be over as soon as I can.

On the way to Nikolai's flat I call into a grocery and select a bunch of flowers and four fat green-tinged mangoes. The grey-haired man behind the till appraises me warily as he takes my note. Before he can drop coins into my palm, we're interrupted by a hoarse shout from the street.

'Death to Arab cunts!'

Amid whistles and hoots of laughter, the shopkeeper's head snaps to the door. I catch sight of the raised fist and retreating back of a tattooed youth with cropped hair. For an instant, as he gives me my change, the old man's fear-filled eyes meet mine. Muttering, he turns to the shelf behind.

I pass the mosque on St Thomas' Road. A crowd surges through the gates onto the street – all males, aged from teenagers to old men. Two uniformed policemen stand on the opposite side of the street watching the exodus. I turn away, recalling news reports of the hook-armed cleric Abu Hamza inciting young Muslims to commit acts of terrorism.

I press Nikolai's buzzer, push open the front door and bound up the scuffed steps two at a time, my footsteps echoing in the stair-well. I rap on his front door. The window beside it is ajar; a draft swirls black dust around the ledge and stirs tendrils of cobweb. I look away quickly, trying not to breathe in the unpleasant odour of the hallway, like stale piss.

Nikolai comes to the door in his underpants and an unbuttoned, crumpled shirt. The colour has gone from his face.

'Careful,' he warns as I go up to him. He pulls his shirt away at his right shoulder, revealing an arm swathed in bandages.

'Oh, my God. What have you done to yourself?'

As I stare, a smile flickers across his face. 'Don't worry, soon I will be like new.' He takes the flowers. 'Thank you, they are beautiful.'

I go into the kitchen to find a vase. The window is shut as usual during the day to keep out the noise. An acidic whiff of damp lingers.

'In there.' He reaches towards the cupboard handle with his unbandaged arm then stops, grimacing.

'Let me,' I say. 'You go back and lie down. I'll bring you a cup of tea.'

'There is a ginger cake there, you will bring?'

There's a look of childish pleasure on Nikolai's face as I come in carrying a tray of tea, cake and sliced mango, which I place on the card table. He lies on the sofa bed, surrounded by CDs and empty Coke bottles. I perch beside his feet.

'I did not expect you so early,' he says.

'Don't be daft,' I reply, placing the plate of cake on his lap and holding out a mug of tea as carefully as I can so he won't have to reach too far.

He takes it awkwardly, spilling some tea.

'You're in a bad way, aren't you?'

'I have been hurt more than this – this is nothing. The doctor says I must rest… I must not work for two weeks.' He groans. 'And I cannot play my keyboard.'

'So tell me what happened.'

'It was stupid thing. I am up on third floor, clearing up after the carpenters. I am the only one there, the others have gone down for lunch. I want to go too. I do not look where I put my feet. I go through hole in the floor – it was not there before. The guys run to help me. The foreman shouts at us. He knows a guy at another site who falls between floors but there is nothing at other end to stop him. After this, he cannot walk.'

He stares into his plate. Voices echo on the landing.

'Why was there a hole in the floor?'

'For the wiring. It is cut yesterday and they cover with plywood. The chief electrician says that someone must take cover away and forget to put back, maybe one of the carpenters. He says it was on floor when he leaves and now it is over by the wall. The ganger man asks us who moves it but no one will say.'

Nikolai leans over to take my hand but stops midway, screws up his face and inhales sharply.

'Shit, I can do nothing.' He flops back onto the pillows. 'I am glad you are here, Miz. Yesterday when you are in Trafalgar Square I worry for you, in case something happens again. Come, kiss me. Make me better.'

I kiss him on the mouth, resting my hand lightly on his undamaged arm, then sit down again, watching the cake vanish into his mouth in a series of snatched gulps. He's using his left hand for everything, with obvious difficulty. Sometimes a too-quick movement triggers a groan and a flash of pain on his face.

His mobile phone, lying on the bed, begins to ring. I pass it to him.

'Hello?'

I can just hear the other person's voice above what sounds like engine noise.

Nikolai shouts into the phone.

'I am all right. I will be back in two weeks. Georgie is here; she is looking after me.' He grins at me. 'I call you soon, OK? Cheers, mate.'

'That was Malik,' he says to me. 'He says anything he can do to help, he will.'

'Are the others still giving him a hard time?' I recall an incident that Nikolai told me about. On Malik's first week back after his 'accident', someone placed a rat in his mug of tea while he went to the toilet.

'Sure they are. Some of them hate foreigners. But even more, they hate Muslims. The other day, Ricky asks me why I am the friend of a Paki. I tell him to fuck off – I choose who will be my friend, it is none of his business.'

I tell Nikolai about the incident in the shop on the way to his flat.

'I hear things too,' he replies. 'The other evening, I am in launderette. I hear some young guys say they will burn down the mosque.'

'It's scary what some people will do.' I look straight at him. 'Are you sure, Nikky, that what happened to you today was an accident? Whoever left that hole uncovered, wasn't it his fault?'

I wait for a lorry to pass and the slow drip of the bathroom tap to resume. Nikolai fingers the frayed edge of the blanket.

'No, I do not think so. I was not careful.' He speaks quietly, not meeting my eyes. 'There is – how you say – bad atmosphere since the bombs go off. Some of the guys, they have no brain; they will say shit about everyone they do not like. But I don't think they will try to hurt me because of this.'

'Are you just saying that to make me feel better?'

'No, I think it is strange we do not have more accidents. Always there are things we should do but we don't. This hole has no fence, this hole is not covered, this man does not wear his helmet – so what? The union say we should follow the rules but no one cares about the rules. The managers, they care only that project is on time and they do not lose money. We have new project manager. He tells site manager we must work harder to finish building on time. We are part of team, we must all pull together to make this project success.'

'At least now you'll have a chance to rest.'

He frowns. 'I am not good patient. I hate to stay in bed like prisoner.'

'Why don't you come and stay with me for a while?'

To be honest, my idea startles me as much as it does Nikolai. I've never shared my home with a man, nor even considered doing so. I'm not that kind of girl.

'Come on, Nikolai. This is no place for you to get better. You can't cook, you can't wash, you can't look after yourself properly. Stay with me till you're well enough to go back to work.'

His expression is half amused, half questioning.

'I will consider. This place, it is difficult for me to work on my music. The trucks, the buses, I hate.' As he speaks, vibrations from another lorry shake the window frames.

'I don't know how you can stand to live in this place,' I say and instantly regret it. This is all he can afford. He told me recently he was grateful to have a studio to himself rather than a room in a house full of immigrants, the kind of place some of the foreign workers he's worked with have to live in.

Nikolai gives me a sharp glance. 'What will your father think if he knows I stay with you?'

'Sod what he thinks,' I toss back. 'Why do you have to use him as an excuse?'

'It is not only that.'

'What else, then?'

He rubs his cheek. 'Last week, when I come home... I think someone is in here when I open the door. I look around, there is no one. But I have feeling someone was here. Some things are different from before.'

'What is different?'

He shrugs. 'It is not important.'

'They'll turn up somewhere. Maybe you threw them out and forgot.'

He looks unconvinced.

'You said it was unlikely that anyone would be able to track you down. Your father paid off the police, didn't he?' And how do you know that this isn't just your imagination, I stop myself from adding. His guilt for killing Ivan seems to have convinced Nikolai that somehow or other he's going to be punished.

'Anton is still out there, somewhere. If he has come for me, it is dangerous for you. It is better that I stay where I am, Georgie.'

'I don't agree,' I say. 'It's better that you stay with me.'

He doesn't reply.

On the way home, I do wonder if I might be putting myself at risk by having Nikolai move in with me. But it seems like a small price to pay.

I'm about to step into the bath I've run. The blind is not quite shut. A row of candles on the shelf flicker in the darkening room.

The sound of my mobile on the chair makes me jump. I've set it to ring like an old-fashioned phone so I won't keep missing calls from the depths of my handbag.

'Hello?'

For a second, silence.

'Hello, who's there?'

Then a soft sound, like someone whispering.

'Bee... '

Bee? What the hell?

I frown, trying to decipher the word.

'... eeechhh... '

The hairs on my neck rise as the sound turns into a soft elongated 'ch' like a kettle coming to the boil. I know what the word is now.

'Who is this?'

'Beeeech.'

I toss the phone away. It clunks against the toilet. I put on my dressing gown and close the blind. My pulse races; my throat is dry. I didn't recognise the voice. But how would I? Whoever it was whispered to disguise their voice – or to freak me out.

Only one name comes to mind.

35

I watch a wasp crawl down an ice-lolly stick into a pool of green goo and sodden *Vaccinate Your Cat* flyers. A rubbish bin is over-flowing onto the pavement. From the road, burning rubber and an exchange of horn blasts. Angry voices spill from car windows.

Queasy from heat and traffic fumes, I shrink back into the shelter's meagre shade. Commuters and tourists jostle around the bus stop, every so often peering in vexation at the timetable and each passing bus. An overweight, heavily perspiring woman ambles towards me and asks how long I've been waiting.

'Half an hour,' I reply, checking my watch. Given the day's events, I left the office at bang on five for a change.

Another bus pulls up, full like all the previous ones. A handful of people get off. The bus belches diesel fumes and departs.

'Fuck me,' blurts a young woman in high heels and a low-cut dress. Beside her, a gnarled-faced man groans and hauls himself upright with the help of his walking stick, saying he's giving up and going to the pub.

For the nth time this afternoon, I ring Nikolai's mobile. I'm meant to be going over to take him out for dinner; lately, he's been surviving on tinned food and takeaways. But just as each time before, a voice tells me: 'Your call cannot be taken, please leave a message.'

I curse as I hang up, wishing I could reach out and shake him, wherever he is. What the hell is he doing, disappearing today of all days?

It started out like any other hot, sticky, late-July Thursday. But once again, bombs have left a bright summer's day in tatters and London in chaos. A few hours ago, bombs packed with nails were left on the number 26 bus in Hackney and inside three Tube trains, supposedly another attempt to form a 'burning cross'. This time, thank God, only the detonators exploded, not the bombs, and only one person was hurt. All the would-be bombers got away.

Unable to concentrate on work, I spent all afternoon checking the Internet for the latest news, and as soon as my last meeting ended, I fled the office. And now I can see for myself: fear is visible on people's faces, a drawn-in, gnawing fear.

With four would-be bombers on the run and the police warning that they could strike again at any time, everyone is desperately trying to get home. But all minicabs are booked, it's impossible to hail a taxi and the Underground has been closed. Earlier, mobile networks were shut down again, which I hoped might be the reason I haven't been able to get through to Nikolai. But they're up again now.

Once again, I go through other possible reasons why Nikolai hasn't replied to my messages. He's at home engrossed in his music with his mobile switched off. He hasn't seen or heard the news and is expecting me to arrive by seven, as planned. He's gone out for a coffee without his mobile, or he's forgotten to charge it... None of these convinces me. I'm considering whether to abandon my trip to Finsbury Park and go home when a bus pulls up several metres from the stop, marginally less full than the earlier ones. Along with everyone else I scurry over. The doors open and we become a herd of cattle stomping into a pen.

'Are you going to Finsbury Park?' I ask the driver as the bus lurches forward.

He grunts something I can't understand.

'Crouch End, darlin',' says the girl beside me. She has black-rimmed eyes and a mass of fluffy pink hair. 'You'll 'ave to get another bus from there.'

The journey is tedious, the bus spending more time stopped, engine chugging than moving. I'm crammed into the downstairs aisle trying not to fall over whenever the driver slams on the brakes. The streets begin to look greener, the houses bigger. The bus puts on a burst of speed, admitting a welcome breeze before resuming another series of window-rattling advances. I swig water, thoughts churning.

What will I do if he isn't in when I get to his flat? Shouldn't I go home and wait there for him to contact me?

But I can't face getting on another bus – and I can't give up on Nikolai.

He'll call soon, I tell myself. He's gone for a walk without his phone and forgotten the time. He'll be home by the time I get to his flat.

I cling to the rail as the bus veers to avoid a cyclist.

''Scuse me, luv.' A tap on my shoulder from candyfloss girl. 'You need to get off at the next stop.'

I thank her and get off the bus, then see the crowd waiting at the bus stop across the street. It'll be years before I get on a bus to Finsbury Park.

I'll walk the rest of the way, I decide. It should take no more than 40 minutes if I take the path along the old railway line. There's plenty of daylight left and the path is well used by cyclists and dog walkers; it heads in a straight line to Finsbury Park, a short walk to Nikolai's flat.

I set off up the hill to the low bridge and take the steps down onto the remains of two concrete platforms.

It's good to be away from the road's noise and fumes. A chaos of wild plants have taken over the space between the platforms – thistles, cow parsley, clouds of dandelions and dock leaves as big as cabbages. Further along the path, a tyre hangs from a branch near the abandoned skateboard rink, engulfed by weeds and graffiti.

Ahead, a tunnel looms, its bricks hidden beneath a violent jostle of multi-coloured paint: declarations of love, four-letter words, words I don't understand. A fish with an electric-blue fin stares at me, its huge mouth agape. Dark against a distant sky, I make out a male figure stooped by the wall by the far end. I walk faster, the stench of cellulose invading my nostrils. The figure materialises into a guy in a hooded top and trainers, spraying red paint onto the bricks.

The path has become hidden from the outside world by a sprawl of green. Though I know it isn't that far from a road at any given point, the exits seem increasingly far apart. Bushes and trees grow from steep banks on either side, their leaves unmoving in the heavy air. No sounds of planes, cars or people, just a cloaking stillness accentuated by fierce bursts of bird chatter. Narrow, vine-choked tree trunks climb into the sky like a patch of sub-tropical rainforest gone astray. I feel a long way from civilisation.

My legs move with increasing urgency. Above, clouds are thickening; the brightness has turned to gloom. The air has become a warm syrup against my skin. I glug lukewarm water, tug my shirt out of my skirt and roll up my sleeves. Once again, I check my mobile to make sure I haven't missed any calls. Once again, I try Nikolai's number, hanging up as his voicemail cuts in.

On top of my deepening frustration comes a rush of alarm.

Something's happened to him. He's got into a fight with the neighbour who complained about him playing his keyboard too late in the evening. He's been picked up by the police for working illegally. He's been tracked down by Russian gangsters.

I set off again. The path goes over a bridge. Below, a set of rail tracks converge into the distance. Ahead, two policemen in rolled-up shirtsleeves and bullet-proof vests talk to a black youth. Way off, the wail of a police siren. Another tunnel encloses me, dark and dank. High above my head arches the original brickwork, untouched by graffiti. I peer into the murk. As I emerge, a thin grey cat streaks across the path in front of me and into the undergrowth, making me cry out.

The path ends abruptly. I follow a footbridge into a large recreation area, breaking into a jog when I see the park gates. Into Seven Sisters Road, past the café where Nikolai and I sometimes go for coffee. Past the delicatessen, where wasps crawl over wrinkled peaches. Past the betting shop, the hardware shop, the Internet café, the £4 barber...

His place, at last. The drab building leers at me, unwelcoming as ever. I press his buzzer, wait. Nothing.

I'm about to buzz again when a long-haired guy in a Che Guevara T-shirt slouches out of the building. I slip inside before he can let the door close and run upstairs.

'Nikolai, are you there? Nikolai?'

I rap on his door again, louder. Shout his name again and again – so loud everyone in the building must hear. Except the one person I need to hear.

Silence gathers. A hopeless, mocking silence.

Foolish girl, it says, what did you imagine? Aren't you sorry you've come all this way? He's not here, of course he's not here.

The spot at the top of the stairs where I wait is hard and not very clean. It will mark my skirt, but there's nowhere else to sit. I check my watch. Ten minutes to eight. I'm fifteen minutes late. I will wait long enough to be sure that he isn't going to turn up.

Something's happened to Nikolai. He's ill, or he's had an accident.

When I finally leave the building, night has fallen. I walk towards the station, thinking vaguely that I might find a taxi. I don't know what else to do, except to go home.

The phone rings as I sleep, its insistent bleat crashing into wisps of dreams. I lurch over to pick up, imagining it's Julian at the other end.

Then I realise it's Nikolai. I struggle to make sense of his words. His dented, frail voice keeps disappearing into the cracks of the bad connection. Footsteps slap on paving stones, echoing into an empty street.

'I am sorry. There is problem. I cannot leave.'

Relief wells inside me. He's safe.

'I didn't know where you were, Nikky. I thought something had happened to you. I was scared.'

Tapping noises on the line.

'I do not mean to scare you. I see Vakha. I am delayed, no signal for my phone... I wait long time for bus, then I walk.'

So he was with Vakha all evening and he didn't contact me?

'Where are you now?'

'I am close to home. In the morning, I will call.'

'Sure, OK.' I want to understand what kept him from phoning me. Surely he could have nipped out from wherever he was to make a call from a pub or somewhere? A hollow, queasy sensation spreads out from my stomach. I know he's keeping something important from me. But what could be worse than what he's already admitted?

36

Nikolai turns up the next evening with a scuffed red holdall bearing the last traces of some Russian words. His jacket is open over his shirt, the buttons not lining up with the holes.

He stands there waiting. I tell him to come inside and close the door.

'You do not believe I will come, Miz?' He drops the bag, puts his hands on my shoulders and softly kisses my mouth. The scent of dry citrus mingles with peppermint.

'Why didn't you call? I would have picked you up.'

'It is OK, I manage. I get taxi. Georgie, I am sorry about yesterday.'

But I'm not going to let him get away with that.

'I don't get why you couldn't call me just once during the evening, given all that was going on in London yesterday afternoon.' I tell him how I caught a bus towards Finsbury Park and ended up walking along the old railway line. My pride stops me from saying how I waited outside his flat for so long; I feel like an idiot.

'It was not possible.' He slumps against the wall, his expression hardening.

'Surely you could have found a way to call me? Didn't you think I might be worried? I really thought something bad had happened to you.'

'I am sorry, Georgie.'

'And you were with Vakha?'

'With Vakha, yes.'

'Where did you go with him?'

'There is pub in Bethnal Green, near the house where he lives. We talk there. It is where we often talk.'

'What about?'

'It is... It is important. When it is safe, I will tell you. I promise.'

I scowl at him.

'You are wonderful woman, Georgie.' He takes my hand and squeezes it. 'I do not deserve you.'

'It's all right, I forgive you.' I smile weakly. 'But you'll have to stay an extra week to make amends.'

I take his bag to my bedroom and put it down by the bedside table I've cleared for his things. 'You'll have to sleep with me, I'm afraid; the spare bedroom's an office.'

'No problem, I am happy to share your bed. You do not snore, I hope?' He removes his trainers and flops onto the mattress with an exaggerated sigh of pleasure.

I ask if he's heard what happened a few hours earlier – several police officers chased a man onto a train at Stockwell Station and shot him seven times in the head. 'They think he was one of the suicide bombers.'

Nikolai whistles. 'I don't believe. London is crazy right now.' Carefully, he climbs off the bed. 'I will take a bath, it is OK? Maybe it will help my arm, it is stiff today.'

As I listen to water gushing in between bouts of splashing and melancholy snatches of Russian folk songs, I peep into the bedroom. At the sight of Nikolai's worn trainers under the chair and his comb, Russian–English dictionary and a pile of music manuscript pads on the bedside table, I feel a surge of happiness.

'Come in!' he calls out when I knock on the bathroom door, and then promptly disappears underwater. He surfaces only as I'm starting to worry, teeth bared in a grin. 'You think I will drown?'

'You –' I scoop up water and splash his face, laughing.

'Are you really going back to work next Thursday?' He looks into the bath water. I sit on a chair in the corner. 'It's only a week away. Why not wait till you're better?'

'I have to go, Georgie.'

'Why?'

'The ganger man phoned yesterday. He asks if I am coming back on time. He wants me to work as hod-carrier for rest of the project – it means moving bricks to the bricklayers. He says if I can't, I must say now and they will ask agency for someone to replace me.'

I help him out of the bath. He steps carefully but shows no signs of discomfort. I pass him a towel from the heated rail and watch his shoulder muscles ripple as he flicks it across his back. He puts down the towel. I go to him, press my face into the valley of his chest, inhaling the scent of herbal bath gel. His hairs tickle my nose. I let my fingertips trail the firm contours of his stomach, down over the ridges of his penis. My drowsy desire of these past days has become something else. I ache for him.

He takes my hand and leads me into the bedroom.

At first I'm worried about hurting him, aware of his murmurs of discomfort when I move too suddenly or too strongly. His body seems strangely unfamiliar next to mine. As he begins to respond though, I can't hold back. My body is no longer mine; it has become part of him.

We lie in silence, arms draped around each other. I feel wonder, exhilaration, joy and sadness all jumbled together. Before, with other men, sex was good enough, most of the time. At times it was little more than the satisfaction of a physical need, as necessary as a coat on a cold day. Other times, it was damned good.

But it has never been like this.

37

At last, another glimpse. You are framed perfectly in the window, all five foot eight inches of you. Blinds left open, no lights on yet. I can't see what you're wearing but I can imagine. You're naked except for the silky gown that just covers your perfect little butt.

Is he in there with you? Is he waiting on your bed to welcome you? Is he at it again, diddling you with that greasy schlong of his? God knows where it's been. Up how many cute little Ruski girls. Boys too, I shouldn't wonder. God help me, I can't think of him with you. It makes me want to puke.

I've found a much better vantage point from this lane beside the row of cottages. Once I've climbed up onto your back wall – thanks to a handy dustbin, that's not difficult – I have an almost uninterrupted view of the back of your flat, including your bedroom window. It's not too much of a leap down into the garden, should I ever wish to try. Probably a bit of a scramble back up, but hey. As luck would have it, your lime tree is right beside the wall, big enough to provide shelter from prying eyes. I'm sitting here, rugged up in my fleece (green, of course), the mini thermos in my backpack full of hot tea. My Nokia is fully charged so I can play Snake on it while I'm waiting.

What am I waiting for, exactly? You may well ask. He's not going to rush out into the garden and give it to you out on the lawn, is he? But the nights are getting even warmer. You'll be leaving the bedroom window open soon enough. I'll be able to hear you and him at it. I want to hear the sound of the two of you going full throttle. Just the once. I know, that makes me sound like some saddo. But I need to hear the cries you make when you're being screwed by him, dear girl. Will you be the same with him as you were with me?

There's a noise again below. Snuff snuff, snuff snuff. A hedgehog? A fox? It's unlikely to be human – it's pretty quiet round here after dark. Too many weird people about, I suppose. The folks in these cottages must all be asleep or watching telly. It's hard to tell, given that the only windows at the front are small bathroom ones with frosted glass. How convenient is that? You wouldn't think the town planners would allow it.

I wonder what your neighbours would think if they spotted me. There's someone up to no good, casing the joint? Who's that creepy git who hasn't yet grown up, playing in his tree house? But no one is likely to spot me up here in the dark, hidden by this mass of leaves.

Oh, nearly forgot. The other night an owl landed on a branch, three feet from my face. I looked into his big yellow eyes and it was like communing with a kindred spirit. Stock still it was, watching out for its prey.

38

We stay inside on Saturday. The weather is rainy and cool, the humidity of previous days gone. Nikolai claims the kitchen table and sets to work, poring over sheets of music with a pencil in hand, occasionally groaning, sighing or shouting in triumph. Often he seems not to know I'm there and doesn't respond if I talk to him. There is a final part to come that's giving him trouble and he's revising the first two parts that aren't yet perfect. I ask how he can do this without his keyboard. The music he's written is in his head, he tells me – he doesn't need to play it.

As Nikolai works, I busy myself around the flat. I wonder what it would be like to have him living with me permanently. Would his moods drive me to distraction? Would my need for solitude make me send him away, or would I grow accustomed to his presence? I smile at myself for harbouring such thoughts. Give up my cherished independence? How could I be considering such a thing?

Late in the afternoon, he pulls himself away from his composition for long enough to eat.

'It's going well, isn't it?' I say, handing him a sandwich. 'I remember when you started this, you weren't sure whether you could finish it.'

'I find something inside, I did not know it was there. Now I have the will to finish, whatever happens – and I find someone to inspire me.' He chomps on the sandwich.

'Me?' As usual, I'm not certain whether he's serious. 'Well, I'll expect to get a recording when it's finished – how long do you think it'll take?'

'I don't know. I am trying to make something that is different from other music. I want people to hear my music and know it is me. That I am not Stravinsky or Kapustin. Maybe people will not understand; they will not like or they will think it is too different. But I must do what I can before it is too late.'

The torrent of words stops. I smile, he sounds so earnest.

'You're still young. You have plenty of time to leave your mark on the world.'

'My head tells me it is true, but something makes me not believe.' He hunches his shoulders, his face clouding. 'Sometimes I am angry at myself that I take this job that robs me of time and makes me so tired I cannot work on my music; that hurts my body so I cannot play. I tell myself that what I want, it will not come easy.'

I leave him to get on with his work, thinking how he has changed over the months I've known him. At first, his energy and resolve to create seemed unfocussed, as if consumed by the effort of simply surviving. But now, his project has taken hold of him and given purpose to his life.

Next morning, I turn on the radio to hear that the police killed the wrong man. The suspected terrorist shot at Stockwell Station wasn't a terrorist, after all; he was a Brazilian electrician. The would-be suicide bombers are still being chased by police in 'the biggest ever manhunt in the UK'. The *News of the World* have offered a £100,000 reward for information leading to the capture of the bombers.

'It is crazy,' Nikolai says as we read *The Sunday Times* over breakfast. 'Now everyone is a terrorist. We cannot even go on train without the police shooting at us.'

Shortly after eleven, the phone rings. I hurry to take it, thinking it might be someone else asking if the barbeque is still on. I set the date last month and invited people. Despite the unpromising weather forecast and recent grim events, I've decided not to cancel. Nikolai has been looking forward to it, and it's ages since I've had friends over.

But it's my father on the phone.

'Hello, Georgie. There's something I'd like to talk to you about.'

I tell him to come over. Though I still haven't forgiven my father for his comments about Nikolai, my anger towards him has lessened. However misguided he might be, I realise whatever he said was out of genuine concern.

I tell Nikolai my father will be here soon. He drops a half peeled prawn onto the plate and stares at me. 'He is coming here?'

'He wants to talk to me about something.'

Smoke puffs into the air. Drops of rain fall, making the glowing coals hiss. I turn the last of the steak and sausages. Around me, voices merge with the thrum of power tools.

All of the gang have turned up, along with some climbing friends and a few others. Nikolai must have said something funny because Ella is having a good old belly laugh, tossing her head back and brandishing off-white teeth. Beside her, Cath is smiling at Tim who's popping a succession of rice crackers into his mouth.

We've set up the barbeque under the lime tree, which protected us from an earlier shower. Instead of the usual topics of house prices and climate change, all anyone is talking about are the recent terrorist attacks. I've encouraged Nikolai to mingle with the guests. He's a natural host, friendly to everyone, seeming to take genuine pleasure in the occasion.

Then Tim signals that the doorbell has rung and heads inside. I put down the tongs and follow. My father steps into the kitchen as Tim goes back to the barbeque. I move halfway towards him and stop, waiting to see if he will approach me. He doesn't.

'So,' I say, 'what did you want to tell me?'

'It can wait a little longer.' He glances towards the garden. 'That smells good.'

'I'm having a barbeque. Stay, if you like.'

I only say it to be polite; that's the last thing I want. But it seems wrong not to invite to him.

He smiles. 'I might stay for a quick bite, why not?'

'Nikolai's here. He had a fall at work.' I tell him what happened.

The furrows on my father's forehead deepen. 'That sort of accident isn't unusual. I've known quite a few like it over the years.' He excuses himself to go to the bathroom.

I warn Nikolai that my father is here.

'Sure,' he replies, as if he couldn't care less.

I introduce my father to some of my other friends and rejoin Nikolai, Ella, Cath and Tim. All four look serious.

'They'll have to catch them soon,' Cath says.

'Christ, let's hope so,' Ella replies. 'These people deserve everything they get. If that's the right word for them. Animals wouldn't behave like that.'

'Many Muslims can't tolerate anyone who doesn't believe what they believe.' This is from my father who appears beside me, glass of wine in hand. 'They think all infidels should be killed. They want to overthrow all Western governments and wage their jihad.'

No one speaks. Nikolai, who's digging into the grass with the toe of his trainer, looks up and laughs disparagingly.

'I think that is not true for most Muslims. If we are afraid of all Muslims, if we hate all Muslims, more of them will join the war against us. Then there will be even more suicide bombers.'

'So you think we should just carry on and let them plant bombs on our trains?'

'I do not say that.' Nikolai speaks in a quiet, steady voice. He draws himself upright. 'I said you must not think all Muslims are terrorists. I have friend who is Muslim. He is good friend. He is not going to bomb the train tomorrow.'

'How do you know?' My father glares at Nikolai. 'He's a damn sight more likely to bomb a train than your typical white bloke, that's for sure.'

'That is stupid thing to say.'

'No, it's not stupid.' My father lowers his free arm to his side, as if about to draw an invisible sword.

'Muslim people aren't all the same,' I say. 'That's the point he's making.'

'No, the point is,' – my father jabs his fingers in the air, addressing everyone in the garden – 'any of them could become a terrorist, tomorrow. A kid hears some imam at the mosque or falls in with the wrong crowd at college or chances on a radical website… Those young men who created carnage two weeks ago – their families didn't think they were terrorists, did they? The way I see it, we *should* be a little scared of *all* Muslims. Who knows what one of them might do next? Because you're either on the side of those fanatics or you're against them.'

No one speaks. Cath fiddles with her silk scarf, Tim rubs his thinning hair and Ella looks at me as if I ought to say something. Nikolai stands ruler straight, eyes blazing.

'Sorry, folks, I'm a bit sensitive at the moment.' My father's cough is vaguely apologetic. 'My godson was in one of the bombed trains.' He checks his watch and turns to me. 'I'd better be off. Enjoy the rest of the party.'

I follow him into the kitchen.

'You might be upset about Sean,' I say shutting the door behind me, 'but that's no excuse for you to talk like that to my friends.'

'You mean your new boyfriend?' His upper lip curls. 'He's moved in, hasn't he? I saw his stuff in the bathroom. After everything I said, you've let him move in with you.'

'For Christ's sake. Since when was moving in with someone a crime?'

My father's jaw tightens.

'Let's get this straight, Georgie. I have no objection whatsoever to you having a boyfriend. What I object to is you sheltering a terrorist sympathiser when my godson was nearly killed because some radical thinks Allah is going to shower him with virgins.'

'A terrorist sympathiser? What are you talking about?'

'I'll tell you what I'm talking about. I found the answer to your question.'

I stare at my father in confusion.

'Don't you remember? You asked me if I could get a police check done on Vakha Dagayev. Jimmy ran a check yesterday. He was taking extended leave after a heart condition was diagnosed, so he couldn't do it before.' My father pauses, stroking his chin, as if enjoying making me wait.

'So? What did he find?'

'Vakha is a known Chechen radical – and Muslim, by the way. The French police questioned him about a year ago. He was part of a group that was planning to bomb a shopping centre in Paris, supposedly to promote the cause of Chechen independence. Their aim was to get Russian forces out of Chechnya. He was implicated with the others but the police didn't have enough evidence to charge him and had to let him go. He's living in Bethnal Green now. That's all they've got on him. But I think it's enough, don't you?'

I can't speak. It's what I suspected. It's what I told myself couldn't be true.

My father stares accusingly at me. 'Do you know this Vakha Dagayev?'

'No, Nikolai told me about him. He's a student at Imperial College. I know they've met up a few times. His parents came to England because of the war in Chechnya.'

'Your boyfriend has some fucking dubious friends, Georgie. I don't know what this is all about, but it sure as hell doesn't look good from where I'm standing.'

'There must be an explanation –'

A derisive snort. 'Oh, yes, I think there's an explanation, a very obvious one. Nikolai is mixed up with violent extremists – terrorists, in other words. Who knows, maybe he's even one himself.'

Voices flow through the open window from the garden. I hear myself laugh, a brittle bark.

'Nikolai a terrorist? It doesn't make any sense. He's Russian, he fought against the Chechens.'

'Some of the most ardent fanatics were originally on the other side. They have to atone for their guilt by going even further the other way.' He glances at the window and lowers his voice. 'Maybe he just likes their company. Only from where I sit it looks a little strange.'

'I don't believe Nikolai could ever be involved in anything like that.'

But as I say this, I know it's not true. I don't know what I believe about Nikolai any more. I try to think clearly, to put aside the conflicting emotions inside me. I want to shout out how wrong my father is. But pushing against this are my own doubts about Nikolai and a desperate need to understand.

When my father finally speaks, his voice is stiff with anger.

'I know this is difficult for you, Georgie. You have quite a thing for this guy, that's plain to see. But I think you should ask yourself if you really want to shack up with some guy who, for all you know, could be a fucking terrorist. Just give it some consideration, that's all I ask.'

'You'd better go.' I fight to keep my voice steady. 'And I'd appreciate it if you left us both alone from now on.'

He marches down the hall and lets himself out. I go back to my guests and make an attempt to be sociable. But inside, I'm seething – and a tiny bit afraid. As soon as everyone has left, I go to lie down. I need to be alone, to try to get my thoughts into place.

Minutes later, Nikolai opens the bedroom door. His faces twists into an ugly mask.

'What your father says out there, I cannot believe. We should be afraid of all Muslims? It is crazy.'

I lift my head up from the pillow and say nothing, hoping he will run out of steam.

'You know what I think? He is afraid of everything he cannot understand. He is afraid that I will take you into a world where he cannot reach you.'

'It's because of what happened to Sean,' I reply, putting my head down again. 'It's frightened him. He'd never talk like that normally.'

Nikolai responds with an openly disdainful expression.

'I'd rather not talk about this any more.' I turn onto my side. 'I'm tired, I need to rest for a while.'

'What is the matter, Georgie? Why are you like this?'

'I'm upset with something my father told me. I don't want to talk about it right now.'

He turns away.

39

My alarm goes off at seven on Monday morning as usual. I throttle it and consider getting out of bed. Cutting through my bleariness, the conversation with my father comes back to me, now laughably unreal. Vakha was arrested last year on suspicion of terrorism? Nikolai is involved with radical separatists? It's absurd, surely.

Even if what my father says is the truth, the police might be wrong about Vakha. They released him, after all. But suppose Vakha *is* some kind of extremist, willing to murder people in aid of the separatist cause. It doesn't follow that Nikolai is an extremist as well. That is a leap too far. Whatever Vakha may have done, I'm certain that my father is wrong about Nikolai. He is willing to believe the worst about Nikolai because he's a manual labourer with nothing to his name and no prospects except his ambition to be a composer. He can't imagine someone like that being a kind, decent person.

But I can't point the finger at my father without pointing it at myself too. I am the one who asked for that information in the first place. I am the one who poked around in Nikolai's personal stuff, made assumptions as to what it all meant and suspected the worst about Vakha. And I am the one who violated Nikolai's trust.

'I have a meeting this morning,' I say, attempting to extricate myself from the warm body beside me.

Nikolai pulls me back. 'Take the day off.'

'I can't.'

Jake has decided that we need to update WholeHealth's image to increase its appeal to men in their twenties and thirties; I am meant to be contributing to a brainstorming session. Just the thought of it depresses me.

'You cannot miss one day?' Nikolai brushes the hair from my face and looks searchingly into my eyes. 'I will be back at work in just three days. We could enjoy this day together, go somewhere.'

It's too tempting. I say I'll phone in sick.

We eat a late breakfast. Nikolai asks what exactly my father has said to upset me. I'm about to tell him everything right now and insist that he explains himself. But that might only make things worse. He would tell me nothing. What's more, he would know that I've doubted him and he'd be furious with me.

One way or another, I need to find out what Nikolai is hiding from me.

In the afternoon, at Nikolai's urging, we take a bus into central London. Everywhere we go, groups of armed police guard entrances to Tube stations and hunker down inside armoured vans, as if preparing for an imminent invasion.

First we go to the National Portrait Gallery, then the National Gallery. My interest is waning, I admit, by the time we've trudged past interminable gloomy paintings with religious or mythological themes. Finally, I attempt to tear Nikolai away from the painting of Diana the goddess of hunting.

'Let's go.' I tug his arm. 'It's nearly five. If we go back any later, we'll be crushed by commuters.'

Back at my flat, Nikolai helps me prepare a lamb stew. He can lift large saucepans now without difficulty.

'You are quiet today,' he says as we eat. 'Tell me, what is the matter?'

'It's nothing,' I lie. 'I'm just tired.'

By the time we've cleared away, it's getting on for 10 p.m.. I leave Nikolai in the office checking his emails and go into the bedroom. On the chest of drawers beside my perfume is his comb, missing several teeth, and below it, his Russian–English dictionary. Something is poking out from inside – a letter, perhaps. He sometimes puts letters he receives in English there so that he can translate any words he doesn't understand.

I take out a sheet of A4 paper folded in half, and open it. The paper is thin – poor quality. Printed on it is a photograph, roughly 5cm by 3cm. The colours are garish and leak into one another. It's of a young man's face – no, a boy's face. It is slender, the features delicate. He's looking past the camera with a warm, open expression. A vague darkness hugs his upper lip. I feel a maternal stirring. He's the sort of boy who might tempt me to become a mother, if that makes any sense.

I turn over the paper. On the back is written in black felt-tip pen: *Akhmed Shoygu Born 18 April 1989 Died 1 February 2005*

My mind scrambles to decipher the meaning of the words. Akhmed Shoygu is a Chechen name, I guess. The photograph shows a Chechen boy who died aged sixteen. How did he die, I wonder.

The usual night sounds intrude into the room, unnaturally sharp: the clack of a distant train, the click of hot water pipes. From the office, a computer bleep, a series of squeaks from the adjustable chair. Footsteps down the hall. I quickly fold the paper, put it back and close the dictionary before Nikolai comes in.

But he goes on into the bathroom. I sit down on the bed, listening to him sing snatches of a Borodin melody as he showers.

We emerge from dark woods into sunshine. I stop and wait for Nikolai to catch up. It's early the following afternoon. I've phoned in sick again, saying I hope to be back at the office tomorrow, Wednesday. Jake tells me to get plenty of rest.

Behind me, harsh panting. 'You are like goat on cocaine, Miz! Only goat is not so fast.'

His limp is starting to show. We're on Hampstead Heath again, this time on a well-defined path.

'We stop at the café, maybe.' He yawns.

'Are you OK?'

'I did not sleep well last night. Bad dreams again.'

We come to Kenwood House. The woman behind the counter in the café stares at Nikolai as if she thinks that any second he might reach for a detonator hidden in his back pocket. Perhaps it's his dark looks. Apart from that, many people are jumping at their own shadows. Police have warned that the men responsible for the attempted transport bombings last week could attack again at any time. This seems to be fuelling a kind of mass paranoia, making otherwise rational people imagine the most unlikely things. I am one of them, perhaps.

'Georgie. You will have Earl Grey?'

'Yes, please. Sorry, I was miles away.'

I lead the way to an outside table well away from the other customers, beside clumps of bee-strewn flowers. Nikolai smiles at a small girl licking an ice-cream cornet. I try to find my courage.

'You are strange today, Georgie. I look for you and you are not there.'

'I'm sorry. I didn't sleep well, either.' He knows it's not why I'm preoccupied, though, I'm sure. His eyes scrutinise my face.

'What else happened in Chechnya, Nikky? It's not just Zara, is it?' Suddenly I have a hunch there's much more that he's not told me, something that troubles him as much as the Chechen woman does.

He drinks his Coke as if he hasn't heard, then glances around. 'Not here.'

I look around too. There aren't that many people; none close enough to overhear.

'Please,' I say. 'Tell me.'

An unfathomable expression crosses his face; I feel a tweak of guilt. Do I really need to know this? Would dredging up yet another piece of his past serve any purpose apart from setting off more nightmares? But I have to know who this man is. I trust that he won't hurt me, yet I know he's capable of extreme violence. He killed while serving his country and killed again as a civilian in a torrent of anger. What more might he have done?

'You remember the boy milking the cow?'

His eyes fix upon my teacup; intermittent sunshine lights his face as he talks. He keeps his voice low and from time to time I have to lean in closer to catch what he's saying.

'After we left Zara's house, we drive him back to base. We all know that he is not who we look for; this boy would not be in yard milking cow if he has just killed our soldiers. But Lieutenant Krizsky must blame someone. The boy is old enough, he says, any boy that age is able to fight. We put him in the lock-up – it is underground room where we keep prisoners. The lieutenant says we must get confession from the boy. He is one of the fighters.

'Leon and Pavel go to question him first. Four hours later, I am writing letter to my sister and the lieutenant orders me to go to the boiler room. He says he has enough of this stubborn boy; I must go now. He will know I am Chechen lover if I don't do this. I must get confession by dawn or we are all in big trouble.

'It is very cold outside but inside this room it is like sauna. Leon and Pavel wear only trousers and boots. The boy is lying on floor with hands tied behind back. He is shaking, his face is bleeding. They have put black cloth over his eyes. "Hey, join the party," Pavel says when I go in. He kicks the boy in knee and laughs when boy cries. He asks names of the men he was with who attack our unit. The boy says it was not him, he knows nothing. Pavel kicks again and asks where they attack from. "It is not me," the boy says again.

'Then it is my turn. I tell the others to go, I take cloth from his eyes and give him my water. I ask who he is. His name is Alihan. He is intelligent boy. He speaks good Russian. His father, mother and sister were killed in a rocket attack, only he is left. He has gentle soul, I think. I am sorry for him. I do not believe he fights anyone.

Leon and Pavel come back. They say we must keep on – they do not want to tell the lieutenant there is no confession. I say no, the boy has enough.

'I take him back to the lock-up. He asks me if I will let him go. I am afraid of what will happen to him, where they will take him to. Then I think of what the lieutenant will do to me. I will be put in cell for helping the enemy, or worse.

'When I go back, Leon and Pavel are drinking vodka. I join them. It gives us courage. At dawn we go to the lieutenant and say we have no confession. He says the boy makes a fool of us. He tells us to get the boy. We go for walk. We go behind the school into the forest where there is no one. The lieutenant tells the boy to stand in front of tree, holds up pistol and shoots him in the head. He tells us to dig hole for body. Afterwards we swear to him we will say nothing to anyone.

'After that day, I feel hate. For the lieutenant and for myself more. I ask myself why I did not help this boy. Why instead I am such coward that I help to kill him. I can never forgive myself for this.'

Nikolai closes his eyes for a while, then wipes his hands on his T-shirt and drinks the rest of his Coke.

My mouth is dry. I don't trust myself to speak. Far away, cutlery clinks against polite laughter.

We leave the café and follow the path around Kenwood House. People do things that seem surreal in their ordinariness. We walk in silence down the path across a smooth, wide lawn. At the footbridge over the lake, I stop.

'Why didn't you leave the army after that?'

Nikolai, ahead of me, leans over the handrail. He peers down into the water.

'I have just one month before they let me go. I tell myself to wait, I will do my duty for my country.'

'Did you ever feel you had to – I don't know – make amends for what happened? I mean, like helping the Chechen people, doing something to make things better for them?'

A furrow forms on his brow. He raises himself to his full height, looking down on me. His stare seems to penetrate my skin.

'Yes, I would like to help them. I believe they have right to want independence from Russia. But I do not wish to fight for their cause.' His eyes narrow. 'You want to know something? I heard about Russian soldier who fought in Chechnya in the first war. He became Muslim. He joined the Chechens fighting in his village, he wore green scarf on his head to show he is on their side.'

'What made him change sides?'

'They say it is after he sees what his comrades do to Chechen prisoners.' He steps closer; I can see the pulse in his temple. 'I am not him, Georgie.'

My heart thumps in my chest. I say nothing.

We carry on through the woods; I hardly notice where we are. The path twists and leads us to a pond covered in green slime. I toss a stone into the water. A ragged black shape appears, quickly swallowed up by slime.

Nikolai stands gazing at the water, his face stony, then speaks without looking at me.

'We go now, OK?'

I don't move.

'There's something I need to know.' I draw a deep breath. 'Why are you meeting with Vakha?'

A shadow crosses his face. 'I am sorry, Georgie. I say again, it is better that you do not know.'

He walks on. I follow a few feet behind. Suddenly, he spins around to face me.

'Why do you ask me about Vakha? What does it matter to you?'

'I wanted to check a few things out. I found out something the other day... Something disturbing.'

'What do you find out?'

My nails dig deep into my palms. 'That this guy you've been meeting with is suspected of being a radical separatist. A terrorist.'

Nikolai moves closer. A muscle at the corner of his eye twitches.

'Who tells you this?'

'I can't say.'

Breathing hard, he grips my arm. 'Georgie, who tells you this?'

I say nothing.

'This person you hear from – they say that I am terrorist too?'

A blanket of cold sweat nestles against my skin.

'I need to know what's going on, Nikky. I know that the police arrested Vakha because they suspected him of plotting to blow up a shopping centre in Paris. I know you've been meeting him and that you never want to talk about it. What am I supposed to think? No, that's crazy, Nikolai wouldn't be involved with someone like that? Tell me, what am I supposed to think?'

I can't stop talking. My voice starts to tremble.

'I know you can't control your anger and I know you've killed someone because of it. You've told me about your experiences in Chechnya. I know you've got a mountain of guilt locked inside you because of what happened over there. How do I know what you're capable of?'

'Fuck you.'

It's no more than a murmur. His fist clenches at his side as he steps towards me. I stand my ground and wait for him to hit me. But there's only a quick sideways movement of his head, like a thought snapping into place, before he turns and walks away.

Nikolai doesn't return till gone 10pm. He lets himself in, comes into the kitchen, walks over to where I'm washing up and looks at the dish of risotto lying on the cooker. Then he looks at me, his expression cold.

'Nikolai, please. Let me explain –'

'You don't need to explain.' He turns away.

'I've made dinner.'

'I am not hungry.' He stops in the doorway. 'By the way, I know it is your father who tells you these things. You don't need to pretend they are from someone else.'

For a moment I'm speechless.

'You're right, my father told me about Vakha. He asked his detective friend in the Metropolitan Police to check the computer to see if Vakha has a police record.' I square up to him. 'He did it because I asked him to.'

'You ask him to do this?' Nikolai digs his fingernail into the door frame, his expression turning darker. I have an urge to run and hide. 'I cannot believe.'

'When I saw that note in your flat, I was worried about what it could mean. Vakha, a meeting, local action… I just wanted to put my mind at rest. I'm sorry Nikky, I probably shouldn't have done it.' I take a deep breath. 'But I did do it, and now I know the truth –'

'The truth?' he wrinkles his nose. 'So now you have the truth, so-called, it is OK for you to check into my stuff and go to police about my friend?'

'Nikolai, listen –'

He is furious as he raises his left hand and slams a fist onto the worktop.

I start at the sound. Nikolai turns and strides away.

40

It's raining steadily when I leave the flat. At the end of the street I stop and consider turning back. I've left Nikolai in my bed; he came back in the middle of the night. I decided I'd let him sleep after he didn't respond to my attempts to wake him. But now I wish I'd persisted and tried to fix things between us.

At Belsize Park Tube Station I join the surge onto the train, squeeze into the compartment and hunch down into my own space, trying to block out everyone else.

The office is much as I left it, filled with the drone of people and machines. It seems like weeks since I was last here, not five days. I switch on my computer. My calendar shows my weekly catch-up with Jake and a marketing briefing in the afternoon. A stack of emails awaits me, the subject lines depressingly predictable: 'Dispute over company direction'; 'Rebranding exercise'; 'New corporate logo'; 'Stylesheets for External Communication'. I delete as many as I can and start the most pressing tasks on my list. But it's impossible to concentrate. My thoughts keep veering towards Nikolai. I imagine him in my flat, wonder if he's pleased I'm not there. Is he still angry with me? Should I have stayed?

Halfway through the morning, unable to put it off any longer, I call his mobile. It goes straight to voicemail. I hang up.

I make myself another coffee. In the kitchen, three people are discussing a dawn raid on a house in Birmingham. A suspected attempted suicide bomber has been arrested. I take my coffee to the window and stare at glistening rooftops. I manage to resist going home until mid-afternoon, then bolt from the building like a child released from school on the last day of term.

The journey takes longer than usual. I fumble and drop my key on the porch in my hurry to get inside. A smell of burned toast lingers in the hall. No sounds of TV or radio, just the kitchen clock's ridiculously loud tick. Beside the sink, a knife on a crumb-specked plate. On the kitchen table, the newspaper is open. Nikolai's music books, scattered at the end of the table when I left, have vanished.

I open the bedroom door. On his bedside table is an empty mug stained with tea, a used travel card and a blunt pencil. His comb and dictionary have gone, and his big holdall is no longer crushed into the bottom of my wardrobe. I check the bathroom. His toothbrush is missing from the mug; there's no striped toiletry bag on the cabinet. Finally, I go into the living room. On the coffee table, on the back of a gas bill envelope, Nikolai's impatient, large-looped handwriting:

Georgie,

I am very sad to hear the things that you said yesterday. I thought you believed me when I said I am on the right path now. I am sad to find out that you do not trust me, despite what you say.

I must be alone now to think about many things. Please do not try to talk to me or come to see me. I will call you when I am ready.

Nikolai

His front-door key is beside the note.

For the next two days it stays damp and cloudy. The weather suits my mood. I torment myself with thoughts that I will never see Nikolai again. I try to imagine never again hearing him laugh, never again holding his hand.

I resolve to do as he's asked and not contact him. Though it won't be easy, I want to respect his wishes, from pride as much as anything else.

I find some solace in routine. I go the office, wrap myself as best I can in my work, then come home and eat dinner in front of the TV.

Events taking place in London are impossible to ignore, providing some distraction from thoughts of Nikolai. On Thursday, pictures of the failed Tube bomb ingredients are shown, including a stash of nails. The next day, the hunt for the would-be bombers reaches a climax when police storm a west London flat and arrest the three remaining suspects. The critical moments are shown on that evening's BBC news: two bare-chested men emerge onto their balcony to police waiting in padded jackets and black balaclavas.

Each day, when I've had enough of the news, I pour a glass of wine and lie on the sofa with my Ray Charles or Nina Simone CDs playing, tears flowing freely at every heart-wrenching song. It is then that I'm most tempted to call Nikolai and implore him to come back.

I spend Saturday alone, finding things to occupy me around the flat.

Cath and Ella both phone to enquire how I am; I tell them Nikolai has gone back to his place as we've quarrelled. I still haven't heard from my father, which is fine by me as I have no wish to speak to him. There's only one person I want to hear from.

I find a close-up shot of Nikky on my phone, taken after he'd been fooling around pulling faces. His dark brown eyes squinting in the sunlight, full lips caught in a huge smile. A lump comes to my throat. I print the photo and put it on a ledge in the kitchen beside Cath's Easter Island postcard.

Later that evening, unable to think of sleeping, I find myself cleaning kitchen cupboards, thinking about Nikolai. For months he has kept so much from me. What else might he still be hiding? Ella's comment comes back to me. *It's that look in his eyes – like something's broken.*

I put down my cloth. How well do I know Nikolai? Is there another man underneath the one I know, who's quite different?

Yes, it is possible. Although he's omitted to tell me important things, he's never actually deceived me, to my knowledge. Quite the opposite – he's revealed a great deal of himself, admitting his own weaknesses, failures and wrongdoings. As far as I can see, he is genuinely striving to overcome the violence of his past. And he believes that there should be peace in Chechnya, not war. It doesn't make sense that he would want to get involved with terrorists.

On the other hand, there are many things I still don't know about him. We've had different experiences, backgrounds and ways of seeing the world. His views often diverge from mine. We disagree over whether footballers should be paid more than social workers. He stands up for the rights of the poor; I argue for incentives to become rich. More often than not, we agree to differ. 'You are capitalist!' he would fume. 'Socialist!' I'd retaliate.

Does he omit to tell me certain things because he thinks there is an unbridgeable gap between us? One of our conversations comes back to me. We were watching a news item on TV about the upcoming trial of the sole surviving captured hostage-taker from the Beslan school siege. Hundreds of people died after being held hostage by 31 armed Chechen separatists, the report said, including 186 children, though it was believed that the botched rescue attempt by Russian special forces caused many of the deaths.

'It's beyond me,' I remarked, 'how any civilised person could consider holding innocent children hostage.'

'The Chechens were wrong to do this thing,' Nikolai replied. 'But I understand why they did.'

Thousands of Chechen children had been killed by Russian bombs and missiles, he said, and countless Chechens had been taken away by the Russian military, never to come back. The hostage-takers acted because the Russian people did not know what their government was doing, and the rest of the world didn't want to know.

'The TV in Russia, it always shows the suffering of innocent Russian people by the terrible Chechens. It does not show the houses hit by rockets and bombs, what happens to the old women and children inside. They are innocent too. I am not saying they were right to do this thing. But they had a reason.'

I hadn't argued. His views didn't surprise me – besides, what he said made sense. I also believed in trying to understand people, even if they seemed beyond understanding.

But now, remembering his conviction, I'm troubled. In a way, Nikolai *has* switched sides, exactly as my father suggested. He understands only too well the hostage-takers' motives – is it possible he might be willing to go further and take some sort of action? He killed as a soldier in Chechnya and after the war he killed Ivan. Given sufficient motive, who could say that he wouldn't be prepared to kill again? I recall how upset Nikolai had got in the café after reading about the assassination of Chechnya's former president. Had that been the trigger for him to get involved with Chechens fighting against Russia?

Shocked by my thoughts I go into my office, suddenly wondering what I might find on my computer. Nikolai was the last person to use it; before he left he was using it most days to go on the Internet. His propelling pencil lies on the desk beside half a sheet of A4 paper torn off my writing pad. The computer has been left in sleep mode, as usual. I open the web browser and click the Show History tab. The most recent site visited is a news report from 19 July headed 'Worst attack in months in Chechnya against the Russian military'.

Separatists fired on a minibus carrying security forces in Znamenskoye, it says. When a second vehicle came to help, the rebels set off a bomb, equivalent to 27.5 tons of TNT, killing 14 people including two children. One was riding a bicycle past the scene at the time. The article concludes that this was the most serious assault on Russian forces since the first months of the Second Chechen War in 1999.

The information does not seem particularly significant, apart from indicating that three weeks ago the fighting was hotting up again between the two sides in Chechnya. I look around the desk; Nikolai has left no other sign of his activity. I glance in the wastepaper bin. It's empty except for a crumpled serviette and a Coke can. I go into my bedroom and look around the chair he was using for his clothes; there's a lighter on the floor, that's all. Inside the wardrobe, his old trainers rest in the lower drawer. I pick them up, intending to put them in the hall to give him if he returns. One shoe has a bulge in the foot. I put my hand in and pull out a clear plastic bag folded into a ball. Inside are some scrunched-up pieces of paper. I smooth them out. They're printed, roughly torn. I place them on the carpet, print side up. When I've finished fitting them together I can make out all of the words:

Caucasus Action meeting 21 July

Target –

Russian Orthodox Church SW7 1NH

10am service Sunday 31 July

Plan –

Kalashnikovs explosives

Hostages

Beslan school siege

Demand –

Russian forces to leave Chechnya

The walls of the small room press in on me. Black letters dance before my eyes.

Kalashnikovs. Hostages. Beslan.

They want to maim people, kill people. They want to create another Beslan school siege – in London.

I try to recall today's date – 30 July. The 31st is tomorrow. They plan to do this tomorrow. I should go to the police. I should show them what I've found and tell them everything I know about Nikky and his connection with Vakha and Caucasus Action, and everything Nikky told me about what he did in Russia.

Then they'll take him away and lock him up and you'll never see him again. Is that what you want? There's no real evidence that Nikolai is involved with terrorists. He has sympathy for the plight of the Chechen people – big deal. It doesn't mean he's in league with violent separatists.

But everything points to that, doesn't it? Vakha suspected by police of plotting a terrorist attack in Paris. Nikolai's secrecy about his meetings with Vakha. This Caucasus Action group. 'Action' clearly means violent action. They intend to take hostages during a church service. Do they hope to come out alive – or are they prepared to die for their cause? Is Ruslan involved in this plot as well as his son? Is Nikolai?

I recall the words I overheard Nikolai say by the River Thames, several months ago: '*I am on your side, Vakha.*' What else could they mean, except that Nikolai has offered support to a violent extremist, one prepared to kill dozens of innocent people? It all fits. What else do I need to know? I must go to the police before anything terrible happens.

I switch off the computer. I'm afraid. Thoughts stomp around my head. Could Nikolai really be helping Chechens win independence from Russia? Could his frustration and rage at the actions of Russian commanders, along with his own guilt and trauma, have pushed him over the line between justifiable anger and a willingness to commit calculated large-scale murder? Could he really be, as near as damn it, a terrorist?

I want to dismiss the idea as far-fetched – no, as totally bonkers. Yet a flicker of doubt refuses to die. The more I try to snuff it out, the stronger it burns.

I start to cry. The tears flow out of me until I'm surprised they haven't flooded the floor. When they finally stop, I crawl into my huge, empty bed and listen to sounds come and go. Rustling leaves outside the window, passing footsteps on the pavement, the clack-clack-clack-clack of a distant train.

He's a good person, a decent person, I know he is. And I love him. I love him more than ever.

41

At 6 a.m. I wake with a dry mouth, exhausted. I've slept badly, had nightmares. I call Nikolai's mobile and get the automated voicemail. I leave a message asking him to call me urgently. In the next hour I leave ten messages.

I drive to his flat and press his buzzer but there's no answer. I wait there for about an hour until 8 a.m., from time to time trying his mobile. Then I drive home and call 999.

My palms are cold and sweaty. I'm going to turn Nikolai in to the police. I am going to betray my lover on the basis of the words on some scraps of paper.

I hang up.

No, I'm not going to turn him in. There isn't going to be an attack on that church. I don't believe Nikolai would be involved with something like that. If he knew that Vakha or anyone else was planning such a thing, he would do whatever it took to stop them.

I run to the café, where there's a payphone. I call 999 again and ask for the police. As soon as I'm connected I say: 'I have information that there may be a terror attack about 10 a.m. today at the Russian Orthodox Church in Ennismore Gardens, SW7. Can someone check this out urgently please and put some security at the entrance –'

A voice interrupts. I hang up and hurry away in case they try to trace the call.

At 10 a.m. I check the TV and radio news, then the Internet. There's nothing about an attack on a church.

For the rest of the day I check the news every half hour and occasionally try Nikolai's number. I can't breathe properly. I keep stumbling into things and forgetting what I'm doing. I drink cups of tea and in the late afternoon I eat a dry piece of toast.

Around 9 p.m., I allow myself to believe that nothing has happened – and that most likely nothing will happen. The relief I feel is indescribable. It's the taste of the most delicious chocolate dessert, the smell of the most exquisite honeysuckle. I lie on the sofa with the lights dimmed and the stereo on low, enjoying the waves of weariness rolling through me.

I'll go to bed soon, I tell myself. It's gone ten. Tomorrow I must get up early and go to work. But the cushions under my head and

hips provide just the right amount of comfort and the familiar reg-
ularity of my Bach CD lulls me to sleep.

I wake with a start. There's a loud clunk, close by.

A fox knocking over the food-waste bin again? But the sound
has come from the garden side of the flat, not the street side.

Another noise, different. Definitely not from outside.

I open my eyes. Someone is inside my flat.

With a pounding heart, I switch off the stereo, straining for the
slightest sound. There's nothing now, except the almost inaudible
swish of traffic.

The next noise is quieter. From the kitchen.

My heart beats hard and fast. The mallet, it should still be
on the toolbox... I get up, pad along the brightly lit hall to the
cupboard housing the water heater. Clutching the mallet, I creep
towards the kitchen door, not quite shut. A thin strip of darkness
shows in the gap between the door and the frame. I push the door
open.

The room is dark except for a faint wash of light from the hall.
I glance around at the cluttered worktops and table, still bearing my
breakfast bowl and an open *Sunday Times Magazine*. The door leading to the garden is closed. Everything looks the same as it did a
couple of hours ago when I took a beer from the fridge and flopped
onto the sofa – except that one of the sash windows is now wide
open.

I stare at the window. It has been opened from the lower end,
and the blind has been pulled up above the opening. I definitely
didn't leave it like this; I always open the kitchen windows from the
top, hoping that fewer insects might come in. In any case I never
open that one much, even in summer, as this is a burglar-prone area.
There's no sign of forced entry, though. I must have forgotten to
lock the window the last time I shut it.

From outside, snapping and crunching sounds. I go to the window and peer through the opening into the dark garden. A dark
shape moves briefly at the top of the wall by the tangle of rhodo-
dendron bushes. Without thinking, I drag the sash down, snatch the
key from the drawer and lock the window. I pull the blind down
and shut the slats, double-check that the back door is locked and
turn on the overhead spotlights.

The brightness is comforting. For several minutes I sit on the
hall step, listening, while my heart thumps as if I've just sprinted up

Parliament Hill. Only the usual sounds, now: a passing plane, faint voices next door. A dentist lives there; I hardly ever see her.

Without switching on the light, I go into the bedroom and stare out into the garden. No movement. No sign of any people or animals. Whoever or whatever it was must have escaped over the wall into the alleyway. It's low enough for someone agile to climb, if they really want to.

I switch the light on and check the bedroom for signs of disturbance. Then I check the office and bathroom, and go back to check the kitchen once more. Nothing has changed anywhere, at least nothing I can be sure of. My jewellery box is still locked on top of my chest of drawers. My passport is still tucked beside my notebooks and photo albums in the bottom drawer. My turquoise and diamond ring is still on my bedside table and the jade necklace still lies next to the washbasin where I left it. The only thing that isn't the same is the photo of Nikolai in the kitchen. I put it on the ledge; it is now face-down on the worktop. It must have fallen over without me noticing.

An odd sensation goes through me, cold fingertips crawling down my back.

It certainly doesn't look like a burglar has been here. So who has?

Julian. I know it's him. I start to shiver, then my hands start shaking. I make a strong cup of tea and try to collect myself. Whoever was here has now gone. I think about going outside and checking in the shed, and decide against it.

I phone the police. Someone came into my flat while I was asleep, I tell the man who answers. I say I'm being harassed by someone who won't leave me alone and I'm scared. I've already reported his emails and anonymous phone calls. The officer advises me to make sure all my windows and doors are locked before going to bed and whenever I leave the house. He says it would be a good idea to have a burglar alarm fitted too. I can ask my phone company to block calls from any unidentified numbers. If the calls continue, I should contact the police again.

I go to bed edgy. Instead of sleeping naked as I always do, I put on my gym shorts and T-shirt, and keep the hall and kitchen lights on.

I wake again around 1 a.m.. More small noises. They all seem to be outdoors. Unable to sleep, I reach for the phone and press Nikolai's number. I imagine him telling me I'm silly for being afraid, he will come right over. But of course he doesn't pick up. Wherever he is, he isn't thinking of me.

On the third ring, I end the call. I won't go crawling back to him like a frightened little girl. I'll stick to my plan and wait for him to contact me.

I go to the bathroom, swig the remains of a bottle of Night Nurse and wait for the drowsiness to kick in. Maybe the window was left open by a burglar, after all. An opportunistic thief who panicked when he heard me.

In the morning I unlock the kitchen door. There are no footprints visible in the flowerbeds. Some of the ivy choking the wall is broken in places, though, near the end of the garden. I stare up into the lime tree. It's close to the wall, too close, really, from a security point of view.

Then I see it, in the grass. A short stub, tube-shaped. The remains of a packet of Polo mints. My scalp prickles. Julian likes Polos. He sometimes carries a packet around with him. It's got to have been him.

42

From Nikolai Alexandrovich Konstantinov
1 August 2005

Dear Georgie,
I am staying with Ruslan and his wife in Leicester. He has spare room and his wife cooks good meals. I have taken time off from work and am not sure when I will be back to London.

Why I am writing this? I do not expect this will change your view of me, but I want you to know what happens and why I do not tell you everything before. I do not wish for you to remember me as angry man who tries to make you believe what you cannot believe. I hope you will be able to think of me as a good man, one who does what he thinks is right.

I will start with the day Zara is killed. You remember how I am in her house with my fellow soldiers and the lieutenant. What I did not tell you — before we leave, I take a letter that I see in the kitchen. The envelope is addressed to Ruslan Dagayev. I remember she tells me she has brother Ruslan, a chemistry teacher, and when the second war starts he takes his wife and son to Leicester, where his wife has cousin. I send Ruslan the letter and write to him that I was friends with Zara when my unit is staying near in her village. I cannot say all that happens to her but I say she was very good woman, always kind to me.

He writes back to come to see him and his wife one day if I am ever in England. That was five years ago. The week I arrive in UK I visit for three days. They make me feel welcome in their house, they do not ask questions. Ruslan asks me if I will do him favour. When I go back to London, will I talk to his son? He is in last year at university and not doing well. He does not study, he misses lectures. Ruslan is afraid he is on bad path. He thinks Vakha will listen to me, we have the same fire inside us. I tell him yes, I am pleased to help. I think it is way for me to amend for what happens to Zara.

Ruslan tells me that Vakha was arrested last summer when he is staying with some Chechen students in Paris. The police watch them for months then go to make arrests. They find chemicals for bombs in their apartments. They say they have plans to attack embassies and shopping centres. Four of them are in prison, they will go on trial soon for terrorism.

They let Vakha go and one other. Ruslan says he does not believe that his son was helping these people but he is afraid for Vakha. His son no longer speaks to him, there is wall between them. He asks me to find out what Vakha is doing now, if he is under influence of anyone at his university. He hopes I can say something to make him look again at his life.

So Georgie, I tell you about Vakha. I meet him for first time in February, two weeks before I meet you. We go to pub near his place. (He shares house with five students, it is not practical to go there.)

What can I tell you? He has face of angel, such a beautiful boy. He talks fast, good English, better than me.

I buy him pint, he lights cigarette. He says he is moderate Muslim, he does not go in for beheadings. He laughs and I see he makes joke. To hide that he is nervous, I think. He is suspicious of me. He asks me who I am and why I am here. I tell him the truth. His father is concerned for him, and asks me to talk with him. He says I must tell his father that he is not terrorist but he has to stand up for Chechnya, it is his real home.

He tells me he wants to do something that will help his friends who stayed to fight the Russians, and for the memory of his twin brother Akhmed. Akhmed was held by the military after friend of his joined some fighters who tried to shoot down Russian helicopter. He was 16. His family get note saying they will not release Akhmed unless his family gives them $1000. Ruslan does all he can do to get this money but he cannot get it all in the time they give. He is told to collect Akhmed's body. Soon after this Ruslan brings Vakha and his wife here, so the family will be safe.

I say I understand why he is angry – I too have reasons to hate the army officers. I tell him what I have told you, about the boy in Chechnya who I do not let escape and because of this he is shot. I tell how nothing can get rid of my guilt, how sometimes I must stop myself from crying when I see boys of his age.

It is strange, when I make this confession I expect Vakha to be angry with me, to push me away. But it does opposite. He shakes my hand, says he is honoured to know me.

We meet again in same pub. I ask how he will help to make Chechnya free – he is student in London. He tells me he knows Muslim students at Imperial who want to fight back. They are angry that Maskhadov is assassinated. A postgrad called Imran comes to him after lecture and asks if he will join group called Caucasus Action.

I tell Vakha he is better not to fight, peace will not come like this. I say my anger nearly destroys my life, it does not help anyone. He laughs, says I am wrong. The resistance is getting stronger, they will never give up.

The next time we meet, he has joined this group. He tells me a little. There are eight in all, three are chemistry students too and the others are mathematics or engineering students. They plan to take action in London against rich Russians who come to live in their mansions in South Kensington. Their aim is to free Chechnya of Russian military.

I do not ask questions, I try to be like a brother, not his father. But Vakha will not talk to me now, he swore to keep the group's secrets. I tell him I am on his side, if he needs my help I am here for him.

It is true. I care very much for him. He is young and full of passion, and he does not understand how dangerous is what he is doing.

I hear nothing from him then until after the bombs on July 7. He calls me. He is very scared. Imran has told the chemistry students in group to make explosives, they must get ingredients from lab at Imperial. The others must get Kalashnikovs and masks. There is secret plan and the new members are not told what it is about. Vakha says his friends in the group do not want to do these things either but they are too scared to go against Imran. I tell him pretend to do what he is told but really he must persuade his friends to join him to go against Imran. I ask if he will tell me about the plan when he knows more of it. My hope is that maybe I can do something to change their minds, to make them stop. If not, I will report them to the police. I take notes of what they say, for evidence.

They have meeting on July 21 after the failed bombs, the day I am due to meet you. Vakha tells me before he will meet me at the pub but he comes late. We go into street where no one will hear. He is shaking. He lights cigarette and drops it. I cannot believe at first what he says. Imran tells group that they will make Beslan school siege in the Russian church in Kensington. On the last Sunday in July they will go into church and take ten hostages with demand for Russian army to get out of Chechnya. Everyone has list of what they must do.

Vakha's friends say the plan is crazy. If they try to hurt people in the church, they too will be killed. Vakha says he does not agree with Imran's plan, he is not suicide bomber. To take this action in the church is wrong and everyone will hate them – it will bring shame on their heads. Imran says Vakha is Judas, he will go to police and all of the group will go to prison.

Vakha says no one is on Imran's side. He asks for vote of who supports plan. No one does. Imran walks out. Vakha and his friends say they will not be in group any more and the others also say this. So Caucasus Action has gone.

It is small victory. I say he is brave, I am proud of him. After this Vakha tells me he is going to Chechnya for summer to see his friends he left behind five years ago. Then he hopes to retake his final year at Imperial.

I do not know for how long Vakha's good intentions will last. But I am glad that things turn out like this, when I think of what else can happen.

Please understand Georgie, I wanted to tell you this before. But I promise Ruslan that I will not talk about this to anyone and I did not want to expose you to more danger than I have already. Also at the end there was another reason, I confess. I was angry with you. I wanted you to believe me but I could see you were not sure if I told the truth. So I decided to let you believe whatever you wish to believe. Until I have time to think – then I know that I must tell you everything, even if you do not believe me.

I am sorry Georgie for all the pain I have caused you. I want you to know I am grateful for the kindness you showed to me. I now understand that I cannot force you to trust me. It is I who must earn your trust. How can I expect you to keep faith in me when I have shown you only reasons to doubt me?

I wish you happiness and many wonderful things in your future life.
Yours,
Nikolai

43

It's on the doormat when I come in from work. As soon I see the writing on the envelope, I know it's from Nikolai.

I read the letter at the kitchen table. The pages are on pale yellow watermarked vellum. There are no smudges, drink stains or traces of grease. The writing is in dark blue ink, legible though not neat. He's written this in a hurry, I guess. I imagine his hand darting across the sheet without pausing, just as I saw him writing music that first time.

When I finish, I leave the letter and go into the garden. I wander among the flowerbeds for a long time, listening to the sounds of the evening. My emotions go in one direction then another. First relief and euphoria at having learned the truth; I have no doubt that what I have read is true. Then I'm angry at myself for having doubted him. At last they settle into an almost unbearable sadness at the thought of never again seeing him. There's no mention of any future contact between us; it is absolutely clear that he doesn't want or expect to see me again.

I wonder why I should be so stricken by this fact. We never made any promises to each other as far as our relationship was concerned. He told me from the start that one day he intended to go back to Russia. I never imagined anything lasting between us, did I? A well-off career girl hooked up with an illegal immigrant – how could that ever have worked?

Anyway, I'm getting ahead of myself. Nikolai doesn't love me. There's nothing I can do about that. There's no point throwing myself at him.

August creeps towards the halfway mark. As the days pass I try to carry on with my life, though I have little enthusiasm for anything. I still don't speak to my father and he doesn't try to speak to me. Work continues. Everyone is slowing down in the hotter weather; no one seems to notice that I've stopped trying. It's suddenly clear to me that I can't stay in this company – in this career – much longer. It's almost too much effort to pretend to be making an effort. I recall how keen I was on biology at 18 and can hardly believe that I didn't study that or biochemistry at university as I meant to.

More than ever, I wish I hadn't listened to my father when he'd gone on about the difficulties of making it as a researcher and the benefits of a business-related career. 'You'll earn a decent salary,' he said. 'You won't be scrabbling around for a permanent position in a university.' To him, academia was anathema. Choosing a career was not about passion, but pay and practicalities.

My mother just said, 'Do whatever your heart tells you; whatever you do is fine with me.' But after she left I stopped listening to her. Whatever my father said became a good idea by definition. I wasn't so sure of myself any more – or anyone else. I didn't know who I could trust. I had a sneaking suspicion that even people I'd known for a long time might suddenly turn on me and hurt me for no reason. And as far as love went... I didn't trust that, either. I knew my dad loved me but I wasn't quite sure my mother did, despite her statements to the contrary. Though she came back quite often, the fact remained that she spent most of her time hundreds of miles away. I felt superfluous, a tatty old coat replaced by something better.

A few months after my mother left, the shock turned into acceptance. I entered some sort of altered state, like after you've watched some really weird movie, only this one came back day after day. My hope that my mother might change her mind withered. On the plus side, the house was no longer filled with angry and spiteful voices, the sounds of love's slow suffocation. And I could stop worrying about what might happen to my parents because the worst already had.

My best friend said my mother was one of those women who shouldn't have had children – that she'd put her own selfish desires above my wellbeing. My father said most women wouldn't do what she'd done but she did love me... in her own way. He didn't say it outright, not for a long time. But I knew he felt she'd abandoned us both.

Perhaps that sense of being united against a common enemy drew us closer. We took the dog on long walks via local pubs, forgot about keeping the house clean, planted sunflowers in the garden (my mother hated them) and did as many things as possible that she wouldn't have approved of. Well, things we imagined she wouldn't have approved of; my mother was pretty easy-going – more so than most of my friends' mothers.

The first Saturday night without her, Dad and I stayed up till 4 a.m. watching Tarantino and Cronenberg films and gorging on chocolate biscuits. On the spur of the moment one Friday afternoon we drove to Nice in the Mercedes with the dog in the back seat, taking four school days off without permission.

My father encouraged me to focus on the future, to see this change in our family arrangements as an opportunity rather than a disaster. A temporary setback. 'Don't let it get you down, sweetie,' he'd say, giving me a hug. 'We've both got some adjusting to do but we'll get there.'

And we did, after a while. My father got on with the business and dated from time to time. I strummed sad songs on my guitar and did extra stuff after school and on weekends, as he suggested – tennis, drama, orienteering… But they were only ways to fill in time, to distract from the pain of being left behind.

Why was she in Spain without me? She wanted to be with her boyfriend, I got that. He couldn't move his job and she could. But she hadn't asked me if I might like to join her. She'd just assumed that I'd want to stay at my school with my friends rather than start at a new school in Spain. And I couldn't even speak Spanish. Yes, of course. But weren't those just convenient reasons? The real reason she'd gone without me was that she didn't want me around to disrupt her romance.

In those moments that I missed her the most, I tortured myself with the worst things I could imagine. Why did she leave me behind? Didn't she love me enough? Did I have some flaw that made me less lovable? I spent hours wondering what the flaw could be. My habit of forgetting what she asked me to do? Or the way I left the house for long periods without letting her know where I was going? My worsening behaviour at school? The money I stole from her purse?

Or perhaps it wasn't anything like that. She hadn't been able to breastfeed me, she once admitted. And sometimes I'd cried for hours and she hadn't known what to do. Ally said it was more likely to be something like that. Perhaps I'd been such a difficult baby my mother hadn't properly bonded with me.

When I mentioned this to my father, he got angry and said my friend was 'talking out of her arse'. My mother had trouble coping with life, he explained; she had 'black moods' that overcame her and made her behave irrationally. 'She's not herself at the moment,' he would say, as if that explained everything that wasn't right with our family.

Whatever reasons I came up with for my mother's absence, they couldn't stop the thought that sometimes arrived in the middle of the night, that I couldn't tell anyone else about. Who else was going to love me if my own mother didn't? I suppose it was around then that I began to keep people on the outside. Not totally, of course. Just enough to know that if they suddenly upped and left I wouldn't end up a quivering lump of jelly.

Now I'm starting to wonder if I should have seen things differently. Maybe I got things a little muddled and came to the wrong conclusion about my mother. Maybe I should have just listened to what she told me, and everything would have been all right.

After work one evening, I get out my address book and turn to the 'F' section. F for Frances, not M for Mum. Her phone number in Ronda is at the bottom of the page, along with an address. It's in pencil, much faded from when I wrote it down nearly ten years ago. She's not moved since, though.

Without thinking I pick up the handset and dial the number.

There's no answer, just an automated message in someone else's voice. I hang up.

On Saturday evening, I invite Ella over for pasta. Afterwards we watch *Terminator*, which is one of Julian's favourite films. It feels odd that he's no longer around.

When Ella leaves, it's late. I nip outside and scan the road to make sure Julian's car isn't parked anywhere.

I've been trying not to think about who it was in my flat that day, as I probably won't ever know for certain that it was him. But I do think about it. Ever since I found that window open I've been jumpy. Before, I slept through most noises. Now it only takes a creak somewhere in the flat after dark for me to be wide awake for hours. The thud of a car door outside sometimes makes me start. I'll wake up with my heart racing, unable to relax. Sometimes, when I'm watching TV or listening to music, I'll mute the sound and listen to what's around me, in case there's something else I should be hearing. Or I'll get a sudden sense of unease and zip around the flat checking all the windows are shut, as well as the curtains and blinds. Just in case.

I've had a burglar alarm installed and have to punch in a code every time I leave the place. I'm not sure it makes me feel any safer, though.

Around 1 a.m., I get ready for bed. I take off the long, beaded earrings and put them in the jewellery box on my dressing table.

The earrings Julian gave me are still tucked away inside the drawer, unworn. It's silly, but I haven't been able to throw them away.

Once in bed I'm not sleepy any more, of course. I read my Murakami paperback from where I left the bookmark, at just gone halfway. I'm sure I've read this page several times, while only half awake. But it doesn't matter.

After about half an hour I turn off the bedside lamp. I close my eyes and without wanting to, I wonder what Julian's doing. Is he asleep yet? Is he in his flat? Is he on his own or with friends – or with a girl? Is he happy? Maybe he's tired after a hard week at work. Maybe he's finally getting the recognition he thought he deserved. I hope so. That at least would help take his mind off me. Maybe he'll forget about me soon and meet someone else who can love him back. God, I hope so.

I'm at my desk, busy making notes ahead of an afternoon meeting with the ad agency. My desk phone rings and I pick up, wondering who it will be this time. A minute earlier it was someone wanting to know if I needed any temporary staff.

'Georgie?'

The voice startles me, it's so deeply familiar. 'Nikolai?'

'How are you doing?'

'I'm OK. How are you?'

'I am sorry I do not call for so long.' A loud buzzing threatens to obliterate his voice. 'I am leaving work early today. Can you meet me somewhere?'

We arrange where and when. When I put the phone down it takes me a minute or so to realise what has happened, then I'm too anxious and excited to do anything except think about what Nikolai might say.

Just after four, I slip out of the building and head to the Regent's Canal. I wait on the bridge where we've agreed to meet. A line of greenish ducklings paddles towards me and disappears into shadow. The sun's hot whenever it emerges from behind cloud, but my hands are cold and damp. I grip the rail, struggling to control the little bubbles of trepidation rising inside me. Is he only coming to tell me goodbye?

'Hi.'

I spin around and there he is, inches from me. No canvas bag, only a light jacket slung over his shoulder. I take in the bulk of his upper body, the tanned muscular arms emerging from his white T-shirt, the streak of dirt on his neck, the dampness of his brow, the untidy hair caught in a flutter of breeze, the smell of man and sweat with that faint citrus overtone.

He smiles. I smile back. I want to kiss him, wrap my arms around him, feel the warmth of his body.

His eyes move slowly over my face. 'It is good to see you,' he says.

'Yes,' I reply. 'You too.'

We take the steps down to the towpath and follow the twisting canal. Cyclists flash past. Men in hats sling fishing lines into the murky water, where squares of bread float among plastic bags. Children lean on bicycles, shouting as they throw stones into the canal. In the distance, sprawled across the sky, an empty gasometer neatly frames the graceful spires of St Pancras Station.

We stop walking and sit on a low wall.

'I am sorry if I hurt you, the last time we speak,' he says. 'I was going to call you so many times. Each time I know what I will say, and each time I cannot say, I can find no words... I wrote the letter to say them instead. If you do not believe me, I will understand.'

A lump forms in my throat.

'I believe you. I believe every word you said. I'm sorry I doubted you. Truly sorry.'

He holds out his hand; I take it. We continue along the towpath. Nettles and weeds spurt from the dry earth, tickling the pockmarked, crumbling walls of abandoned warehouses. Narrowboats rock against the sides of the canal. The path veers to reveal a huge chunk cut out of the earth, extending in either direction as far as you can see – the site of the new Channel Tunnel link at St Pancras, Nikolai informs me. Above, two cranes form a giant cross in the sky.

We come to a lock. People are basking on the grass, talking and smoking. We climb some steps and sit on a bench. The gush of water fills my ears. On a narrow island in the centre of the lock, two pigeons tap each other's beaks.

'There is something else I must tell you,' he says.

I wait. Somehow I know already what it is.

'My father is not well. He is getting worse, he is thin now. My mother writes that he does not do what the doctor says.'

'Do you have to go back?'

'It depends on my father – and other things.'

'You could be put in prison. Or killed.'

'It is not only because of my father that I must go back.' He gazes at his hands with their long fingers and dirt-encrusted nails. 'I have enough of running away. My home is Russia, not London. I will take my chances with the police, with Anton's gang, with Ivan's father and brothers. Maybe I will go far away from Urals, where no one knows me. I will work on my music and try to fix what is broken inside me.'

In his eyes, I see only sadness. He touches my cheek.

We walk back, past office workers congregating on the terraces of warehouses turned café-bars. The towpath ends. Ahead, the canal disappears into the tunnel's black mouth. At the other end, suspended in gloom, a tiny half-moon.

Nikolai stands in front of me, not quite touching, his eyes locked on mine.

'So,' I say, 'is this goodbye?'

'That is what you want?'

'No.'

He kisses me with wide, warm lips. I kiss him back with all my heart.

'Miz.' He pulls me close, his lips touching my ear. 'I love you. I have loved you for a long time, don't you know? I want to be with you. I want to hear you laugh, I want to hold you to me at night so I can feel your heart go thump thump thump.'

I smile. 'That's what I want too.'

He holds me at arm's length, eyes on my face, as if taking in the essence of me. As if he's found my soul.

44

Nikolai puts down the shears. 'It is better, no?'

I look up from the rose bush I'm pruning, unable to suppress a smile at the sight of the forsythia hedge that earlier this morning poked up from the side fence like a punk haircut, and is now flat enough to lie on.

The evening is warm. Birds twitter, the light is hued with gold. I carry on pruning while Nikolai rests on the patio wall.

He's come over after work to help me with the garden. He stays at my place more often than not, and has given notice to his landlady after I told him it would be stupid to waste any more money on rent. We do things that lovers do: lazy weekend mornings in bed, walks hand in hand on drowsy summer evenings. I wonder how I've managed to live without such things.

'Do you think,' he says suddenly, his voice loud after the long silence, 'I am – how you say – tempting fate, if I go back to Russia?'

He hasn't said anything else about going back since our walk on the canal and I haven't mentioned it, hoping by some miracle that his father's health might improve.

'I don't know. You left because you didn't want to be arrested for killing Ivan – or someone killing you in revenge. Why should you be immune to those things now? It's not even a year since you left.' I snip off another deadhead. 'But as for fate, I don't believe in it. Fortune tellers and old women who read teacups – that's a load of old bollocks.'

Nikolai gives me a bemused smile.

'I do not believe a fortune teller can tell me my future,' he replies, 'or that my sign is Aries so I will have money when Mars comes in line with Jupiter. But I remember how the guys in my unit would say, "If it is your day to die, there is nothing you can do to stop the bullet." At first, this is stupid to me. Then I start to think like them. I stop thinking, if I make one little mistake I will die. I think, if I am meant to die on this day, I will.'

'I understand,' I say. But I can't really imagine what it would be like, day after day facing the real prospect of death.

'Once,' Nikolai says, 'I believe there is a God and he will look after me.'

'And now?'

'If there is a God, he does not care.'

I sit on the wall next to him. He touches the large ruby on my right index finger. I put the ring on this morning – for years it's been stored away in my dressing-table drawer.

'This is beautiful,' he says. 'I have not seen before.'

'My mother gave it to me for my eighteenth birthday.'

'Why do you not talk about your mother? Always you tell me of your father.'

'What do you want to know?'

'What is her name?'

'Frances. She was an art teacher for fifteen years – until she left for Spain.'

I feel a brief flutter in my stomach. It comes back sometimes, that first shock of seeing her gone. Her dressing table without her hairbrush, just a few blonde hairs lying on the dark wood where it used to be. The lingering smell of her perfume, reminding me of cloves and ripe apricots. And the old questions, unanswerable.

'I knew my parents weren't happy together,' I explain. 'But I didn't realise she was having an affair. I'd never even heard the guy's name. I had no idea what was going on.'

'Your father knew?'

'He never believed she would leave him. It's ironic – Julio never married her. After five years, he left her for someone else.'

It's strange to be talking about my mother. It's also a relief. A tear rolls down my cheek, then another. I can't stop them. I wipe them away with the side of my hand but more come.

Nikolai puts his hand over mine and waits for me to wipe my face. 'When did you last see her?'

'She sometimes comes over for my birthday. I haven't see her for a few years, though – things haven't been that good between us.'

'It is sad for you that you lose your mother,' he says. 'And it is sad for her that she loses you.'

His words linger. For the first time, it really is that simple.

Over our evening meal Nikolai retreats into silence, despite my efforts to reach him. Later, he says he's going for a walk. I ask if I can join him.

We walk side by side through leafy streets, a short distance apart, neither of us speaking. It's on the cusp of darkness. Birds whistle above late bursts of traffic.

'I was not going to show you this,' he says suddenly, stopping and removing from his bag a folded sheet of white A4 paper. 'I thought it is better you do not see. But now I must ask you something.'

He unfolds the sheet of paper and passes it to me. In the middle, the printed words:

GO BACK WHERE YOU CAME FROM RUSKI
OR YOUR NEXT FALL WILL BE YOUR LAST

I shiver as I stare at the words.

'It was in my jacket pocket when I leave work. I leave my jacket in drying room all day. Anyone can put it there.' Nikolai folds the note and puts it back in his bag. 'Do you know who sends this?'

'No, of course I don't. How could I know that?'

'Maybe your father sends this message.'

'No. My father would never send something like that.'

Nikolai doesn't reply.

'My father isn't behind this note,' I insist. 'I know he isn't.'

'So who is?'

'The guy who drove into those bricks that fell on Malik – Ricky. Maybe it's him. You said he could have done it on purpose.' I try to think clearly. 'If it's not him, maybe it's one of the others you've told me about, the ones trying to stir up this anti-Muslim thing.'

'You know what I think?' His eyes bore into mine. 'I think your father knows who leaves this note. I think he asks someone to do this for him, someone who knows which is my jacket and who has security pass. It is not difficult. He finds out that Malik was in accident. He knows that I am hurt in accident too. He leaves this note so it will look like it is Ricky who makes trouble for me. Then no one will guess what he is trying to do.'

'What the hell are you talking about? What is he trying do?'

'He wants to get me away from you. He will do anything to get me away from you. Even if he must kill me.'

'That's total nonsense,' I say. 'I can't believe you just said that.'

He doesn't reply.

'I'd appreciate it,' I say firmly, 'if you would stop blaming my father without a shred of evidence.'

Nikolai's face clouds.

'You should know something, Georgie,' he says in a low, steady voice. 'When someone thinks they can make me afraid, they are wrong. When someone tries to hurt me, I will fight them back. I will never give in to them. You understand? The person who makes this threat, he should watch out. I am not joking. Please tell this to your father.'

Later that night, while Nikolai is in the bathroom, I pick up the phone.

I know what I'm doing is probably not sensible. If by some infinitesimal possibility my father is responsible for that note, he is unlikely to admit it. If he isn't responsible – and for all his mistrust of Nikolai, I can't believe that he has anything to do with this note – I could alienate him further. But I have to ask.

'I'm sorry to call so late.' I take a deep breath and rush on. 'It's about Nikolai. He's received an anonymous note. It says he'll have an accident if he doesn't go back to Russia. A fatal accident.' I wait. 'Do you know anything about it?'

I count the seconds of silence. One, two, three...

'Are you seriously suggesting I could write a note threatening to kill someone?'

'I'm only asking if you know anything about it.'

'If I wanted to get rid of this bloke, do you honestly think I would go to the trouble of sending an anonymous note? I would just call the police and report him as an illegal immigrant, one who may well be involved in terrorism to boot. In the current climate, that should go down well.'

I nearly spit down the phone. 'He's not involved in terrorism, Dad. He's not a Muslim – he doesn't even believe in God, for Christ's sake. He's explained everything to me... Oh, what's the point, you wouldn't understand.'

'In that case,' comes the terse reply, 'I suggest he goes to the police with this note. Maybe they can help him.'

A cough, then a long pause.

'I'm sorry that it's come to this, Georgie. I never thought things would get this bad between us. And I'm sorry you've gotten hooked up with this young man. As far as I can see he's brought you nothing but trouble.'

'You're wrong. He's just what I've always needed.' As I say this, I realise it's true.

'Well, good luck to you both.'

The line goes dead.

I've made the rift between us greater than ever, I think gloomily. But at least I'm sure now that my father has nothing to do with that note.

I recall news reports of a black teenager who not long ago was murdered with an ice axe for walking down the street with his white girlfriend. Could fascists at the building site be trying to intimidate Nikolai? Could the person responsible for Malik's 'accident' have set his sights on Nikolai because of their friendship?

Or does whoever threatened Nikolai have no connection at all to his workplace?

Julian, I think suddenly. Julian is responsible.

But that's crazy. Julian wouldn't leave a note threatening to kill someone. He's a professional engineer, a responsible adult. He votes, pays his taxes, puts litter in bins. Anyway, how could he have put that note in Nikolai's jacket? He doesn't even know where Nikolai works, does he?

I put the phone back in its holder on the hall table and slump against the cupboard. The more I think about this, the more the strands of my thoughts twist together into an impenetrable knot. In the week since Nikolai's return, I've felt almost normal again, bolstered by his presence. But I start to realise that his presence alone will not make me safe. Nikolai himself is not safe.

A ripple of fear goes through me. That same apprehension is back inside my body, like a tiny electric fizz inside my muscles and my skin, speeding my heart and tightening my scalp. I'm wired up, waiting for whatever it is I must face.

45

In the dregs of daylight, I approach the warm stink of Nikolai's block. Vapours of overripe mangoes and rotting fish slink up from the line of dustbins. The rattle of a passing police siren cuts through stereos blaring from open windows and intoxicated laughter.

Before going inside, I study the cars parked opposite: all are unoccupied. The lamp above the entrance to the flats reveals withered shrubs. The entry system is broken again – this time the door is held open by a brick and a stack of phone directories. I climb the stairs into a fug of stale air and rap on Nikolai's door. He opens it, unsmiling, and takes my bottle of wine.

The usual mess of newspapers, CDs and unwashed mugs has gone; the manuscript pads are stacked in a single pile beside the keyboard.

I flop onto the worn leather armchair Nikolai bought for fifteen pounds on eBay, roll up my sleeves and kick off my sandals. Despite the open windows, it's like sitting inside an oven. Nikolai switches on a fan, more noisy than cooling. He hands me a tumbler. I take in his below-the-knee shorts, T-shirt and sandals. His shoulders hunch over and his eyes are shadowed, one of them bloodshot. The scar on his wrist is a livid white against his tan.

He sweeps the hair from his eyes with an impatient gesture. We drink the wine, not speaking.

I put my empty glass down. 'I'm worried, Nikky. That someone might try to hurt you.'

'No one will hurt me. Whoever is trying to scare me, I will find them and make them stop.'

'It isn't my father. I've talked to him, I told you. He wasn't lying to me.'

'He tries to turn you against me. He makes you think I am some crazy guy who throws bombs at people.'

'That's different from threatening to kill someone.'

Nikolai scowls. 'Of course.'

'Why would my father want to threaten you?'

His glass stops halfway to his mouth. 'You are joking, no?'

'He really doesn't like me being with you, I'm not denying that. But he'd only have to report you to the police or Immigration if he wanted you out of the country.'

He clanks his glass down on the keyboard. 'Maybe there is rea-son why your father does not report me – he is scared what I will say about him. Maybe there are things he would not like the police to know.'

'It isn't him, Nikolai.'

'If is not your father,' he says, eyes narrowing, 'who leaves this note?'

I swallow to relieve the tightness in my throat, unable to say the name. Could Julian really have done such a thing? What would be his motive? Does he think that simply by leaving a note, Nikolai will take fright and disappear? Or does he still think he can make me leave Nikolai?

We leave the wine unfinished and stroll through the back streets of Finsbury Park. Night presses against us, silken and alive, smelling of honeysuckle, curry and cat piss. At a patch of grass and one or two spindly trees, we sit on a bench. Houses across the street leak their indifferent light over us. A breeze stirs my hair, shifting the shadows. I wonder if anyone could be crouching behind the bushes, or if I've become paranoid.

'I wish it wasn't like this,' I murmur.

'How would you like it to be?'

'For us to be somewhere far away. Where no one will bother us.'

'You want us to run away together?'

Yes, I want to run away with you.

I touch the vein pulsing on the top of his hand, imagining blue smoke rising from a cottage chimney, and no other houses in sight. Somewhere far away from the real world.

A helicopter throbs low across the sky.

'We should go to the police,' I say. 'Threatening to take some-one's life is against the law.'

He throws his hands apart. 'You think I am stupid? You think the police will look for the crazy idiot who makes this message? You think they will make me safe?'

Of course, he's right. What could the police do? They would write down a few details then do nothing – at best. Or they might start asking awkward questions and find out Nikolai is working ille-gally, and put him in a detention centre. What if they find out he's been meeting with someone who the French police suspect of being a terrorist? They might arrest him and lock him up.

It's too much. I lower my head in my hands.

'I am sorry I shout at you. This fucking message – it is making me crazy.'

'I know you told me you're not scared. But *I* am. What if someone tries to push you in front of a Tube train or something? What if someone tries to shoot you?'

'No one will get chance to shoot me, Georgie. If someone comes for me, it will be me who shoots him.'

'You can't go round shooting people. That would be just repeating everything that's gone before, don't you see? The anger, the violence that simmers away inside you. You need to let it go, somehow or other.'

'Why? I could be the cowboy of Finsbury Park!'

He springs to his feet and mimes drawing a gun from each hip. I can't help laughing.

Back in Nikolai's flat we lie on the sofa-bed, surrounded by a warm glove of night air. Snatches of a saxophone riff, the thud–thud of car stereos and intermittent grumbles of lorries. My head rests on Niko-lai's slowly moving chest. I'm in a small boat riding ocean waves.

It's dark when I wake. Nikolai is still asleep. He's saying something in Russian, a short phrase repeated several times with increasing force and desperation. I've heard it before, on other nights. I can't bear to listen. I reach across and kiss his forehead, illuminated by the yellowish street light.

'Nikolai, wake up,' I whisper. 'You're having a bad dream.'

His head jerks on the pillow. I gently nudge his arm. He sits upright, staring straight ahead, his eyes shiny with tears. Then he looks around the room as if lost and drops down onto the mattress.

'I see a man come towards me,' he says. 'I know why he comes. He is going to punish me.'

I feel a slither of dread.

'Who is he?'

'I don't know. He has no face.'

He lies on his back looking up at the ceiling.

'You must forgive yourself, Nikky. Otherwise the guilt will eat you up.'

'And you, Georgie. Do *you* forgive me?'

'Yes, I forgive you. But it's not my forgiveness you need.'

I lie awake in the dark while Nikolai sleeps beside me. At each creak of the floor, each tap or rustle, I imagine an intruder ready to attack.

Julian is waiting out there, somewhere, preparing to carry out his plan. Nikolai is in danger. I can't just wait and let something happen to him.

As grey light creeps into the room, I wake from my own dream.

In it I'm walking in a wood. Trees loom, dark shapes in the mist. I have to find Nikolai. If I don't get to him quickly... I turn this way and that, stumbling over roots and uneven ground. My foot catches on a log. Only it isn't a log.

I reach out and touch a cold arm.

Then I see his lifeless face.

46

Next morning, on the way to work, I call Julian's mobile. I leave a message asking him to call me back ASAP.

It's a Friday, which means the weekly team meeting. I need to prepare for it but my brain has turned to sponge; concentration is impossible. Julian could call any minute, I keep thinking, wanting and not wanting him to at the same time.

Nikolai calls mid-afternoon to say he can't see me that evening, as planned – he's going to the pub to talk with a union guy from work. He'll tell me about it tomorrow, he has to get back to work.

As the day grinds on, I'm more and more certain that this meeting is to do with my father, and feel increasingly angry with Nikolai. He wants so badly to blame someone for that note, he's willing to turn my father into a murderer.

The call I'm waiting for comes that evening. Dripping from a shower, I grab a towel and run into the bedroom.

'Georgie.' A diffident tone, formal. My body tenses.

'Julian. Thanks for calling back.'

What the fuck do I say? A whole script has been waiting in my head, if only I can find it now.

'There's something I need to talk to you about.'

'Oh, yes?' His tone isn't encouraging.

'It's about –' I stop. Suddenly, I know there's no point trying to talk to him on the phone; he'll deny everything. 'Can we meet somewhere?'

A pause at the other end. 'I'm quite tied up at the moment.'

'It won't take long. How about straight after work next Monday? I'll come to that pub down the road from your office.' It's a noisy barn of a pub full of bleeping machines. I used to meet him there after work occasionally, an age ago.

Another pause, longer.

'All right then. Six o'clock, Monday.'

'OK, see you then.'

I wander around the flat, full of trepidation. This is going to be difficult. But I have to find out if Julian is the one who threatened Nikolai. In the meantime, I have to hide my suspicions from

Nikolai. Though he's vowed to control his anger, I know what he's capable of – and that frightens me.

It's nearly 2 p.m. when Nikolai turns up on Saturday. He comes into the kitchen, breathing hard.

'Sorry to be late. I was at the library, on the Internet.'

I get him a glass of water. He approaches the table, which still bears the remains of lunch. He scoops a dollop of hummus onto a piece of pitta bread and devours it.

'So, what have you found out about my father? That's what you've been doing, isn't it?'

Whatever he has discovered, I tell myself, I will be prepared. No longer do I believe my father incapable of anything less than perfection.

Without sitting down, Nikolai takes more pitta bread, fills it and takes several bites.

'Yesterday I talk to this guy from the union.'

'And? What did you find out?'

'I ask him before if he knows of your father's company. Yesterday, he brings papers with him.' He hesitates. 'He tells me about the accident.'

'The accident?'

'Last year, there is accident on building site near Hemel Hempstead. Your father's company is in charge of the excavation. You do not know?'

I dig into my memory. There was something last year. My father and I were having lunch one Sunday afternoon. He'd mentioned an incident at work.

'It was last spring – March or April. He said three men were hurt because they hadn't prepared the ground correctly. Is that the one you mean?'

'It is the same, yes. March 2004. Three men are working in trench. The walls fall down and they are crushed. One is killed.'

Killed. The word blares in my ears. My father didn't tell me the accident was serious. I asked what happened to the men involved and he'd said something vague like, 'They'll be back on their feet again soon'.

'The inspectors say the trench was not made properly,' Nikolai goes on. 'Your father's company had to pay forty thousand pounds because he and his managers do not give shit about safety.'

He delves into his bag and hands me a sheet of paper. Printed on it, the details of a Health and Safety Executive prosecution:

Company: Cameron Construction Ltd
Offence date: 8/3/04
Total fine: £40,000 plus £19,000 costs
Summary:
Prosecution following a trench collapse resulting in the fatality of one sub-contractor employee and serious injury to two others. Poor training and risk assessments. Poor standards seen on site on previous occasions. Failure to manage safety and to prevent recurrence of unsafe act three weeks earlier when man found in unshored trench by HSE inspector at same site in contravention of company's own procedures. Pleaded Guilty.

Then he hands me a photocopied newspaper article, headlined 'Poor Management Led to Death at Local Construction Firm'.

I read quickly. One man died five days later from his injuries; the other two suffered crush injuries that would leave them permanently disabled. All three were casual labourers from Eastern Europe. Below is a summary of the judgement, which puts the blame for the accident squarely with management. The large fine reflects 'the failure of senior management to manage safety despite previous warnings of poor safety practices… '

I hand back the paper.

Nikolai leans back in his chair, observing my discomfort.

'My father never said anything about all this,' I protest, to myself as much as to him.

Then I remember what he told me about health-and-safety officials inspecting one of his sites just recently. Could that have been prompted by this accident? A sweat breaks out in the small of my back. My father runs the company, doesn't he? It is he who tolerated the lack of safety. He is responsible for that man's death, through his inaction.

'It does not make Mr Cameron look good,' Nikolai says.

I go outside and sit on the kitchen step. Crisp leaves fleck the lawn.

Something my father said a few years ago comes back to me. I'd commented on some startling statistics in the newspaper about the high number of accidents in the construction industry.

'Accidents are always going to happen,' he replied, 'especially in this industry. One hundred per cent safety is impossible and in any case would be too expensive.' I recall also his frequent complaints about the burden of excessive rules and regulations on business. Now I know just how far he is prepared to go to avoid following them. For a long time I sit there, shock and dismay washing over me, and a sense of something important gone for ever.

I find Nikolai. He switches off the TV and waits for me to speak.

'It's wrong what my father did,' I say. 'What he did – or didn't do – caused that man to die. But it doesn't mean he goes about killing people on purpose or that he'd ever threaten to kill you. That's ridiculous.'

'You are right. It shows only that your father is not such good man as you think, and he is not so careful about people's lives.' He lowers his voice. 'And maybe you should not believe all that he tells you.'

'I've told you already. If he wanted you out of the country, he could just report you for being illegal.'

'Maybe he *has* reported me. What are they going to do to? Put me in handcuffs and take me away? There are thousands like me. I am not causing trouble, I am not fanatic Muslim preaching *jihad*. I work, I am part of their system. Your father and all the others like him, they make money out of people like me.' His voice gets louder, his face fiercer. I stare at him, mesmerised. 'We are padding in pie – they put us in with the good meat. They take us out, pie falls in. We come here, a few months later we are gone. We work in shit jobs, they pay us shit in return. When they have enough of us, they spit us out. No one notices us unless we break our necks.'

I think he's going to spit on the carpet, he's so angry. But he turns and stares out of the window.

'I will go to him,' he says eventually. 'I will tell him that I know he tries to push me away from you.' His voices fills with contempt. 'I will tell him that I will not be scared away. If he tries to hurt me, he will regret.'

I let out a sigh of frustration. 'It isn't him, don't be so stupid.' My mind leaps ahead. I can't let Nikolai go near my father, not in this state. 'I'll go and talk to him.'

47

Next morning, I wake up feeling as if I haven't slept at all. Overnight, a disturbing thought has taken root and spread like a weed inside my head. Could Julian and my father be colluding to get Nikolai out of my life?

I'm in no state for conversation with my father. But I know I'll have no peace until I've talked to him. I reach for the phone beside my bed.

He picks up straight away.

'Hello?' It sounds more like goodbye.

'Sorry to disturb you, Dad. But I need to speak to you.'

Silence.

'Dad?'

'It's not convenient now, Georgie. I've got to go out shortly. Can you call back in the afternoon?'

'I want to ask you something, it won't take long. When did you last speak to Julian?'

A pause. In the background there are voices.

'A week or so after the party. He phoned me. He was worried about you and your... situation.'

'You talked to him about Nikolai behind my back?'

'I simply told him I was concerned about your boyfriend and his background, and his possible intentions towards you. We shared our views of Nikolai, which happened to be quite similar. It's a free world, Georgie.'

'And you haven't spoken to him since.'

'No, I told you. Why do you ask?'

'The guy's been stalking me. Sending me creepy emails, making weird phone calls.'

'I can't believe Julian would –'

'I'm not making this up, Dad. You haven't made some kind of arrangement with him, to do with Nikolai?'

At the other end, the sound of my father's breathing.

'Do you think I'm lying to you?' His anger isn't concealed.

'But you've lied to me before – how do I know you won't again?'

At the other end, the sound of a door closing. The voices disappear.

'I lied to you? When did I lie to you? What the fuck are you saying?'

'I'll tell you later,' I reply, hanging up.

Even before my anger dies down, I know I've said too much. Of course my father isn't in league with Julian.

Alicia answers the door, a tight smile on her face.

'I've come to see my father,' I say. My anger has been simmering all afternoon.

'He's on the phone, Georgie.' She uses the wary tone of a secretary guarding her boss against unwanted visitors.

'I'd like to speak to him.'

She opens the front door a fraction wider. 'He's in the study... Vincent! Georgie's here!'

I stride down the hall, Alicia's warning coinciding with my entry. My father is reclining on his leather chair in front of the computer, hand on mouse. He continues to stare at the screen as I stand there.

'Sorry to disturb you. But this is important.' I perch on top of a drawer unit, ignoring Alicia hovering in the doorway as if not sure whether to usher me outside or offer me a cup of tea.

'It's OK, Alicia,' my father says.

Once she's closed the door, he swivels his chair to face me.

'Well, Georgie? What else did you want to say to me?'

'That accident last March near Hemel Hempstead? The trench that collapsed –'

'The accident, yes. What about it?'

'I know what really happened, Dad. I know your company was fined forty thousand pounds by Health and Safety. You told me that it wasn't anything to do with you, that it was the fault of those men because they didn't do their job properly. But that wasn't true, was it? It was you who didn't give a damn about their safety. I read what the judge said. You'd had previous warnings about safety but you ignored them. The inspectors found your methods of working weren't safe weeks before the accident. You didn't do anything, you let everything go on as before.'

My father loosens his tie. I take a breath.

'You didn't even have the guts to tell me what really happened. But you're used to deceiving people, aren't you?'

The words are out of my mouth before I can think better of it. His eyes make small, rapid movements.

'What the fuck are you talking about?'

'Why didn't you tell me a man was killed in that accident? And two others were seriously hurt?'

His voice is quiet. 'When I told you about the accident, Georgie, that man was still alive. He died in hospital nearly a week later –'

'You could have mentioned it then, couldn't you? But you didn't.'

He doesn't answer for a while.

'I felt bad about it, that's why. I didn't want you to see me as… some sort of cowboy.'

'Well, that's what you are, isn't it? That man might be here now if you'd done the right thing.'

I've never seen my father look so uncomfortable. And I've never spoken to him like this in my life.

'I admit it, Georgie. That accident was one we could have avoided – should have avoided. I knew we didn't have all the procedures in place.' He sighs. 'Things were done the quick way to save time – no one was making the safety checks, they just ticked the boxes. I did what I could to change things. But change wasn't easy. I had a shitload of things to think about – cancelled jobs, staff leaving, you name it.'

'You're making excuses,' I say. 'You don't really care about safety at all, do you? You use people; you get what you can out of them. You hire cheap foreign workers who can't complain when things go wrong.'

My father drums his fingers on the desk.

'What you're talking about – people exploiting other people – it's the way it's always been in this industry. It's business, Georgie. It's not easy in my position. Things are never so clear at the time. There are always mistakes – things one could have done better with hindsight.'

'Yes, and there's always excuses. All this time I thought you had principles. But it's not true, is it?'

I wait for him to respond. But he only gets up to open the door.

'You've said enough, Georgie. You'd better go.'

I feel empty inside. I want my old dad back. The one I can rely on, the one who always does the right thing.

48

The traffic is lighter than I expect as I drive through north-west London. But I can't enjoy the leafy lanes or the early evening sunshine, and don't bother to put the roof down.

I arrive ten minutes early, park in a lane between the woods and the golf course and walk down towards the junction with the main road. The pub car park would be full, probably. Besides, a short walk will help me relax.

The pub is much the same as I remember, large and unpretentious. I peer past swirling smoke to the crowded bar. No sign of Julian. I go outside and perch on the low wall between the car park and the pavement, watching each passing car. Then, in the distance, a thick growl, rapidly increasing in volume as a black Jaguar XK8 approaches. I watch it turn left at the junction and disappear up the lane I've just walked down. He'll be with me in just a few minutes. My heart taps out a new rhythm in my chest.

It's not too late. I don't have to go ahead with this.

I hold my damp hands out to dry in a half-hearted breeze, wishing I'd changed out of my work things. I'm still in my smart shoes, tailored skirt and jacket. Jeans and flat sandals would have been more comfortable, not to mention practical.

Julian strides along the pavement towards me. His hair is blonder and shorter than the last time I saw him and his face is tanned. I stand and watch his long legs eat up the space between us.

'Hi there.' His voice is surprisingly warm. 'Long time no see.'

I edge back in case he tries to touch me. 'Hello, Julian.'

We stand on the pavement sizing each other up. He has a flicker of scent. Dark grey suit trousers but no jacket, no tie. The top button of his shirt is left undone.

'Let's go in, shall we?' he says with a quick movement of his hand.

I go the bar and order us a couple of beers. Julian hangs back, busying himself with his phone. I hand him his glass and lead the way to a quieter table.

'How are things with you, then?' I say before he has a chance to speak. 'Still working as hard as ever?'

'It's pretty full on at the moment, yes. I'm working on a new bridge with one of our top designers – he chose me for the project.'

He's lying, I think.

'Congratulations. And how about... everything else?'

'I'm OK now, don't worry.' He gives a little chortle. 'I don't fall asleep thinking of you any more. Actually, I've been seeing quite a lot of this ballet dancer – she's half French, half Portuguese.'

Sure you have.

'And how's your Russian friend?' Julian glances around the bar as if he's not really interested.

'He's OK.'

'Thought you might have finished with him by now.' There's an edge to his voice. He shifts in his seat.

'No,' I reply. 'We're still together.'

'Is he still at the building site?'

'He's got a few weeks left till his contract ends.'

Julian looks sharply at me. 'What will he do then?'

'He's planning to go back to Russia.'

'Really?' His tone is polite again. 'So, Georgie. What did you want to see me about?'

Around us, silvery white coils of smoke unwind. Coughing, I gulp down the rest of my Becks.

'How about we go and sit outside? This smoke is really getting to me.' I have to be alone with him. That's the only way I'll get through to him.

He checks his watch. 'Actually, I haven't got much time... I'm seeing Maria later.' A beam of sunlight strikes his face. It shows no sign of emotion.

'But you said –'

'Walk back towards my car with me, if you like. I'm parked in the lane beside the golf course.'

'OK,' I reply, stopping myself just in time from saying, "So am I". Of course, it would be safer not to go anywhere with Julian; this could be a trick. But I have to find out the truth.

We climb the narrow pavement. The lane is hugged by woodland. Beside us rises a bank of deep shade, silent except for an invisible bird, whistling a melancholy five-note song. I hurry to keep up with Julian's long strides, my jacket and handbag slung over my shoulder. A cyclist passes. No pedestrians, no traffic. As we reach the string of parked cars, mine among them, I slow. I'll have to say something soon.

'I want to ask you something, Julian.'

'I'm all ears.'

I try to breathe normally. 'Someone put a threatening note in Nikolai's jacket.'

'Oh, yes?'

Again, that casual-verging-on-arrogant tone. In the distance, a thwack of golf club against ball.

'You did it, didn't you?'

'You must be off your rocker. Why would I want to write Nikolai a threatening note?'

I stare at him. Have I got it wrong? Am I only making an idiot of myself?

'You're jealous of him,' I say. 'You said so yourself in those messages you sent me. You can't bear the thought of him being close to me.'

One heartbeat, two...

'It's different now, Georgie. I couldn't give a monkey's about your boyfriend. I'm getting on with my life. I'm not the sad git you seem to think I am.'

'I'm sorry, I don't believe you.'

His head jerks towards me. 'What?'

My heart kicks like a crazed stallion in my chest. A roar fills my ears.

'I don't believe you have a girlfriend waiting for you. I don't believe your life is suddenly perfect. And I don't believe that you didn't threaten Nikolai. It was you who made those creepy phone calls, wasn't it?'

His eyelids are flickering. He's breathing fast, his mouth open a fraction.

'You can't accept that I didn't love you back, that I chose some-one else over you. You can't stand me wanting him and not you.'

His face contorts. 'You... bitch.'

That word again. I clench my bladder muscles tight. I'm really scared now.

'Admit it, Julian. You can't let go of me. You're trying to scare off Nikolai – and scare me into leaving him.'

I wait. A muscle at corner of his mouth twitches. His voice is quiet, controlled.

'I'll have to try a little harder then, won't I?'

'I'm not going to leave him. He'll leave when he's ready to leave, not because of you. He's not a coward, you see. He's got more courage than anyone I've ever known.'

'Courage? That Ruski cunt? I think you should talk to your

father about him. Your father knows what he's like; he's told me all about Nikolai. How he's been trying to sponge off you ever since he first got his leg over.'

My face flushes. I want to punch him in the gut so hard he'll be writhing on the ground.

Julian leans against a tree behind him. Two of its lower branches have fused together.

'Nikolai's a loser, don't you get it? A no-hoper, a fucking waste of space.'

'He's worth more than a hundred of you put together, you little shit.' I can't hold in my anger any longer. I want to spit in his face. 'He's more of a man than you'll ever be!'

Before I know it, Julian has grabbed my arms and shoved me against the tree trunk. My bag falls. His breath is hot on my face. I feel the tip of his finger move slowly across my lips. It makes my skin crawl.

'I'll pay you back for that,' he whispers.

'Let me go!' I struggle to free myself from his grip.

'Give me a kiss first.' His mouth, distorted by a sneer, moves towards mine. 'For old times' sake.'

His tongue forces its way into my mouth. His body presses against mine. I'm crushed between him and the tree. My yell of outrage comes out as a pathetic bleat. His hand moves under my skirt, pulls at my underpants. I push against his chest but he doesn't budge, just forces me even harder against the tree. Then he pushes his fingers up between my legs.

I gasp. I have to do something.

'Is that nice, Georgie?' His lips twist into a cold smile. 'I've got something else for you, right here. Something even better.'

He unzips his trousers and tries to push inside me.

I don't know where it comes from. My anger is instant and overpowering. Before he can do anything, before I can even think what I'm doing, I kick him in the shin as hard as I can.

'Fuck!' He lets go of me and leaps back, his face scrunched up.

I grab my bag and bolt up the lane. A woman jogs towards me from the other direction, earphones plugged in, oblivious to my distress. Where the hell is my car? It wasn't this far up, was it? At last I spot it. Panting, I climb in behind the wheel, not daring to take the time to look behind me. I drive up the hill past Julian's empty Jaguar and away into country lanes.

I know I'm driving too fast. Every few seconds I check the

rear-view mirror, expecting Julian's Jaguar to appear. A white van behind me honks as I veer into the next lane without signalling.

Stop the car, I tell myself. Get a cup of tea and calm down.

But I don't stop until I'm safely inside my front door.

After checking all the windows are locked and the curtains and blinds closed, I pour a large gin with a dash of tonic and sit at the kitchen table. My hands tremble as I drink. I feel light-headed.

My phone bleeps. A message from Nikolai asking what I'm up to, when can he see me.

Will call tomorrow. I text back. *Tough day, going to bed.*

Part of me wants Nikolai to comfort me, protect me. But first I'd have to tell him what happened. And I can't. Not yet. What's happened is all my own fault. I went alone to a secluded place with Julian, despite the risk, then I pushed him too far.

I see again his horrid smile as he leaned in to kiss me. If I hadn't got away when I did… I shudder. But now I know it's him. He is responsible for that note in Nikolai's pocket.

And despite the horror of what he did to me, I feel relief to know this for certain.

Now, surely, any fantasies he may have harboured about some-how getting back into my life must be dashed. He knows without the slightest doubt how I feel about him. And he also knows Nikolai is going back to Russia, so he'll give up this pathetic game of trying to scare us. He'll leave us alone from now on – won't he?

A pipe creaks. I start. My mouth is as dry as bone.

If Julian comes here, I think, I'll call the police. I'll scream the place down.

I get a glass of water and secure the kitchen window, then go to the living room, open the curtain a fraction and sneak a look into the street. I can't see Julian's car.

I pick up my phone. I'll tell the police Julian admitted threat-ening Nikolai's life. I'll tell them he assaulted and attempted to rape me, and they'll arrest him.

I put the phone back down.

He would deny everything. It would be my word against his. He probably wouldn't even be charged. I went with Julian voluntarily to a quiet lane beside the woods; I made it easy for him, that's what they would say.

I take a long shower then go to bed half dressed, leaving the hall light on. A succession of small obscure noises makes sleep impossible.

Julian can't come in, I remind myself, over and over.

49

I wait until mid-morning the next day to phone Nikolai, during his tea break.

'Sorry I couldn't talk to you yesterday,' I begin.

'Are you all right?' His voice is harsh in my ear. 'I think something happens to you.'

'I met Julian yesterday, after work.'

A pause.

'Julian? Why do you see *him*?'

'I had to find out if he was behind that note. I know it was him, Nikky.'

'How do you know this?' He sounds incredulous.

'I can't tell you over the phone.'

'I meet you at the café after work?'

'I'm at home. I'm not going into the office today.'

'So I will come to you when I finish.'

'OK, see you later... You'll be careful at work today, won't you?'

I stay in all day. Twice the landline rings, sending my heart racing as I ready myself to hear Julian's voice. But the first call is a wrong number and the second is someone asking if I'm interested in a double-glazing quotation.

Nikolai arrives just after five. He walks past me into the kitchen and helps himself to a glass of water. I follow him. He turns to me, his face set firm and his shoulders pulled back. The power of his upper body is clearly visible under his thin T-shirt. He doesn't sit down.

'You say it is not your father who threatens me, it is Julian? This guy who was your friend a few months ago?'

I lean against the back of a chair, staring helplessly at the smudge of dirt on his cheek.

'When you told me about the note I had a feeling it could be from Julian. I didn't say anything because I wanted to be sure. I knew he was jealous of you, but this – it seemed so crazy. So I arranged to meet him to find out.

'Someone came into my flat one night when I was asleep –

about a month ago, when you were away. I think it was him having a nose around.'

'How did he get in?'

'Through the kitchen window. I must have left it unlocked.'

Nikolai is pondering my words, I realise, as one might examine a teacup to find a hairline crack.

'Why is your friend so jealous of me? It is strange, no?'

'He isn't my friend any more, I told you.'

'Julian, you were fucking him?' Nikolai's eyes lock onto mine. He's moved closer and is standing right in front of me now.

'Only the once,' I say. 'It was just before I met you... I've never loved him, I never promised him anything.'

'You play around with this guy? You go to bed with him, then you push him away?'

'It was a mistake to have sex with him. It was stupid of me. But I didn't mean to hurt him.'

Nikolai looks away from me, saying nothing.

'Nikky?' I touch his arm, afraid he will leave.

'So, your friend, he has wound to his pride, he puffs out his big chest and tries to frighten you – frighten us both. But now he is going to kill me?'

'He just wants to scare you away, I think.'

'He admits that he leaves this note?'

'Not in so many words, no. But I know it was from him.'

'How does Julian get note into my jacket? How does he know which one is mine? There is no name marked where it hangs. And how does he get inside the building? No one can go on site without security pass.'

'I don't know. He must have got in somehow.'

Nikolai continues to look sceptical. Then he touches the skin just above my left elbow. It's tender. A bruise has formed there, I noticed as I dressed this morning.

'He did this?'

'He pushed me against a tree.'

'He hurt you?'

'He insulted you... I said something back. It made him angry.'

His expression darkens. 'How does he insult me?'

'It doesn't matter, Nikky. Look, I know it was Julian who threatened you. He thinks you've stolen me from him and he can't bear it.'

'He fucks you again, Julian?'

'No. No, he didn't.'

'What does he do to you?'

I say nothing.

'You are going to tell me?'

'He kissed me and…' I can't say the rest; '…I kicked him in the leg and ran away.'

Nikolai doesn't reply. His face is impossible to read. I feel my strength crumble, and turn away from him. Tears form behind my eyelids.

'I don't care what you believe,' I say, a hot drop rolling down my cheek. 'I just want you to be safe.'

I feel his hands, gentle on my shoulders.

'It was crazy thing you do.' He pulls me close to him; I can feel his heart beating. I feel overwhelmed with relief. 'You will be OK now, I promise. I will make sure this idiot does not hurt you. The two of us, we are stronger than him. We will show him we are not scared of him and he will go away with tail between his legs.'

'How can you be so sure?'

'If he wants to fight, I will fight him back. And I will win.'

50

I come home after work and check my emails on the computer. There's a message from Julian.

25 August 2005 11.01
To: Georgie Cameron
From: Julian Lewis
Georgie,
    I repeat, I know nothing whatsoever about an anonymous threat to Nikolai. I am disappointed that you could consider me capable of such a thing.
    I am extremely busy at work ahead of a month's trip to Italy and have no time to waste on these ridiculous allegations. Please do not contact me again.
Regards,
Julian.

My first reaction is indignation. The formal, cool tone is so at odds with the anger he showed a few days before. And his insistence that he knows nothing about the threat to Nikolai... He's lying, trying to confuse me.

And that thing about him being out of the country for a month. Is it some kind of trick?

I read the email to Nikolai.

'What do you think?' I say, sitting down on the sofa beside him.

He frowns, taps the table. 'You are sure we are not – how you say – barking up the wrong tree?'

'He's lying. He just wants to confuse us.'

'Maybe he is planning his final assault.' He laughs. 'My execution is coming soon.'

'Don't joke about it, Nikolai. You've no idea what he might be capable of.'

'I don't think he is capable of very much, actually. He is like cockerel strutting around with big chest, who falls down when someone blows at him. Maybe he thought he could have you if he can frighten me away. But now he knows he cannot frighten me, it is he who runs away.' As his eyes steady on mine, the humour drains from Nikolai's face. 'We must forget him now, Georgie. Understand?'

'I'd be only too glad to forget him, believe me.'

'Come, I will cook you good meal.' He takes my hand. 'And you will be happy again – that is order.'

After dinner, we sit in the garden. The last traces of blue fade from the sky. When it gets cool and stars appear, I move closer to Nikolai and bask in his warmth.

It feels natural to be with him like this. Whether as a result of God, fate or coincidence, I realise I've been given the chance of a different life, before my heart hardens irreversibly.

I'm relieved when Nikolai's last day at the building site comes that Friday. The building is nearly complete; casual labourers are no longer needed.

'What are you going to do now?' I ask.

'I will work on my music. It is time that I finish this thing. Every day it waits patiently for me, asking me to give it my attention.'

'How much have you got left to do?'

'I am nearly finished. I must finish before I go home.'

'Home?'

'Russia, I mean.'

'When will that be?'

'I don't know. One day, I must go back.' He looks at me sadly, then smiles and takes hold of my hand. 'But for now I want to show my girl a good time.'

51

It's no use closing the curtains, I know you're in there, little lady.

I'm back in my favourite spot behind the dustbins, nicely out of the way. Don't know why you never think to look here. There's enough room, just. A bit of discomfort is quite tolerable when one knows it won't last for ever.

My shin still twinges, by the way. I think you've caused permanent damage. Did you enjoy it, that swift kick you gave me? Did you think that'll teach him a lesson, the sad git, still pining after me, can't get it into his thick head that I don't give a rat's about him any more?

You were everything to me, Georgie. You filled my days even when you were far away, even though I couldn't tell you because I knew you would run away faster than a cat from a bucket of water. I never stopped thinking about you. I've never stopped thinking about you.

I kept hoping that things might change. Only a little while ago, I was counting on Ruski van Winkle falling from a ledge or stumbling into the path of a fortuitously passing high-speed train. I had the faint yet lingering hope that after you'd shed a few tears for him you might be receptive to the offer of a DVD and consoling bottle of wine at my place.

I wouldn't have been in any rush. We could have played one of our silly games again. The most embarrassing things we've ever said, the stupidest things we've ever done. You were good at coming up with ideas for those. But you've made it quite clear that the game is over between us.

Bye bye, Georgie. I'll always love you.

52

During the warm, mainly fine days at the end of summer, we go out often – concerts at the Royal Festival Hall, opera at Covent Garden, dining in restaurants, a cruise on the Thames... Nikolai pays for most of it. He's saved enough money to repay his father; now he wants to spend some money on me. I don't argue. I feel his pride in being able to take me out to places he's previously never been able to afford. Sometimes I catch him looking at me with a tender, melancholy expression, and a lump comes to my throat. Neither of us says anything about him leaving.

I come home from work on a Friday evening looking forward to a long weekend with Nikolai. It's 9 September, three days short of my 30th birthday. Nikolai has promised to take me somewhere on the day to celebrate. He won't tell me any more.

I pour a glass of wine, grab some nuts, put on the TV and settle back to flick through channels. Nikolai is collecting some clothes from his flat and isn't due over for a while.

My body tenses at the bang of a car door. Then I think I hear footsteps approaching the gate. My heart beats faster. Several times in the past week, I've had a feeling that there's someone outside my flat. There'll be a creak of the gate but when I peep out through the window or scurry onto the pavement, there's no sign of anyone. This time I don't bother to look. I know it's just me getting over-anxious.

I check the time again. It's just gone 7 p.m.; Nikolai probably won't be back till 8 at the earliest. I finish my glass of wine and pour another. Though on arriving home I was in good spirits, now a deep gloom presses on me, an almost physical sensation.

To lighten my mood, I watch a repeat of *The Two Ronnies*. While I'm laughing, the front gate creaks again. I jump, spilling wine onto my skirt. My heart beats erratically.

I mute the TV, creep to the front door and peer through the spy-hole. No one's there. I open the door a crack, feeling like a frightened old woman. The gate is open but there's no sign of anyone. I go out and look up and down the road, then close it and go back inside. Someone must have come to the flat since I got home ten minutes ago, and gone away without shutting it.

For the first time I wonder if I'm losing it. Perhaps I should go to the doctor and get some medication.

When Nikolai gets home, I ask if he's seen anyone hanging around the flat.

'You've got the heebie-jeebies, baby,' he says, laughing. 'It is probably parcel for Mrs Dentist, or Mrs Talky Talky upstairs come again to say she has leak in her pipe. It is not Julian with axe in his hand.'

I laugh too, feeling foolish.

Later, while Nikolai is engrossed in his music, I drive over to Camden Lock. It's only a few minutes away. I want to reassure myself as much as anything.

There are no lights showing in Julian's windows and there's no answer when I ring on his door, nor any other sign that he's in. I buzz his neighbour's intercom.

A woman answers. I vaguely remember talking to her in the lift once.

'Do you know if Julian's around, by any chance?'

Julian asked her to keep an eye on his flat, she tells me. He's been gone for a week; he will be staying in his uncle's house in Perugia until the end of September.

Relief flows through me, as welcome as water to my erratically tended pot plants. Time to stop being paranoid, I tell myself sternly.

Nikolai is in the kitchen in the morning when I go to get breakfast.

'Good morning,' he says glumly, scarcely looking at me. 'I make you tea?'

His music is still spread out over half the table. He's moved practically all his stuff into my place; his keyboard is squeezed into the space beside the French windows, where there's plenty of light. For the past few days he's been working solidly to finish his composition. But for once he isn't hunched over his keyboard or sitting, pencil in hand at the end of the table scribbling into music books.

'What is it? I thought you'd be hard at work by now.'

'I have email,' he says, rubbing his brow as if he has a headache. His eyes are glittery, distracted. 'From my mother. It comes this morning.'

'I thought she didn't use email.'

'My sister sends for her.'

A dart of fear threatens my composure. 'What does it say?'

'My father has more problems with his heart. They take him to the hospital. The doctor says he will not last for much longer – three months, if he is lucky. Both my sisters have come back to see him. I must go too.'

'You must go, yes. I understand.'

A lump blocks my throat. Clouds of steam swirl above the kettle. I watch them whiten the air before disappearing.

'I've got used to you being around,' I say at last.

'I am sorry, Georgie.' He comes to me and speaks softly. 'I must go. I will write to my mother that I will be with her soon.'

Nikolai goes into the garden, leaving me with my mug of tea. From the kitchen window I watch him tread slowly down the path, his right leg heavy and his shoulders drooping, until his figure merges with the shade.

His return to Russia is what I've expected. Only now it is about to happen, I can't make myself believe it.

For my birthday, Nikolai gives me a rose-quartz pendant.

'You like?'

He moves the tray of breakfast things and sits on the bed beside me. He's already dressed, having been up for ages while I slept. I'm still in my dressing gown, scarcely awake.

'It's beautiful. Thank you so much.' I attach the silver chain around my neck and kiss him, tears in my eyes. 'I love you.'

'There are no diamonds, no rubies. But it takes my eye.' He smiles. 'You must wear it and think of me.' His voice is serious.

'I promise,' I say.

'You will open your parcel? The stamp is from Spain.' Without waiting for a reply, he passes me the large package. I remove the brown paper and withdraw a wool wrap in yellow, red and rusty orange. Nikolai reaches across and strokes it. 'It is good material, very soft. Put it on.'

'My mother's great with clothes. She probably made it herself.' I drape it over my shoulders and go to the mirror. It looks great, as she knew it would.

Inside the card, a folded sheet of notepaper brimming with my mother's handwriting:

Have a wonderful birthday, darling. I've been making this for ages – hope you like it.

Missing you very much, it seems ages since I last saw you. Would you like to come and visit? Autumn is marvellous here, not as frazzling as summer. I have finished doing up the guest room – it has a fabulous view from the terrace, by the way. You would love this place, I'm sure.

Latest news – I'm teaching again part-time at the local college. Oh yes, last week I sold my first painting – for 200 euros!! It was on sale at a shop in the village. I am thrilled, you can imagine.

Much love,
Mum

Nikolai leaves the room saying we should go soon or the day would be gone; he's got everything ready. I take off the wrap, fold the letter and put it inside a drawer, contemplating my mother's offer. I've travelled through most of Europe but never to Spain, though my mother has invited me countless times. Ronda is a special place, she says. And it would be interesting to see how she was living over there…

But no, it's too convenient. Does she really think that just because she has a room ready for me, suddenly everything will be OK between us?

A yell breaks into my thoughts.

'Hurry up, Miz! What are you doing?'

'Be there in a sec!' I pull on a T-shirt, jeans and trainers, grab my bag and a denim jacket.

Nikolai picks up the bulging backpack by the front door. 'Let's go.'

53

Nikolai stops and pulls a map scrawled on a folded envelope from his pocket. I remove my jacket and put on my sunglasses. Ahead, a footbridge stretches across the Thames. Below, white hulls glint in the sun and fishermen hunch over their lines, staring into the water. As we pass, one begins to reel in. A silver-blue fish flaps in the air.

We come to a narrow island and cross a further bridge to join the towpath on the opposite bank. A boat chugs noisily out of Teddington Lock, accompanied by sloshing water and whirring machinery. My stomach growls again. I try to peek inside the backpack.

'What have you got in there?'

Nikolai breaks into a run; I can't catch him. Then he turns and walks backward, grinning.

'Now you are old lady, I must be careful. Old ladies are very bad tempered, no?' He lets me catch up, ducking as I swing my bag at him.

We walk hand in hand along the riverside, pass by bicycles, walkers, small screaming children and a dripping dog.

'It is pretty here,' Nikolai says. 'At home, it is not like this.'

He has used the word 'home' again, which he rarely does.

'You miss Russia very much, don't you?'

'When I come to London, I believe I must stay away from Russia for very long time. I think that some people can live anywhere and be happy, maybe I can too. But now I know I am not like that.'

I don't reply. With a jolt of surprise, I realise what I want him to say: come with me to Russia.

'What is wrong?'

Nikolai puts his arms around me. I press my head against his chest. Tears wet my cheeks.

'I don't know what I'll do without you,' I say.

He wipes away my tears with his fingers. 'I don't want to leave you, Georgie.'

'But you will.' I separate myself from him.

'I must go back to make peace with my father – and I must make new life. I must stop running away.'

'And what if the police catch you?'

'It is ten months since I leave Perm. The police in Russia have short memories. I think they forget me by now. But if they arrest me, I will tell them truth. I will tell them what happened.'

'You could be put on trial for murder. They'd put you in prison.'

'It is risk I take.'

I stare at him.

'If it is my punishment,' he says slowly, 'I will accept.'

'What about Anton – and Ivan's relatives? What if they find you? You could be killed.'

'Anton has taken his revenge on my father. I think it is enough. They will forget me soon.'

'And if they don't?'

'I will take my chances.'

His voice is resolute. I know there's nothing I can say to stop him.

We carry on along the riverside path. After a while, Nikolai exclaims in Russian and scrambles down through the undergrowth, calling for me to follow.

The spot is screened from the towpath by a tangle of creeper and wildflowers. Weeping willows hide the view along the river. Their long green fingers tickle the water and small boats bob against the opposite bank.

Nikolai opens the backpack and pulls out a rolled-up mat, followed by an unbelievable amount of stuff: a bottle of champagne inside a plastic cooler, two long-stemmed glasses, two china plates, a packet of Serrano ham, a jar of mushroom pâté, boxes of shortbread biscuits...

I pick up a heavy silver fork.

'Where did you get all this from?'

'It is my secret.'

'I didn't expect this,' I say, blinking back my tears.

We lie side by side under a parasol of leaves, the sun warming our bare feet. The champagne is gone and we've eaten all we can. I close my eyes, listening to water slap against the bank and the rumble of passing boats.

'Will you come to see me, Georgie? In Russia?'

I can only just hear him. But the question cuts through my drowsiness.

'Yes, I would love to. If you want me to.'

'I will show you my city, all the places I love since I was child.'

He looks at me sideways, a flicker of mischief in his eyes. 'Or maybe you will not want to see me. When I leave, you will find another man who will make you happy.'

I shake my head, unable to speak.

'Please. You must not cry. If you cry, I will cry.'

His tongue is warm on my skin, drying my tears. Then his mouth is on mine and his fingers on my breasts, and I want him with every cell in my body.

He unbuttons his jeans and my shirt, unhooks my bra.

Tilting my head I see a motorboat receding to the far bank, where a row of dark houses overlooks wide, smooth lawns.

I help Nikolai remove the rest of my clothes. I don't care that we are in view of passing boats; my need for him takes over. As he moves against me, stones dig into my back. Then I stop noticing anything except my lover. His hair, volcanic black against the sun, flops against his brow. His mouth, speaking words I can't understand. The delight that spreads over his face as I climax.

We grip each other, panting. I run my finger over drops of sweat on his brow. From willow tendrils above, a high-pitched warble and the flutter of wings. Two small birds dart out and over the river.

Still naked, Nikolai gets to his feet and jogs down the slope over to the water shushing against a strip of gravelly sand.

'Georgie!' He waves at me, a big grin on his face. 'Come in!'

I follow him, not bothering to put on any clothes either. Yelping at the cold water, I lunge towards Nikolai's bobbing head. His body slides over mine, water goes up my nose. I start to giggle. Then we're both at it, laughing like children.

We can't stay long in the river, it's too cold. We take turns to dry ourselves with the rug then dress and pack away the remains of the picnic.

'This has been my best birthday ever,' I say, bringing Nikolai close. 'Thank you.'

'It is my pleasure. I wish you to remember this day always.'

We scramble up the bank onto the towpath, me behind Nikolai. I stop beside him. His body is rigid.

'What is it?'

He doesn't answer. I follow his gaze to a lone figure four or five metres away. Instantly I recognise the wavy blond hair, the high brow, the oversized red rugby shirt and the yellow-tinted aviator-style Ray-Bans. And that familiar gawkiness, as if the limbs don't quite belong together. Julian is watching us so intently his head seems to pull his neck forward, like a plant drooping after heavy rain.

'I don't believe,' Nikolai says under his breath.

'Let's go, right now.' I'm not afraid – I simply have a strong urge to be as far away from Julian as possible.

'The guy is crazy. What is he doing here?'

'Please Nikky, let's go.'

He pulls his arm out of my grip and runs towards Julian.

It takes me a few seconds to start moving. Though I run faster than I've run for a long time, I'm not fast enough. Nikolai and Julian disappear into the mess of greenery beside the towpath. I slow, panting. My ears fill with the roar of a huge waterfall.

'Nikolai!' Panic bubbles up through my body, chilling me. 'Nikolai!'

A girl walks towards me, pointing to a narrow track leading away from the path. Her yellow hair curls around a pair of large purple-framed sunglasses.

I jump over stinging nettles, passing creeper-smothered trees, catching my clothes in the undergrowth. In the distance, flashes of red. Moments later, the white of Nikolai's T-shirt. The path opens out into meadows: tall, sun-bleached grass strewn with thistles and gorse. Two figures are clearly visible in the distance, unmoving. No one else is in sight. I run on past clumps of wiry, rough-barked trees to a clearing littered with fragments of bark. A plane drones low across the sky.

The two men stand facing each other. Nikolai is a body length or so from Julian, his back to me, backpack on the ground beside him. As I approach, gasping for breath, Julian waves to me. His eyes are hidden behind mirrored lenses. A scuffed tan leather bag like a school satchel hangs from his shoulder.

'Look who it is,' he says. 'Here we all are again. Nice day for a picnic, isn't it?'

'Go, Georgie.' Nikolai gestures towards the river. 'Leave us!'

Ignoring him, I go up to Julian.

'What the fuck are you doing?' Specks of saliva shoot out of my mouth. 'What's wrong with you? Did you follow us all the way from my flat?'

His smile is insolent.

'I waited outside your place all morning. I guessed you'd come out eventually. I nearly lost you on the Tube, trying to keep out of sight. And it was a bit tricky crossing the river – I was certain one of you would look round and see me.'

A chill goes through me. My heart thuds wildly. 'You weren't in Italy at all, were you?'

'I was for a few days. I came back early. I was hoping I might get back to normal over there.'

Nikolai takes a step towards Julian. From the corner of my eye I see his hand clenching and unclenching at his side.

'So it is you who left that note,' Nikolai says.

'Of course,' casually, not looking at Nikolai. 'I thought it might put the wind up you, even if it didn't actually get rid of you.'

... get rid of you. The words jolt the air out of my body.

Julian turns to me.

'I got the idea from your father, actually. He told me there'd been some trouble at Niknik's building site. A lot of racist stuff going on.'

'He knew about the note?'

Julian looks at me as if I'm an idiot. 'No, he didn't have a clue.'

'You asked someone to put this fucking note in my jacket?'

'It was easy enough.' Julian smiles unpleasantly, curling his upper lip. 'I started going over there and chatting to the guys in hard hats coming out on their breaks. One of them didn't mind running a few errands for me... for a small inducement. He didn't like you, Nikolai. When I mentioned your name he practically began to growl. But I digress.'

Nikolai breathes harshly beside me. He seems to be straining to keep still.

'You asked him to follow me?'

Julian sniggers. 'No, I did that myself. I've been keeping tabs on the two of you for quite a while.'

The back of my neck prickles. So Julian was the one watching and following us all along.

'I did ask him to set up your little accident a while back. But he botched that up. It was meant to be more of a grand exit than a minor tumble. I think wiring buildings is more his thing.'

He wants to kill us both. I gulp in more air. My head feels light, I'll faint soon.

'And now you follow us here.' Nikolai's voice is tight with anger.

'Yes, I saw your little picnic. Two lovebirds cooing to each other, it was quite touching. Then things started to get a lot more interesting.' Julian rests his hand on top of the satchel. 'I couldn't see much. But I worked out what was going on, all right.'

Nikolai raises his fist and takes a step towards Julian.

'Is that all you can do?' Julian withdraws a large, old-fashioned pistol from his satchel and points it at Nikolai's chest. 'What do you say now, Ruski? Not so cocky now, are you?'

My eyes fix on the silver-grey octagonal barrel and follow its slight swaying motion.

'Julian,' I say, a tremble catching my voice. 'Please. You don't need to do this.'

'It's the real thing, believe me. It's part of my grandfather's antique collection – I don't think he'll miss it.' Another mirthless laugh. With his free hand he cocks the hammer, which gives a loud metallic rap.

'You are jealous of me? This is why you do this?'

I glance at Nikolai. His hair is damp with sweat. His T-shirt clings to his chest.

'Put the gun down, Julian,' I say. A cold, clammy toad-skin is spreading over my body. 'Please, put it down. We can talk, can't we?'

Julian smiles without moving the gun away from Nikolai. 'What would you like to talk about?'

'Nikolai's going, Julian. He's going back to Russia. '

'Bully for him.'

'Please, listen to –'

'Put the gun down, Julian.' Nikolai's voice doesn't waver. He takes a step forward.

'Stay away from me.' Julian tilts the gun barrel upwards so that it points midway between Nikolai's eyes. 'I'll do it. I'll finish you off, right now.'

I fight an urge to scream. 'Why, Julian? He's done nothing to you.'

'Georgie… Don't you understand?' For a few moments Julian's lips contort, moving wordlessly. 'He's stolen you from me, this fucking Russian prick. And you, you've gone gaga at him; you can't control yourself, screwing him right in front of everyone like a fucking bitch on heat.'

The barrel swings up to point at my head. I open my mouth to scream, no sound comes. The horizon wobbles. Distant poplars sway, ready to topple. Nikolai launches himself at Julian's legs. Julian totters and collapses. The satchel falls; the gun spins through the air. Two bodies grapple together, a blur of limbs. Julian thrusts his hand into Nikolai's face and pushes himself away. He's back on his feet, so is Nikolai. I watch it all as if this is a film in front of me. I can do nothing. Fear has paralysed me. Then a blunt sound like a mallet striking wood as Julian head-butts Nikolai. Nikolai bends over, staggers a few steps. Suddenly he straightens and throws himself at Julian, his hands reaching for Julian's head.

I run up to them. Julian now lies on the ground beside his twisted Ray-Bans, spluttering and spitting soil, his legs thrashing. Nikolai's hands encircle his neck.

Julian stops moving. His eyes bulge and a horrible choking sound comes from him.

'No!' I shout. 'Nikolai, don't do it! Remember what you promised.'

Nikolai meets my eyes. On his face, turmoil and bewilderment. He lets go of Julian, who moans and raises his head.

'Go on, Ruski, why don't you? Go on, kill me. Don't you have the guts?'

Nikolai climbs off Julian and kicks him in the side.

'Get up.'

Julian gets to his feet, wiping dirt from his eyes and mouth. Nikolai stands facing him, head held high, legs apart, arms at his sides. There is defiance on his face.

'OK,' he says. 'You want to fight? Let's fight.'

Julian steps back, moving his head from side to side.

Nikolai laughs scornfully. 'What do you say now? You point your gun at us, and now you have nothing to say?'

Julian lowers his head. He looks done in.

'Leave us alone, Julian,' I say. 'Just go away and leave us alone.'

He picks up his satchel and the sunglasses, which he puts inside. Then he turns and walks slowly away in the direction of the river. I stand there, dizzy, hardly daring to believe that it's over.

Suddenly, Julian changes direction. He runs towards a straggly patch of weeds and dives onto the ground. Before I realise what's happening, Nikolai is running towards him. Julian scrambles to his feet, holding the gun with both hands in front of his body. It's pointed at Nikolai's chest.

'Stop! Stop or I shoot!'

Nikolai stops, holding up his arms. Julian steps closer, still pointing the gun at him.

A cold dread grips me. I begin to creep towards Julian. I'm off to Nikolai's left-hand side at enough of an angle, I hope, that Julian won't see me approach. Please God, don't let him notice me, I think.

'Why do you do this?' Nikolai calls out. 'What is it you want from me?'

'I want you dead, Nikolai,' Julian replies. 'I want you never to be able to touch her again.'

I'm maybe three or four metres away when he sees me. The gun swings across to point at my face. The barrel opening glints in the sun, a perfect circle. I close my eyes and wait for him to kill me.

A blast rattles my eardrums. I open my eyes. He cocks the hammer once more and straightens his arm.

But already I'm running towards him. Moments later, my foot finds his groin. He makes a grunt tinged with a yelp, like a dog whose paw has been trodden on. His body hinges at the waist and the satchel falls from his shoulder.

The gun is still in his hand. He raises his arm.

I lunge at the gun, knowing I have one last chance. My hand grips his, firmly clasped over the handle. The gun wavers between us, pointing at the sky, at him, at me…

Then everything is silent.

I watch Julian's long figure topple onto the grass. His foot twitches several times, then he's completely still except for a bright red shape spreading from the centre of his chest, like the unfurling petals of a beautiful rose. I sink to my knees, gulping air, drawing it deep into my lungs. Muffled sounds come and go. Nikolai appears beside me, his lips moving. No words come out.

When I open my eyes, Nikolai is holding my hand. Julian is still lying on the ground. In the distance, a teenage girl crouches behind waist-high grass. She looks straight at me, then frowns and rubs her eyes as if she can't believe what she has just seen. She has pale, bony shoulders; a purple bra beneath a flimsy, half buttoned blouse. Beside her is a boy, almost hidden by the grass. He draws himself upright, revealing light brown skin and hair braided in rows across his head. Pink lipstick is smeared across his mouth. He stares at me, eyes wide open.

Then they are gone.

I look down at Julian's body. His eyes are open, their irises that same unnatural blue.

I hear Nikolai's voice as if he's talking through a thick cloth. He has his phone to his ear. A pause, then more words. I can't understand them. The sounds blur, clanking together inside my head.

'He's dead,' I say in the strange silence that follows. I scarcely recognise my own voice.

I make an effort to stand but my legs are unsteady and my head seems to have no weight at all.

Nikolai catches me as I fall. I cling to him, inhaling the acrid smell of his sweat.

Quietly at first, sirens begin to wail.

Four policemen in uniform. They move closer, watching us carefully the whole time, as if at any moment we might try to point a gun at them.

I pull away from Nikolai, startled. He moves my head gently so that my face is opposite his. I notice the large reddish bump on his brow just above his eye.

'Listen, Georgie. You must tell them. I will not be here if you do not kill him.' Tears fill his eyes. 'You saved my life.'

The police order us to separate and stand with our arms and legs apart. Everything happens so fast, I can't make sense of it. As they pat us down I feel I'm going to fall over, my legs are shaking so. A woman officer appears beside me, holding open a pair of handcuffs.

They're meant for me? I turn to Nikolai for guidance but he is already cuffed and being led away. I watch the back of his T-shirt recede, the cotton streaky with sweat. Behind him, in the distance, several people are gathered, watching us. The girl I saw on the towpath is talking to a policeman, her purple sunglasses propped on top of her head. She stops talking when she sees me and her mouth hangs open.

The handcuffs click shut.

'I am arresting you on suspicion of murder,' the policewoman intones. 'You do not have to say anything. But it may harm your defence if… '

54

I climb into the back of the police van as instructed. My mouth tastes of metal. I'm shivering and my top is soaked in sweat.

The journey is short. The policewoman helps me down from the van. She leads me into the police station and on into a room where she removes my handcuffs, leaving me with another policewoman standing behind a counter.

'Where's Nikolai?' I ask. 'The guy I was with. Can I talk to him?'

'He's been taken to another cell. He'll be questioned separately. You can talk to him after they're finished with him.'

A chill goes through me. Finished with him?

'You'll be here for quite a while, I should think.' She sounds weary. 'Do you want me to phone someone for you and inform them you're here?'

'My father,' I say, and give his mobile number.

The number is busy, she tells me, putting the phone down – she'll try again later and make sure to leave a message if she can't get through. She hands me a sheet of paper. 'You have the right to talk to a solicitor at any time. Sign here to show you've understood.'

'A solicitor?' My voice rings out in alarm. 'I haven't done anything wrong. Julian was trying to kill us –'

'Don't worry, you'll get the chance to explain everything soon.'

She takes my bag and spills its contents on the counter. 'Sachet of tissues, bar of chocolate, house keys, mobile phone, pencil, nail file… '

Next she asks me to remove my watch, jewellery and belt. Everything is put inside plastic bags. She asks me to raise my arms and pats me down.

'Name and address?' She stabs at her keyboard. A long list of questions follows: do you take prescription drugs, and so on. Then I'm photographed, fingerprinted and taken to another room. DNA swabs are taken from my hands and mouth. As I stand there with my mouth open, it finally sinks in. They think I murdered Julian.

In my cell are a mattress and a partly walled-off toilet. There's no washbasin. The clang of the door resounding in my ears, I use the toilet. It's a worn, distinctly unsanitary looking object. When I'm finished I fumble for toilet roll. There's a battered box with no paper inside. I resort to the scrap of tissue in my jeans pocket and lower myself onto the stained mattress.

How long will I have to spend in this place? Will Nikolai be put through all this too? Don't they know he didn't shoot Julian? He didn't touch the gun. Surely, they'll work out that the finger-prints on the gun aren't his.

They might be suspicious, though, at first. They might find out that he's overstayed his visa and try to contact the Russian police.

I can't think any more. Julian, once my closest friend, has just tried to kill me. If I hadn't done something, both Nikolai and I would be dead now, not him.

It's as unbelievable as someone saying that the world has just turned bright orange.

There's a rap on the door. Keys rasp and the door swings open.

'Yer dinner, miss.' The copper who delivered me to my cell places a tray bearing a plastic carton and a cup of water on the floor in front of me. I leave the carton untouched and drink the water.

Later, I'm stirred from rambling, semi-conscious thoughts by a sus-tained rapping on the door.

'Get yerself up now, miss!'

The constable takes me to Interview Room 1, in which there is little besides a man and woman in plain clothes sitting behind a table. The man, DI something, clears his throat, gestures for me to sit in the chair opposite and starts the tape recorder in front of him.

'This interview is being tape-recorded and may be given in evidence if your case is brought to trial. We are in an interview room at Teddington Police Station. It's twenty hundred hours on the twelfth of September 2005.' His voice has the residue of a Merseyside accent and the texture of a scouring pad. He notes who we all are and tells me I don't have to answer their questions. But if I don't, that could harm my defence should this matter go to court.

He exhales the odour of cigarettes. 'Do you wish to speak to a solicitor now or have one present during the interview?'

'I don't want a solicitor,' I insist. 'I haven't done anything wrong.'

'Are you sure you don't want me to get the duty solicitor?'

A flush of panic comes over me. I'm not thinking straight. I do need a solicitor, don't I?

I'm taken back to my cell.

After a long wait, I'm taken to the interview room again where a young black woman with cropped hair is waiting. She's well turned out in a dark suit and heels. She stands and shakes my hand, sort of smiles and says her name loudly. Miss Pile, it sounds like.

We sit down and she asks me what happened earlier. I try to recall it all and to translate my experience into words. But patches of my recollection are sketchy, and much of what I do remember doesn't make sense. It's like trying to see fish through pond water.

'I had to do it,' I say in the end. 'He was going to kill us.'

Miss Pile tells me I shouldn't tell the police that, or anything else that sounds like an admission of guilt, because it might incriminate me. 'If they ask you something you don't think you should answer, say "No comment".'

Before I can process this or reply, there's a knock on the door. The detectives come in without waiting. My solicitor looks away from me, sits up straighter in her chair. The DI sets up the tape recorder again, repeats the introductory bit, then rolls up his shirtsleeves. It's warm in this room.

'Miss Cameron, you are being held in connection with the shooting of Julian Lewis this afternoon near Teddington Lock.' Forensic tests are being carried out on a gun that has been found next to the body, he explains, holding up a sealed plastic bag. 'A Remington Rider Pocket Revolver, made in the 1880s. Kept in good nick, clearly... ' He puts the bag down. 'Miss Cameron. We need to ask you about this afternoon so we can establish exactly what happened.'

I glance at Miss Pile. She looks nervous, hot or both. Droplets of sweat cluster on her brow. Her hands are fastened in her lap. Her back is rigidly upright, her neck taut as a ballerina's.

'Georgina.' The woman officer, a DC I think, smiles crisply.

'Georgie.'

'Georgie. Can you tell us how you came to be at Teddington Lock this afternoon?' She has precision-cut hair and an accentless voice.

'I was with Nikolai,' I tell her.

'Nikolai?'

'Nikolai Alexandrovich Konstantinov. He's my friend – he's Russian. We'd been having a picnic beside the river to celebrate my birthday. It was a surprise. He'd brought loads of food. Then... '

I hesitate, wondering whether to mention the impromptu sex and our swim.

'Please tell us everything that happened Georgie, just as you remember it.'

I glance at Miss Pile who nods, two small, bird-like movements. I take a long drink from the plastic cup of water in front of me. Then I tell them how Julian appeared ahead on the towpath and ran to a meadow behind the river, then while we were talking brought a gun out of his bag and pointed it at me and Nikolai. How the gun went flying, the two men fought and finally Julian walked away from us, apparently defeated. How all of a sudden he made a run for the gun and pointed it at Nikolai. How I crept up on Julian, he fired at me and missed, then I struggled with him for the gun. How I kicked him in the groin to make him drop it, then in desperation tried to tug the gun out of his hand. How we struggled once more until the gun went off a second time and Julian fell down dead. I leave out just one thing.

'Thank you, Georgie,' says the DC.

There's a gap filled by the sound of pens on paper. Miss Pile smiles at me awkwardly as if she's forgotten how. She's worried, isn't she? I've said something I shouldn't have, perhaps. The strip lighting overheads buzzes loudly. I take another drink of water, feeling like I'm in an exam I haven't prepared for. One answer might make the difference between pass and fail.

'How did the gun go off exactly, the second time? The shot that killed Julian.' The DI asks the question.

'I was trying to get the gun away from Julian. He was pointing it at me. I pushed it back at him... The gun was moving about between us. It was all over in a couple of seconds. The gun just went off. He dropped it and fell down.'

'Where was the gun pointed when it went off?'

I hesitate. I must be careful what I say. 'The gun must have been pointed at him, I suppose, or he wouldn't have been shot.'

The DI leans forward. 'Who pulled the trigger?'

As I open my mouth to speak, Miss Pile raises a hand to stop me. 'Be careful how you answer.'

'I don't know,' I say eventually. 'Julian must have pulled it. He must have accidentally pulled the trigger.'

The detectives exchange glances.

'Where was Nikolai all this time?'

'He was behind me, I couldn't see him. When Julian shot at me and missed, Nikky called out something – he was quite a way off then. When the second shot fired he was much closer. I heard him panting behind me. He must have run over to us.'

My heart begins to thump. They don't believe me. I sneak a glance at Miss Pile, rigid beside me. She's biting her lip now.

'How exactly did you try to take the gun from Julian, just before he was shot?'

'I grabbed his hand, the one that was holding onto the gun. I grabbed the gun with my other hand. The barrel, I think.'

'Why did you try to take the gun from Julian? What was your plan?'

'Excuse me, my client –'

The DI growls, his especially noisy throat clearing cutting off Miss Pile.

'I just wanted to get the gun away from him,' I reply, determined to say my piece. 'It was self-defence. I didn't have a plan.'

Silence. Miss Pile dips her head.

'Julian had been going to shoot Nikolai,' I repeat, feeling as if I'm talking to a brick wall. 'If I hadn't stopped him, he would have killed us both.'

The DC taps her pen on the desk, a puzzled look on her face.

'How well did you know Julian?'

'He was a friend from university – until earlier this year. He got jealous of Nikolai and I had to end the friendship.'

'When was the last time you saw Julian, before today?'

I tell everything: the pleading phone calls and emails, the anonymous calls, the intruder in my flat, which I reported to the police immediately afterwards, and finally how Julian pushed me against a tree and tried to rape me.

'How well do you know Nikolai?'

'I met him in February. We're close.'

'Sleeping together?'

'That's right.'

'Did Julian meet Nikolai before today?'

'Once, at my father's party.'

The DI takes over, probing into my relationship with Julian. After a while, all their questions seem to merge into a big, sticky trap.

'Miss Cameron, please tell us what really happened. Did you and Nikolai plan to shoot Julian?'

I realise the DI is frowning, awaiting an answer to his question.

I pull at my damp top, hoping it hasn't gone transparent. Their position is now horribly clear.

'Excuse me,' interjects Miss Pile. 'That's a leading question. Could you rephrase that, please?'

The DI exhales loudly. 'Miss Cameron, please tell us about your plan to shoot Julian.'

'That's pure speculation –' Miss Pile begins, but I'm too riled with the DI not to answer.

'We didn't plan anything. It was Julian's gun, how could we have planned to kill him? He told us it was in his grandfather's antique collection. He took it out of his bag and pointed it at us.'

The DC scribbles furiously. The DI carries on.

'Why would you have put your own life in danger? You could have left Julian and Nikolai and gone to get help.'

'If I'd done that, Nikky would be dead now.' I'm starting to feel hopeless. Then I remember. 'What about the witnesses? Haven't they told you what happened?'

The DI clears his throat again and glowers at me.

'Georgie,' the DC says firmly, 'no witnesses to the shooting have come forward.' The police have talked to a young woman and an elderly man who was walking his dog in the meadow, but both turned up only after the second gunshot.

'What about the couple in the grass? The teenagers?'

She looks at me blankly.

'They were only a short distance away,' I insist. 'They must have seen everything.'

No, they haven't talked to any teenagers. They have appealed for any witnesses to come forward, but none has as yet.

'Let's break for ten minutes.' The DI flicks off the tape recorder.

Miss Pile pulls a phone from her bag, studies the screen then scrapes back her chair and rushes out of the room. I'm taken back to my cell.

I'm so desperate to use the toilet I go ahead despite the lack of paper, which I've forgotten to ask for. My hot stream pelts against the ceramic throat, loud enough surely for everyone in the police station to hear.

I sink onto the mattress. I want to go home, take a hot shower, put Etta James on full volume and yell at the top of my voice. Why, Julian? Why?

Back in the interview room, it's the DC's turn.

Where is Nikolai from? How long has he been in London? Why did he come here? I try to be vague but she stops me.

'Georgie,' she says in a grave voice, 'you can't help Nikolai unless you're completely honest with us.'

Miss Pile nods.

'You know Nikolai and I didn't plan to shoot Julian, don't you? Isn't it obvious?'

'We have to look at every possibility I'm afraid, Miss Cameron.'

The questions go on. Do I know of any other names Nikolai uses, or any others he's used in the past? Why didn't Nikolai go to the police when he received the threatening note? Did I know he's staying in the UK illegally?

The DI takes over.

'Miss Cameron. Why would Julian want to try to kill you and Nikolai?'

'He became obsessed with me, he wasn't thinking straight.'

He moves his face towards mine. I smell stale smoke again.

'Why did you run towards Julian when he had a gun in his hand?'

'I told you. To get the gun away from him. To stop him shooting Nikolai.'

'But you could have been killed.'

I don't know what to say.

'You can say "No comment",' says the solicitor.

'No comment,' I repeat robotically.

'And then Julian pointed the gun at you, fired and missed, yet you confronted him once again?'

'I've already told you. It was in self-defence. It was the only chance I had.'

Another break. Miss Pile comes to the cell and tries to talk to me about what happened when Julian was shot. But I can't take anything in. Her questions echo around my head, blurring into each other. When I try to speak my words come out wrong. She starts to look at her watch and finally leaves me in the cell alone.

My thoughts begin to drift. I have no idea of the time. I lie on the mattress looking at scratches and imperfections in the wall. My heart beats faster, like waves crashing through my body. I close my eyes. Again I see the opening of the gun barrel, pointing at me for an eternity, my brain telling me that any second now I will be dead.

Then I see Julian lying on the ground, lifeless, a red rose blooming from his chest.

Miss Pile sits opposite the detectives, her hands clasped in her lap, head dipped. She looks up and smiles as I enter, a momentary stretching of the lips that's over almost before it's started. A jolt goes through me. I'm going to be charged, I know it.

The DC looks at the DI, who looks at me sheepishly.

The two teenaged witnesses I mentioned have come forward, he tells me. Their evidence supports my statement, as does Nikolai's. He accepts that I unintentionally caused the gun to go off while attempting to defend myself and Nikolai; they aren't going to charge either of us.

They've informed the Crown Prosecution Service who will consider the matter further, but he considers it unlikely that they would wish to press charges. I'll be bailed to appear at this police station in one week, after any further evidence has been reviewed. If there are to be any charges brought, or if there's a decision to hold a coroner's enquiry into whether the shooting was lawful, I will be informed then. I can go home now.

I stare at the DI, not convinced I've heard him right.

'You're free to go, Miss Cameron.'

55

Nikolai sits on the low wall outside the police station, his backpack at his feet, drawing on a cigarette. As I go towards him, the exhaustion on his face turns to relief.

'Thank God. I think they will never you let you go.'

He smothers the cigarette against the wall, stands upright and opens his arms wide. I let him hold me. He feels solid, warm and wonderfully alive.

My legs are unsteady again. I lower myself onto the wall.

'Nor did I. I thought they were going to charge me with homicide or whatever it's called. They didn't seem to believe anything I said at first.'

Nikolai sits down beside me. I reach out to touch the damaged part of his forehead, bulging and turning purple.

'I look like boxer,' he grins, 'who loses.'

We get a taxi back to my flat. On the way, Nikolai clasps my hand tight. The taxi radio dispenses a mix of adverts and DJ banter. I have that disconcerting feeling of coming back home after a long time away. I'm dazed and disorientated. All I can do is sit back and watch the night streets go by.

When we get to my flat I check my mobile. There are 18 messages from my father.

'What's happening?' he demands when I call. 'Are you out of there?'

'They let me go,' I tell him. 'They're not going to charge me.'

'Thank Christ!' I almost feel the flick of his spit against my skin. 'I've been worried sick.'

He's spent the past three hours on the phone trying to track down a good criminal barrister for me, in between calls to the police station, and was about to head over there. He throws questions at me. What happened? Why did they arrest you? Why didn't you call before?

I start to answer but my brain seems to be well into a system shutdown; I can only manage a few words at a time. 'I have to go, Dad,' I tell him after a bit. 'I'll tell you the rest tomorrow.'

Nikolai puts his hand on my arm. 'Here, take this.'

I drink the Scotch whisky he gives me. Its fiery tingle kicks my brain back to life. Nikolai pulls out a couple of chairs and the two of us sit down.

'What happened to you, Nikky? They didn't charge you either? They were asking me questions about your visa. I didn't know what to say.'

'I tell them the truth. My visa is for six weeks but I stay longer. It is not for working but I must pay my rent. I say that in ten days I will fly to Moscow to see my father, he is dying.' His eyes narrow. 'They say they are going to hand me to Immigration, I am in serious trouble. They ask what I do before I come here. I tell them I was in Russian army. They say I know how to use guns, I know how to kill. They ask if it is my gun, the one they find, if we use to shoot Julian. Then they ask if it is our plan to kill him, if you and I agree our story before we murder Julian.'

He strokes his stubbled chin, eyes flashing.

'I tell them it is Julian who tries to murder us. They do not believe. I think how strange it is that I kill a man in Russia and I am free – and for this crime I do not commit, I will be punished.' Nikolai meets my eyes, a bitter smile on his face. 'But they try to scare me, that is all. I expect that they will talk with Russian police and find I am wanted for Ivan's murder. But they say nothing of this.'

'So your father's bribe worked?'

He shrugs. 'I think that they do not bother to check on me. Or maybe there is nothing on my record. The police in Russia, they wiped it. Who knows? Anyway, the next time they say, "Go take care of your girlfriend", and I think that fate is kind to me.'

I press his hand and swallow the rest of my whisky, hoping that the alcohol, shock and exhaustion combined will soon take me into oblivion. I don't want to see Julian's face any more. It keeps coming back. His twisted lips. His eyes staring at me, bluer than blue, wide open, astonished.

'I didn't tell the police everything,' I say, half to myself.

'What didn't you tell them? Georgie?'

'When I was trying to get the gun off Julian, at the end... ' I don't know if I can say this. 'The gun was pointed at his stomach. I pushed it so it pointed at his chest and squeezed on his hand really hard to make him pull the trigger. I wanted to kill him, Nikky. I didn't want him to get up again.'

My breath comes in shallow gasps. I had killed Julian. I'd shot him on purpose. The police ought to have charged me, surely? I pick up my glass, which trembles in my hand. But there's no whisky left.

'Look at me, Georgie.' Nikolai takes both my hands and holds them still. 'Julian was crazy in the head. If you do not shoot him, we will not be here now. I will not be here now. What you did was in self-defence. It was the right thing that you do.'

I say nothing. I don't know if what I did would have been shown to be self-defence in court, or if it had been the right thing to do. But I do know I had no choice except to kill Julian. If I were able to go back and relive those final moments, knowing that this time I had the chance to save him, I wouldn't save him. I would do it all exactly the same.

56

The funeral is to be held at a church in west London, not far from where Julian's parents live, in a house close to the river. I've been there twice and briefly met his parents and his sister.

I go, in the end. Because Julian was my friend – and because I will never have the chance to tell him that I am sorry for my part in his suffering.

I arrive five minutes before the service is due to start. In the churchyard, people in dark, formal clothing cluster in the shade of a yew. Two of them stand apart from the others. A slender man with thinning hair taps ash into the flowerbed. His long neck and high forehead are familiar, but I can't place him. Grabbing on to his arm, a girl with pink-streaked hair in a grey cardigan and black jeans stares forlornly at me. She has the same slender build. Father and daughter, I think.

Then I realise who they are: Julian's father and sister.

I slip into an empty pew near the back behind two small boys and their parents, willing no one to turn around. Julian's father and sister will be sat at the front, safely out of sight. There are around eighty people in the church. A chorus of coughing echoes through as the vicar begins to speak, his face fleshy and melancholy as a Basset Hound's.

'I am sure that we all feel great sorrow at the passing of this young man in the prime of his life. It is a shocking and terrible thing for a young life to have ended in violence, for his potential to be so abruptly cut short…'

During long pauses, sweet-sucking noises erupt from the pew in front. I keep perfectly still as he speaks, certain the slightest movement will draw the attention of the entire assembly.

After the vicar's address, Julian's father gets up from the front pew and lopes towards the lectern.

'My son,' he begins, 'meant the world to me.' He sounds so like Julian: the same fluid, polished tones only deeper.

'His sudden death is difficult for me and my family to comprehend.' His gaze travels over the pews in the assured manner of someone used to addressing large gatherings. 'Actually, I couldn't believe it, not until I saw my son's body. It was the sort of death that should never happen to anyone… Least of all, to one's own son.'

He grips the lectern and his eyes sweep over the congregation – this time, I could have sworn, he looks directly at me.

Mr Lewis loosens his tie. Silence, save for the din of my heart.

'I'm not going to say anything about what happened on that day – an inquest will be held to examine all matters pertinent to Julian's death.' I study the hymn book resting on the ledge, the worn lettering and disintegrating fabric at the ends of the spine. 'The actions of my son... ' Mr Lewis struggles to keep his composure. 'They were not the actions of the young man we knew.'

As Mr Lewis talks about the Julian he's known and how much he would be missed, I think of how little I really knew Julian and which version of him I will keep in my mind. I think of the cake from Harrods that he bought for my 25th birthday, and how, after guzzling too much of it followed by an hour's aerobatic flight in an open cockpit, we'd both been sick, and how later on, in a country pub near the airfield, this seemed inordinately funny. I think of long Sunday afternoons on his terrace, the hours chatting as we listened to CDs and the wacky conversations we will never have again. Then I think of the lapis earrings still in my drawer. And the gun he pointed at me.

Finally, Mr Lewis returns to his seat. I glance up at the girl with a narrow face and pink-streaked hair as she begins to speak in a shaky voice.

'I don't have much to say, I've never been much good at speaking. Just that I'll miss Jules... ' She dabs at a make-up-smudged eye. 'He was the best brother in the world.'

A quiet sobbing begins from the front pews, then someone else gets up to speak. The sobbing keeps on through Julian's favourite songs, starting with 'Come Away With Me' by Norah Jones. I leave during the third song, 'Reasons to be Cheerful'.

The sun is bright and there's a sweet after-rain softness to the air, and suddenly I'm overwhelmed with happiness.

'I'm alive,' I whisper. Somehow I feel as if I truly understand this for the first time.

57

I'm with my father at The Spaniards, a popular pub beside Hampstead Heath. It's on the cusp between summer and autumn. People sit in the garden and the open windows let in snatches of laughter. My father takes another generous sip of red wine. I finger the stem of my own glass, its contents untouched.

It was his idea that we meet in person – I had my bail visit to the police station this morning, and there are things he needs to say. But now we're face to face a gap still separates us, blocking the easy exchange that for so long I took for granted.

'So, they're not going to charge you,' my father begins. 'Thank God for that. You've just got to get through the coroner's enquiry. I can't imagine that will change anything though.'

It's scheduled for six months' time, I've been told, at Kingston Crown Court. I wonder if I might tell the coroner the truth about those final moments. I didn't tell the police this morning and I haven't told my father.

'You're going to leave work, then. Any thoughts as to what you're going to do?'

'I've got a few ideas... nothing definite.' Not knowing feels exciting, and a tiny bit scary. All I know for sure is that my next job will have nothing to do with food supplements. Whatever I end up doing, it will be something I care about.

Another gap stretches out between us.

My father leans onto his elbows, fingers interlocking.

'How could he have done something like that, come at you with a loaded gun? Julian always seemed such an affable, reasonable guy. A bit quirky but what the hell.'

'He had another side to him that I didn't see,' I reply. 'Maybe no one saw. Something that made him lose his reason.'

'He must have had something seriously wrong to do that, for Christ's sake.' My father makes a noise of disgust and drains his glass.

'I should have let him down more gently, maybe.' Julian was the brother I never had, I've realised.

'He could have killed you, Georgie. It's not your fault, no one in their right mind could think that.'

I say nothing.

'You're not the only one with regrets, you know.' My father

lowers his head. 'I was wrong about Nikolai. But after what happened to Sean… I'm sorry I didn't listen to you and I wasn't there when you needed me. I was so concerned about Nikolai, I couldn't see that Julian was the dangerous one.' Before I can reply, he goes on. 'I want to apologise for something else too. That accident last year – I should have been straight with you. But I didn't want to lose your good opinion of me.' He fiddles with his watch strap. 'I've thought about it a lot lately. I've started to change how things are done at work. Everything should be in place by the time I leave.'

'You said you weren't going to retire yet.'

'I've changed my mind.'

My father goes to the bar, and I think about what he's said. He sounds sincere in his regrets; I should forgive him, shouldn't I? Everyone makes mistakes. I've made too many myself to stand in judgement.

'There's another thing.' My father places his refilled glass on the table and sits down. 'I wanted to tell you before but somehow I never got round to it.' I watch his hands, restless on the table. 'It's about what happened before your mother left. It's something you should know.' He frowns, shifts in his chair. 'Our marriage was over years before Frances left. Her depression – I didn't understand it at the time, but looking back it was always there. She'd be all right for a while, then the blackness would come back… I let her slip away from me, stopped trying to get things back on track. When I found out about her affair she promised to never see Julio again. Then a year later she told me she was in love with him; she was off to live in Spain.'

His words come out in a rush. I lean towards him, stuck like a wasp in a glass of lemonade.

'She wanted to buy a flat in London so she could spend more time with you. She was worried about how her being away was affecting you. But I said she should stay where she was; I'd take care of you – you didn't want her around and neither did I. She said she'd go to court for custody. I said they would never grant it, not after she had abandoned you.' He speeds on, a bowling ball in a ten-pin alley. 'I wanted her out of our lives, Georgie. I didn't want to be constantly reminded of what I'd lost… That's why I told you things about her that I shouldn't have.'

'What things?'

'I said your mother was too busy with her new life to see you. It was maybe six months in, a year. I distorted things. I didn't pass on her messages to you, I said she was on holiday with him. I needed to make sure you stayed with me. I didn't want to lose you as well.' He dabs at the corner of his eye with a paper serviette. 'Say something, Georgie.'

His words are trying to find a place to settle. I can't find any of my own.

'I didn't want to let you down. I know how much you look up to me – looked up to me. But I wanted you to know the other side of things. Your mother is just trying to get through life as best she can. She loves you as much as I do.'

'Does she know about this? Did you tell her?'

He says he told her a few years ago. Some of it, anyway.

'Why didn't she talk to me? She never said anything.'

'I think she knew it was too late. Whatever she said, you wouldn't listen. Her affair, her decision to leave home – she thought she had to pay for it by losing you.'

So, nothing is as it appears. My father helped to turn me against my mother. Why did I listen to him and not her? Why didn't I see what was really going on?

'Georgie. I'm sorry, love.' Tears smudge his eyes. 'You don't hate me, do you?'

I know he seeks forgiveness but I have to look away. I get to my feet.

I call her that evening.

'Hello, Mum.'

'Georgina,' she says slowly as if savouring each syllable. I don't mind her calling me by that name any more. Suddenly, I love my name. 'How lovely to hear from you.'

Her voice is velvety and warm. I imagine her in her cool house in the hills, surrounded by canvases and brushes, her body worn now and her face wrinkled, but her eyes still bold. How could I have forgotten that she's my mother?

'I'm sorry it took me so long to call back,' I say. 'Would it... Would it still be OK for me to visit?'

Her laugh is unexpected, as fierce as the Spanish sun.

'Yes, darling, of course! Of course it's OK for you to visit.'

And it's arranged. I will visit my mother in Spain as soon as I finish my notice period at work. For a week, a month... I have no fixed plans. I might even look for some work there.

My imagination leaps ahead. Ronda will still be hot in October.

I'll watch my mother paint and maybe we can go to exhibitions together. We'll go for early morning walks and sit in cafés and cook meals.

And at sunset we'll sit out on the terrace looking at the Andalusian hills, and try to make up for all the years we've missed.

58

Shortly after nine on a clear September morning, Nikolai and I climb into the MG. Destination, Dorset. It's our last trip together before he leaves for Russia. In three days, Nikolai will board a plane to Moscow.

We arrive at a village – a grocery shop-cum-post office and a few stone-walled cottages a mile or so inland. We knock on the one with a B&B sign in the window. A man in slippers with a pipe in his mouth leads us up to a low-ceilinged room with floral wallpaper.

When he's gone, Nikolai dumps his bag on a chair and flops onto the mattress. The bed creaks loudly. I open a window overlooking a garden and breathe in the scent of honeysuckle.

'Please, Georgie. Don't be sad.'

I turn to him, wondering how I could not be.

'When I am famous composer,' Nikolai says, 'I will live in a big house. It will have big garden with statues and fountains, beautiful flowers and birds of every kind. And you will be with me. Every evening I will play you my latest work on my piano.' He smiles. 'After this we will make love and all the birds will sing to us.'

We walk to the nearest pub, a mile down the lane. The sky glows with threads of violet and gold. We eat in a quiet alcove, side by side. Through a fine haze of cigarette smoke I look at black-and-white photographs of local scenes.

All of a sudden, Nikolai puts down his knife and fork. 'I don't want to leave you, Georgie.'

I turn to him, surprised to see tears in his eyes.

Stay. The word hovers behind my lips, but I don't say it. I put my arms around his neck.

'Kiss me,' he whispers.

Tears slip down my cheek and merge with his, making our kiss taste of salt.

I wake to warm sunshine, frying bacon and two yellow butterflies flitting at the open window. Beside me, Nikolai sleeps on. I listen to his slow breathing. The cover is pushed off him, revealing muscular brown limbs and a band of white around his middle. Below his belly button, the ridge of his scar. It's changed since he first showed it to me, months ago: the wound is smoother and flatter, and has faded to a whitish pink. Gently, so as not to wake him, I kiss it.

We're standing a few metres from the cliff edge. I gaze at the foamy rocks far below, glad that my feet are on solid ground.

'Come,' Nikolai says, pulling my hand.

Ahead, green-iced cliffs ripple upwards into the far distance. We turn and walk in the other direction, resting on a grassy bank sheltered from the wind. On either side of us is a great sweep of coast.

Nikolai puts his arm around my shoulders. I close my eyes, absorbing his faintly lemony smell.

'I am scared to go back,' he says softly.

'Because you might be in danger?'

'It is not that. It is because of my father. He might not want to see me. I worry he will tell me to go away, he does not want me in his house.'

'He doesn't know you're coming back?'

'My mother says it is best for him not to know. She thinks if I am standing at his door, he will not turn me away... Every week he is getting worse. He lies in his bed, he does not speak or go out of the house. My mother says he is waiting to die.'

'You must see him. Before it's too late.'

'I have decided, Georgie, I will get job in Perm teaching piano – I think I will do this well. When I am not teaching, I will write music.'

I tell him it's a wonderful idea.

'Also, I will apply to Moscow Conservatory to study composition. It is possible, I think.'

'You should, absolutely. You'll write and tell me all about it, won't you Nikky?'

'I promise.' He reaches for my hand. 'Now you must promise me something. When I am settled in my new life – next spring, maybe – will you promise to visit me?'

I squeeze his hand. 'Yes, I promise.'

'You will fly to Moscow, I will meet you. We will take train to Perm. I will show you everywhere and then we will stay in mountains. And maybe when you come, you will not want to go back. You will want to stay with me.'

'You would want that, Nikky?' I look at him, not daring to believe.

'Yes, I want.' A pause. 'But to live in Russia... It is not easy. Your home is here.'

'I don't need to stay in the same place forever. We could find a house together. A house overlooking the river, somewhere beautiful. You'll write your next sonata and I'll keep goats and make scarves or something, and –'

'We will have children.' He's smiling now. 'Two, it is enough?'

'No, I want three at least. I'm an only child, remember. I want a big family.' Where this comes from, I don't know. I've never realised I want children until now.

'And a dog, Georgie, don't forget. Three children and dog. We will have wonderful life.'

On our way back down to the village, we pass a tiny church.

'Wait, will you?' Nikolai pulls his hand from mine.

After ten minutes I go inside. My footsteps echo in the cool silence. The pews are empty, apart from one at the back. A shaded figure sits, head lowered.

I walk back towards the entrance, pausing to study the Latin words carved into the stone columns, thinking of all the people who have come here to pray through the centuries. I've never properly believed in God – at least I've always been more doubting than believing. Yet this sign of another's belief touches me.

A few minutes later, I look up as Nikolai approaches. His expression is lighter than before, as if all his doubts and worries have fallen away.

'It was time,' he says. 'I find him.'

I watch the pile on my living room floor grow bigger. Nikolai's stuff. Fifteen numbered music manuscript books in various degrees of dog-earedness; six packets of tights from Selfridges for Nikolai's sisters; a Wedgwood teapot and two matching cups wrapped in a *Cats* T-shirt for his mother; a model of an E-type Jag in British racing green for his father. CDs, clothes, a pair of black leather shoes, new Nike trainers, his folded Spurs scarf, his battered Russian–English dictionary and the book of Federico Lorca poems I gave him.

Nikolai opens a shortbread tin and takes out the letters from his mother and sister along with the pictures of me he's taken, and puts them beside the other things.

'That's it,' he says.

I help him stuff everything inside his holdall. Finally, we get it zipped shut and he lugs it to the front door. I stare at his name written in large capitals on the tag, followed by an address in Perm, and try once again to imagine six months without Nikolai, a life without Nikolai. How will I live without him?

I know the answer. Somehow, out of all that has happened since Nikolai came into my world and Julian went out of it, I've discovered how precious and fleeting life is. I'm not going to waste any more of it. No longer will I live timidly, nibbling off little pieces at a time, fearing what can happen. I'll take whatever chances I have to find love and happiness. If they don't work out, so be it. Perhaps I'll go to Russia, live with Nikolai and one day bring up our children. Or perhaps I'll fall in love again, with someone I have yet to meet.

'How do I look?' He has his leather jacket on. His hair is neatly combed, his face clean-shaven.

'Different.'

He laughs. 'You prefer me to be the bad guy, no?'

I check my watch. I've booked him a cab to the airport; he refused my offer to drive him, saying he wanted us to say goodbye in my flat.

'It is not yet time,' he says. 'Let's wait outside.'

We stand on the patio in gentle sunlight; the flowerbeds are brimming with roses.

'This is for you.' He reaches into his jacket pocket. 'I make recording the day I sell my keyboard.'

I take the CD case and read the label. '"Piano Sonata Number 1" by Nikolai Alexandrovich Konstantinov. For Georgie.'

I thank him, blinking away my tears.

'It is because of you that I finish this,' he says. 'You listened to me, you made me see that I must not waste my life. You make me understand that I am not truly bad person.'

'Well, I must thank you too.'

'For what?' He grins. 'Giving you so much trouble?'

'For giving me the kick up the backside I deserved. No, seriously. You gave me something I didn't expect to find again.' I look into his dark eyes, now fixed on mine. 'I love you, Nikky.'

'And I love you, Miz. You have taken my heart.' He touches my cheek. 'It is always with you.'

From the road, two horn blasts. I fling my arms around Nikolai and hold him as tight as I can. Then I let him go.

Acknowledgements

I'm grateful to all the wonderful people at Unbound who have helped to make this book what it is, along with my editor Rachel Rayner (the pain was worth it in the end) and cover designer Mark Ecob.

Thanks to the many people who helped with my research, including Elena Driver and Richard McKane for information relating to Russia and Chechnya, Patrick Shanahan for his advice on construction industry practices, and Stevyn Colgan for his help with police matters.

I found these books particularly helpful:

Chienne de Guerre: A Woman Reporter Behind the Lines of the War in Chechnya by Anne Nivat (PublicAffairs, 2001)

The Oath: A Surgeon Under Fire by Khassan Baiev (Pocket Books, 2004)

A Dirty War: A Russian Reporter in Chechnya by Anna Politkovskaya (Harvill Press, 2001)

Chechnya: Calamity in the Caucasus by Carlotta Gall and Thomas de Waal (New York University Press, 1998)

Russia: Experiment With A People by Robert Service (Pan Books, 2003)

My thanks to those at the WFCG (Gail Cleare, Ann Warner and everyone else) and the many Scribblers and ex-Authonomites who have provided their feedback and encouragement. I don't want to leave anyone out so I won't name names, but you know who you are. Also thanks to members of the former novelists' group (especially Iris Ansell, Hilary Bailey, Margaret D'Armenia and Gail Robinson) and the Richmond Writers Circle, who long ago commented on early drafts of 'Nikolai' and 'Ghosts of Chechnya'.

Lastly, thank you everyone who supported *Blind Side* on unbound.com – not forgetting my two anonymous donors. This book wouldn't be here without your generosity.

Patrons

Sandra Armor
John Auckland
Jason Ballinger
Jackie Bates
Blanka Be
Jacquie Bloese
Richard W H Bray
Bridget Brewster
Carla Burgess
Caroline Burgess
Janey Burton
Scott Butcher
David Calcutt
Mel Cash
Carole Cassidy
Lynn Chaundy
Tom Christian
Gail Cleare
Dave Cohen
Euan Corrall
Jacob Crees-Cockayne
Margaret d'Armenia
Max Danker
Jim Demetre
Elena Driver
Fiona Dunbar
Robert Eardley
Angela Elliott
Ian Farewell
Peter Faulkner
Lisa Galdal-Gibbs
Barry Gill
Nicole Gotch
Jacki Hall
Ray Holland
Laura Holm
Stephen Hoppe

Margaret Howie
Johari Ismail
Daniela Iuliana
Roger Jefferies
Stephen Jones
Peter Kelly
Olga Kenton
Niall Kishtainy
Deborah Knight
Jo Lampard
Gautam Malkani
Janet McCunn
Martine McDonagh
Stephen McGowan
Victoria McLoughlin
Robert Mitchell
Kate Murdoch
Mohan Nair
Kali Napier
Jack O'Donnell
Brian O'Reilly
Daphne Pearce
Simone Philpott
Maurice R
Annabel Ripin
Mihai Risnoveanu
Sebnem Sanders
Jacqueline Saphra
Catharine Scholnick
Ian Skewis
Justine Solomons
Kieran Stallard
Kate Stanyer
Anthony Stickland
Richard Stickland
M Taylor
Neil Taylor
H Tucker
Peter Turner
Alexandra Wood

Karen Yeulet
Clive York